THE UNGENTLEMANLY GENTLEMAN

"You are no gentleman!" Elizabeth angrily accused the viscount.

"Oh, but I am, my dear," he answered. "If I were not a gentleman, I would not have listened to you when I awakened in your bed." He reached out with a long arm and drew her to him. "Now be quiet." He ensured her compliance by kissing her, softly at first. Then his tongue began to tease her lips, urging them to open, sending flashes of fire along her spine.

Startled, she tried to pull away. One hand on his chest slid inside his shirt to the warm, furry skin beneath. "Robert," she whispered, pulling him closer, her arm around his neck.

He pushed her back into the chaise, letting his body hold hers in place. "Ah, sweet," he breathed as he kissed her again.

By this time, Elizabeth was no longer thinking, only feeling . . . and what she was feeling was very dangerous. . . .

BARBARA ALLISTER is a native Texan who enjoys reading and traveling. A̶ ̶ ̶ ̶ ̶ ̶ ̶ ̶ ̶her, Ms. Allister began writing as a ho̶ ̶ ̶ ̶ ̶ techniques to use in he̶ ̶ ̶

SIGNET REGENCY ROMANCE
COMING IN JULY 1989

Katherine Kingsley
A Dishonorable Proposal

Ellen Fitzgerald
The Player Knight

Carla Kelly
Miss Chartley's Guided Tour

THE MIDNIGHT BRIDE

BARBARA ALLISTER

A SIGNET BOOK

NEW AMERICAN LIBRARY

A DIVISION OF PENGUIN BOOKS USA INC.

PUBLISHER'S NOTE

NAL BOOKS ARE AVAILABLE AT QUANTITY DISCOUNTS WHEN USED TO PROMOTE PRODUCTS OR SERVICES. FOR INFORMATION PLEASE WRITE TO PREMIUM MARKETING DIVISION, NEW AMERICAN LIBRARY, 1633 BROADWAY, NEW YORK, NEW YORK 10019.

SIGNET TRADEMARK REG. U.S. PAT. OFF. AND FOREIGN COUNTRIES
REGISTERED TRADEMARK—MARCA REGISTRADA
HECHO EN DRESDEN, TN, USA

SIGNET, SIGNET CLASSIC, MENTOR, ONYX, PLUME, MERIDIAN and NAL BOOKS are published by New American Library, a division of Penguin Books Inc., 1633 Broadway, New York, New York 10019

First Printing, June, 1989

1 2 3 4 5 6 7 8 9

PRINTED IN THE UNITED STATES OF AMERICA

Thanks to the following people who convinced me I should try something new and kept encouraging me along the way: Elaine S., Elaine C. and Walter, George Ann, Rosemary, and last but definitely not least, my mother, who tells all her friends about her daughter who writes.

1

The soft spring breeze stirred the early flowers near the recently planted fields, bringing their sweet scents to the lady who gazed wistfully out the carriage window. The first signs of green were beginning to show above the brown fields. Spring and another Season had arrived. Members of the *ton* had begun their pilgrimages to London. Eager young ladies dreamed of dashing, handsome young men. Mothers dreamed of distinguished matches while fathers opened their pocketbooks reluctantly.

Most carriages on the road were headed south. Just that morning the coachman had seen three men he knew headed toward the capital. He snapped his whip, wishing he were one of them. But he knew that London was the farthest thing from his mistress's mind. "She don't even go there for her clothes," he said under his breath. He remembered the way it used to be, longing for a chance to join his friends at the snug tavern they had discovered. "Wonder if Nell is as friendly as she used to be?" he asked the other coachman beside him. The young boy looked at him and shrugged. He had learned early on that most of the older man's questions did not need answers.

Inside the carriage his mistress took a deep breath and looked over the fields. The afternoon sunlight made everything sparkle. The small pools of water beside the road glittered. It was the type of day she had always loved. She stared at the fields today, however, as though she had never seen them before, their spring colors vaguely dissatisfying, disturbing.

Elizabeth Beckworth sighed and lowered the flap over the carriage window, creating a soft gray world inside the vehicle. She settled back into her seat and tried to drift back to sleep again, but her eyes refused to stay shut. She glanced over the other figures, her chaperon and their maids, and then reached for the flap again, dropping her hand only seconds before it completed its task. The restlessness and vague longing that had been her companion all winter had returned. Even Amelia, her best friend, had noticed it.

"You need a change of pace," Amelia had urged. "Come to London with me. Or go to your stepmother's. You cannot tell me she would not be glad to have you." Elizabeth had simply smiled and shaken her head just as she had done for the two previous years. "Come to London this year. I need someone to talk to. With John so involved in politics, he hardly has time for his family. You would save me from boredom on the evenings he cannot accompany me," her friend urged.

Elizabeth laughed. "Do you mean you will give up your admirers if I agree to spend the Season with you this year?" she asked teasingly. "I am certain John would be surprised and delighted."

She laughed softly once again. The yearly spring visit to Ravenwood had been enjoyable as always. But something had been missing this year. Uncertain and uneasy, she had hugged her friends' children once more and set her maid to packing. She was needed at home, she explained. But to herself she was more honest. The estate, as much as she loved it, was in capable hands. Her father had ensured that by installing Carstairs as its agent soon after he bought it. Maybe she should—

The carriage hit a rut, jolting all of them, putting an end to Elizabeth's thoughts. Her chaperon awoke. Louisa Beckworth yawned delicately, patted her fringe of faded blonde hair, and straightened herself. She tied back the window flap and turned to Elizabeth. "You really must speak to that man again, Elizabeth," she complained. "I knew when he told you that the road would be repaired by the time you returned home, your agent was merely trying to appease you. My dear, you simply must see about hiring someone new."

Her cousin simply smiled at the familiar complaint before saying as always, "You must remember that Carstairs has been with our family longer than I have. I'm certain he has a good reason for the delay, Cousin Louisa."

"Humph! He always does. Why you cannot have an agent like the one Lord Ravenwood hired is beyond me."

"So you can set up one of your flirts closer to home, Cousin?" Elizabeth asked teasingly. The older woman turned pink and simply shook her head. The two women glanced at each other, laughed softly, and began to straighten their bonnets and shawls.

"How wonderful to know we will be sleeping in our own beds this evening. Not that Amelia does not have the best available," Louisa hastened to add. "There is simply something special about having your own things about you." Elizabeth smiled at her cousin and nodded as the carriage pulled up to the door. But coming home had not dispelled her general uneasiness. Taking a deep breath, she told herself that everything would be back to normal very soon.

Before long Elizabeth and Louisa were in the dim entry hall, their bonnets and cloaks dispatched to waiting footmen. Sending the footmen and maids on their ways, Jeffries, Elizabeth's butler, announced, "Tea is ready whenever you wish, Miss Beckworth." He watched with approval as his mistress fluffed her golden brown hair. The short curls, a result of her friend's insistence that she have a new, more up-to-date style, were quite becoming. Because his face was carefully impassive, Elizabeth had no idea that he was making note of the changes in her appearance in order to compliment her maid when the servants had their tea later that evening.

Satisfied that she was as neat as could be expected after a long carriage ride, she turned to her cousin. "Where shall we have our tea, Louisa?" Elizabeth asked, almost certain she knew the answer.

"Upstairs, of course, if I am to show my face later this evening."

Just then a burst of raucous laughter spilled from the billiards room as the door to the hall opened. The smile on Elizabeth's face froze as she asked, "Guests, Jeffries?"

"Your brother and some of his friends, Miss Beckworth. They arrived last week." The butler was impassive yet somehow forbidding. "If I could have a few minutes of your time after you have had your tea?" he asked, his voice carefully impersonal.

"Charles! What a wonderful surprise," Louisa said, her face alight with happiness.

Elizabeth sighed. "You go on upstairs, cousin.

I'll have tea down here and talk to Jeffries. I know you want to look fresh for Charles."

Louisa laughed and hurried up the stairs. "To think of that naughty boy slipping down here without telling us. What a wonderful surprise! Tell him I am angry that he did not send us an advance warning so we could be here when he arrived," she said as she paused on the landing.

Turning away from the glass, Elizabeth rubbed her temples and headed toward the morning room, her private sanctuary, where no one disturbed her without permission. She opened the door and paused in the doorway. "Bring my tea in here," she told her butler. The man in the comfortable chair close to the window placed the book he had been reading on the table beside him and stood up. She was much more beautiful than he had remembered. Her skin had a peach glow that seemed more vivid even under the frown she wore. He too admired the short, tousled curls, noting the way they curled around her ears and fore-head, and made her hazel eyes more prominent. He smiled sweetly, noting the most dramatic change; a delightful, womanly shape of soft curves. Elizabeth entered the room without noticing him, muttering under her breath and rubbing the back of her neck. Then she saw him and stopped.

"Miss Beckworth? How pleasant to meet you again," said the tall man who stood by her favorite chair. His dark brown hair and midnight blue eyes reflected the sunlight streaming through the window. Elizabeth stood frozen for a moment, trying to put a name to his face. During her Sea-sons her inability to remember names had been a constant embarrassment. She simply stared at him, noting almost unconsciously his handsome face, his height, and his broad shoulders encased neatly in a dark blue coat that matched his eyes.

"Of course, you probably don't remember me. I arrived in town only at the end of your second Season," he said quietly, deciding that he had startled her.

Realizing that she had been staring, her face flamed with more embarrassment than she usually felt when struggling for a name. Then there was a scratching at the door, a distraction Elizabeth welcomed. She nodded to her butler, signaling him to put the tray on the table in front of the bronze and azure blue velvet settee. That task completed, the butler asked quietly, "Will the Viscount be joining you, Miss Beckworth?"

"No, thank you, Jeffries," Robert Clarendon, Viscount Dunstan said quietly, "I did not plan to intrude. I will look forward to renewing our acquaintance this evening, Miss Beckworth." Crossing to her, he took her hand and bowed. The tension she kept from her face was evident in her hand. He looked at her again curiously, but was too well mannered to remain. Until the door closed with a snap, Elizabeth watched the tall figure carefully, unaware that she was holding her breath.

"Should I know him, Jeffries?" she asked. The butler, a man whose family had served the Beckworths for generations, knew her inability with names. In fact, when she had moved to the manor, she had chosen him for her butler because he had always found a way to give her information on who people were. Even when he was only a footman and later an under butler on her father's estate, he had tried to prevent her being embarrassed by her poor memory.

"Perhaps, Miss Elizabeth." Although Jeffries was always careful to address her by her proper title in public, often in private he reverted to the name he had called her when she was growing up. "He is Robert Clarendon, the second son of the former Viscount Dunstan and the grandson of the present Earl of Darington." Jeffries checked the tea tray carefully. He straightened the cup on its saucer and stood back to take another look. He continued, "He came into his father's title quite unexpectedly when his father and elder brother died in a carriage accident. I believe his grandfather was rather pleased at the way things turned out."

Elizabeth raised her eyebrows at that. Then something he had said made an impression. "Dunstan? That name is so very familiar. I suppose I met him during my Seasons?"

"Yes."

"What is he doing here, Jeffries?" She poured herself a cup of tea, added a lump of sugar and a thick dollop of cream, and sat back, trying to force herself to relax.

"He came with your brother, Miss Elizabeth. But I don't understand why. He certainly has not been a part of all their activities." Jeffries' face, usually very pleasant, now wore a grim look.

"What has been the problem this time, Jeffries?" Elizabeth asked, wondering if she really wanted to know the answer. She loved her brother dearly, but she was also the first to admit that he had been spoiled. And she had to take part of the blame.

"At first everything was going well. The gentlemen in the party took out their guns or went fishing during the day. In the evenings they played cards or billiards. There was a mill in a town nearby; they went to that." Elizabeth waited patiently for her butler to come to the point. From long experience she knew that telling him to hurry would do no good. "Then one day someone spotted a fox. The next day they took the dogs and went after it. Your agent has been working with the farmers to repair the damage ever since."

"Is that all?"

"No. It began to rain." Remembering the downpour that had drenched her friend's plans for a spring picnic, Elizabeth nodded. Jeffries hesitated as if he were not certain he should continue. Then taking a deep breath and keeping his face calm only by strict discipline, he hurried on, his eyes carefully fixed on the ceiling. "Very soon they became bored with other games and decided to make sport with the maids. Before the housekeeper and I realized what was happening, there was a serious incident."

Elizabeth blanched. "Is the girl all right?" she asked, thinking about some of the tales she had heard at school.

Her butler nodded and continued. "Apparently the silly girl believed everything the man told her. At least that is what she claims. She thought he would marry her. The upper staff believe the incident may have occurred because of a tiff she had. From what I can discover, she has been walking out with one of the grooms. They quarreled when he would not agree to marry her. And the silly girl decided to pay him back by making up to the gentleman." His tone revealed how foolish he believed the maid to have been. "I have had her kept in her room since the incident. Of course, the housekeeper moved the other maid out." He cleared his throat nervously. The incident was the lowest ebb in his career. He glanced at his mistress and then fixed his eyes on the ceiling again. "We would have turned her out immediately, but she claims she will go to the magistrate if she doesn't get some compensation."

"Who is this girl?" Elizabeth's voice was as calm as she could make it. Remembering the gossip and scandal in the neighborhood when an engaged couple had been found together in the woods, she controlled it with difficulty.

"Susan, Miss Beckworth." Jeffries looked at her coldly. This time Elizabeth could read his mind. He had tried to convince her that hiring girls from the workhouse was not a good idea, but she had refused to listen.

"Is she the only one involved?" She had hired three young girls at the same time.

"Yes."

"Send her to me, Jeffries. And thank you for your discretion." Elizabeth rubbed her forehead. The headache that had been nagging at her since Jeffries had asked to speak to her now was raging. She closed her eyes, dreading the coming interview. She began to take deep breaths. Then she refilled her cup and drank another cup of tea and tore a piece of bread and butter into pieces. Finally she had the tray cleared away and sat reciting the books of the Bible, a task her governess had required whenever Elizabeth had been sent in disgrace to wait for her father to pronounce the punishment she had usually deserved.

At last the butler returned, followed by the housekeeper, who pulled a reluctant maid behind her. The girl's bright, brassy golden hair barely showed beneath the white cap all of Elizabeth's servants wore. But even the gray uniform could not hide the girl's full-blown curves. When she saw Elizabeth, her eyes widened. "It's Master Charles I should be talking to, not an unmarried lady," she said, her voice contemptuous.

"I am afraid he would give you short shrift. You would do better to be honest with me." Elizabeth pulled herself up to her full height and glared at the maid. "Was my brother involved with you?"

"Him? He couldn't see me for anything but a maid. Just like the other one, the one with the dark blue eyes. Too good for the likes of me, they were." She tossed her head and smiled slyly. "But one gentleman promised to marry me, he did," the girl said belligerently.

"And you believed him? You believed that a gentleman would marry a girl from a workhouse?" Elizabeth looked at the girl, her eyes clear and straightforward. The maid's eyes dropped at once.

"I hoped . . ." she began. Then she straightened up, her eyes angry. She looked at the room and then her mistress, elegant as always even in the plainest of her traveling gowns. "I thought it was a chance to get away from all this, scrubbing floors, polishing windows, dusting. Besides, he promised. He's a gentleman and gentlemen keep their promises."

"Only if it is a promise to pay gambling debts. They rarely keep them to women." Elizabeth's tone was bitter. "I am sorry that you had to learn your lesson so cruelly, but you must see that the gentleman did not mean what he said. And in these circumstances you cannot stay here." Elizabeth spoke quietly and much more gently than she had first intended because she too could remember the hurt of broken promises.

"You won't turn me off. Not with what I can tell." The girl glared at her mistress. "I won't be treated like some garbage to be thrown away once its usefulness is gone." She took off her cap and tossed her hair so that it hung wildly around her shoulders and down her back. The housekeeper moved toward her as if to force her to cover her head, but Elizabeth put up a hand to stop her. Susan ran her fingers through her hair, arranging it so that it hung around her face in tangled curls, giving her a gypsy-like appearance. Satisfied, she said. "You may hide in the country once a gentleman discards you, but I won't." She smiled belligerently.

Elizabeth's cheeks paled. She straightened her back, all her charity forgotten.

Her two servants were horrified. They both reached the girl at the same moment. "Be quiet!" Jeffries had the maid by one arm while the housekeeper had the other. They pulled her to the door. "Be quiet, girl!" Jeffries hissed. "Miss Beckworth took you from that place, gave you a chance, paid you an honest wage. How dare you insult her!" Together they rushed Susan from the room, the girl still screaming her threats.

Elizabeth, horrified, stood frozen to the spot. She was still there a few minutes later when the butler returned. He glanced at his mistress and hurried to a small table by the wall where a decanter was always kept. He poured her a glass of port and, putting the glass in her cold hand, led her to her favorite chair, its deep azure a perfect background for her golden brown hair. Wanting to offer more comfort but afraid of overstepping his bounds, he stepped back and waited. Finally Elizabeth drank the port and handed him the glass. Her voice was as colorless as her face when she said, "Get rid of her. Give her a reference and tell her to see my agent."

"You don't mean to give her any money?" Jeffries asked, horrified.

"Her wages and something to tide her over until she finds another job. I'll write a note to Carstairs immediately." She crossed to the small desk where she dealt with her correspondence. "I want her gone tomorrow." She dashed off the note and sanded it. "And keep her away from the men." Elizabeth's face was as cold as she felt.

Her butler cleared his throat, hesitated, and then hurried on. "Master Charles wishes to speak with you. He has been waiting in your rooms." He bowed slightly and walked stately out into the hallway, glad that for once he would not be a party to the argument he knew would follow.

Elizabeth's head now seemed to pound with a thousand drums. She rose from her desk and left the room, heading up the staircase. Charles was waiting to see her. With each step she climbed her anger grew. Her brother invaded her home with a party of his friends, and she was the one who had to bear the insults. So deep in her own thoughts that she was oblivious of anything else, she ignored Dunstan, who passed her on the stairs with a pleasant greeting. Surprised at the cut, he stood still for a moment and watched as she moved gracefully up the stairs, the skirts of her traveling gown moving in the same swaying motion as her hips. When she disappeared, he continued on his way, wondering what had caused that glazed look on her face. He wondered too at his own reaction. He glanced upstairs once more and then turned, walked down the hall, where members of the hunting party whiled away their time, waiting for another meal.

Tension filled Elizabeth's sitting room. "Elizabeth, where have you been? Cousin Louisa said you would be up in a minute," her brother said, his voice anxious. "You really should come visit Mama so that I don't have to come all the way here to see my big sister. I miss you." Charles smiled, the impish, boyish smile that had made his governesses fall under his spell and continued to enthrall young women. He reached out and hugged Elizabeth exuberantly, pressing her face into his cravat. He never remembered that she was not as tall as his six feet plus.

She remained stiff in his arms. He pulled away from her, his face worried. "What's wrong, Elizabeth? Is anything the matter with Amelia and the brats?" Taking her silence as a no, he pulled her to him, reaching behind her to massage her neck. "Is your head hurting? What can I do to make it better? Shall I call your maid?"

Her head pounding and her spirits bruised, Elizabeth for once failed to see the love shining out of her brother's bright blue eyes. His affection for her was evident in the worry on his face. She pulled away from him and walked across the room her back to him, her face set in a calm mask. "You could leave," she said, her voice as cool as water off a glacier.

Charles stepped back. Puzzled, he ran a hand through his already carefully disheveled gold hair. "Leave? But you just got here? I thought—"

"No, you didn't. You never think. You do what you want and let others pick up the pieces." Elizabeth turned and glared at him, her sense of outrage magnified as she took in the casual elegance and almost classical beauty he achieved without effort. In the last few years his appearance, a sharp contrast to her own, had been a constant reminder of her own inadequacies.

"Elizabeth, what's the matter? You just got home." Charles tried to put his arm around her again, striving as he always did to reassure her with a hug.

"And what met me when I arrived? My brother,

without letting me know, has brought a party of—of how many men?" She paused for his answer, tapping her foot impatiently.

"Seven. Eight counting me. But you—"

"You didn't even have the decency to write to let me know you were coming?"

"You weren't here. So what difference would writing have made?" Charles's face had lost its usually pleasant expression. He glared at her.

"Good manners require that the mistress of the household be warned if guests are coming to her home. Perhaps if you had discovered I was not at home, you could have made your visit later. This is my home. I should have the right to decide if I want guests." By the time she had finished, Elizabeth's low and throaty voice had risen several octaves.

"Well, if you want to talk about whose home this is, let me remind you that Papa left this manor to me. You only have the right to live here until you marry. So don't talk to me about who has rights." Little realizing how much like a nursery argument their discussion sounded, Charles shook his finger at her.

"Then I suppose you want to talk to Carstairs about the fields your friends destroyed during that fox hunt " Elizabeth asked in the prissy voice he had always hated.

At that Charles had the grace to look embarrassed. He mumbled, "I tried to get them to stop, but the fox was just ahead. No way to stop the dogs. I told Carstairs I'd make the damage good."

"For the damage to the fields and to the crops too?" He nodded. "Good." Then she looked at him scornfully. "I wish you could make good the damage to Susan." Elizabeth, who had been standing near the door during the last exchange, crossed to a chair and sank into it. She closed her eyes, trying to ignore her brother.

"Susan?" Charles's voice was indignant and his face flushed. "That maid is a hussy. She's the one did all the chasing. And she didn't care who it was." Charles laughed ruefully. "After Robert turned her down, she tried all of us before Sebastian finally took her up on her invitation."

"Sebastian? Sebastian Hartley? He's not here?" Charles nodded sheepishly. "You promised Mama and me at Christmas that you would have no more to do with that man." Elizabeth was worried. "You know what Lord Ramsburg said about him."

"My stepfather thinks anyone but his colleagues in Parliament is a loose screw. Sebastian is a good chap." Charles glared at his sister and sat down on the chaise, crossing his long legs and admiring the shine his valet had put on his boots. Since it was a simple hunting party, all the men had agreed that there was no need to dress for dinner.

"Good chap is he? Susan said he promised to marry her." Elizabeth stood and walked over to her brother. She stood in front of him, glaring. "Charles, I had to turn her off and pay her to keep quiet!"

"Pay her off? Elizabeth, if you gave that bit of muslin a sixpence, it was more than she deserved. She knew what she was about. She tried to trap Hartley." Tired of feeling as though he were on trial, he stood, looming over his sister. "You should have talked to me before you did anything."

"And what would you have done? Allowed her to go to the magistrate? Allowed her to smear our name across the country? Or perhaps you would have married her yourself?" She crossed to the bell pull and gave it a yank. "I'm tired. Please give my excuses to my cousin. I shall have my meal in my room." She turned to stare at him haughtily as she had done when they both were in the same schoolroom and she had grown tired of their arguments.

His earlier delight to see her again forgotten, Charles let his hurt feelings and guilt take control of him. "Hiding away again, are you? Well, let me tell you, sister dear, that had you shown some ability to get married yourself, this incident would never have happened. I could run this estate any way I pleased without your interference." Charles stalked to the door and put his hand on the latch. "Now you are too cowardly even to look anymore," he said scornfully. Elizabeth stepped back as though she had been struck. She kept her hurt from showing on her face but only with supreme effort. "I will be happy to give your message to Cousin Louisa. We have no need of a Friday face in our gathering." He walked out and slammed the door behind him, his face a thundercloud.

Inside the sitting room, Elizabeth once again sank to a chair, rubbing her head, already regretting her hasty words, their hasty tempers. Even as children, an angry word from one or the other could cause a flash fire of anger to sweep over both. Each had learned to strike the other where it hurt the most. Elizabeth laughed ruefully, thinking what her old nurse would have said to them. Charles and she usually were the best of friends. Most of the time Charles was a loving and caring brother, if a little self-centered, she reminded herself. Then she frowned slightly as she realized she was making excuses for him as she always had done. Just then her maid bustled in, noticed the frown, and hurried her mistress to bed. "A cold compress and you will be feeling more the thing. You shouldn't let Master Charles upset you, with that headache and all. He never thinks," Miller said soothingly. From the moment that she had been hired as Elizabeth's maid, Miller had aligned herself with her mistress, trying to ease her life. And lately Charles had been the chief source of her mistress's worry.

The words were different, but two floors below, Sebastian Hartley had Charles Beckworth as much in hand as his sister's maid had her mistress. Seeing Charles come storming down the stairs, his face angry, Sebastian had made one of his usual quick decisions. Ever since Christmas, he had noticed a slight cooling in Charles and was not yet willing to let this pigeon escape. Nor could he afford to. Charles, whether he knew it or not, would be providing Hartley's support until the next quarter day. He took a moment to survey the situation, running a hand through his pale blond hair, already thinning to a degree that worried his valet. He straightened his waistcoat and felt for the fob he always wore, its surface smooth from his rubbing it unconsciously

"Charles, just the man I was looking for," he said in his heartiest voice, taking his friend's arm. "I'm looking for someone to blow a cloud with. We even have time for a quick hand or two." He smiled his winning smile.

Just then a voice rang out from above them. "Charles, darling boy. Why didn't' you stop by my room to see me before you came down?" They looked up to see Louisa tripping down the stairs, her blonde locks covered by a lace dowager's cap that matched the lace on her gray-blue silk gown.

"I forgot. I had to wait to see Elizabeth," he said quietly through clenched teeth.

"Well, where is she? Jeffries is ready to announce dinner and she isn't down yet." Louisa laid her soft white hand in its lace mitt on his arm and patted his cheek in a way that always embarrassed him.

"She's not coming. She said to tell you she will be having her meal in her room."

Both his cousin and Hartley looked at him, the hostility in Charles's voice evident. Louisa patted his arm to get his attention. "Did the two of you argue again?" He nodded, already ashamed but still angry. "Charles, how could you? And on her first day at home." Then determined that even that little unpleasantness would not spoil her evening with such handsome young men, she said soothingly, "Now, take me into dinner as soon as I have greeted the others." She moved away to speak to Viscount Dunstan, a face she remembered from Elizabeth's Seasons.

"It was her fault," Charles muttered, too low for Louisa to hear because she was talking to Dunstan, but Hartley heard it well.

Later that evening, after Louisa had gone up to bed and the men were gambling and finishing off the port, Hartley smoothly maneuvered Charles to a table far enough removed from the others to make their conversation private. Seating Charles with his back to the others, Hartley took the place opposite, his pale blue eyes checking the room once again. As he glanced at another table, he frowned as he watched Dunstan pull in yet another winning pot. He had lost more than he could afford to the viscount that afternoon. His eyes narrowed.

Hiding his thoughts, he turned back to Charles, who slumped over the table. The young man, having consumed more than his share of wine at dinner, was almost castaway.

"Tell me, Charles, what's disturbing you? You

haven't been yourself all evening," Hartley said in as encouraging a voice as possible.

"My sister," Charles began and then stopped, putting a hand over his mouth. He burped. Then he smiled. "Elizabeth told me have bad manners." He frowned again.

Hartley asked quietly, "Elizabeth?" Charles nodded and then held his head. "Older sisters can be such a problem."

"Problem,' Charles agreed, slurring his words. "Think they know what's best for everyone."

"Especially for younger brothers."

Once again Charles nodded. "Tries to choose my friends. Thinks you—" He paused and reached for his glass. Finding it empty, he reached for the bottle. It too was empty. He started to haul himself out of the chair to get one of the full bottles on the table nearby.

Hartley grabbed him, pulling him back into his seat. "I'll get another. You stay here." His eyes almost half closed, Charles simply smiled. Hartley used the few seconds that it took to reach the other table to consider Charles's remark. He would simply have to be more careful. With all his charm, he assured himself, he would be able to win all the ladies to his side. He had done so before. He hurried back to the table and poured Charles a fresh glass. "Tell me what started your argument?" he asked, his voice sympathetic.

"Not arguing with you. Like you. You're my friend." Charles sank farther down in his seat. He smiled like a happy baby.

"Not me. With your sister?" With effort Hartley kept his voice soothing, his contempt for the younger man carefully hidden.

"Thinks she's in charge here since my father left her life interest. Don't remember I own it.

Always trying to be in charge. Can't even arrange a marriage properly. Messed that up. Chose a stupid man. Now she'll live here forever." Charles emptied his glass and reached for the bottle again. "I'll never be able to see it. Hand in glove with Mama, that's what she is. My mama, not hers." By this time Charles was mumbling almost incoherently.

"What about your mama?" Hartley asked, prodding him awake.

"Won't let me join up. If Elizabeth were a boy, she could join. My mother never denies her anything. Not fair. She's my mother. Should love me best."

"And she doesn't?" Hartley took a quick look around the room to see if they were being observed. Dunstan raked in another hand. Couldn't the man lose?

"No. If she did, she'd marry Elizabeth off so I could sell this place. Or she'd buy me colors herself. I know she told Elizabeth not to give me the money. Elizabeth helped me before. Bought me a hunter. Doesn't mind sharing her money." Charles straightened up some. "Not jealous. Everything'll be fine when get rid of the trustees. Then I'll do what I want. No one stop me," he mumbled.

"Your sister has more money than you?" Charles nodded. "But she's a girl. How did that happen?"

"She's older. At least that's what lawyer said. I'm the heir, but she has money—lots and lots. Her mother left her pounds and pounds." Charles sighed, once again caught up in self-pity. "Not even that'll get her married off down here. All available married." He lifted his glass. "Needs to get married. Then I'll get rid of this place. And be off. To the Peninsula." Proud of himself for completing the thought, Charles smiled and held out the empty bottle. "Find another."

Across the room a chair was shoved back from the table. "No more tonight, Dunstan. I'm cleaned out. Accept my marker until we are back in town?" The young man ran his hand through his hair as if embarrassed to admit his lack of funds.

"Certainly. Anyone else want a game?"

A chorus of groans broke out. "Not now. You've the luck tonight."

"Every night."

At the table where Hartley and Charles sat, the older man sat up straighter. He glanced over at the table where Dunstan now sat alone, thought for a moment, and then turned to Charles. "You want to get your sister married, don't you?" His companion nodded and then regretted the action. "How would you like Dunstan as a brother-in-law?"

"Dunstan? Never offer. His grandfather has plans for him."

"We'll make certain he will have no choice. Then the manor will be yours," Hartley said, smiling coldly as he began to develop a plan.

Across the room, Dunstan now sat alone. The viscount glanced around the room, wishing he were in London or at Clarendon. Had his superior been a little later that evening at the club he could have been. He had been playing cards with Charles and a few others when Charles had issued his invitation. Dunstan had been about to refuse it when he felt a hand on his shoulder. He looked up to see Lord Seward, standing behind him. "Can I see you for a moment, Lord Dunstan?" the older man had asked formally. "I have a message from your grandfather."

Amid groans and murmurs of consolation, Dunstan followed him across the room to a more secluded corner. "Sit facing the room," his superior had said, his gray eyes stern. Dunstan obeyed. "Did Beckworth include you in his invitation?" Dunstan nodded. "Accept it. No, I know it is not what you will like, but we need you there. The place is little more than an hour from the coast. Make a habit of riding out alone in the morning. Someone will be in touch with you." Dunstan sighed and agreed. He had pushed his chair back before getting up when the older man stopped him. "Make certain you seem one of the group."

"What does that mean?"

"Do what they do. Play deeply, lose occasionally, and let them see you in your cups. Sobriety frightens some people," Lord Seward said, his tone implying more than his words.

Those words now echoed in Dunstan's ears. He sighed, remembered the message he would be carrying back to London, and called for another bottle.

Hartley glanced over at Dunstan, his hand curving around the stem of his empty glass. He watched as a footman filled the glass again, leaving the bottle on the table. His eyes narrowed dangerously, Hartley inspected the room. Then he sauntered over to the largest table and separated the two youngest members from the group as easily as a sheepdog cuts ewes from the herd. "Dunstan looks lonely. Why don't we join him?" he asked, smiling sardonically.

"Too serious," the youngest complained. "Won't play with me anymore. Said he wouldn't take my vowels. Almost called him out over that."

"Me too. Told me to wait until I sobered up," the other added. "Not had as much as he has this evening."

"Maybe that will make a difference. He is a bit on the go tonight," Hartley said encouragingly.

"Still no money. Meant what he said."

The older man slapped them on the back and smiled, at least his mouth did. He drew them to the side of the room, talking quietly. Finally they nodded.

"Give me your vowels," Hartley said, pulling from his pocket the roll of blunt he had won from Charles. "Keep him busy for a while. I'll join you shortly." He watched as they crossed the room and sat down with Dunstan, their young faces shining with mischief. They he rejoined Charles.

"Shouldn't have gotten angry at Elizabeth," the younger man said, his words badly slurred. "Never mean to." He slumped forward on the table.

Hartley leaned over and pulled Charles back in his chair. He signaled a footman. "Tell my valet I wish to see him in my room," he said quietly. "And get your master some coffee." When the man hurried away, Hartley walked around to Charles, his face serious. "I want a fresh pack of cards. I'll be back in a moment."

In his bedchamber he found his valet waiting. "Mix up one of your potions for Charles Beckworth, something to sober him for a time. And do not tell me how late it is. I know. On your way." He waited until the door closed behind his man and then took a vial from a case on his dressing table. A short time later he was across the table from Charles again.

During the next half hour or so, he dealt one hand after another, pushing pen and paper toward his host and accepting his vowels. He also made certain Charles drank only coffee and the potion Hartley's valet provided. By the end of that time, Charles was no longer sagging so disgracefully in

his chair. His quarrel with his sister hung heavily
on his mind.

"Do something about it then. It is not too late.
Ask if she will see you. Tell her you wish to apologize," Hartley urged.

Charles brightened. Then his face fell. "Never
agree. Said some terrible things." He sighed
disconsolately.

"Try. Sent Jeffries or her maid to ask her."

Finally Charles agreed and sent a footman on
his way to find his sister's maid. He looked at the
bottle of brandy beside him and reached for it.
"Drink to celebrate."

"Just the thing. Take some wine up to share
with your sister." Hartley held up the bottle of
Madeira he had kept beside him.

"Brandy."

"Here's Jeffries with your answer. We will ask
him to decide."

"What she say, Jeff—Jeff—Jeffrries?" Charles
finally managed to get out.

"She will see you, sir." He stood back, his face
impassive though his eyes were disapproving.

"Mr. Beckworth wishes to share a drink with his
sister, Jeffries. Which do you recommend—brandy
or Madeira?" Hartley asked, his face carefully
unconcerned.

"Madeira, sir." Charles shrugged his shoulder.

"Get a tray and glasses. Here's a bottle of Madeira I just opened. You take them. I'll see to Mr.
Beckworth." Hartley watched as the butler arranged
the bottle and glasses on a tray and then helped
his friend up. Slowly but steadily they climbed the
stairs.

"That's the one," Charles said, pointing to the
door. Hartley glanced at Jeffries, who nodded
disapprovingly.

"You go on in now and apologize. You don't need me at a time like this," Hartley said encouragingly. For a moment Jeffries allowed his approval to show. Then his face was impassive again.

As soon as Charles entered the room, both Hartley and Jeffries headed back downstairs. When he entered the card room, Hartley glanced at the table where Dunstan and the others sat. Picking up a bottle of brandy, he made his way over to them. "Who is winning?" he asked, his face only mildly curious.

"Dunstan," the others groaned. Hartley glanced at the notes in front of the man in the dark blue coat, and his eyes narrowed. "That calls for a drink." The others pushed back their chairs.

"None for us. I'm for bed." The other nodded and yawned. Dunstan, already awash in more brandy than he usually drank, tried to refuse, too, but Hartley would not hear of it.

"We are celebrating your winning. Wouldn't be the same if you did not take part," he explained, laughing.

"One more hand. Then just one glass," Dunstan said, slurring his words more than he had intended to do. The hand won, he tossed down his drink and stood up, weaving slightly.

"I am ready for bed. I will walk with you upstairs," Hartley offered. He waved away a footman who stood ready to help. "See to the others."

2

The morning sunlight was still only pale streaks on the horizon when Elizabeth awoke the next morning. A faint uneasiness plagued her. She shoved it aside, enjoying the cozy warmth of her bed, her headache still faintly nagging at her. After a while her maid would be there, ready to help her dress for another day. She breathed deeply. At least she and Charles had settled their differences the evening before. She smiled sleepily as she remembered how worried he had been about her forgiveness. If he only knew, she had never been able to maintain her anger with him for longer than an evening. Still, he had made a sweet apology.

However, the longer she thought of the previous evening, the more distressed she grew. Even at ten o'clock, her brother's speech had been slurred, his walk unsteady, and his breath strong with brandy. Reminding him of his promise to curb his drinking would do no good. She would have to write another letter to her stepmother. Charles needed something worthwhile to do with his life before he became so comfortable with his role of drinking and gambling that nothing would save him. If she could only convince her stepmother to let him do as he wished and join the army.

She sighed and closed her eyes once more, still

drowsy even after the peaceful night's sleep in her own bed. Enjoying the cozy warmth, she snuggled farther down in the feather mattress. Then all her sleepiness forgotten, she crouched at the head of the bed, the covers drawn tightly around her, her eyes wide, and her mouth open in a silent scream.

There was someone in bed with her. Her breath came in gasps. Her chest heaved. Once more she tried to scream but couldn't. Then she noticed the bare arm covered with a light dusting of brown hair. Creeping even farther up in the bed, as close to the edge as she could possibly get, she gulped and pulled even more covers around her. The move was a bad one. The covers now around her had been hiding more than an arm. She could see two long legs also dusted with hair poking out of the covers. Elizabeth closed her eyes and tried to calm her breathing so that she could call for help.

She was in bed with a man. Or was he in bed with her?

She opened her eyes. This was her room. The man groaned and turned slightly. Hastily Elizabeth closed her eyes, but that did not erase the vision of a hairy chest and a shock of brown hair.

Controlling her fear, she opened her mouth to scream and then shut it hastily. She considered her choices. If she screamed, someone would come running. Picturing the turmoil that would cause made her blanch with fear. She had been through one miserable scandal in her life and once was enough. She opened one eye for a peek and then shut it quickly. Only the edge of a sheet, vividly white against his skin, had kept her from her first look at an unclothed adult male. Still breathing irregularly, she opened her eyes again, telling herself she needed more information before she could decide what to do. Just then, the man, chilled in the cool air of the spring morning, turned again and reached for the covers.

Elizabeth refused to give up her hold on them, clutching them even more tightly around her. Once again she closed her eyes, realizing the inevitable. She would have to wake him up. Then she heard the creak of the coal and wood hoist. The servants were up. Soon a maid would arrive and light a fire on the hearth.

Acting quickly, Elizabeth held on to the bedpost tightly and angled herself. She doubled up her feet and kicked, knocking the man to the floor.

"What the hell?" Dunstan groaned, not knowing whether to hold his head or his sore elbow.

Who was he? Elizabeth wondered, noting his handsome, sleepy face and deep blue eyes, still half closed. She knew his face. Then she remembered. She had met him yesterday. Using a few choice words she remembered from the last time she had heard Charles complaining in the stables, Elizabeth muttered under her breath. Her miserable memory. Realizing that knowing his name was not going to solve her problem, she said quickly, "Get under the bed!"

"Huh?"

"Get under the bed!" Elizabeth took a quick look to see if he was following her orders, but he was just sitting there as handsome as ever, holding a pillow in his lap, not a stitch of clothing on him. She closed her eyes again, gulping nervously. "The servants will be here at any moment! Get under the bed! Now!" This time her tone made an impression on him.

Dunstan looked at Elizabeth and then around the room, a room he had never seen before. His clothes were on the floor around him, just as he had left them since he was a small boy, to the despair of his nanny. Then they both heard the quiet conversation in the hall. Grabbing what clothes he could gather quickly, he yanked up the bed skirt and slid under the bed.

Elizabeth hopped out of bed and collected his coat and neck cloth and shoved them under the bed, too. Dunstan, entranced, wondered if he should tell her that bending over in a low-cut nightrobe could be revealing. But she was obviously not thinking of her clothing. Her robe was sheer and the morning sun, now shining more brightly, silhouetted her figure against the embroidered linen. Before he had a chance to say anything, Elizabeth was back in bed. Dunstan, now that his distraction was gone, lowered the bed skirt and plunged himself into darkness. He banged his head on the edge of the bed and groaned.

"Be quiet!" Elizabeth said, her voice trembling. Then they both heard the scratching at the door. Elizabeth burrowed under the covers, her heart pounding as her head had done earlier. Dunstan froze, hoping that he would not sneeze from the dust under the bed hangings. Elizabeth would have to check on her servants more carefully, he thought. Then realizing the absurdity of his thoughts, he almost chuckled.

Elizabeth? He had been in bed with his hostess! The thought made his heart stop for a moment. This could not be true; it could not be happening to him. This was an incident from his brother's life and not his own. He would wake up in his own room and find that he had simply dreamed the entire situation. Even though he tried hard to convince himself that he was right, he did not move or make a sound. What if it wasn't a dream?

In the few minutes that the servant spent making up the fire, time that seemed like hours to the two of them, Dunstan and Elizabeth each had ample opportunity to review the morning. Dunstan, his first memory of the morning an uncomfortable thump to the floor concentrated on his companion. Even the day before in her traveling gown, Elizabeth Beckworth had attracted him. If he were honest, he would have to admit that he had been attracted to her when she was in her second Season. But then he had been a mere second son—not a bad position in some families. But his father was a rakehell, a man heading down the path to ruin as fast as he could, impeded only by Dunstan's grandfather's refusal to release additional income or to die and allow him to inherit the earldom.

Dunstan's presence as an extra man had been welcome at balls and other social events; he had known, however, that even though he had an impeccable reputation himself, no father would consider his suit, not with his father's and his brother's reputations for squandering vast sums of money. So he had watched Elizabeth at the balls and held his tongue.

Even later, there was no thought in his mind of an offer. Then she had disappeared. Honest with himself as he always tried to be, he had to admit that as attracted as he had been to her, when she left London, his attention was easily distracted. This time she would be harder to forget. The vision of her through her thin nightgown seemed burned in his mind. He thought of her lying in bed above him and almost groaned. The clank of the coal bucket reminded him of the situation. He held his breath for a moment.

What was he doing in her room? He began to review the events of the evening before.

As hard as she tried, Elizabeth could remember nothing after her talk with Charles. In fact, she could not even remember her brother leaving.

For Dunstan the evening had been much like those earlier in his visit. After the meal he had played a few hands of cards, winning most of them. He patted his coat pockets lightly. At the first rustle of vowels and clink of coins, he stopped and listened. The maid did not pause in her duties. He exhaled quietly. How had he gotten from gaming to his hostess's bedroom?

Minute by minute he tried to recall the details of the previous evening, but they were uncharacteristically fuzzy. Dunstan knew he had played a hand or two with almost everyone in the house party; the satisfyingly full pockets told him that he had, as usual, been lucky. Once again he was struck by the irony. He, who cared little for games of chance, won; his father, who had lived to gamble, had beggared himself with his losses. He chuckled ironically. Then he remembered where he was and froze, checking to see if the maid was going to react.

She did not pause in her work. Elizabeth, however, trembled, certain the man's presence was going to be discovered. Who was he? She ground her teeth for a minute and then relaxed her jaw. Jeffries had told her his name when he appeared with the tea tray. Tea—Teasley? Elizabeth shook her head, dislodging a pillow. The maid turned, her eyes on her mistress. Elizabeth forced herself to breathe deeply, feigning sleep.

As soon as the maid returned to sweeping the hearth, Elizabeth relaxed. Not "A," she thought, or "B." "C"? Yes, that sounded right. Or was it "D"? Clarke? Clare? Clarendon! That was it. But didn't he have a title? Was Clarendon his name or his title? She tried picturing him once more as she had seen him the previous afternoon. The sight of him on the floor beside her bed kept getting in the way. Her face a flaming red, she burrowed deeper in her pillows, a tiny smile on her lips. He was certainly more intriguing than the rest of her brother's friends.

The thought of her brother almost brought Elizabeth out of bed. A quick peek at the windows told her it was still early, far too early for Charles to be up. Once again the thought of his slurred speech made her want to shake him. She had seen what a constant round of drinking and gambling could do to a man. She did not intend her brother to go the way of her fiancé.

"Dunstan! Viscount Dunstan!" she whispered under her breath. The details came flooding back. Jeffries had said the man had inherited the title recently. Now that the name was firmly in her mind, the gossip her stepmother insisted on sharing came to the surface.

Viscount Dunstan was a name associated with the wildest parties, the deepest gambling. If Charles were running with that crowd, she had better contact her stepmother soon.

So intent was she on these thoughts that she did not hear the door close behind the maid. "Miss Beckworth? Elizabeth? May I come out now?" a deep voice asked.

Elizabeth jumped. "No!"

"Do you plan to keep me here forever?" he asked with a laugh. "If so, I do hope you plan to give me a duster." The danger now past, he could see some humor in the situation.

Elizabeth could not. "What are you doing in my room?" she said, her tone angry.

"Sleeping," he said as casually as though he were in his own bed at his grandfather's estate.

"What?"

"Apparently I spent the night with you. You did invite me, didn't you?"

"*Me*? How dare you! Just wait until my brother hears about this!" She slid out of bed with a thud and dashed across the room to the bell pull, stopping only when she realized the futility of the gesture.

"You plan to tell your brother?" Dunstan asked, his voice reflecting his confusion.

"You invade my chamber and expect me to accept your insults. Of course, I am going to tell my . . ." As she realized what she was saying, Elizabeth paused. She could not call for anyone, not if she wished to keep the encounter a secret. And it had to stay that way. She was not ready to face another public scandal.

Two long, well-shaped legs poked out from under the cream lace and turquoise satin bed skirts. Elizabeth stared at them, shocked, for a moment. "No!" she said loudly. "Get back under there."

"I do not plan to stay here forever," Dunstan said, his voice more calm than he believed possible. "It is far too dusty."

"Dusty?" she asked, confused.

"I recommend that you speak to your housekeeper. Someone has been shirking this job," he added with a laugh. "I will give you a minute to cover your eyes. Then I am coming out."

"I'll—I'll go in my dressing room. Then you can get out," Elizabeth said hurriedly. She moved across the room, and he heard the door close behind her. What he did not realize was that she was leaning against the other side of the door, trembling. Her heart pounding, Elizabeth breathed heavily.

What was happening to her? Never in her life had she acted the part of a wanton. Why was this happening now?

On the other side of the door, Dunstan crawled out from under the bed. He crossed to the pitcher and bowl and poured some warm water to wash away the dust, pausing for a moment to wonder once again how he had gotten there. He looked at the door and smiled. Gathering his clothes and shaking them, he quickly dressed. Then he knocked on the dressing-room door.

"What?"

"I'm dressed."

"Then leave." Elizabeth said, relieved.

"I'm afraid there is more to this situation than simply leaving will solve," he said quietly.

"What do you mean?"

"Come out. We need to talk." His voice was quiet and sincere.

Elizabeth pulled away from the door. She stood up straight. "I'll be out in a minute," she said quietly.

Although she thought it impossible, Dunstan realized how difficult those simple words must have been for her.

When she appeared a short time later, he held his breath for a moment. She had donned a deep amber velvet dressing gown trimmed with blond lace. The deep collar of lace formed a frame for her flushed face, and the soft gathers of the high waistline emphasized her figure.

Elizabeth too stopped for a moment. He was standing by the window, his handsome face highlighted by the early morning sunlight, his dark brown hair tousled becomingly over his forehead. It did not seem like the face of a man who was known for hard living, but Elizabeth had learned the hard way that a person's nature is not always reflected on his face.

For a few moments neither spoke. They looked at each other and then at the floor, color flooding their faces. Dunstan cleared his throat; Elizabeth raised her head and looked at him. "Ah, Miss Beckworth, Elizabeth," Dunstan said, his voice cracking as it had not done in years, "you must believe that I did not intend to do you harm." He paused, thinking in embarrassment of what he had said while he was under the bed. How could he have acted as though what had happened had been a silly prank? He cleared his throat again when he realized that she was not going to say anything. "There is no other apology I can give for my behavior." He took a deep breath and then hurried on, spitting out the words in one breath. "Miss Beckworth, I request that you do me the honor of becoming my wife." He stood there looking at her, his deep blue eyes sincere.

Ready to accuse him of plotting her ruin, Elizabeth stood speechless for a moment. She stared at him as though he were an exhibit at the fair. Then she closed her eyes, trying to make sense of the situation. She had awakened early as she usually did; she had gotten more comfortable in bed and prepared to go back to sleep. That was it; this was a dream. She opened her eyes, hoping that she was right.

"Elizabeth?" Dunstan asked.

"You are still here," she said tiredly.

"Did you think I would go away without discussing what has happened?" he asked, his voice stern.

"I was hoping you had never been here at all," she explained. She sank into an ivory velvet chair beside the window, her face somber in the early morning light. "Why don't you go away?"

"And where will I say I have been? If the maid has been in to light your fire, won't someone have been to my room as well?" He walked over to stand behind her, wanting to smooth her hair but resisting the impulse.

"Oh." She closed her eyes again, her shoulders slumping. Then she sat up straight. Her eyes were wide. "What room are you in? Is it close to my brother's?"

"On the same floor." He crossed to stand in front of her. "Why? What difference does that make?"

"Jeffries will not allow a maid to work there. Our footmen must serve more rooms than normal. Are you at the end of the hall or near the stairs?" She got up quickly. Then she realized how close he was to her and sat back down.

"At the end." He paused and took a deep breath. "Elizabeth, I asked you to be my wife. Do you plan to ignore me forever?" Dunstan asked, his voice harsher than he had planned.

"Good. Now if you only hurry . . ." She got up again and rushed toward the door to the hall, ignoring what he was saying.

"Elizabeth!"

"What?" She turned back toward him, annoyed to find him standing in the same spot as before.

"Are you going to marry me or not?" No matter how she tried to pretend the situation had never happened, Dunstan knew that it could not be ignored. He had worked too long to preserve his reputation. Even now, a year and a half after the deaths of his father and older brother, people still wondered about him. He did not plan to give them any more ammunition to use against him. And she met his grandfather's requirements as well as his own.

"Not." He stared at her in shock. "If you hurry, you can return to your room and no one will be the wiser." She tried to make herself appear composed and calm, as though finding a man in her bed did not disturb her. "Come. I'll check the corridor and be certain it is clear." She turned back to the door, her hand on the latch.

"No." Dunstan sat down in the chair she had just left. "We must talk before I go."

Elizabeth froze. Then she whirled around, the amber velvet swinging around her like a swirl of gold. She hurried over and stood in front of him. "What are you trying to do? You broke into my room, climbed into bed with me—against my will, I might add—and now refuse to leave. Jeffries told me that certain members of my brother's houseparty were no gentlemen. Now I believe him!"

"I climbed into bed with you?" Dunstan rose and stood glowering over her. "How did I get here? I must have been invited. I never go where I am not wanted." His blue eyes snapped angrily.

"Invited? You—you. . . ." Elizabeth raged at him, standing so close to him that he could feel her chest heaving. She longed to slap him, but gradually she gained control of herself. She took a deep breath. Realizing that words alone were not going to convince him to leave, she moved back, her eyes on his face. "If I agree to talk to you later, will you go now before you are discovered here?" she asked. Her voice was as calm as she could make it. If she could only get rid of him so that she could find out what had happened.

"How much later?" he asked suspiciously. Dunstan knew the problems his being found in her room could cause and wanted to avoid them as much for himself as for her sake.

"At eleven." Elizabeth almost heaved a sigh of

relief as she watched his face relax. In a few minutes he would be gone, and she would be safe again.

"Where?"

"My morning room." She was holding her breath, hoping he would agree.

"You promise you will come? The word of a Beckworth?" he asked, not at all certain whether this was merely a ploy to get rid of him.

Elizabeth gritted her teeth silently. Then she smiled. "I promise." Even if I do have to see him again, it will be better there than here, she thought. She glanced at the bed and blushed as she remembered the sight of him on the floor.

"Check the hallway." Quickly he made certain he had all his belongings. Then he crossed to the door, where she waited impatiently. Certain he was ready to leave, Elizabeth opened the door cautiously. There was no one in sight. She signaled for him to go. He slid past her, at the last moment before he went out the door impulsively turning and kissing her on the lips. "Eleven," he said softly. Then he hurried away.

The door safely closed, Elizabeth sank to the floor, a hand over her mouth. "Eleven."

3

Elizabeth sat with her back against the door to the hall for a few minutes, long enough for her feet to feel as though they were becoming icicles. Finally, moving as though she were in a dream, she climbed back into bed, pulling the covers over her head as she had done as a child whenever she had had a bad dream. If only that were what had happened now.

In her safe world of warmth and semidarkness, Elizabeth tried to relax. He was gone. No one knew that he had been in her room or in her bed. The last thought made her shiver. Once again she saw that arm, those legs, that chest, and those smiling blue eyes. Now she was trembling. How had he gotten into her room without her realizing what had happened?

Over and over again Elizabeth reviewed the morning's events, always stopping when she saw him on the floor with the pillow as his only covering. He had been as surprised as she. He had simply sat there, shocked. Her mind had a vivid picture of him imprinted on it. His chest was so broad, and his legs had seemed to go on forever. The way they had poked out of her feminine lace and silk bed hangings brought a smile to her face for a moment, a very brief moment.

"At least I will never forget his name," she whispered quietly. The knowledge did her little good. She would never be able to look at him again. How would she get through the next few days? Had Charles told her how long his guests were staying?

Charles! If he ever found out what had happened, he would kill the man. And everyone else would know what had happened, she thought ruefully, remembering her brother's habit of speaking before thinking. He would never know, she promised herself. She pulled the covers from around her head and straightened her body until she was lying as precisely positioned as if she were in a coffin. Then she laughed quietly. If Dunstan had reached his room successfully, Charles would never know. They were safe. She smoothed the silk coverlet as though she were petting a cat.

But how had he gotten into her room? Remembering how she had been plagued by fortune hunters during her first Season, Elizabeth could not help wondering if Dunstan's gambling debts had led him to her room. A rich wife would solve many problems. Then why would he have left so easily?

"He didn't." She sat up straight in bed as she said it, her eyes flashing. "I agreed to meet him at eleven. I gave my pledge." She lay back down and began to close her eyes when another thought brought her out of bed completely. "What if someone has seen him?"

Too agitated to be still, Elizabeth paced from one end of the room to another. Dire scenes filled her head. Dunstan planned to trap her in marriage, get his hands on her money, and gamble it away. She could see herself in a few years, penniless and living on her brother's generosity. "And Charles's wife probably will not like me," she said to herself. "Even Cousin Louisa has a better life than I will have." She whirled around, a hand over her mouth. "Cousin Louisa!" How would her cousin ever be able to hold her head up in town again? She would feel as though she had failed the family. Big tears began to form in Elizabeth's eyes as she thought of the consequences the morning might have.

Then her eyes grew wider. He had been in bed with her—with no clothes on. Could he have—? Hastily she ran her hands over her body. She climbed back into bed, looking for the signs that gossips said always followed that type of action. She could find nothing. The lack did not reassure as it should have. She wasn't sure what she was looking for. She felt much the same as she had the evening before. In fact, with her headache finally gone, she felt better. The thought made her more nervous.

What was she going to do? One trip across the room brought her close to the clock on the mantel. It was only eight o'clock. How would she ever get through the morning? She crossed the room to her bed, climbed the steps, and lay down again. This time her chill did not dissipate with the warmth of the covers. She had to meet him at eleven. She had no choice if she wished to avoid a scandal.

A scandal—the words sent her back under the covers again. After her last experience of being the object of scorn for society, Elizabeth wanted nothing more to do with scandal. She remembered the day as clearly as though it had happened six minutes ago instead of six years. Only the evening before her fiancé, Cousin Louisa, and she had been to a ball, leaving early because Jack had said he had an early morning engagement he wanted to be fresh for. She had laughed and teased him about it, trying to get him to explain, coaxing him to stay for one more dance. But even her sweetest smiles and softest words had not swayed him. He had found Cousin Louisa and sent for their cloaks, putting her pomona green velvet over that lovely white muslin sprigged with a matching green. She shook slightly as she remembered how Jack's hands had caressed her shoulders, his kiss had brushed her cheek lightly. She could not force herself to wear that shade of green again, a shade she connected with betrayal.

Their carriage ride home had been quiet except for Louisa's chatter. Jack had sat across from her, his dark brown eyes fixed on hers and a smile on his lips. He had escorted them inside and waited, seemingly impatiently, for Louisa to say her good nights, waited for the brief minutes that an engaged couple were allowed. He had gathered her into his arms, kissing her so passionately that she had protested a little, her eyes frightened but sparkling. Then he had gone, leaving her to dream of him and their life together.

It was the last time she had seen him. On her breakfast tray the next morning there had been a note explaining that he had to leave England unexpectedly. He would not be returning for some time. He was certain she would want to place an announcement ending their engagement in the papers. She had stared at the note, stunned. Tears poured out. The maid, returning for the tray, found her crying so hard the girl was frightened. Hurriedly she had sent for Elizabeth's stepmother.

For that week Elizabeth had stayed in her room. The announcement appeared in the papers, adding fuel to what was already a hotbed of gossip. Not until Elizabeth made her first foray into public again did she learn the rest of the story. Several of her acquaintances were only too happy to tell her. Her fiancé had not left alone; the ladybird over whom he had fought a duel and killed a man had gone with him. After learning that, Elizabeth noticed how a buzz began when her name was announced, followed by a dead silence and then renewed buzzing. People watched her. After the second ball when she sat out every dance, Elizabeth refused to leave the house. She had not wanted to go to the second ball, but her stepmother had persuaded her.

Finally her father called her into his study. "What are we to do, Elizabeth?" he asked, his voice soft.

She was only able to cry at first. Then she managed to whisper, "Let me go home."

Her father looked at her sharply. Then his eyes narrowed as they did when he was considering an idea. "But your mother wishes to stay in London."

"Cousin Louisa will go with me."

"Is it fair to ask her to do so?" her father asked quietly.

She hung her head, ashamed. "No," she said, her face sad.

Her father looked at her, the stern look disappearing as he noted the way her mouth turned down. "I suppose we could ask what she thinks of the idea," he said reluctantly.

Of course, Louisa, as determined as anyone to save Elizabeth pain, had agreed. Within a week they were at home. Charles, sent down from Eton because of fisticuffs with someone who laughed at Elizabeth, tried to cheer her up. But she spent most days alone in her room. At last Louisa had enough. Elizabeth smiled as she remembered the way her cousin had attacked her, calling her a layabout, a person with no bottom. She needed to remember who she was, hold her head proudly, and show the world she could not be affected by the scandal.

Elizabeth tried, she really did. But she would burst into sobs at the most inconvenient times. Even Amelia was almost ready to let her drown in her tears. She was the talk of the country.

Finally she learned to put a shell around herself when she went into public. She danced with people and even gossiped a little during the Christmas holidays that year. She reluctantly returned to London for the Season. To her parents' dismay, however, she had become ill after only one ball, and the doctor suggested removing her to the country to allow her to recover. She never returned to the capital.

Later that year her father bought the manor and established Carstairs there. She spent the fall helping her stepmother redecorate the place. When her father died suddenly that winter, Elizabeth was not at all surprised to learn that he had left her a life interest in the manor. With most of his property entailed he had ensured her independence in the only way he knew. When her stepmother returned to society after her mourning, Elizabeth moved to the manor. Gradually she was accepted by the country gentry. And all might be lost because of one night.

Too restless to remain in bed any longer, she reached for the bell pull to summon Miller. She would dress, perhaps in the new apricot sprigged muslin; she was not going to let Dunstan see that she was worried. She had learned something from her earlier brush with scandal—presenting a calm exterior helped quiet the gossiping tongues. Somewhere deep inside another motive was lurking. She wanted Dunstan to see her at her best.

Had she known it, as far as Dunstan was concerned he had already seen her at her best, her hair tousled, the morning sun shining through her nightgown and illuminating her figure. It was that picture that kept recurring as he lay in his bed waiting for eleven. She had to marry him.

But like Elizabeth, Dunstan was worried. As far as he knew no one had seen him as he made his way to the room assigned him. But he wasn't sure. What if a servant had come into the hallway behind him? It would not be the first time someone had tried to trap him into marriage.

Since he had inherited his title eighteen months earlier, he had been astonished to find himself the object of matchmaking mothers as well as his own matchmaking grandfather. But remembering Elizabeth's shocked face, he had to acquit her of trying to trap him. Her innocence did not absolve others, though. Her cousin? He shook his head slightly; the lady had been too busy questioning Charles and flirting lightheartedly with her captive audience to plot something so devious. Charles? The thought gave him pause for a moment. Then he shook his head again. Charles had been so castaway by early in the evening he would have been unable to think of it.

Or had he? Once again Dunstan tried to review the events of the previous evening. They had dined early, keeping country house. The meal, since Elizabeth had not been there to plan the menus, was a simple one, only three removes. The chef, determined to reveal his expertise to a more varied audience, had prepared crimped cod and smelts, cutlets à la Mainteon, beef Tremalon, oyster loaves, and black caps served with fresh spring vegetables from the forcing house. Remembering how much they had eaten the evening before made Dunstan's stomach feel queasy. But he would have to get the recipe for black caps from the cook, he reminded himself. His grandfather enjoyed apple desserts, especially if they were made with apples from their own orchards.

The thought of his grandfather made Dunstan stiffen. Had the man been so lost to propriety to somehow arrange this? No, he had to admit that even to see him married, his grandfather would not use those methods. Besides, he knew the girl his grandfather had in mind. Because of her he had not been to the country estate since Christmas. Briefly he compared his grandfather's choice to Elizabeth: the girl was pretty in a typical sort of way—blonde, blue eyed, angelic; Elizabeth was stunning, everything a man could want in a wife. Dunstan laughed as he remembered the look on her face when he had refused to leave. He settled back more comfortably into his pillows, his face calm. No matter who had arranged this, he was going to marry her. There would be no scandal.

Scandal was something he had lived with for most of his life—not his own but his father's and elder brother's. They had run with the Prince of Wales's cohorts. There was nothing they would not try. After his mother's death, his uncle, his mother's brother, had grown tired of Dunstan's father and his constant borrowing. His father's scandalous behavior had made him turn them off the estate. Dunstan remembered the last interview with his uncle. After the gentleman had given the viscount his notice to quit the place, he turned to Dunstan. "You are welcome to stay, Robert," his uncle assured him. "I will send you to school and will treat you as though you were my own son."

He looked up, startled. But his father answered for him. "If a viscount is not good enough to live on your estate, then neither is his son," he shouted. Then he grabbed him and dragged him from the room.

For Robert, then eleven, the next year had been frightening. His father took them first to London. There the older man and his eldest son began their careers as gamblers. Somehow—Robert never wanted to know how—his father found someone to finance him and later to introduce him to the people he wanted to know—the wealthy or presumably wealthy crowd that surrounded the heir to the throne. Left alone in their grim rooms with only a haughty valet for company, Robert read, regretting the lost opportunities for an education. After the first time he knew not to ask his father for anything, choosing rather to run errands for people to earn his food. Gradually the valet came to respect him; now Graves was his own valet, the only way the older man would allow him to repay his many kindnesses.

As he grew older and more like his grandfather, whom he had never met but whom his father blamed for his lack of money and position, Robert's life became a constant struggle to stay out of his father's way. With Graves's help, the viscount was persuaded to send him off to school, his first year's tuition in his pocket. After that his father forgot he had a another son. Had it not been for his grandfather he would not have been able to complete his education; his father did not continue to pay the school's fees. Only an appeal by the headmaster to his grandfather, the Earl of Darington, changed his life.

The older man, then in his late fifties, decided to see the grandson he had never known. To both their surprise, the man and boy became friends—tentatively at first but later firm and steadfast. The two Roberts spent all of the younger's school holidays together. And Darington made certain that Robert, unlike his father, was well trained in estate management and in business.

For the first time in his life Robert had someone whom he could love and trust. His father had cared only for himself; his mother, only for her eldest, Edward. Neither trusted the earl; they had quarreled with him early in their married life, leaving his estate for that of Robert's mother's brother. Although his maternal uncle was fond of Robert, the boy knew that his uncle often regretted his impulsive invitation to his brother-in-law, an invitation that had cost him twelve years of support for a man he had learned to hate. Robert too regretted those early years, years he could have spent with his grandfather whom he had learned to love. Only on two things did Dunstan ever argue with his grandfather: buying a set of colors and marrying the daughter of the family who owned the next estate.

The first, buying a set of colors, he decided to forgo. His grandfather introduced him to a friend in the Home Office who found interesting work for him to do. Sometimes it was interesting, he reminded himself. Other times, like the house party, it was decidedly dull. The post would have gotten the message there as fast as he did, and he would not have needed to endure the endless round of gambling and meaningless activities he disliked so much. Of course, he would not have renewed his acquaintance with Elizabeth either, he added to himself.

Acquaintance? he asked himself. Then he laughed quietly. "She probably has another word for it," he said, startling the footman who had quietly entered to make up the fire on the hearth.

"Did you say something to me, your lordship?" the man asked.

"No." Dunstan lay back on his pillows, struck once again by the subtle plotting that might have been his undoing. Had he not been in his bed when the footman came in? He could imagine the stories that would have gone around belowstairs, especially when it was discovered that he had not been off the estate.

Remembering the humiliation of listening to the whispers about his father and his brother, he was determined he would not be the subject of gossip again. The years of being snubbed or being regarded as a fortune-hunting gamester had made their mark on him. Now he lived his life as circumspectly as possible, not even his closest friends knew his liaisons. In the last years his reputation had begun to improve. He did not intend to change that fact.

Like Dunstan, Hartley did not intend to change his way of living. The money he and the others had lost to Dunstan would have to be replaced. That thought was the first in Hartley's mind as he awoke that morning to the noise the footman was making on his hearth. "What's the time?" he demanded, his voice rough with sleep.

"It's past seven, sir," the footman said quietly; he had already seen Hartley's displeasure when the man thought his importance had been slighted.

"Seven!" At first Hartley reached for the heavy candlestick to throw at the servant who had awakened him so long before his usual hour. Then he remembered. He sat up in bed, pulling the sheet around him. "Who else is awake this early?"

"Lord Dunstan spoke to me when I was making up his fire." The footman paused in his work and looked at the man in the bed. The man's face was mottled with anger. Quickly the footman finished his work, hoping to be through before the wrath spilled over onto him. "Is there anything I can get you, sir?"

Hartley waved him away, not noticing how fast the man made his escape. Dunstan was in his own room. The frown on Hartley's face grew darker. Somehow the man had cheated him again. Hartley lay there silently for a long while. Then a sly smile crossed his face, making it light up in a ruthless way. He slid out of bed and crossed to the bell pull.

A few doors down the hall, Dunstan listened to the minutes tick away and tried to remember the details of the previous evening. No matter how hard he tried, the details eluded him. Finally he rose, dressed, and headed down to the usually empty breakfast room. As he walked across the threshold, he stopped in surprise. For once the others were before him.

"I say, Dunstan, you look chipper this morning. Did you sleep well?" asked the youngest, a brother of one of Charles's closest friends. He winked at Dunstan.

"Yes," the viscount said quietly. "Until the footman woke me as he lit the fire, I slept wonderfully well."

"You should have," the young man said, laughing. The others quieted him quickly.

"What do you mean?" Dunstan looked from Hartley to the others suspiciously

Hartley stepped in quickly, flashing an angry look at his companions. "You were so castaway when you went up to bed that we made bets whether you would be able to rise today," he added, his voice smooth as treacle.

Dunstan laughed. "I am lucky that I have such a hard head. I rarely feel the effects of the evening before. But that does explain why my stomach is so unsettled this morning. Now, who bet on me? I'd like to give him my congratulations."

"None of us," Hartley said quietly, a slight edge

to his voice. "Charles is the man you must congratulate."

"Charles? I will have to give him my thanks for his confidence later." Dunstan looked around the room, his face unconcerned. "What has Cook provided for breakfast this morning?"

While the others continued their conversations, Dunstan selected his breakfast from warming dishes set along the sideboard. Recognizing the difference between appetites, the cook had prepared not only the usual buns, cakes, coffee, chocolate, fruit, and preserves, but also a ham of noble proportions. Dunstan had the footman slice him some, adding it to his strawberries and bun, and made his way to the table. His stomach still slightly unsettled, he ate slowly, adding a bit to the conversation here and there when someone addressed him.

Although the others drifted off to find amusements at the stables or in the stream, Hartley stayed behind to keep Dunstan company. He signaled for the footman to fill up the other man's cup. Then he leaned casually back in his chair. "I never thought you were much like your brother Edward until last night," he said musingly.

"My brother?" Dunstan's face became a mask of disinterest. "How did you know my brother?"

"We met occasionally," Hartley told him. "Had some friends in common. Last night you reminded me of him."

The viscount stood up, knocking his chair to the floor. As a footman hurried to set it upright, Dunstan asked, his voice icy and quiet, "How?"

"Oh, nothing specific. Perhaps just the way you were playing or perhaps your drinking."

"Thank you for the warning."

"What?"

"I do not consider the comparison a compliment."

"Nor, dear boy, do I," Hartley assured him.

"Your brother was as big a scoundrel as I ever hope to meet." And stupid as well, he added to himself. Dunstan, he knew, was anything but stupid. "Remember that scandal he caused with the daughter of some cit? Had the poor girl believing he would marry her. It did make an amusing story at the club."

Remembering the flurry of gossip that had surrounded the event, Dunstan had to agree, but his face never changed. He merely nodded and walked out of the room, heading outside to the garden. After walking through the quiet pathways for some time, he found a marble bench in an isolated corner and sat down, allowing his anger to show on his face. Would he never be free of the reminders? He laughed sardonically. Of course he wouldn't, not as long as men like Hartley wanted to keep the memories alive. And for some reason Hartley did.

Wondering what his brother had done to the man, Dunstan reviewed what Hartley had said and what he had seemed to say. "Damn! I don't trust him," he said under his breath.

" 'Scuse me, sir?" A gardener stood only a few feet away, pruning shears in his hand.

Startled, Dunstan got up, nodded to the gardener, pulled out his watch, and headed to the house. The morning was far advanced. Only a half hour until his meeting with Elizabeth. She had to agree to marry him; he refused to let his name become part of a scandal again. His stomach began churning again, and he rubbed it, wishing he had eaten less that morning.

4

Upstairs in the master's chambers Charles Beckworth had just begun to stir. His first movements caused disastrous results. Only his valet's knowledge of him kept him from ruining his bed. Porter stood beside the bed, a basin in his hands until Charles finished heaving.

"Don't look at me like that, Porter," he said huskily when he could speak again and his valet had returned.

"I am sorry, Master Charles. Tell me what you do not like about my expression, and I will be happy to change it," the older man said soothingly.

"You can start by calling me Mr. Beckworth," Charles said as he had often done before, regretting that he had allowed his mother to persuade him to keep his father's valet for himself. There was something intimidating about a valet who had known you before you were even in short pants.

"Of course, Master Charles." The other man continued to lay out the clothing his master would need for the day. "How was your visit with Miss Elizabeth?" he asked with the familiarity of an old retainer.

"Elizabeth?" Charles asked. The fact that even his older sister was still a child to Porter soothed his feelings somewhat. "We had a rare dustup."

"Somewhat quicker than normal, wouldn't you

say, sir?" Porter continued with his duties as calmly as if Charles had told him that Elizabeth and he were getting along well. "How were Lord and Lady Ravenwood and the children?"

"All right, I suppose." Charles climbed out of bed, heading for the dressing room. "Why does this always happen, Porter?"

"What, sir?"

"These arguments. Devilish uncomfortable having Elizabeth angry with me. Have to go to see her and make up." Charles ruffled his hair and then poured water over his head and neck. He frowned at the man in the mirror and then caught sight of the arrested expression on the face of his valet.

Porter stopped. He laid the shirt he had in his hands on a chair and crossed the room. He handed Charles a towel, stepped back, and asked, "Did you quarrel with her last evening?"

"No. Yesterday afternoon was enough. She was angry with me, and I must admit she had a right to be. I must see her and apologize immediately." Like his sister's, Charles's anger was quick to disappear, a flash fire that quickly burned away. There were times, however, the anger smoldered for days, weeks, but those were usually when someone else had been hurt. Had he been able to find his sister's fiancé six years before, he would have shown him what a Beckworth's anger was like when it was left to smolder. Even when he thought of the man today and remembered his sister's weeping, his anger began to burn as hotly as ever.

"But Master Charles?" Porter paused, unwilling to admit that he had been gossiping with the other servants. But the matter was too important. "You saw her last evening. From Miller's account, we assumed that you had already made peace with her."

"When? Last evening?" Charles turned around, rubbing his wet head with a towel. His shoulders, broader than they appeared when he was dressed, rippled with muscles.

"Apparently you insisted on seeing her. Took a tray of Madeira with you."

"Madeira? I don't even like the stuff."

"But I believe Mr. Hartley persuaded you it was more proper for a reconciliation drink with your sister than brandy." Porter handed Charles the first of his clothes. The valet's face was stiff with disapproval. Although too loyal to his master to mention the matter to others, he did not approve of Sebastian Hartley. Even his valet was second-class. A gentleman's gentleman knew these things.

"Hartley? I was talking to Hartley about Elizabeth?" Charles ran his hand over his face, wishing he could remember more about the former evening. "What have I done now?"

"Perhaps you should ask the gentleman," Porter suggested quietly, "in a discreet way, naturally."

"And how am I going to go about that? You know me, Porter. Discretion is not something I am good at." Charles sat down and pulled on his pantaloons.

"Would a simple question or two be too difficult?"

"A simple question or two? I can just see myself now. 'Hello, Hartley. Nice day, isn't it. What did I tell you about my sister?' Elizabeth will never forgive me if I have said anything I shouldn't."

"Now, Master Charles. You know your sister will forgive you almost anything."

"It's the 'almost' that is worrying me. If I've created a scandal, we may as well leave for the colonies tomorrow." Charles shrugged into his coat, adjusted his cravat slightly, accepted a handkerchief, and walked to the door. "Ask around, Porter, maybe one of the other servants heard something." He put a hand in front of his face and laughed mirthlessly. "If Elizabeth could hear me. I'll try to stay out of her way until luncheon. I'll meet with Carstairs and then head to the stables. If you find out anything, let me know." He shook his head. "Now I'm asking you for the same kind of information you gave my father." He opened the door and peered out cautiously. He looked at the empty hall and breathed a sigh of relief as he headed for the back stairs.

He was no sooner inside the door that hid them from view than he heard someone coming down the hall. "Interesting breakfast," one man said, his voice calm and clear.

"Most fun I've had in days. Dunstan seemed not to know what we were talking about. Clever of Charles to give us such a diversion. Never saw Dunstan so castaway before. Too bad he wasn't that way when we were playing," a young-sounding voice said gleefully.

"Lost deep, did you?"

"Not more than I can bear. Dunstan don't like to win too much from us 'innocents,' he says. Someday I will beat him, and then we will see who is so innocent." Charles heard a door slam and footsteps continue down the hall.

Charles bit back a curse. Not certain who was still in the hall and not wanting to take a chance on being discovered, he hurried down the stairs, heading for the kitchen and a quick escape to Carstairs's office. "No use asking them about last night. But what did they mean about my providing them an amusing diversion? Elizabeth will never let me hear the end of this," he muttered as he entered the kitchen.

"Mr. Beckworth, is there something I can get

for you, sir?" Jeffries asked, rising from the table set for his morning tea.

"Coffee." After the butler had prepared it just the way he liked it, Charles took a long drink. "Has my sister been down yet?"

"No, she slept later than usual. I imagine the Madeira you took her last night made her sleep." The butler remained standing, casting a wistful look at his own quickly cooling tea.

"Sit down, Jeffries. I'll be gone in a minute. Just tell me what you mean about the Madeira," said Charles, waving the butler's protests away. His face, normally smiling and pleasant, wore a grim frown.

The butler wore a solemn expression. "You insisted that you had to speak to the mistress last night, had to apologize. You demanded I send a footman with a bottle of brandy to her bedchamber. But Mr. Hartley intervened. He convinced you to take a bottle of Madeira he had beside him on the table. Master Charles, Madeira is more of a woman's drink than brandy." He paused, concerned that Charles had shown such decided poor taste. Charles merely nodded. "I carried the tray to Miss Elizabeth's room, where you took it from me. You were absent from your guests quite some time. Several people wondered about you. Then you reappeared, said your good nights and went to bed." Jeffries cast an anxious look at his master to see if he was ill.

"How long did I spend with my sister?"

"More than a few minutes, sir."

Charles winced. "Let me know when she comes down, Jeffries. I'll be with Carstairs in his office." He turned to walk out the door to the back garden, but then he paused for a moment. His house party had been disastrous since the rain began.

For a minute the room was silent as Charles thought about the turmoil of the last few days, wondering how he could gracefully suggest that his guests return to their homes. Then, remembering the attention span of most of them, he smiled wryly. "Jeffries, spread the word that I have been thinking of challenging the record from here to London. And have Porter make a fuss asking for my trunks to be brought down from the boxroom."

"It will be my pleasure, Mr. Beckworth." The butler allowed the slightest smile to cross his face as he thought of the scurrying that this news would cause. He watched as his master crossed the yard.

"Good morning, sir." Carstairs stood as Charles entered his office. Then he sat behind the desk as Charles took a seat, stretching his long legs out before him, staring seemingly at his boots' brilliant shine. "How may I help you?"

"Tell me about the wretched girl, what's her name?"

"Susan," Carstairs said dryly.

"That's the one. Did you get her off?"

"Yes, sir. But she is the kind to make trouble. Even with the paper I had her sign, she may not keep quiet." Carstairs looked at him steadily, not sure he liked the changes he could see in the young man. Already he could see signs of dissipation. If only the young man's mother would pay some attention, he thought restlessly. Well, he had done what he could.

Charles frowned. "What kind of trouble, Carstairs? She was the one who offered."

"That is not the story she tells. And you know how gossip spreads. I instructed the man I sent with her to put her on the stage to London. Maybe there she will find a wider market for her wares."

"My sister said something about paying her off. Did you?"

"That's why I had her sign the paper. She can read, you know. Your sister gave her a full year's wages. I was against it, of course. She is setting a precedent, I am afraid." The agent shook his head. He held out the document to the young man.

Charles took it and looked it over. "Did you explain this to Susan?"

"Yes."

"Then I am certain she will be quiet. She admits her plotting here." Charles leaned farther back in the chair, smiling. "How are the repairs coming on those fields?" For the next half hour or so they discussed the problems the tenants were having replanting. Then a messenger from Jeffries arrived and Charles left.

He walked back to the house. "Where is she?" Charles asked as soon as he had found the butler.

"In her morning room."

"Tell her I wish to see her."

"She told me she did not wish to be disturbed until half past eleven," Jeffries said apologetically.

Charles frowned. "Tell her I will be in the library. And don't let her put you off." He walked down the hall, his face serious. The talk with his agent had been more sobering than he had expected.

When he entered the library, Charles found Hartley sitting there, recent newspapers in front of him. "You are up early, Sebastian," he said sardonically.

"I might say the same of you," the man said, his mouth curled into a slight sneer. The morning had not gone as he had planned. "What is this I hear about your returning to London? Jeffries told me you had told your valet to pack." Hartley put the paper down on a table near the comfortable chair in which he sat. His eyes narrowed dangerously.

"My friends have done enough damage here. I cannot afford any more incidents," Charles explained, closing his eyes and rubbing his forehead.

"I hope you are not including me in that group," Hartley said coldly.

"Of course not. I told Carstairs the girl had made advances to you, not the other way round. Besides, she's gone for good, I hope. She left this morning."

"Susan was an eager piece. I'll be sorry to see her go." His friend laughed, remembering the incident.

"That is not to happen again. Not even if someone else offers. Do you understand, Hartley?" Charles asked. His voice was stern and harsh.

"Turning Methodist on me, Charles?" The older man smiled maliciously. "What will our friends say?"

"No, but I do respect my sister's right to live here in peace. We shouldn't have come without her permission."

"But you told me you own the place." Hartley enjoyed nettling him. "Last night you said Elizabeth was trying to take it away from you."

Charles blanched. He cleared his throat. "You especially should know that you should not believe everything I say when I am in my cups."

"Do you mean you don't want her to get married so that you can sell off this place?" Hartley got up and walked closer to the fireplace, where a small fire smoldered. He poked it and turned around, his face carefully unconcerned.

"What are you talking about?" Charles asked, horrified.

"Oh, just a conversation we had last evening." Hartley walked over and looked him in the eye, his pale blue eyes clear and cold. His smile never reached his eyes. Charles's eyes dropped. He turned away from Hartley.

"What exactly did I say?" Charles asked hesitantly, afraid of what Hartley was going to tell him. He reminded himself that what a man said when he was drinking was often discounted. But that did not make him feel better.

"We discussed how unfair it was that your father had not left this estate outright to you. You mentioned it would come to you when your sister married." Realizing his advantage, Hartley went on. "You said if I could arrange a marriage for your sister, you would give me twenty-five percent of what you make when you sell this estate." He pulled out a piece of paper and handed to Charles, whose face blanched as he read his signature under the words.

"And you believed me?" Charles's voice reflected his astonishment. "After what I apparently drank?"

"But, dear boy, you gave me your solemn oath on it, word of a Beckworth and all that." Hartley moved across the room and leaned casually against the back of the chair. "Do you mean you will not honor your debt of honor?" His tone reflected just the right amount of horrified amazement.

"No, no. But you must have known I was in no state to promise anything . . ." Charles let his voice trail off into nothingness, remembering how many times he had seen a drunken man bet his family's fortune on the roll of dice or a turn of a card. They had paid up; so must he. He gulped and controlled himself with effort. "Besides, Elizabeth never goes anywhere to meet anyone eligible." He breathed a sigh of relief as he realized the truth of his remark.

"So you said." His friend plucked a small piece of lint from his otherwise flawless dove-colored pantaloons, looked at it coldly, and threw it in the fire. "You leave everything to me." He walked toward the door and then paused, his hand on the latch. "I think it might be best if the two of us remained after the others leave. What do you think?" When he looked at Charles, the faint smile on his face chilled the younger man.

"Of course." Charles had never intended to leave with the others anyway. "Keep it to yourself, though. We wouldn't want the rest to change their minds." He watched Hartley leave the room and then took his first deep breath since they had begun the conversation as the door clicked closed. "Idiot, that's what I am. Now how can I get out of it without my sister finding out?" he asked himself. "I am never going to drink again." Hearing a noise in the hall, he took a deep breath and squared his shoulders.

He yanked the bell pull. "Where are my friends, Jeffries?" he asked when the butler arrived. Before long he had seen off all of them except Dunstan. With only a few complaints they had all agreed with him; the country was dull. With company returning to London, there would be more excitement there.

The person he had had the most trouble convincing was his best friend's brother. Charles had promised David Ashcroft he would keep an eye on his younger brother while the older was away on the Peninsula. Today he wished the brat at Jericho. Stephen insisted on gambling too deeply, drinking too much, and now he wanted to stay and see how Dunstan liked "losing to an innocent." Charles promised to keep him informed. "It won't be the same," Stephen complained. But finally when a friend suggested a little wager on who would reach London in the fastest time, he laughed and dashed out. "Catch me if you can," he told the others, accepting their wagers.

Within a short time the five young men had eaten a meal of bread and cheese, ordered their clothing packed, their horses saddled, and headed out toward London. Charles, who had gotten out of the race by reminding them of his obligations, gave the command to begin. As the five raced down the long road away from the manor, he longed to dash carelessly after them, his responsibilities forgotten. It was a state of mind in which he often lost himself.

A clock chimed somewhere in the background, and Charles looked up, appalled. "It's twelve."

"We've plenty of time for a game before luncheon," Hartley assured him, certain that he would have more of the Beckworth money in his pocket before the meal.

"Not now. You go ahead," Charles said quietly. "I have someone I must see immediately." He turned and walked quickly toward the stables. Hartley stood staring after him, an unpleasant look on his face. Then he turned and walked back into the house.

Charles continued on his way until he was out of sight. Then he quickly changed direction, heading for the back entrance to the kitchen.

"Jeffries," he called as he entered the kitchen, frightening the youngest maid so much that she dropped the meat pie she had been carrying. She burst into tears. "Tell her to stop immediately," Charles said, his voice harsher than he intended.

"Silly girl, be quiet," an older maid said and cuffed her on her head.

"No! You are not to hit her again," Charles commanded, holding the older girl's arm in a tight grip. She turned pale, fearing that he would hurt her. His grip on her arm was tight.

The younger girl stopped crying and ran to her friend's protection. "Oh, sir, she didn't mean anything by it. Cook will wallop me when she discovers what I have done," she explained.

"Do you mean my servants are beaten?" Charles demanded. Totally ignoring the two girls' protests, he yelled, "Jeffries."

"Yes, Mr. Beckworth," Jeffries said quietly, coming up behind him.

"Glad he don't look at us that way," the older kitchen maid said to the younger. The other girl nodded.

"Jeffries, that girl said Cook will beat her when she discovers that she dropped a meat pie. Is that true?" Charles drew himself up to his full height, an inch or so above six feet, and looked down at the butler, his face impassive.

"I didn't say she would beat me, sir," the young maid tried to explain to Jeffries. "He"—she pointed to Charles—"wouldn't let me explain. Besides 'twas our meat pie, for our dinner." Her face was mournful.

Jeffries did not say anything for a moment. He simply looked from the maids to his master. "You girls, find something to clean up this mess," he said quietly. "We will discuss it later." Hastily they made their escape. "I thought you would be in the library, sir. I sent someone to find you only minutes ago."

"Won't do, Jeffries. You may have gotten around me for the moment, but I want an answer. Are maids beaten in my household?" From the time he and Elizabeth had been old enough they had made free use of the kitchen and lower regions of the house. As a result they knew of the rules his mother had laid down. No one was to be beaten; their wages could be docked, but no one was to suffer physical harm. Charles blushed as he realized he had allowed one of his guests to violate one of his mother's major edicts. He had allowed one of his servants to be taken advantage of; worse, he had not protected Susan as he should have.

The butler, never afraid of the man whom he had known since before he was in short pants, raised his chin and said proudly, "Miss Beckworth and Lady Ramsburg follow the same policy, sir. The girls are new; they joined the household when Susan did. I will do my best to inform them that they are not to fear a beating. Losing their favorite dinner will be enough."

"Make sure that Cook knows, too," Charles ordered. "Is my sister still in her morning room?"

"She was a short time ago. Shall I seek her out, sir?" Jeffries looked at his master with more interest. Only yesterday he had declared that the young master was a wastrel and nothing more. Maybe he was wrong. Perhaps Master Charles would mature to become the landholder his father had been.

"No, it will be quicker if I go myself." Charles crossed the room hurriedly. He paused at the doorway. "Tell Cook that we will be five less for dinner, will you, Jeffries?" He dashed up the stairs, taking the narrow steps two at a time.

"And I'm certain she will be as happy to hear that as to hear the meat pie for our luncheon was ruined," Jeffries muttered, knowing that the man had planned an elegant meal. Then the butler's face brightened. "With them gone, we will have our fill of Cook's best dishes."

5

Well before the appointed hour she had so reluctantly agreed upon, Elizabeth was in her morning room, dressed in the apricot sprigged muslin. She discussed the menus with her housekeeper, checked with Jeffries about Susan's departure, and ordered that the space under her bed be totally dusted.

When her housekeeper asked her about the latter, she stammered something about a shoe she had misplaced. With effort she kept herself under control, but as soon as her two retainers were gone, her face flamed. She drew a sheet of paper from the drawer, planning to write a thank-you note to Amelia and her husband. Staring at the white paper, all she could think about was the white sheets covering those wide shoulders, those long legs poking out of the hangings on her bed. A fierce longing engulfed her. Her hand tightened and she crushed the quill she held. Not even a stern discussion with herself could erase those memories.

Dunstan, like Elizabeth, had found that the memory of that morning adventure could not be forgotten. Elizabeth, despite her rounded charms, was not really classically beautiful; even Dunstan had to admit that she would never be acknowledged an *incomparable* by the *ton*. But she had something that would never fade, an inner fire that delighted him. He could hardly restrain his impatience to see her again. By the time he decided he had waited long enough, he had forgotten her anger and had convinced himself that she would agree to be his.

When they met again, neither was prepared for the shock, the embarrassment. Dunstan had entered quietly, so quietly that Elizabeth, concentrating on her letter, had not heard his footsteps. "Good morning again," he said, his voice low and caressing.

She jumped, splattering ink on the letter, fortunately only half finished and largely incoherent. She looked up and then lowered her eyes quickly. To his surprise, Dunstan was as embarrassed as she. Both their faces flamed. The clothes they were wearing did not matter. Neither could see them because the memories of that morning kept getting in the way.

Falling back on the polite behavior she had been taught from childhood, Elizabeth asked, her voice not as steady as she could wish it to be, "Would you like some tea?"

"No." Dunstan cleared his throat nervously. "No thank you." She motioned that he should take a seat and positioned herself as far from him as she could. For several minutes neither of them said anything, each waiting for the other to break the silence.

"Miss Beckworth." "Viscount Dunstan," they began at the same time. They they both fell silent again.

Dunstan sneaked a look at her. She was staring at the floor, her cheeks a rosy red that clashed with the ribbons on her dress. This time he could appreciate how she looked, her dress a soft, creamy muslin sprigged with flowers of rich apricot. Around the neckline and under the bust were ribbons of the same apricot color. Through the short brown curls her maid had laced another ribbon that matched the others. "Miss Beckworth," he began hesitantly. "I can never tell you how surprised I was by the incident this morning."

"Nor I," she added quickly. "How could you do something like that. If you had been caught . . ."

"I didn't do anything."

"You must have. You were in *my* room," she reminded him with a shaking voice.

"And that poses quite a problem, doesn't it? How did I get there?"

"You are asking me?" Elizabeth rose and went toward the window, her skirts swishing angrily.

"Well, it is your home, and I was in your room." He followed her, standing behind her.

She turned hurriedly. "You can't believe . . ." She stepped back hastily, startled by his presence so close to her. Her hand went to her throat. Elizabeth regretted that the need for secrecy had caused her to forgo her cousin's cheerful and protective presence.

"All I know is that I ended up in your bed." His dark blue eyes stared into her hazel ones as if to force her to deny his story.

"How?" She tossed her head, setting her curls dancing. Flouncing across the room, she sat down, primly straightening her skirts. Determined to stop his ideas before they grew more outrageous, she asked, "Did someone come to your room and ask where you had spent the night?"

"The only people who came to my room were your footman and my valet, and neither of them discussed the matter." He paused for a moment, thinking of the conversation at the breakfast table but dismissed the idea quickly. "Perhaps your brother had something to do with it?"

"Charles? He would kill you if he found out what had happened!" At that she blanched, realizing the truth of what she said. "Charles. If he should hear of this . . ."

"He will not hear it from me, I promise you that." Dunstan crossed the room until he was across from her. Dragging one of the delicate Chippendale chairs she liked so well from its position against the wall, he sat down in front of her. His face serious, he straightened the sleeves of his dark blue coat nervously. She drew back slightly and closed her lips firmly, startled by his closeness.

"Elizabeth?" She looked at him as if to ask why he used her given name. He began again. "Miss Beckworth, have you discovered any information about how the incident happened?"

She stared at him aghast. "And how was I supposed to do that, pray tell? Ask my maid if she let a man in my rooms last night?"

"She did."

Elizabeth gasped. She opened her mouth, but nothing came out. She tried again.

"When I asked to see your brother this morning, I was told he was still sleeping. The footman was very pleased to supply the details. Apparently you and Charles quarreled and then made up last night. As you stayed in your rooms last evening, I assumed he saw you there." He tried to make his voice as calm and matter-of-fact as possible, but it wasn't easy. All he could think of was how lovely she looked the first thing in the morning. And he had decided that he would have the exclusive rights to that loveliness.

"You do not know what happened last night? Weren't you there?"

This time he was the one who was embarrassed. "According to the breakfast gossip I indulged rather heavily last night."

"You mean you were drunk. That's how it happened. You came to the wrong room by mistake. I've almost made the same mistake before in a strange house, and I wasn't drinking heavily." Now that the matter was at least partially explained, Elizabeth felt momentary relief. Then her imagination took hold. She frowned. Perhaps he had just pretended to be drunk.

"But why didn't you wake up? Are you normally such a heavy sleeper?" No matter how much he had had to drink, Dunstan knew he had a good sense of direction. He had never lost his way at a house party before. His conscience reminded him, however, that never before had he been so drunk he could not remember the evening.

She flushed again. "I do not believe my sleeping habits are any concern of yours, sir," she said in her haughtiest tone. She straightened her back and stared at him.

"They were not until this morning. They are now." His voice was as haughty as hers. His eyes took hers prisoner, forcing her to glare at him.

"But we have decided what must have happened."

"No, Miss Beckworth. We have discovered a possible reason, but nothing has been established for certain."

"You sound just like a magistrate," she muttered so low she did not expect him to hear her.

"My grandfather is the magistrate for his county. I hope to follow in his footsteps someday; therefore, I have often been to inquiries with him," he told her quietly. She glanced up, surprised. "I don't spend all my time in the beds of ladies I admire," he said, startled by his ability to make a joke when the situation was as serious as it was.

Elizabeth did not think the remark funny. "Only in those you wish to cause problems for, I suppose."

"No. You—" Elizabeth glared at him as if daring him to finish his thought. He started again: "I never meant to harm you."

"Then you certainly should consider the results of your actions more carefully," Elizabeth said, her anger beginning to build. "If anyone had seen you—"

"But they didn't. I arrived at my room safely, I think."

"What do you mean, you think? Did someone see you or not?" Elizabeth jumped up, feeling too agitated to keep still for much longer.

"They didn't," he assured her, also standing up. "But I do not feel that is the main concern. We know." He stopped and drew himself up, standing as stiffly as a life guard. His brain muddled by her presence, her scent, he tried to remember one of the logical arguments he had developed that morning.

"Well, I do not plan to tell anyone. Do you?" For Elizabeth the answer to that question held the answer to her safety, the guarantee that her life could go on as it always had. She wondered why the thought gave her so little pleasure.

"No."

"Then as far as the incident is concerned, I think we both should forget it. Good-bye, Viscount. You will understand if I ask that you leave the manor as soon as possible." Elizabeth swept to the door, her head held high.

"Wait." His command stopped her, froze her in place. "What if someone did see and has just held his tongue. What then?"

She turned slowly, her face a calm mask. "You said no one saw you. Were you lying?"

"No." He walked across the room to stare out the window at the garden with its early blooms. "You probably will not understand, but something about this bothers me."

"A great deal about it bothers me," she said sharply.

"I don't mean you. Have you ever been in the woods or in town and felt as though someone were watching you, and later you discover it is true?" His voice was low, so low that it was obvious that he did not really want to speak his thoughts aloud.

She shook her head. Then realizing that he could not see the gesture, she said, "No."

"It may sound as though I should be in Bedlam, but that is the way I am feeling now—as though someone were watching me, someone who is waiting until the right moment to reveal himself to me." He turned around and crossed the room to her. "We cannot afford to have that happen."

"What do you mean?" Her normally throaty voice sounded hoarse. She waited impatiently for his answer, her face as impassive as she had learned to make it.

"Well, can you afford to be involved in a scandal?" Dunstan had turned back to the window, remembering how embarrassed he had been when his father or brother had been the on-dits of the *ton*. Because he had his back to her, he did not see her face become stony.

"That must have been what you were counting on." The anger in her voice was so evident that Dunstan, caught up as he was in his own emotions, could not fail to hear it.

"What?" Dunstan turned around, startled.

"How long did you intend to fool me?" she asked bitterly. "Did you intend to convince me that you cared for me too?"

"Elizabeth—Miss Beckworth"—he was growing accustomed to those fiery glances—"all I want, as I said this morning, is for you to marry me. Then I will be able to protect you."

"Oh? And what advantage will you have?" Her voice was as cold as a mountain stream during a thaw.

"I will not have to live through another scandal," he said quietly. His face was as determined as she had ever seen it.

"And I will avoid one, too? How convenient!" Elizabeth whirled around and put her hand to the latch again. "Good-bye, Lord Dunstan, I do not believe that we have anything further to discuss. I appreciate your offer." Her voice dripped with sarcasm. "But I regretfully decline."

"But you can't . . ."

"I believe that at my age I have that right." Her face, once red with embarrassment, blazed with anger. "I have asked you to leave, sir. If you are any kind of gentleman, you will respect my wishes."

The last shot was too much for Dunstan. All his life he had borne insults so calmly that no one had known when they affected him. This time was different. "Had you been the lady I expected you to be, I would be happy to oblige."

Elizabeth drew back as though struck. "What do you mean?"

"After what happened between us this morning, I had assumed you would want the protection of my name. I see I was mistaken." He started past her when she put a hand on his arm.

"What do you mean by 'after what happened'? What happened?"

"You must be very accustomed to finding men in your bed, Miss Beckworth, if you do not remember." Each word held the cutting edge of a sharp knife.

"Oh, that." Elizabeth sagged against the door in relief, closing her eyes.

"Yes, that." He stopped short, noting the way her face and body had relaxed. "What did you think I meant?" he asked curiously, intrigued against his will.

Her face flamed again. She simply shook her head. Her reluctance to answer finally told him what he wanted to know. "No, no, Miss Beckworth, that cannot be true. I am certain I would remember . . ." He broke off in confusion, turning hastily to hide his embarrassment.

Elizabeth was more embarrassed than she had ever been in her life. She wanted to sink to the floor, but chose instead to walk to the settee on trembling legs and sat down. "Then why did you insist . . ."

"On marriage?" She nodded her head. He thought for a moment, trying to find exactly the right words. Finally he just blurted out what he had said before. "I simply could not bear to go through another scandal." His voice was not as clear as it should have been.

"But your life has been nothing but scandal," she said, confused.

"My life? What do you mean? Who told you about me?" The questions flew so fast she felt that she were being hit from all sides. She put a hand up in front of her face as if to ward off blows.

Embarrassed by his tactics, Dunstan dropped into the chair he had occupied only a short time before. He waited quietly until she lowered her hands. "Please, tell me who has been gossiping about me," he said in a soft voice.

"Jeffries told me you were Viscount Dunstan. You are, aren't you?" She looked at him questioningly for a moment and then lowered her eyes again. He nodded. "My stepmother told me that you are known for your gambling and disgraceful behavior."

"Me?" Are you certain she said me?" he asked astonished.

"You are the Viscount Dunstan," she reminded him.

Then as though a candelabra had been lit, his face changed. "When did she tell you about me? During your Seasons?" he asked as gently as he could. As embarrassing as it was to admit his father's and brother's villainy, it would be a welcome relief to know that the gossip she had heard had not been about him.

"No. Oh, I heard gossip then," she added, "but this was later. Something to do with a girl." She paused and then looked at him curiously, noting his pallor. "Jeffries said you had come into your title recently. What did he mean by that?"

"Until eighteen months ago I had no title and no prospects other than a small income from my grandfather," he told her, his voice as warm as he could make it. He laughed ruefully. "Until today the only scandals I have known has been of my relatives' making. And they made enough to last me for several lifetimes." Then he ran a hand through his hair, embarrassed for having given so much away. Now it was his eyes that were glued to the floor. A faint line of red showed above his collar.

"You did not crawl in bed with me to create a scandal?" Elizabeth asked, not certain whether or not to believe his story. She could ask Charles, she supposed. He loved to gossip. But one thing she was certain of was that her brother would never do anything to harm her, would never introduce her to someone who was bad *ton*. Sebastian Hartley crossed her mind momentarily, but she dismissed the thought as quickly. Even her stepmother had to admit that the man was still acceptable to the *ton*. And she knew Dunstan was a better person than Hartley. Somehow, though she could not explain how, Elizabeth did not want to believe that Dunstan was guilty of anything but having too much to drink and a poor sense of direction.

Dunstan rose, towering above her like a great oak. "If I wanted to create a scandal, I could have made sure the maid found me there on the floor," he reminded her firmly. Her face blanched. "All I want to do now is make certain no gossip about this incident can touch either of us." He smiled sweetly, certain she was ready to yield. Soon she would agree with his proposal, and they could begin to make the arrangements.

Just as he was picturing himself beside Lord Ramsburg, helping to write speeches that changed the nation, a quiet, throaty voice asked, "You are telling me that what happened this morning was an accident, totally unplanned?" Elizabeth still could not believe that it was true.

"That's right." He sat down in the chair in front of her and took her hand in his. She looked at their clasped hands pointedly, but he ignored her. "But I cannot be sorry the incident happened."

"What?" She pulled her hand back as quickly as if she had touched hot coals.

"No. No. I didn't mean that."

"It seems to me you frequently say things you do not mean, Lord Dunstan." This time Elizabeth stood up and crossed to the window. "If you have anything further to say, please hurry. I have many duties waiting on me."

"But you can't go. We haven't arranged the marriage." All of Dunstan's plans evaporated. He stood up to follow her. But she glared at him and he sat back down, feeling slightly foolish. How had the situation gotten out of hand?

"What marriage?" Elizabeth's mouth was set in a firm line.

"Ours. Yours and mine." This time his tone was more tentative.

"I have told you before that I do not plan to marry you," Elizabeth said firmly. "If you do not desist, I will have to believe that everything that has happened has been a plot." For a moment she had believed him. Her wealth was too great a temptation, she supposed, remembering the lectures she had been given the first time she had gone to London. Even then she had been taken in. Remembering the humiliation she had faced that time, the quality of her own judgment, made Elizabeth stiffen her back. "If you are as innocent of wrongdoing as you claim, I am certain you are enough of a gentleman to do as I wish. I will bid you good-bye." She stood by the window, a perfect picture of spring, her eyes determined.

Realizing that for the moment he had no choice but to agree or be labeled a cad, Dunstan nodded. He walked to the door. His uneasiness and guilt made him pause just before he opened the door. "I shall be in London for some time. I can be reached at Darington House, Berkley Square, or at the Home Office." He swept her a bow worthy of a duchess. He turned to leave and then stopped again. He hesitated and then faced her. "You would do well to discourage your brother's interest in

Hartley," he said quietly. Then he opened the door and left.

"Darington House? Berkley Square?" Elizabeth swept to the door and opened it. Dunstan was gone. "I suppose he gave me his direction because he thinks I will change my mind," she said angrily. Not for anything would she admit that she wondered what would have happened if she had only said yes.

6

When Charles burst through the door as energetically as he had when he was a schoolboy, Elizabeth, once more in the throes of writing her friend, jumped. Her pen left a jagged hole in the paper, and the point on the quill broke. "I have been looking for you," Charles said, his voice carefully cheerful, not at all certain how she would greet him.

"I have been here all morning," Elizabeth said quietly, a smile on her face. He sounded just like he did when he was a small boy in trouble with his nanny or tutor.

"Jeffries said you were busy. So I saw the others off first." Charles dragged a chair across the carpet and sat down beside her desk.

"Where are they going?" Elizabeth looked at him in surprise. "I rather thought you would be out with them on a morning like this."

"Oh, they are going back to London. I decided to stay with you a while, if you will have me." His voice was properly humble. He glanced at his sister to see how she was going to react. She was waiting for him to look, laughter in her eyes.

"Caught you," she said, laughing. "Cousin Louisa will enjoy your visit." She could not hide her pleasure. She sat there quietly smiling, waiting for what she was certain would follow.

"I am sorry. You do know that, Little Bit?" His use of his childhood name for her made her smile even more. Charles looked at her, still confused about the easy way she was taking his apology.

"You told me that last night. I am glad we settled it before we went to sleep. I dislike going to bed with our arguments unresolved." She glanced at him, trying to discover any ill effects from his excesses of the evening before. "I only wish you would learn to drink more moderately."

"Now you sound like Mama," he said a trifle petulantly. He paused, still uncertain, and then hurried on. "I was a bit on the go last evening, wasn't I?"

"A bit? Charles, you were so far in drink you could hardly talk." Indulgent though Elizabeth was at times, she did not approve of his recent habits. "If you are not careful, you could be ruined." She turned to look at him, taking his hand between both of hers. "I don't mean to preach. You get enough of that from Mama. But I wish you could find something to do that would make you happy."

Charles let her clasp his hand for a moment, running a thumb over hers. Then he pulled away, his face darkening. "Little Bit, can you try again with Mama? I know what I want to do with my life, and it is not sitting around my estates watching my agents work." He stood up, running a hand over the back of his neck. Then he began to pace.

"I have tried. But since your cousin's death, she is even more adamant. As the heir to two vast estates, you cannot be risked." Elizabeth sighed, remembering the last letter she had received from her stepmother. Indulgent as the lady was, she was determined that her only son and her brother's heir besides would not risk his life on the Peninsula. She had told Elizabeth that the decision had nothing to do with her and that if she wanted to keep their relationship intact Elizabeth was to say nothing further on the subject. For such a pretty flibbertigibbet, Lady Ramsburg had a will of iron about some things. "I will try again but not immediately."

Then she remembered Dunstan. Before Charles could open his mouth to ask her why she would not sit down that very day and draft a letter, she asked, "Why did you bring Lord Dunstan here?"

"He was at the club when I was forming the party. Would have been rude if I had not offered an invitation. I was rather surprised when he accepted," Charles said, not at all pleased to have her attention diverted from his problem.

Elizabeth was carefully casual with her next question. "Is he the same Viscount Dunstan I have heard so many stories about?"

"Robert? Doubt it. Straight as an arrow. Knew him at school. He was in his last year when I entered. Now, his brother and father—they were the subjects of every gossip monger from London to Scotland—even made the papers, made your scandal look like a mere bagatelle." He laughed heartily.

"My scandal?" Her voice was dangerously low. As hurt as she was by his careless reminder, she also breathed a sigh of relief to discover that at least Dunstan had been honest with her in that part of what he had said.

"Now, Little Bit, you know what I mean." He glanced at her, trying to determine just how far he could go. Her eyes were sparkling, whether from anger or from laughter he wasn't sure. "It has been four years, Elizabeth. Even you should have gotten over it by now."

"Gotten over being the center of attention, having everyone gossiping about me?" She was angry. Charles cursed under his breath, regretting his impulsive mention of the affair. "Even the next year they were talking about me. I heard them when I went to fix a torn flounce. 'Too bad even all that money cannot keep a man. I suppose she will have to set her sights lower this Season. After all, it is her third.' I knew whom they were talking about." She sat down, covering her face with her hands, shaking as though it had happened only minutes before.

"Oh, Little Bit," Charles said as he wrapped his arms around her, patting her comfortingly. "You never liked being the center of attention, did you? Even at your birthday parties, you wanted me beside you." She shook her head against his shoulder. "How did you ever survive your Seasons?"

She pulled away, straightening her dress. "That was easy. I had Amelia the first Season. She didn't mind being the center of attention."

"Too true," Charles said laughingly. "Remember when she got her hair caught in John's waistcoat buttons?"

"I was so embarrassed, and there she was snuggling against him." Elizabeth's face lit with laughter. "He did propose the very next day. I have often wondered how she managed that."

"What else could the poor man do? He was hopelessly compromised," Charles reminded her. Although she knew that her two friends had been deeply in love, Elizabeth lost some of her color at the word "compromise." If John had been compromised by simply having Amelia so close, what would Charles think about what had happened to his sister that morning? She took a deep breath, visualizing exactly what he would do, her face losing even more color. Charles watched his sister's face and wished that he had held his tongue.

"Elizabeth, you know John had already made an appointment to see Amelia's father. You told me so yourself. I was simply joshing."

"You must think I am silly," she said quietly, wishing that she could be as fun-loving and easygoing as her brother was.

"No. I think you have convinced yourself that all those people of the *ton* do is talk about you."

"Even I am not that self-centered. But you must admit that gossip is one of their chief occupations." She sounded very bitter.

"What do you expect from people who have nothing better to do with their lives? And don't tell me that when you and Amelia get together, she doesn't bring you up-to-date on what has happened."

At that Elizabeth had the grace to look ashamed. She did enjoy her visits with Amelia and the gossip they shared. "But we do it in private."

"And that makes it all right?" Charles walked across the room and stood beside the mantel, carefully considering his next words. For the first time since she had returned home abruptly after the beginning of her third Season, she was talking about what had happened, and he did not want her to stop. He thought for a moment or two and then said, "Elizabeth, do you remember the first time I got to ride by myself?" She nodded, not certain why he had asked. "I fell off into that big mud puddle." He looked at her to make certain she was listening. "Do you remember what my groom made me do?"

"Get back on and ride home."

"That is what you should have done. Little Bit, the *ton* cannot touch you if you don't care what they are saying."

"But I do care. It makes me ill to think that people are talking about me. 'Poor Elizabeth.' I heard enough of that when I was a child." She got up and walked over to him. "I love your mother dearly, but she never understood how hard it was for me to accept her, to call her Mama. Then the servants, at least the ones who had known my mother, kept reminding me. 'Poor Miss Elizabeth. So young to lose her mother.' For a long time I thought I was the one who had caused her to go away, to die. All I could think about was what I had done to 'lose' her." Her eyes filled with tears as she remembered how she had hid in the schoolroom with her nanny, trying to escape the changes in her life. "Then just when everything was going so perfectly, it happened again. 'Poor Elizabeth.' I thought I would die. Charles, I simply could not go through it anymore." She put up her hand to wipe the tears from her cheeks. Instead he dabbed her eyes with his handkerchief. When she was calm again, she went on, "Father understood. At least I think he did. I have always thought that was why he bought the manor and tied it up the way he did." Thinking of his conversation with Hartley that morning, Charles flinched. "Oh, Charles, here I have been able to get away from the past. People accept me for who I am; they don't pity me." Her voice was earnest, pleading with him to understand.

"I do understand," he assured her. "You forget that I have been part of the *ton* for a couple of years now." He paused for a moment, thinking about how eagerly he had left the university for the last time. "At first it was fun, heady, exciting. After my cousin died, things changed." His face was pensive. He drew her arm through his and walked to the settee. "After George died, I became an object of great interest. I received more cards for balls, breakfasts, picnics than I ever imagined possible. But all anyone wanted was for me to marry one of their daughters."

"Marry? Charles, are you serious about someone? You are so young." Accustomed as she was to her society, Elizabeth saw nothing unusual in that remark. Although girls were expected to marry before they reached twenty, men waited.

"No. But Mama has joined the ranks of the matchmakers," he said angrily. "Every time I am invited for dinner or to a ball there is a new young lady for me to meet. You saw what happened at Christmas." Elizabeth nodded, for the first time realizing why so many of her stepmother's cousins and their families had joined them. "And you should see some of her choices." Charles rolled his eyes.

"Remember I have been through this, too. Mama was determined that my second Season would be my last as an unmarried lady. If I had not accepted Jack when I did, I think she would have had a spasm." For the first time Elizabeth could laugh at the events of that year. She giggled, thinking how chagrined her stepmother had been when she had accepted a mere "Mister" after refusing a viscount and a baron.

"Well, whatever she didn't have over you, she is having with me. She is driving me to drink." Elizabeth raised her eyebrows suggestively, and he had the grace to blush. "Don't lecture me." Charles ran his hand through his hair, disarranging his curls. "I think that if I would agree to marry, she would suddenly find that she could somehow find the courage to let me go into the army."

"Charles!"

"That is all she ever talks to me about, Elizabeth. Why do you think I came to the country?"

"I had hoped it was to see Cousin Louisa and me," she said dryly.

He had the grace to look ashamed. "It was." Then he added before she could get out the remark she was getting ready to say. "At least partly. Little Bit, you know I enjoy being with you."

"When I am not preaching to you, don't you mean?" she teased.

"That too. But you were right to be angry last night. I shouldn't have brought anyone here without your permission." His face was more serious than she had ever seen it. For the first time Elizabeth began to realize that her little brother, six feet and more of him, was a man.

"Maybe. But I was wrong, too. Charles, this property does belong to you. You have the right to visit it anytime you like," she said quietly. How could she have missed seeing that he was no longer the little boy she had teased and protected?

"But no right to treat it as I have." Too restless to stay seated, Charles began to walk around the room. "I talked to Carstairs this morning. The fields are being repaired, and I arranged to pay some compensation to the farmers as well as paying for the new seed." He paused and looked at her. She smiled back. He walked slowly around the room as if the movement made it easier for him to speak. "Elizabeth, I am sorry about Susan. But she was no innocent. After she could not attach Dunstan or me, she made a go for Hartley. We had bets on who would be next."

"Never dreaming your 'friend' would take advantage of her, of course." Elizabeth twisted around on the settee until she could look at him again. Her face was stern.

"Dash it, Elizabeth. If anyone was taken advantage of, it was Hartley." His sister raised her eyebrows and didn't say another word. Charles cleared his throat. He needed to tell her about Hartley's still being there. But before he could get the words out, the butler opened the door.

"Lord Dunstan is leaving at this time. He wishes to convey his thanks."

"I'll see him off and be back," Charles said, grateful for the reprieve. He hurried into the entry hall, where Dunstan waited, caped, ready to go.

"Thanks for the fishing, Beckworth. I enjoyed the visit. You must let me return the hospitality soon," Dunstan said quietly. He glanced around as if expecting someone else to appear. "Tell your sister that I hope to meet her again soon." Charles's eyebrows went up so that Dunstan hurried on. "We met briefly yesterday afternoon."

The door to the library clicked shut. "I'll see you in London," Charles said quietly as he walked Dunstan to the door. So Dunstan knew Elizabeth. Had that been the cause of this morning's distress? Although his farewells seemed sincere, Charles's mind was far away. At that moment he wished his mother, as meddling as she had been lately, were close at hand.

As Dunstan galloped down the long drive, he frowned. As much as he had been regretting his presence at the manor the day before, he now regretted leaving. "Blast. Why wouldn't she listen to me?" he yelled, spurring his horse. The cows in the home meadows turned their heads curiously and then went back to their grass. Dunstan galloped for a few minutes, letting his horse's speed blow his anger away. When he could think more clearly, he smiled, remembering the assignment that had brought him there in the first place. "If there was a message here this month, might there be another next?" he wondered.

In the library at the manor, Hartley stared at the door he had just closed, anger in his eyes and in his bearing. Dunstan was leaving. After the man's coolness at breakfast that morning, Hartley had been certain that something had gone wrong. And the constant suggestions and innuendos by that young friend of Charles's had kept him from being able to delve more deeply into the matter himself. Hartley threw himself into a large comfortable chair and considered the situation.

For a few minutes he simply stared into space, his fingers rubbing the fob he wore. Had Charles seen him at that moment he would have agreed with his mother and sister's view of the man. Hartley's pale blue eyes were narrowed to slits; his mouth shaped in a snarl. He was still concentrating minutes later when the bell for luncheon called them to the small salon.

To Hartley's delight, Elizabeth Beckworth's eyes grew wide as he walked into the salon. She turned to her brother. Before she could ask him the question that trembled on her lips, Charles walked across to her. "Elizabeth, have you had a chance to renew your acquaintance with Mr. Hartley? He has agreed to stay on for a few days to keep me company." He turned to his cousin, who stood beside his sister, bending to kiss her cheek. "A guest adds spice to any gathering, don't you agree, Cousin Louisa?" He looked at his sister as if pleading with her to hold her tongue. Not pleased to have a limit on his visit, Hartley nevertheless kept his expression pleasant.

"A handsome man is always welcome," Louisa said, dropping her eyes coquettishly. "I was beginning to wonder if I had bored all your friends at dinner last evening."

"You, boring? Never! You are one of the most

fascinating ladies of my acquaintance," Hartley said with a bright smile. He came up beside her and held out his arm. "Will you be my luncheon partner, my lady?" Louisa Beckworth fluttered her eyelashes at him in much the same way she had at her long-deceased husband. She took his arm, allowing him to lead her into the dining room.

Elizabeth and Charles, used to their cousin's flirtations, simply smiled and followed a little way behind. "Thank you for not making a fuss about Hartley's presence, Elizabeth," Charles said so quietly the others could not hear.

"Would it have done any good?"

"No."

"That's what I thought. How do you plan to entertain him?"

Before Charles had time to answer, they were in the dining room with the others. Because good manners demanded they pay attention to the others, the brother and sister did not have a chance to talk alone for some time. Elizabeth was the gracious hostess, a fact for which Charles was profoundly grateful. His sister, when she decided to be rude, was quite formidable.

Louisa was in her element. Her two "children" and a handsome gentleman who was not above flirting with her made her day complete. As Elizabeth watched her cousin with the younger man, she felt guilty. Louisa had given up so much when she had agreed to retire to the manor with her four years earlier.

Because of her cousin, Elizabeth had been accepted by the society of the county. She sighed, remembering what the cost had been. Louisa did love parties and flirting. She would grow wistful when others in the neighborhood packed up to return to London, but she never said a word. Left a childless widow when she was barely thirty, she had spent her life caring for Elizabeth and Charles, selling her own estate to be a resident on theirs because their father had convinced her she was necessary to them; she did so want to be needed. Just when Louisa had been making plans to return to a more social existence in Bath, Jack had deserted her little girl. Since then she had been Elizabeth's constant companion and defender.

Watching her flirt with Hartley, Elizabeth could not deny Louisa her amusement. She held back the sharp remarks she had ready for Charles and did her best to ignore her unwelcome visitor.

Over the next few days she was very successful. She saw Hartley at meals and with Charles, but he seemed to recognize that Elizabeth preferred to be alone. After her stepmother's stories and the scandal that had awaited when she returned home, she had expected him to be endowed with horns and a forked tail. Instead he proved to be pleasant. He provided interesting tidbits of gossip to enliven the evenings, never grumbled that he was bored. And he was always willing to visit the tenants with Louisa or play a hand of whist with her in the evenings for penny stakes more often than not. But even though Elizabeth admitted his good manners, she could not forget his reputation or the way he had taken advantage of Susan.

One afternoon as she rode across country with Charles, leaving their guest to take a nap, she asked curiously, "How did you and Hartley become friends?"

Charles looked at her sharply, not really wishing to admit the truth. "What does it matter?"

"Is it something you are ashamed of?"

"Yes."

"I knew there was something not quite right.

You have been avoiding him whenever you could. Why don't you ask him to leave?" Elizabeth pulled her horse to a halt, forcing Charles to do the same. She turned to look at him. "Well, are you going to tell me you want him to stay?"

"It is not the thing to do." Her brother avoided her eyes, turning to survey the fields on the horizon. "Besides, he amuses Louisa." And, he admitted to himself, as long as Hartley was at the manor the man could not hope to collect on that piece of paper Charles had signed.

"Come, now, Charles. You can think of a better excuse than that." Elizabeth said sardonically. "Why does he want to stay? What could be of interest to him here? We have no gambling."

"Every time I go looking for him, he is with Louisa. Maybe she is the one who should explain," her brother said in a teasing voice.

Elizabeth glared at him and spurred her horse into a gallop, the rich azure blue veil on her riding hat trailing behind her like a war banner. Charles followed for a while and then passed her, heading back toward the manor. When she reached the stables, he was waiting to hand her down. "Charles, try to get him to leave. He is already the subject of rumors in the area. Servants, no matter how well trained, do talk to their friends on other estates. And you know how your mama feels about him. If she hears that he is visiting you here . . ." She let her voice trail off suggestively.

"Then my hopes for a commission are forever gone." She nodded and headed toward the house. Charles stood and watched her until she disappeared.

"Damn!" Charles slammed his hand against the side of the barn.

"Something wrong, sir?" asked a groom who

was hurrying forward to take the reins of the horses from him.

"No. Nothing." Charles handed him the reins and plunged off toward the house, taking the familiar route through the kitchen.

No sooner had Elizabeth entered the front entry hall than Jeffries appeared. "Your mail, Miss Beckworth," he said quietly.

"I will take it upstairs with me. Was there anything for anyone else?" Every day she hoped Hartley would receive a message recalling him to town.

"Only for Mrs. Beckworth and your brother." Jeffries stood quietly waiting for further orders.

"Send my maid up to me, please," Elizabeth said as she looked at the letters from Amelia and her stepmother. There was an unfamiliar handwriting on one that puzzled her. "Oh, tell her I will want a bath," she added as she headed up the stairs, turning the letter over to see if she recognized the seal.

As usual her maid had already anticipated her desires; Miller had the tub ready. Elizabeth gratefully disrobed and climbed into the copper tub, shivering for a moment in the cool air. Miller quickly poured another bucket of hot water in, waiting for the sigh of satisfaction her mistress always gave when the water was exactly right.

Elizabeth closed her eyes for a moment, letting the warm water soothe her. Then she reached out a hand. "Hand me my mail, Miller." She quickly opened her stepmother's letter, noting that once again it began with an invitation and a command. "She wants me to come to London now or at least to Brighton for the summer, Miller. Do you think she will ever give up?"

Her maid, if she had been asked her opinion,

would have agreed with Lady Ramsburg. Miss Beckworth needed more people around her. Miller did not want to be the maid of a crotchety maiden lady all her life. When she had taken the position as lady's maid to her mistress, she had envisioned dressing her for all the famous *ton* parties, of being sought after for her unique way of curling her mistress's hair. For the first Season it had been everything she had dreamed it would be. One mother had begged her to take charge of her less-than-beautiful swan, but by then Miller had grown accustomed to her mistress. Had the questions been asked during the last four years, the answer might have been different. She still had hopes. She noticed Elizabeth shiver and added another bucket of hot water. She turned to ring for more.

"Well, we will not be seeing Lord and Lady Ravenwood for a time," Elizabeth said, her voice disappointed. "He feels that they must be in Brighton for the summer."

"Brighton seems a popular place." Miller laid out her mistress's clothing on the bed, then hearing a scratching at the door, hastened toward it and admitted a maid with two more buckets of hot water. They added the hot water to the bath, putting towels around the floor to catch the overflow.

Finished with her letter from her friend, Elizabeth handed it to Miller and broke the seal on the third, the mysterious letter she had been deliberately saving for last. As she read the signature, her face flushed. Her hand shook so badly she almost dropped the letter into the bath water.

Her maid noted her reaction, stepping close to the tub with a towel. "You have been in there long enough, Miss Beckworth. The skin of a prune is not becoming to a lady."

For once Elizabeth did not take exception to her maid's tone of voice. She stepped from the tub and allowed Miller to wrap her in the towel. Without stopping for further clothing, she walked to the chaise, the letter still in her hand. It was from the Viscount Dunstan—"your Robert" as he signed himself. He simply reminded her that his offer of marriage stood, that he did not plan to accept her refusal as final, that he hoped she remembered him with as much fondness as he remembered her.

Remember him? She could not forget him. Every night her dreams were filled with a handsome, sleepy face, warm lips, long brown legs, a broad, brown, muscular chest, and blue, blue eyes. She blushed once more as she thought of how wanton those dreams had grown. Not even during her engagement to Jack had she awakened reaching for someone beside her in her bed. Resolutely she put down the letter, resisting the impulse to run her finger over his signature one more time. "Your Robert" indeed.

7

A few evenings later Hartley watched the ladies leave, his eyes narrowed dangerously. Finally he turned to Charles. "I am very disappointed in you. I hope you have not forgotten the note you signed, my friend," the older man said quietly, a hint of steel evident in his voice.

"Promise?" Charles asked innocently. Hartley held up the slip of paper that had not left his person since the night it had been written. "Oh, that. Well, even if you do provide a husband Elizabeth will accept, I am not certain I want to sell this land." He walked to the billiards room and picked up a cue, missing the look of anger on Hartley's face. Hartley hurried after him. "Carstairs believes this place could produce more income if it were managed less conservatively," Charles explained.

Hartley picked up his own cue and stood there for a few minutes, his fingers clenched around it. "I suppose that now you have decided that you do not want to be in the army either," he said quietly when he could control his anger. His voice seemed unconcerned.

"Never." The determination in his voice as clear as ever, Charles watched as Hartley made his shot. "Even my mother would have to let me go if I had the money for a commission." He sighed. "How I wish there were more men in my family."

"What do you mean, more men?"

"For the last three generations our family has produced only a few men. My father was an only child; his closest relative was a cousin, Louisa's husband, who died when he was only thirty-two. On my mother's side, there is only her brother and her sister's son, a five-year-old." Charles put down his cue and crossed to the table where the brandy was. He poured himself a glass and offered one to Hartley. "At times I have wished for six brothers or at least more cousins."

"Speaking as someone who is a cousin, especially one of those who always had to wait to be invited to family events, I can assure you that a large family is not always pleasant." Hartley threw back the brandy and held his glass out for a refill. His eyes glittered angrily. "I would prefer to be in your situation."

"You say that now. When my mother started in on you about marriage, you would change your mind." Charles drank another glass of brandy, relaxed now that he had explained his position to Hartley.

"Marriage. You would soon be bored," Hartley said as if thinking aloud. "Come. I am feeling in a lucky mood tonight. What about a wager?" And if he were lucky, Hartley would be able to add some more cushion between himself and the moneylenders, enough to tide him over without having to use the small quarterly allowance that would soon be due.

His winnings that evening only whetted Hartley's appetite. He waited impatiently for another opportunity. But Charles and Elizabeth spent the afternoon engrossed in a chess game. Finally when the dressing bell rang for the evening meal, Elizabeth sank back into her chair and looked at the board. In another few moves he would have her trapped. "Shall we call it a game?" she asked, stretching. Then she jumped slightly as she noticed Hartley sitting where he could watch them, his eyes on her.

"Does that mean you admit I will win?" Charles asked, a grin on his face. He had noticed Hartley arrive, but had been so engrossed that he had ignored him.

"I suppose," his sister said grudgingly. "Good evening, Mr. Hartley, have we been ignoring you long?" She smiled at him as if asking his forgiveness.

"I understand. Chess can be absorbing." Hartley rose as Elizabeth got to her feet.

"Please excuse me. I must change." She turned to her brother. "Do you plan to go up?"

"You go ahead. I will be up shortly," he assured her, turning to the man who was making him feel more uncomfortable every day. "Did you find something to occupy your time this afternoon, Sebastian?" he asked, a forced smile on his face.

"Counting my winnings helped, Charles." He smiled, the quiet, confident smile of a man who knows he holds the winning cards. "Perhaps you would like a rematch later?"

"Neglecting my sister and aunt last evening was enough. I do not believe I should desert them this evening too." Charles smiled, hoping Hartley would accept the statement.

Hartley looked at him for a moment, started to speak, and then thought better of it. He nodded, his expression carefully bland. "Then we shall invite the ladies to stroll in the garden and to play a hand of whist." He pulled the cuff of his dark brown coat down and walked to the mirror over the mantel to check the folds of his cravat. "Do you think I need to redo this?" he asked Charles.

"If you plan to change, Beckworth, you had better be at it. The changing bell rang some time ago."

Charles made good his escape. By the time he returned to the salon in a light blue coat that had arrived from London only that day, both Elizabeth and Louisa were before him. And Jeffries was hovering in the hall, waiting to announce the meal. Although Cook was at her best, the lobster patties and fresh peas with mint, usually Charles's favorites, disappeared without comment. "Something is bothering the master," Jeffries said, consoling the woman later that evening.

"And why does it always have to happen just before a meal? I ask you, Mr. Jeffries, how people can expect me to work if they do not appreciate my talents?" Cook asked, her face mournful. Only the arrival of a footman with an empty syllabub bowl soothed her. Jeffries breathed a sigh of relief, but his own mind was as disturbed as Cook's. He had delivered the brandy to the billiards room the previous evening, his eyes narrowing in dismay as he noticed the condition of his master.

Leaving the men to their port, the women retired to the salon, but they were not alone long, merely enough time for Louisa to ask, "Did you and Charles discuss how long the two of them plan to stay?" She picked up a cup, its floral design of the soft blue of her gown. The matching turban pinned with her favorite sapphire brooch made a frame for her wispy bangs and soft face.

"No." Elizabeth put the teapot back on its tray. "I did everything in my power to avoid discussing any topic that might have upset him. The afternoon was quite a pleasant one." She twitched a bow that was loose back into place.

"Here they come," Louisa said softly, her face carefully bland as the door to the room swung open. "Are you gentlemen ready for some cards?"

The next morning found Hartley in the breakfast room before anyone else. Elizabeth, following her usual routine, descended about fifteen minutes later. Startled to see Hartley, she paused in the doorway for only a moment, her eyes wide. Then she turned to Jeffries and spoke quietly. A few minutes later Charles appeared, his eyes still blurry and his clothing less than his pristine best. As the two men talked quietly, or at least Hartley talked and Charles mumbled, Elizabeth wondered what she would have done had she discovered Dunstan waiting for her. At times her memories of their meetings were so clear she found it hard to believe that they had happened over a week earlier. Even the thought of Dunstan caused a faint flush to rise in her cheeks. Although she would not admit it to herself, each day she waited impatiently for the mail to arrive. The letter she had received was hidden in her desk, carefully put out of sight and away from harm.

Secure in Charles's presence, she laughed lightly and was as gracious as she could force herself to be. Only the stray thought that her stepmother would have been proud of her made her realize how easily she was hiding what she was feeling. Once again she thought about Brighton.

"Miss Beckworth? Do you agree?" Hartley asked, smiling at her, his determination to win her approval of Charles and his friendship. She looked at Hartley, trying to remember what he had said. "Will you join me in the garden later this morning?" he asked again, hiding his annoyance behind a smile.

Elizabeth tried to think of a logical reason for refusing him. "Well," she began and then realized how rude her attitude seemed. "We do need fresh flowers. What time do you suggest?" The arrangements made, she left. Charles, still sleepy, made his way out with her, heading back to his bed for a nap. Elizabeth hurried upstairs, knowing her cousin would be awake and enjoying a comfortable coze in bed.

She knocked on her cousin's door. When the maid answered, she entered and then stopped, startled. It was dark, the curtains pulled against the outside light. "What's wrong?"

"She has one of her heads. I gave her the medicine the doctor left for her," her cousin's maid said in a soothing tone. "With a few hours sleep she should be fine."

Elizabeth frowned. Well, Charles would simply have to be in the garden with her. She made soothing statements and left.

By the time Elizabeth finished her morning conferences and got a bonnet to wear outside, her brother was nowhere to be found. Elizabeth drew in a deep breath and then let it out slowly. A frown creased her otherwise smooth brow. The frown increased a few minutes later when she remembered that it was her maid's day off. Finally she found a young maid and pressed her into service as a companion.

When she met Hartley, she could see his eyebrows rise. "Today is Miller's day off," Elizabeth said hurriedly. As Hartley smiled and walked toward her to take her arm, Elizabeth quietly told the maid to walk behind them.

The farther they went from the house, the closer Hartley held her arm. Finally Elizabeth could tolerate it no longer. "Sir, I think you are growing familiar with me!" she exclaimed in a laughing tone that hid her growing nervousness. She pulled away and sat down in the center of a nearby bench, carefully arranging the skirts of her yellow muslin dress around her.

Hartley hastened to her side. In spite of her distaste, he took her hand. She tried to pull away, but he would not let her. "Being able to share such a quiet visit with my friend in the midst of his family has meant so much to me. It is so long since I have had a real home. I appreciate you sharing yours with me." He paused, a thoughtful expression on his face. "If I can win your respect I will be happy."

At that Elizabeth gave her hand jerk, pulling it free. She stood up, her face set in stern lines. "You are my brother's friend, sir. That should be enough for you." Her voice was dangerously low and quiet.

"Are you refusing my offer of friendship?" Hartley asked. He moved a few feet away, but his eyes were fixed on her face.

She retreated. For a moment after she had put a sufficient amount of space between the two of them to feel comfortable, she simply looked at him. "Mr. Hartley, you are my brother's guest. I do not wish to be rude."

His face darkened with anger. "Are you so perfect to sit in judgment on me? I think not."

Elizabeth's face turned red and then as pale as the whitest roses on the bushes around him. She turned away, hoping to catch sight of a gardener, but the only other person nearby was the maid, who stood beside the climbing roses down the walk. Elizabeth's voice was very soft and surprised as she said, "I did not say—"

"But you implied it." Hartley let his anger show, realizing that he would never gain her support. "You have looked down on me from the first moment you met me. I suppose you and Lady Ramsburg are jealous of the friendship between Charles and me. I could see it in your eyes this morning. So this is the famous hospitality that English landowners are famous for. You only welcome those of equal rank and look down on the rest of us."

Elizabeth took several deep breaths to calm her nerves. Then she said in a voice she was proud was clear but steady, "Obviously, Mr. Hartley, we will never agree. Perhaps you will feel more comfortable in your own home."

"Leave. Why, you . . ." Hartley reached for her, but Elizabeth drew back. The maid, her eyes growing wider, darted forward and stood close by her mistress's side. Hartley pulled himself up as tall and menacing as he could. "We shall see what your brother has to say about this. And then we will talk again," he said, his voice seeming to promise retribution. This time Hartley did not try to hide the anger in his face or in his voice. He plunged past Elizabeth, giving her only a moment to pull back and to avoid being knocked to the ground.

8

As soon as she walked into her home, Elizabeth told the maid who accompanied her, "Find Jeffries. Send him to me immediately." The girl nodded and scurried away.

His face stiff and his back ramrod-straight, Jeffries listened as Elizabeth explained that it was imperative that she see her brother immediately. He frowned slightly at her tone. "Mr. Hartley has also been inquiring for him," he told her stiffly.

"Did he find him?" Elizabeth asked, her face carefully unconcerned although her voice shook a little.

"No. He left word with me that I was to tell Mr. Beckworth that he needed to speak with him immediately." For a moment his stiffness evaporated. "Miss Beckworth, I believe he is not a good companion for the master. His attitude to me was not that of a true gentleman. Is there a problem?"

"Make certain Charles sees me before he sees Hartley." She looked up at the tall man, his light brown hair just beginning to gray. "With my luck and your skill we should brush through this nicely," she assured him. He blushed and hurried away.

A short time later Charles walked through her door, his face concerned. "Jeffries sent me word that you needed to see me immediately. What has happened? Is it Louisa?"

"If only it were that simple."

"Elizabeth! Make sense, please." His close inspection of her revealed that she was more agitated than he had seen her lately with anyone but himself. "What have you found out about me now?" he asked defensively, running through his latest actions like a small boy who reviews his misdeeds while waiting for his father's judgment.

"You? What are you talking about?" she asked as she walked over to where he stood close to the door. Her curls, still disheveled from her bonnet, bounced as she walked. Her hazel eyes snapped.

"Are you telling me that I left a sick horse for nothing?"

"No." Elizabeth whirled to face the window, the soft yellow muslin that she wore spread out like a bell. Admitting to Charles what had happened would be bad enough, she decided. She did not have to face him to do it. She hesitantly pulled back the drapes. There in front of her was the very place where it had happened. She stiffened her back and turned to face her brother once more. "Charles, I told Sebastian Hartley to leave." She was rather surprised to hear how steady her voice sounded.

"What?" Charles's words were almost a shout. "How could you be so rude? Have you lost your senses?" His long legs made the distance between them disappear. He grabbed her shoulders, pulling her around to face him. "How could you do something like that?"

"Actually it was quite simple."

"Elizabeth!"

"Charles, the man said I was a snob just because I did not agree with him. Had I been a guest in this house I would have thought twice before insulting my hostess. And he said I had bad manners. I would not feel comfortable in this house with him." She paused, letting her words sink in.

"But if you prefer that he remain, Louisa and I will leave." She tossed her head, and her eyes flashed.

"No, there is no need for you to leave. I will see him, smooth everything over." Charles frowned. "Have you told Louisa what happened?"

"No. She has one of her headaches. But she will agree with me." She thought for a moment and then added, "Had he been a true gentleman, he would have offered to leave immediately." She glared at her brother, remembering how quick Dunstan had been to tell her of his departure. And if Charles had chosen his friends more carefully . . .

"I suppose you expect me to oversee this departure?" Charles stopped and looked at her, disapproval written heavily on his face.

"Yes. But be careful. He is not going to like hearing you agree with me," Elizabeth said with a sigh. She rubbed her head again, wishing she could curl up on the chaise with her eyes closed and sleep the rest of the day away as Louisa was doing. Then she smiled suddenly and sat up straighter. "I do not plan to leave this room until you can tell me he is gone. Tell Jeffries I will have luncheon in my room."

Regarding his sister with some anxiety, Charles crossed to the door. "You could change your mind and see him with me," he suggested.

"Not unless you want to see me have a temper tantrum to put my old ones to shame," she said, her voice a deep, throaty promise of destruction.

Charles, recognizing the danger, opened the door slightly. "You are certain?" She nodded her head imperially. He straightened his shoulders and left. As soon as the door closed, Elizabeth slumped back down on the chaise, her face hidden in her hands.

When he had changed from his riding clothes, Charles walked slowly down the stairs, his face somber. With every downward step he took, he could see Hartley waving the note he had signed in front of his face.

"He is in the library, sir," Jeffries told him when he asked where his guest was.

Reluctantly Charles headed down the hall. He stopped in front of the door, drew himself up until he was standing as straight and tall as he possibly could, and walked boldly into the room. "Jeffries told me you wanted to see me," he said quietly, looking more stern than he usually did.

Hartley lounged in one of the big leather chairs, his face determined. When he saw Charles, it changed. "Your sister has thrown me out, Charles. Talk to her, tell her who is master in this house." His pale blue eyes glittered angrily.

Embarrassed, Charles fell back a step or two. He cleared his throat. "I am master here, but my sister is the mistress of the house. She has the right to be comfortable in her own home." He crossed to a chair opposite the one in which Hartley sat. "If it were only my views to consider, you could stay here for the rest of your life. But the ladies—"

"Always knew you would crumple under pressure," Hartley said with a wry laugh. Charles flinched. "Well, I would not want to upset your household. I'll be on my way as soon as my valet packs." He walked to the door. "Have the coach ready in an hour." He looked at Charles and noted his look of surprise. "You did remember that I came with you, Beckworth? If you want me to leave, you will have to provide me transportation. Or you could leave with me." He smiled at that thought knowing how much it would disturb Elizabeth to see her brother depart with him.

"I cannot. But I will accompany you for a time. And I will see you as soon as I return to London."

Hartley laughed, the kind of laughter that mocks. "Ride at your own risk. You do not want to incur your sister's anger." He laughed again and slammed the door.

9

While Charles accompanied Hartley on the beginning of his journey, another rider galloped up smaller roads leading from the coast to the manor. From the look of his horse, the farmers he passed could tell that the man and his beast had been on the road for some time. He paused at the gates of the manor, wishing he had had time to pack at least a clean shirt. Then he spurred his horse on.

A few minutes later Jeffries opened the door. "My lord," he said in amazement, looking at the viscount, who was covered in dust. "Mr. Beckworth is not at home," he began correctly enough, but his shock caused him to ask, "Was he expecting you?"

"I did not come to see Charles, Jeffries." Dunstan caught sight of himself in a mirror. "It is Miss Beckworth I seek. But first, is there somewhere I can wash away a little of this dirt?"

"Certainly. I will have a footman bring some water and towels to the bedroom you had when you stayed with us. Would you like some tea also?" Jeffries, determined to show the nobleman the proper respect, was still not certain. "Will your luggage be arriving shortly?"

"I am only here for an hour or so. I must be in London by tomorrow morning," Dunstan explained, stretching. After hours in the saddle, he needed a rest, but there was no time for one.

At that, Jeffries' impassive face showed a flicker of concern. Then he said firmly, "After you have had time to freshen up, I will tell Miss Beckworth you wish to see her."

"Tell her simply that she has a visitor. Do not tell her it is I." Dunstan winked. Jeffries, scenting a romance, hurried on his errands.

Less than a half hour later, Dunstan was once more in the morning room, pacing up and down. During the long ride he had told himself that he would not try to see Elizabeth again. But here he was, his heart racing furiously.

The door opened, and Elizabeth walked in, expecting to see one of her neighbors. She caught sight of Dunstan and stopped, her stillness a measure of her surprise. "Lord Dunstan, my brother is not here."

"Jeffries told me." His voice was dry and raspy. "I am here to see you." He took a step toward her, his blue eyes holding her hazel ones in check.

"Why?" she asked huskily, her voice no more than a whisper. He looked so tall, so strong in his rumpled clothes.

"To see if you had changed your mind." She was more desirable than he had remembered. He could smell the sweet scent of her perfume from where he was standing.

She turned and walked over to her small desk, picking up his letter that she had put there that morning. "I was going to answer you," she said, her hands turning the letter.

"Now I have saved you the trouble." Dunstan took a step closer, and she retreated. He stepped back and took a deep breath. "Will you be my wife?"

"Dunstan, we have been over all of this before. No. I cannot. My reasons remain the same." She looked at him longingly, wishing she could trust him enough to change her answer.

Once again he stepped back, almost as though he did not want to frighten her. "Change your mind," he pleaded.

"No."

He looked at her again, coveting her soft, red mouth. Taking a deep breath, he smiled. "Don't forget me," he said quietly and left the room.

Forget him? Elizabeth thought. Dunstan in clothes was as devastating as Dunstan wrapped in a sheet or pillow. She sighed deeply and went back upstairs.

Finding Hartley's company less than hospitable, Charles traveled only a short way with him. Then he returned to the village inn, seeking the company of men.

Before nightfall Hartley was well on his way toward London, the uncomfortable jostling of the coach provided by his former host an unpleasant reminder of the ending of his visit. With every jolt his expression grew harder.

Thinking back over his visit, he admitted to himself that perhaps his timing had been less well chosen than usual. Apparently Elizabeth was still distressed over the episode with the maid. That morning she had not tried to hide her condemnation. For a moment his face blackened with anger; then suddenly he smiled and leaned back on the gray velvet squabs, his hand clenched on the strap beside him.

The first week of his visit had gone extremely well. That Susan was a saucy piece. He grinned as he remembered how eagerly she had fallen into his hands. No matter what the girl had claimed, she had been as eager as he. "Damn all maiden ladies who try to spoil our fun," he muttered, remembering the accusatory look in Elizabeth's eyes. If she and that silly cousin of hers had stayed away for a few days longer, he would have been able to quiet Susan and win enough money to ensure he would not have to worry about finances ever again.

As usual when he was alone and one of his schemes had gone awry, he began to review the situation. He smiled mirthlessly, his eyes glinting blue ice. Dunstan, he would have to send him the money he had lost to him as soon as he arrived in London. With quarter day still some time away, he would need to practice economy, something he hated. Still, he could not afford to have people questioning his ability to pay his gambling losses. Thinking of the comfortable existence he had been forced to give up for his small rooms made his anger flare again. He flung open the small curtain between him and the driver. "Spring 'em," he said, his voice harsh.

"But, sir—"

"Spring 'em." This time the command was quiet, so quiet that the coachman stopped trying to argue and sent his whip crackling over the backs of the pair he was driving. He ordered the groom to watch closely for approaching vehicles, for the road was bordered by rock fences and was so narrow that if another coach approached, a collision would be hard to avoid.

Just when the coachman was beginning to believe he was clear of the danger, he heard a loud crack as he hit a particularly deep rut. During the next few minutes the coachman had all he could do to keep the coach upright and to stop the horses.

"What happened?" Hartley demanded, jumping

from the coach. His face wore an angry expression that boded trouble for someone.

"The wheel, sir. And one of the horses has come up lame," the coachman said, his face worried.

"How bad is it?"

"We'll need a wheelwright to fix it. There's a town up ahead. We stop there sometimes on our way to London," the man assured him.

"I'll take the other horse. You stay here. I'll send someone back for you when I reach the inn. I suppose there is an inn," Hartley said, his voice mocking.

"Yes, sir, the White Hart. It's not large, but the innkeeper is honest," the coachman assured him. He wiped his sweaty forehead with his sleeve and loosed the last rein; then he led the horse over to Hartley. "He's sound enough, sir. You should be at the inn shortly." He took off his hat and dusted it against his trousers. "Don't know what the master will say about this."

Hartley glared at him. Taking the reins, he mounted. "Make certain nothing happens to my clothes," he ordered. Then he turned the horse and headed down the road.

"Don't know anyone who'd want the things. Too perfumy and tight for anyone I know," the coachman muttered as he watched Hartley spur the horse onward. "Hope he remembers to send someone for us. The older chap don't look so good." He nodded toward the wall, where Hartley's valet sat, his back against the wall and his head in his hands, for once totally oblivious to the damage he was doing to his clothing by sitting in the grass.

Breaking his usual silence, the groom said in a dry voice, "As long as we got his clothes, he will." Together they both chuckled. Bending their shoulders to the rear of the coach, they worked to move it from the road. A short time later the mail coach lumbered by, the passengers on top laughing at their predicament.

At the White Hart, the innkeeper listened to Hartley and gave instructions: the best bedchamber prepared and men sent out to bring in the coach and the servants. Soon Hartley was sitting in a private room, a glass of wine in his hand, waiting for his meal. He stretched lazily, looking around him with interest.

When the door opened a short time later, he sat up. "It took you long enough," he said angrily. Then his eyes opened wide. "Susan?"

"What are you doing here?" she asked, her voice hostile. She tossed her guinea-gold curls proudly.

"I could ask the same of you, but I can see you've landed soft." He laughed at her expression. "I thought they paid you off."

The girl plunked the dishes on the table, sloshing the soup onto the top. She swung around and faced the man, her hands on her hips. The kerseymere dress a deep red, much too good for a girl in her position, swirled around her. It hugged her curves and amply displayed her full breasts. "You have no call to laugh at me, sir," she reminded him. "Thanks to you and the mistress I am my own employer. Or I will be soon."

"What do you mean?" Hartley leaned back in his chair again, smiling winsomely. He caught her hand and brought her over to him. Running his finger around the low neckline of her dress, he smiled and winked.

"I'll have none of you, Mr. Hartley. Now I know your ways, I know better than to trust you."

"You don't have to trust me for what I have in mind," he said, his voice soft and coaxing. He tried to pull her onto his lap, but she pulled away.

"What's the matter? Do I need to offer you money now?"

Her eyes glittered angrily. She whirled and crossed to the door. Lazily, Hartley rose and followed her. Just then a hearty voice called, "Susan? Here's the mail. Where are you?"

"I have to go." She reached for the latch, but his hand caught hers. "Please, I have to go. We have only a short while to get them back on the road."

Hartley pulled back. "Will I see you again?" he asked, his voice caressing.

Hesitantly she nodded. As he bent to kiss her, she opened the door and rushed from the room. Hartley stood there for a moment, looking after her. Then he headed back to the table. His face set, he came back to his meal, ripping a leg from a capon. He ate hungrily, his ears listening to the rumble of noise from the public room. When after less than a half hour the noise died and he heard the mail coach lumber away, he rang for the innkeeper. "Bring ingredients for a punch," he said quietly, taking the man's measure.

Within minutes the ingredients were assembled: lemons, nutmeg, arrack, brandy, sugar, and the rest. He watched carefully as the innkeeper heated the irons in the fire and mixed the ingredients, his round face earnest. When the punch was poured into Hartley's cup, he took a cautious sip and then nodded his satisfaction. "Have my servants arrived yet?"

"No, sir. But the only horse I had to send is a walker. Hard to make him go. They should arrive shortly. Will there be anything else?" He stood there quietly for a moment, wishing the gentleman would hurry.

"The girl who came in here before? Who is she?" Hartley asked, his voice carefully neutral.

"Susan?" The man beamed. Hartley nodded. "My wife-to-be. Plan to marry as soon as my sister returns. It was my lucky day when she arrived." Warming to his subject, the innkeeper forgot his pressing business and rattled on. "You see, my sister left to get married. I couldn't begrudge her wanting her own home. Left me in quite a bind, though. No one to supervise the women. And that meant I could hire only a certain type, if you know what I mean, sir. No one to serve the noble ladies who stop here occasionally. Quite a problem." He shook his head. "Then Susan got off that mail coach. I took one look at her and struck up a conversation. Luckiest day of my life, I tell you that. Forced to leave her job because of unwelcome advances by the gentleman of the house, she was, and looking for work. Had some money of her own too. Together we'll make this the best inn in the area. That's our plan." He smiled and rubbed his hands. Realizing the rank of the man to whom he was talking, he stopped and stammered, "Sorry to ramble on, sir."

"No, I asked you. Did she tell you who had forced his attentions on her?" Hartley asked. His voice was guarded.

"Didn't need to hear. That's what I told her. Many a young girl without a family has the same problem. Now she has me. I'll take care of her now." The set look on the innkeeper's face kept Hartley quiet. Recalling his other duties, the man asked, "Will there be anything else, sir? Susan makes good tarts. Some will be fresh from the oven soon."

"Tarts?" Hartley laughed. "Have her bring me some while they are still warm." Nodding, the innkeeper bowed and left. Hartley sipped another cup of punch, his mind replaying the vision of

Susan in that red dress. Before his dream became too vivid, the door to the room opened again. "Your servants have arrived, sir. Do you wish to speak to them?"

"The coachman perhaps. And send my valet up to put out a change of clothes for me." Hartley's voice was lazy.

" 'Fraid he can't, sir. Coachman had me send a boy for the doctor. Seems your man has been hurt." The innkeeper fixed his eyes on the gentleman stretched out in the chair, his eyes half closed.

"Hmmm. Definitely send me that coachman." This time Hartley's tone carried the force of a whip. As soon as the door closed behind the man, Hartley stood up, crossing to the only mirror in the room. He was standing there adjusting the lapels of his dove gray coat and the folds of his cravat when Charles Beckworth's servant entered. Noting the straight shoulders under the close-fitting jacket, the coachman kept his distance, saying nothing until Hartley finished.

Finally the silence grew more than he could bear. The coachman asked, "You wished to see me, sir?"

Hartley let a few more minutes go by in silence. He polished the fob of his watch on his handkerchief, straightened his cuffs, and checked the shine of his boots, somewhat dimmed by his ride. Then he turned. "Who gave you the authority to call the doctor for my man?" he asked, his voice almost so quiet the other man could not hear.

"He was hurt, sir. Knew you wouldn't want to let him go without care." The coachman shifted nervously under the pale blue gaze that fixed him to the spot. "Mr. Beckworth told me to see that you got to London safely, to take care of everything."

"Then you should have done a better job." Just

then a knock cut off his angry words. Calling his permission to enter, Hartley smiled as he watched the coachman's face change as Susan walked in. "Ah, my dear, I believe you know this man. Come in and say hello."

Susan, tossing her head defiantly, put the plate of warm tarts on the table. She flashed an angry look at Hartley and glared at the coachman. Without saying a word she hurried from the room.

"Cor, what's she doing here? And all dressed up like the lady of the house?" the coachman asked, his dread of Hartley forgotten.

Hartley laughed at the look on his face. Then he said, "Go and make certain we are ready to leave in the morning." As the other man reached the door, Hartley added, "And send Susan in. I wish to compliment her on her baking." The door closed behind the man, and Hartley returned to the mirror. The punch he had drunk had brought a flush to his cheeks. The sight of Susan created the sparkle in his eyes.

By the time she entered some time later, his smile had slipped. His cheeks were more red because of the punch he had consumed. And his temper was on edge. When he looked up to see her, he said, "I called for you long ago." His eyes raked her as though he were evaluating a horse.

"I'm not yours to command, Mr. Hartley. I am my own mistress."

"Mistress. Now, there's a fine word. Yes, mistress." Hartley slid farther down in his chair, stretching his legs out before him and holding out his cup for more of the punch. He watched as she filled his cup, warming the drink with hot pokers first. When she started to move away, he grabbed her wrist. "Wonder what your innkeeper would say if he knew I were the gentleman whose attentions you were escaping. Then I just happened to show up here." He smiled up at her, chilling her as he had done the day he had laughed at her and told her he would never marry a mere maid.

She tried to pull away, but his hand tightened around her wrist. She bit her lips, turning this way and that, knowing that the bruise around her wrist would soon be visible. "What do you want from me now?" she cried.

"Aha! She can talk," he whispered, grinning at her. He pulled her closer to him. "Talk. And more if you do not want the innkeeper to discover your little secret." He leaned back so that he could look up into her face more clearly. "I wonder what you would do to keep your true past secret?"

By the time he left the next morning he knew. He smiled as they drove off. On the box above him, he could hear the angry rumble of voices. Once he heard "Lord Dunstan."

A few minutes later, the other voice, loud and harsh, shouted, "That Susan's no good. The mistress turned her off. Of course, she'd want to say something bad about Miss Beckworth. But I don't believe her. And you should keep your trap shut!" Hartley stretched out, tilted his hat over his face, a faint smile still on his lips, and began reviewing his acquaintance with all the young men recently come to town for the first time.

10

A few days after Dunstan's surprise visit another letter arrived for Elizabeth. This time she recognized the hand; the other letter from Dunstan rested in her desk. Every time she decided to discard it, something stopped her.

Taking her letter, she retired to her room more anxious than she wanted to admit. Cautiously she broke the seal, running her finger over the signature. Once again he was "your Robert." She unfolded the paper, running her fingers over the words as she had often dreamed she had run them over his chest.

Had anything been said by anyone at the manor? He had seen several of the men who had been there when he was; their questions had led him to believe their story was known. Was she certain no one had said anything?

Elizabeth gasped and lowered the letter. Her hazel eyes grew serious. Why hadn't he mentioned the gossip when he was here? Quickly she tried to remember everything that had happened the last few days. The servants were gossiping; his surprise visit had seen to that. But there was nothing malicious in it. Hartley? she asked herself. But in spite of her mistrust of the man, he was one of her brother's closest friends. She sighed, admitting that Dunstan's presence was the reason for the gossip. Even though she had not answered his first letter, she would answer this one and tell him to leave her alone. Telling herself she needed to be able to answer him well, she read the letter again. Why didn't she come to London, he asked. They could announce their betrothal; she could enjoy the last of the Season. Then they would marry, joining the rest of the June weddings at St. George's, Hanover Square.

Ignoring everything but the last few words, Elizabeth laughed, more relieved than she would admit to herself that his letter had not been a graceful farewell. Throwing her usual habits to the wind, she climbed up on her bed, her light gold muslin dress a pool of vivid color against the turquoise of her satin bed coverings. But climbing into bed was a mistake. When she closed her eyes, she could remember him there, his long legs poking out from under the covers, his chest brown against the white sheet. Drifting off into a semi-sleep, she turned over, her dress crumpling around her, only to waken to a thump. She turned hastily, expecting to see Dunstan on her floor, but her maid stood there, a box on the floor in front of her.

"Sorry for waking you, Miss Beckworth. It won't happen again, I assure you," the maid said quickly, surprised to see her mistress curled up in bed on a sunny late spring afternoon. "Aren't you feeling well? Should I fetch a compress for your head?"

"No, Miller, I am fine." Elizabeth climbed from the bed, the letter still clutched in her hand. She glanced down at her wrinkled gown. "You will need to find me something fresh to wear, though." The maid nodded. Elizabeth walked across the room to the window, staring sightlessly out into the beautiful rose garden below. Then she looked back down at the letter.

Crossing to her desk, she sat down, smoothing the creases from the paper, letting her eyes follow the sweeps and strokes of Robert's strong strokes that covered the page, remembering him all dusty from a long ride just to see her. Before she realized it, she began to see the two of them, walking, dancing, sleeping ... She stopped. Leaving the letter on top of her desk, she let her maid help her change into something fresh. But often she would find herself looking back at the crumpled sheet of paper.

During the next few days she more than once picked up a pen and wrote a few lines, only to throw them away seconds later. She was so lost in her own world Charles grew worried. After Elizabeth drifted through the salon, ignoring him completely even though he spoke to her several times, he sought out Louisa.

Propped up in bed with her latest novel close at hand and a box of her favorite chocolates beside her, Louisa was enjoying her ill health. When her headache had continued, more from boredom than anything else, her doctor had recommended some time in bed. And she had taken him literally. During the day she indulged herself, rising from her "sickbed" only in the evenings. Then she would lie on the settee in the salon, wilting interestingly. Elizabeth and Charles always hovered nearby and tried to cheer her up by keeping her informed of what was happening on the estate and who had returned home early from the Season because a marriage was in their future.

If her plan went well, Louisa looked forward to an interesting summer in Brighton with her cousin. The letter she had received that day from Lady Ramsburg had renewed her determination that she and Elizabeth would enjoy the balls, the Venetian breakfasts, and the walks on the Steine this summer.

Picking up another chocolate and nibbling it, she read on fascinated while the heroine, trapped in an ancient castle filled with evil, foiled the villain once again. Then the door to her room burst open. Louisa jumped, dropping her book. She looked up frowning. Then her face became concerned. "Charles, dear boy, what is the matter?"

"Elizabeth! Louisa, have you talked to her lately?" Charles ran his hands through his hair as he usually did when he was upset. He walked nervously around the room, brushing small tables containing porcelain figures.

Louisa held her breath and closed her eyes, certain that at any moment her treasures would go flying. When one of her favorite Sevres vases trembled precariously, she was no longer able to remain silent as she waited to hear what he was thinking. She said firmly, "Charles." He looked up, startled, as if he had forgotten where he was. "Sit down before you break something."

He had the grace to look embarrassed. Then he pulled a chair next to the bed and sat down. Realizing that he could not see his cousin's face from that angle, he sat down beside her on the bed and picked up her hand. "I'm sorry," he said quietly. "But Elizabeth is acting so strangely."

"Tell me about it." Louisa patted his hand encouragingly.

"My valet said that Elizabeth's maid found her in bed asleep this afternoon. I was worried. When I tried to ask her about it, she ignored me." He paused for a moment, his brow creased. "No, that isn't right. She did not seem to hear me. Do you think she could be ill? I have heard that maiden ladies . . ."

"No, dear boy." Louisa stopped him, trying not to laugh. "When I saw her last evening, she was fine. She may have had something else on her mind."

"But she has never ignored me before." This time even Charles recognized how childish he sounded. "That is not what I meant. You must know, Louisa, how I worry about her."

"Yes, my dear, I do. And you must not. Elizabeth is a sensible person. You know that. Maybe there was a problem with the servants." Louisa reached up and brushed back a lock of blonde hair that had fallen over Charles's forehead. "By tonight I am certain she will be her usual self. If not, I will discover what is wrong. Will you leave it to me?" she suggested, putting her finger under his chin and raising his head until he had to look her in the eye. She had perfected the gesture when he was small.

He nodded. Then he smiled and reached down to hug her, picking her up from her pillows and disarranging her lace cap that covered her fading blonde curls. "I love you, Louisa," he said quietly.

"I know, Charles, and I love you." She patted him on the shoulder. Then she straightened up. "Now go talk to Carstairs or someone so that I can continue my ill health in peace." He laughed and slid off the bed.

Just before he opened the door, he turned. "And how long do you plan to be ill?" he asked, his face mischievous.

"You leave that to me, you young scamp," she said firmly, her face reflecting his laughter, her cheeks delightfully rosy.

When she came downstairs that evening, the roses were gone. Wearing a brown silk gown that she had purchased in a moment when she was feeling old and neglected, she drifted lifelessly into the salon. As she had discovered when it arrived, the gown made her look sallow. As a result she had hidden it away in the back of her clothespress, determined that she would be rid of it as soon as she stopped feeling guilty over wasting so much of her cousin's money. But for this evening it was perfect. She lay back in her chair, her eyes closed. Charles smiled. But when Elizabeth walked in a few minutes later, his face was suitably worried.

Elizabeth glanced from Louisa to Charles, suspecting something, but then she looked at Louisa closely. She hurried to her side. "Why did you try to come down, dearest, if you were not feeling well?" she asked.

Louisa opened her eyes, lifting her lids as if even that small amount of effort took more energy than she could possibly bear. "I am so bored with staying in bed," she explained, allowing her voice to drift off plaintively. Charles had to bite the inside of his jaw to keep from laughing. Louisa held out her hand, and Elizabeth took it.

"Perhaps tomorrow we should send for the doctor again," Elizabeth suggested, her face worried. If anything happened to Louisa, she would be lost. Louisa opened her eyes; then she frowned. Charles hastily wiped the grin off his face.

"I will be all right. Having the ones I love around me is all that I can ask for," Louisa said weakly. "I am certain I will be well soon." Elizabeth looked at Charles, her face worried. "Now tell me what has been happening to you." Louisa held out her hand dramatically until Charles rushed to her side. "Help me to the settee, dear boy." He helped her to her feet and across the foot or so that separated her chair from the settee. When she was comfortably settled, he stepped back. "Now, Elizabeth, sit beside me and tell me what has been happening."

For the rest of the evening Louisa kept Elizabeth at her side, asking her questions about the estate and about their neighbors. When she had at last retired, pleasantly tired and ready for bed, Louisa let her maid undress her and see her comfortably established in bed, then she waited.

As soon as Charles saw Elizabeth to her room and assured her that he too was worried about their cousin, he furtively walked along the corridor to his cousin's room. A short time later, he asked, "Well, what do you think?"

"She is definitely not ill. And nothing seems wrong on the estate. Has she been anywhere lately?" Louisa asked. Elizabeth had the look of someone lost in a dream.

"No. Oh, she visits the tenants. That is all since Hartley left." His face clouded. "She can't be still upset about my friendship with him, can she?"

"Hartley? No. She has put him out of her mind for now," Louisa said quietly, still thinking about what he had said. After a few minutes of silence she asked, "Has she mentioned anyone else?"

"Only Dunstan. She asked about him this morning." Charles stopped abruptly, his blue eyes growing wide. "You don't think? But she only met him once."

Louisa simply smiled. "Tell me more about the viscount," she said, her voice pensive.

Charles sat down across from her, stretched his feet out in front of him. "He is a member of my club. And he wins when he plays," he began.

11

While Louisa was plotting with Charles, the man who was in the center of both of their minds was in London. When Dunstan was not running errands for the government, he was carefully amassing a remarkable body of information about the people who had been present at the house party. As he sifted through the reports his informants sent him, his face darkened with suspicion. Hartley, known for leading innocents astray, was an acknowledged master of the underhanded trick. But he only used trickery when it would gain him some advantage. And to Dunstan's dismay he could not find any reason why Elizabeth's and his predicament would help the man.

To make his dismay even more complete, Dunstan received his first letter from Elizabeth that evening. Gentle as her tone was, the message was clear: no. A black depression fell over Dunstan, blacker even than the one he had felt when he realized that his father had totally abandoned him, left him alone at the school at the mercy of unknown people. But then, he reminded himself, the headmaster had known what to do.

His depression blotting out his reason, Dunstan spent that evening deep in his cups. By the time the butler and a footman helped him to his room, he was babbling. "Don't send me away. Must be married. No scandal," He repeated in a slurred voice. The two men raised their eyebrows and then shrugged. They had heard the stories about his father.

Over the next week or ten days, Dunstan's behavior deteriorated even further. Once a member of only the best clubs, Dunstan left the safer haunts of St. James for the hellholes, staking huge sums on the turn of a card. Gambling and drinking until dawn, he would stumble in, falling into bed without removing his clothes. Waking later, he would swallow the gruesome compound his valet held out, dress and head back to the latest hellhole. He gambled and he won.

"Don't play with him," he heard one man say loudly to another as he walked into yet another club. "Too lucky." The two men stared at him suspiciously.

In the background a man so tall he stood half a head taller than anyone else in the room followed the two men's gaze. Although impeccably dressed, the man had obviously seen rougher days. He looked at Dunstan carefully, his eyes narrowed dangerously. For the rest of the evening he was Dunstan's shadow. But Dunstan did not notice.

Hours later, when he was several thousand pounds richer, Dunstan weaved his way to the door. Before he crossed the threshold to the street outside, a hand as large as a kettle grabbed his arm, pulling him around. Staring into a shirtfront was not usual for Dunstan. Slowly he raised his head, a slightly bewildered look on his face. "Tall, very tall," he said, slurring his words.

The man ignored him. "You are no longer welcome here, my lord," the man said in a voice as deep as a kettledrum and as quiet as a whisper.

Dunstan jumped as though the words had been

a shout. "What do you mean?" he said blusteringly, his voice much louder than the other's.

"We do not allow Captain Sharps here." This time the tall man's voice was louder also.

Dunstan stepped back, his eyes flashing in anger. "I do not need to cheat," he said, his voice rising dangerously and his words more distinct than they had been in hours.

Glancing across the room at his employer, the tall man gently but firmly swept the protesting viscount from the room. "Do not return here, my lord, if you care for your life," he said. Then he waved at a hack waiting nearby.

Behind them in the club the gossip had begun. Once again Viscount Dunstan was the center of gossip. living up to his father's memory. One afternoon about ten days after he had received Elizabeth's letter, Dunstan wandered into his office. He had been there less than five minutes when a messenger appeared.

As he stood in front of his superior a few minutes later, Dunstan hid his discomfort. Lord Seward finished the letter he was writing, reread it, sanded it, and handed it to his secretary before he even acknowledged Dunstan's presence. Then he looked up, his cold gray eyes staring into Dunstan's. The younger man resisted the impulse to loosen his cravat and tried not to show how nervous he felt. He had heard of this type of conference, but he had never expected himself to be part of one.

The silence continued for several minutes, hours to Dunstan. Finally the older man waved him to a chair. Dunstan collapsed into the nearest one. "Am I to expect your resignation?" Seward asked coldly.

"My resignation?" Dunstan's face paled. Then he stood up, his back ramrod straight and his face carefully blank. "If that is what you wish, my lord. You will have it on your desk within the hour.

Seward straightened. "Sit down!" he said, his voice as forceful as it had ever been on the battle-field. "What is the matter with you, Dunstan?" asked his grandfather's friend, the man who had given him his place in the government. "Are the rumors I have heard about you true?"

"What rumors?" Dunstan asked, ashamed to admit that he had to ask. He straightened in his chair, wishing he could think more clearly.

"That you have grown more profligate than the Prince of Wales, visiting the hellholes and wagering thousands on the turn of a card. And you protested when I asked you to pretend a tenth of this when you visited Beckworth." The older man tapped his fingers against the arm of his chair while he waited for an answer. His cold gray eyes seemed to bore into the younger man.

"The gossip mongers give me more credit than I deserve," Dunstan said. His attempt at humor brought a darker frown to Seward's face. Dunstan lowered his eyes and tried to think of an explanation.

"Is this behavior going to continue?" The man's tone was as cold as a stream fed by melting winter snow. "If it does . . ." his voice drifted off suggestively.

"No, my lord," Dunstan sat up straighter. "I promise you I will regain my control." Except for the oblivion he gained from the alcohol, his actions the last few days had not brought him any closer to happiness. Ashamed of his weakness, he squared his shoulders and raised his eyes to stare into the older man's.

What he saw seemed to satisfy Seward, for he nodded and waved his hand, signaling Dunstan to leave. On the other side of the door, the younger man slumped against a wall and ran a hand over his face. Then he straightened and headed back to his office and the desk covered with papers.

As he began clearing his desk, he found once more the report on Hartley and frowned. But those thoughts led to Elizabeth. At that thought his eyes darkened. He pushed her to the back of his mind and began once more to sort through the material that had been awaiting his attention.

Finally, his desk was clear and no new problems waited for him. He pulled a letter from his pocket. Creased, wrinkled, and wine-stained, it was his one link to his dreams, to Elizabeth. He read it again, smoothing its wrinkles carefully, his eyes darkening as they always did when he looked at it. But then his mouth took on a determined line. He put the letter in the center of the desk and leaned back, tapping his fingers together thoughtfully.

Dunstan glanced at the letter on his desk, shoved it aside, and picked up a pen. "And if Elizabeth does not accept me this time, I will simply write her again," he whispered, his dark blue eyes shadowed. He pulled a sheet of paper closer, dipped his pen in his ink, and began: "My dear Elizabeth . . ." He closed his eyes, seeing her wrapped in her covers, her eyes wide. Then he remembered the sun shining through the lawn nightgown, and the way she had looked when she had told him good-bye. He closed his eyes for a moment, trying to fix her image in his mind. Then he opened his eyes and continued the letter.

When Dunstan arrived at Clarendon House on Berkley Square that evening, he discovered that the gossips had been busier than he had imagined. Planning to dress and join his friends for an evening of cockfighting, he had gone home to change later than usual. As soon as the door to the house opened, he knew. The earl had come to town.

"Where is my grandfather?" he asked the earl's personal footman, who stood beside the door.

"In the library, your lordship." Dunstan's eyebrows rose. Quickly the man continued. "We arrived several hours ago. He has been waiting for your return."

As soon as Dunstan set foot in the library, his grandfather's barrage began. "How dare you embarrass me!" his grandfather said angrily. "You are the talk of the *ton*!"

Dunstan, who had been prepared to make his apologies, stiffened, a red tinge showing in his cheeks. "And it is nice to see you again, Grandfather."

"That will be quite enough from you, sir. I did not travel to town to be insulted by my heir."

"Why did you come?"

"You ask me that, you who are the center of gossip." The earl stood up, his blue eyes faded now but still almost as deep a blue as Dunstan's blazing under their droopy lids. He tilted his head back a little more so that he could see more clearly. "A little time in the country with your fiancée will give the *ton* a chance to forget your excesses," the old man said firmly as he walked toward the bellpull.

"Grandfather, I have work to do here." Then he stopped. His face grew stern. "What did you say?" Dunstan asked, his voice harsh.

"You will be spending time in the country."

"Not that part. The other about my fiancée!" Dunstan glared at the older man, who let his eyelids almost cover his eyes.

"Marriage is just the answer. Get you settled down."

"And make me bored for life. No, Grandfather, I refuse. I am needed here."

"For what? To bring ruin on yourself and me? When you come to your senses, we will talk again." The older man stormed out of the room, leaving his grandson staring wordlessly after him.

During the next few days Dunstan avoided the earl as much as possible, a task made more difficult because his grandfather made a point of seeking him out. No matter how hard he had tried, Dunstan could not make his grandfather understand that what had happened would never happen again. As far as the older man was concerned, the only answer was a quick marriage to settle him down, a marriage to Miss Cecile Westin, the cherished granddaughter of his closest friend. And he was not willing to listen to any refusals.

Finally one Saturday after the earl had been hammering away at him all day, Dunstan exploded. "Never! I will never marry her!"

"You are just like your father, a wastrel," his grandfather shouted. Remembering his actions after he had received Elizabeth's latest refusal, Dunstan held his tongue, finding more truth in the statement than he would have admitted earlier. His silence angered the older man even more. "I suppose you will next tell me you have run off with an opera dancer," the earl had said bitingly.

"I promise I will never knowingly disgrace you," Dunstan finally said, stammering like a schoolboy in front of the headmaster.

"What does that mean, sir?" His grandfather had risen to stand behind him, his blue eyes boring into his back. Then more than ever before, Dunstan realized how the quarrel between his father and grandfather had begun.

He rose and turned to face the older man, marveling as he always did at the ramrod-stiff back and proud head tilted back so his grandfather could see under his droopy eyelids. "I promise that I will never behave again as I have done recently."

"And you will prove your love for me by marrying the girl I have picked out for you?"

"Just because I do not care to marry a girl over a decade younger than I does not mean I do not love you or respect you, Grandfather, " he said quietly. The older man closed his eyes for a moment and then glared at him again. He started to speak, but Dunstan cut him off: "I want to choose my own wife."

"Choose your own wife? Well, I have not seen any evidence that you are doing much to find one." His grandfather pulled himself up even straighter. "And I doubt you will find one whose lands march as well with yours as this one's do."

"And lands are the only reason to marry, aren't they?" Dunstan turned his back and walked across the room to the fireplace, where a small blaze burned to eliminate the chill of the evening. He pulled the sleeves of his black evening coat down and straightened a fold in his cravat. Hearing his grandfather clearing his throat, Dunstan turned around, his eyes snapping. "According to you and my father, even lands could not make your marriage a happy one."

"I will thank you to keep a civil tongue in your head, sir. My marriage is no business of yours." His grandfather had crossed to the door and had a hand on the latch. "At least I had the good taste to choose a woman of quality. All you associate with are the bits of muslin who are out to line their pockets."

Dunstan said quietly, so quietly his grandfather had to strain to hear, "My wife will be quality. And my marriage will be my concern only." He

waited breathlessly for a reply, but his grandfather glared at him once more, his head tilted back
at its usual uncomfortable angle. Then the earl
left the room silently. The next morning he left
London without another word.

Dunstan's third letter arrived at the manor shortly
after the coachman and groom returned from
London with the carriage loaded with supplies.
Elizabeth breathed a sigh of relief. As soon as she
had posted her answer, she had regretted it, certain that she would never hear from him again.
Once again Elizabeth took one look at the handwriting and slipped away, her cheeks rosy. Louisa
watched her thoughtfully, her eyes narrowed. She
reached up and straightened her lace cap and
followed her cousin, a letter from Lady Ramsburg
in her hand.

She swept into Elizabeth's bedroom unannounced,
taking in the sight of Elizabeth sitting there on the
chaise, her hand tracing the lines of the signature.
"Elizabeth, Charles's mother insists that we spend
some time with her in Brighton this summer. She
has already left London, pleading exhaustion, but
I believe it was simply a chance to set up her
household before everyone else arrives. I think we
should go." Louisa watched her cousin closely.

Looking up, Elizabeth, surprised, jumped. "Did
you want me for something, Cousin?"

"I just told you." Elizabeth blushed and looked
at the letter in her hand again, her face softening.
"Your stepmother insists that we join her in
Brighton."

Her cousin looked up, smiling. "You go if you
want. I plan to stay here. There are too many
things for me to do here. Besides, most of our
neighbors will be returning soon. They would think
it strange if I did not entertain them in return for
their hospitality this winter."

"You know that I will not go off and leave you alone here. What would people think?" Louisa sank down on the opposite end of the chaise. "I really believe the visit would do me a world of good."

"Of course it would. You go visit Stepmama, and I promise I will not entertain until you return," Elizabeth said, smiling not at Louisa but at the letter.

"No."

Startled, Elizabeth looked up. "But I will not be alone. Charles will be here."

"That is another problem. Lady Ramsburg suggests that he return as well. She had hoped that he would select a young lady as his wife during this Season. And she is most upset that he remained here with you." Louisa raised her eyebrows suggestively. "Do I need to remind you what happens when she is annoyed?"

Thinking of the schemes and plans she had been prey to during her second Season and the way she had been badgered until she agreed to return to town for her third, Elizabeth shook her head, dislodging the yellow bow that held her soft curls in place. She ran her hand over the skirt of the yellow muslin dress she wore, noting a grass stain at the hem her maid would fuss over. "Stepmama will not come here. She has not been here since I have made the manor my permanent home."

"Elizabeth, you know how determined she can be. If she decides to come, neither you nor I will dissuade her," Louisa said quietly, wondering if the last letter she had sent the lady had been too strongly worded. It would never do to force Elizabeth to Brighton against her will. "Of course, with most of the members of the government finding reasons to summer by the shore, she will probably be too busy to come very soon," she said, reassuringly. "But I advise you to think about the suggestion. It will be lonely here without Charles. And he will need to return to the *ton* soon."

When Louisa had gone, Elizabeth spread the letter from Dunstan out again, reading it word by word. This letter was different. In it Dunstan told her about his days, about where he had been and whom he had seen. He even told her about his grandfather and his demands. When she reached that part, it seemed to her that her heart stopped beating for a moment. Dunstan married? The thought brought her pain. She rose and laid the letter on her desk, not wanting to read another word in case he had written only to tell her that he had agreed to his grandfather's demands or had accepted her letter as her final word. She hurried out of the room. But before five minutes had passed, she was back. She picked up the letter, gritted her teeth, and turned it over. Then she sighed. He had told his grandfather he would choose his own wife. She took another deep breath. And he wanted her. She smiled. Once again she laid the letter on her desk and then walked to the chaise. When she rose later, she could not resist the impulse that led her back to where the letter lay. This time her hand lingered on it caressingly for a moment before she turned away to change for the evening, her manner so distracted that her maid wondered at her.

Her maid was not the only servant to wonder about the mistress of the manor. A chance remark by the groom and coachman who had gone to London caused a flurry of whispers in the stables. And before long the gossip had invaded the manor itself. It stopped whenever Jeffries or the housekeeper approached, leaving a gaping silence filled only with embarrassed coughs.

One afternoon Miller was hurrying down the back stairs, her arms filled with a soft pink muslin dress that needed to be pressed. Before she entered the kitchen, she heard two of the youngest maids talking. "I still say it weren't right of Miss Elizabeth to turn off Susan without a character for doing the same thing she was doing," said one.

"You heard Georgie, it was Susan who told him what she had seen—that Lord Dunstan sneaking out of the mistress's room." A pot clanked against a table. "Watch out; we don't want Cook screaming at us again," the girl scolded.

"Susan! I wonder why she bothered with Georgie. Course she was always sweet on him anyway. Tried to get him to marry her, I heard."

"Well, you heard wrong. Susan and I had plans, I tell you. She wouldn't get involved with no gent, no matter what they say."

"Then what's she doing at that inn? Georgie said she and the innkeeper were cooing and lovey-dovey."

"Georgie! If you believe him about Susan, why not about Miss Elizabeth? Wouldn't be the first time that Quality has let someone slip between the sheets."

"And what do you know about that?"

"What I heard, that's what! Why do you think Lord Dunstan came here all travel-worn the last time? It was not to see Mr. Beckworth, no matter what Mr. Jeffries says."

Before the conversation could deteriorate into an argument, Miller, her face carefully impassive, pushed open the door farther and walked in. Instantly the girls became silent, their eyes meeting. A look of dread crept onto their faces. Miller glanced around the room, noting the pots waiting to be scrubbed, and then raised her eyebrow ever so slightly. Immediately the girls were hard at work. Her face thoughtful, Miller finished pressing the dress and took it back upstairs.

As soon as she had put the dress away and had laid out her mistress's clothing for the evening, she hurried from the room. Finding the housekeeper, she led her to the small room where Jeffries was working. She checked the hallway and then shut the door tightly. "There is trouble," Miller said quietly. Then she related what she had heard.

"I knew that Susan and the other workhouse girls would be nothing but trouble," Jeffries muttered, his face an angry red.

"Some people do not know when they are well-off," Mrs. Lewis complained. "I told Miss Beckworth that giving Susan money would lead to trouble."

"What can we do?" Miller asked.

The other two looked at each other. Then the housekeeper sighed. Jeffries cleared his throat. "If they are discussing it in the stables, there is very little. I just hope Master Charles does not hear." He rubbed a hand over his forehead as if he could wipe away what was happening as easily as he could remove the moisture on his brow.

"What are the chances of that happening?" Miller asked.

The two looked at each other again. This time Mrs. Lewis answered. "Not good." She looked at the floor and then at the maid. "You do not think the story is true, do you?"

Miller hesitated a moment, a moment too long. The butler and the housekeeper gave each other a worried look. "Of course it is not true," Miller finally said, her voice firm. There was no need to mention the man's handkerchief she had found weeks ago under her mistress's bed. She exchanged looks with the others. "Does this sound like something Miss Beckworth would do?" she asked.

Avoiding her eyes, the other two shook their heads. Jeffries cleared his throat again. He asked, "Then how did the story get started?"

"Georgie saw Susan. She is the one who told him. At least that is what the maids are saying," Miller explained.

"Georgie? I will have a few words with that young lad myself," Jeffries promised.

"Don't do anything rash. Just find out where he saw her and if Susan really started the gossip about Miss Beckworth. We don't want to make the rest of the household suspicious." Miller's face was set in hard lines.

Mrs. Lewis stood up and straightened the crisp black skirt she wore. "Should we tell Miss Beckworth what is being said?" she asked. Her voice was tentative.

"No!" The word burst from both the butler and the maid.

"She has had to endure too much gossip already. I am afraid how she would react to this," Miller said firmly.

"You were not with the family then," Jeffries said. His tone toward the housekeeper was condescending. "You can have no idea what her reaction could be. We must avoid her finding out at all cost."

"I do not understand how you plan to do that," Mrs. Lewis replied tartly. "Someone is certain to say something to her soon."

"Or to her brother." Miller's words caused them all to freeze.

"If Master Charles hears a word of this," Jeffries' words trailed off. Then he straightened up. "Get back to work. We will keep our wits about us and be prepared for anything," he said majestically. "If it is true, we will consult Mrs. Beckworth." Nodding, they left, each hiding a secret fear.

Before long their fears were realized. One afternoon Charles came into the stables, restless, looking for a good gallop to clear his mind. Not seeing any grooms about and in too much of a hurry to seek one out, he lifted a saddle from the rack and entered a stall. He stroked his horse's nose and put a blanket over his back. Before he could lift the saddle in place, the door to the stable swung open again. Two men stood in the open door, their faces hidden by the sunshine and shadow.

"Did you see the mistress today with all her airs of being so good?" one asked.

"You've no call to talk about her like that. She took care of you last winter when you were ill," a younger voice scolded.

"If I had known then what I know now . . ."

"You keep your bloody mouth shut. Miss Beckworth is a good person."

"Not according to what we were told last night."

"And now you're believing the same man who cheated you at cards last week?"

"May not play cards with him again, but why would he lie about the mistress?"

"Maybe because he was sweet on Susan, and the mistress sent her away."

"Or maybe Lord Dunstan did spend the night with Miss Beckworth. A lady has been known to take lovers same as a maid." All during this conversation Charles had stayed where he was, hidden from view. Now, his anger more than he could bear, he stepped out of the stall.

He shouted, "Would you care to repeat to me what you just said?"

The grooms looked at each other. If Charles had been able to see their faces, he would have been delighted at the horror there.

Charles dashed to the doorway, but by the time he reached it, they were hidden. "Damn them," he muttered, his eyes hard and his face set in hard lines. He marched toward the manor.

"Jeffries! Jeffries!" he shouted as he walked into the entry hall.

"Sir?" The older man's voice was as quiet as though Charles had whispered.

"I need Porter in the library. Immediately," Charles said, his face red. He was frowning. He plunged down the hallway. Jeffries started to follow him, but stopped when he noticed the housekeeper and Miller standing by the door that led down to the kitchens. They looked at him anxiously. With an almost imperceptible nod the butler sent them on their ways. Then he sent the footman for the valet.

Charles, his long strides carrying him from one spot of the book-lined room to another, whirled around when the door opened. Porter took one look at his master's face and closed the door firmly behind him. "Yes, Master Charles?" he asked, his face worried.

For once Charles let the manner of address slip by without comment. Porter noted the exception and frowned slightly. He stood still waiting until Charles made another circuit of the room and came up to him. The two men stared at each other for a moment. Then Charles ran a hand over his face. He crossed to a large leather chair and sat down, hitting his fist against his other hand.

"What has happened, Master Charles?" Porter asked quietly. His face revealed his worry.

Charles finally sat back, running his hands through his hair. He stood up again and crossed to his valet, putting his hand on his shoulder. Porter, startled, stepped back. "Master Charles?"

"You must tell me what you know. Promise me that," Charles said as he tried to get his anger under control. The valet nodded, his face puzzled. Charles took a deep breath and said in one breath, "What are the rest of the servants saying about my sister?"

"Your sister?" Porter asked, his voice breaking. He cleared his throat. His face was pale.

"Tell me."

The older man took a step back. "The other servants, especially the younger ones, do not tell me anything," the valet said hesitantly.

"That never stopped you from knowing the gossip before," Charles said, the frown on his face reflected in his voice.

"Master Charles," Porter began. He stopped and cleared his throat again. "You do not want to know," he finally said softly.

"Then they are talking about her?"

The valet looked ashamed. "Yes," he said quietly.

"And Lord Dunstan?" The valet nodded. "I will kill the man," Charles shouted, heading for the door. "Get my clothes ready. We leave for London immediately." He threw open the door and hurried down the hallway.

"Shouldn't you talk to Miss Beckworth first?" the valet asked, appalled at his master's reaction. He was almost running trying to keep up with Charles's long strides. Charles simply ignored him.

12

Elizabeth, totally unaware of the turmoil in her carefully protected world, went about her regular duties while Charles headed to the stables. Warned by his shouts, the younger grooms made good their escape, leaving the head groom to saddle his master's horse himself. "Send a driver with Porter in my curricle," Charles said sharply as he swung into the saddle. He pulled his hat down over his eyes. "And when I return, I want to talk to everyone who works in the stables. Is that understood?" he asked. The head groom nodded, certain now what had set his master in action. "And do not let anyone leave. Tell anyone who asks that Carstairs does not have the authority to pay him off." Glad that he had not been the one who had revealed the gossip, the groom nodded again. He watched as Charles took the road, pushing his horse hard.

When she walked toward the salon for tea, Elizabeth stopped, startled. There in the entryway stood Jeffries, his face solemn as he shut the door. "Was there a message, Jeffries?" she asked.

"No, Miss Beckworth. I was seeing Porter off."

"Porter? What kind of errand has Charles sent him on now?"

The butler kept his face impassive. "He is following Master Charles. Of course, it would have been better to make the trip tomorrow, but the master has already left. Porter hopes to be in London only a few hours after him."

"My brother has left for London?" The butler nodded, his eyes carefully neutral. "When?" Before Jeffries could answer, she fired another question. "Did he say good-bye to my cousin or leave me a note?"

The butler straightened, becoming even more rigid than before, his expression carefully wiped clean of all emotion. "I believe he left not quite an hour ago. And Porter did not mention any messages. Shall I question the footmen and grooms?"

"No. But it is strange." She walked down the hall, a frown on her face.

Jeffries, relaxing a trifle, frowned. Catching sight of a footman who was trying to reach the door to the lower stairs without being seen, he called to him. The young footman gulped and turned, ready for the dressing-down he was sure would follow. To his surprise Jeffries simply said, "Take a tea tray to the the ladies in the salon." The young man nodded and hurried away. Jeffries stood there for a moment, looking down the hallway toward the salon. Then he headed toward the housekeeper's office.

When she reached the salon, Elizabeth discovered her cousin sitting quietly, turning a piece of material in her hands. "Louisa, did Charles tell you he was leaving?" she asked, her face still perplexed.

"Leaving? When?" The older woman's face reflected her disappointment. She dropped her hands to her lap. "Can't you persuade him to stay for at least another week?"

"He is already gone." Elizabeth sank into her favorite chair, a worried look on her face. "I am so worried about him. He was enjoying his stay. I know he was. This is totally unlike him."

Controling her own disappointment, Louisa laughed lightly. "Of course he was enjoying his visit. What male would not enjoy two women doting on him. But you are wrong, my dear."

"About what?" Elizabeth asked. Her face registered her surprise that Louisa was taking the news of Charles's departure so well.

"About this being so unlike Charles," her cousin said, her face pleasant. "Remember the time he bet someone around here that he could beat the record to Bath?" Elizabeth nodded. "Then he left after supper." Noticing the footman with the tea tray, Louisa signaled him to place it on the table before her. "I believe he won the bet, too." She poured a cup of tea.

Elizabeth stood up hastily, startling the footman. The cup he had been about to hand her rattled. She accepted the tea and sat back down. "But there is no one here to suggest such a wager." Her eyebrows went up. She glared at her cousin, a fierce light in her eyes. "Louisa, you didn't?"

"Of course not, Elizabeth. I always bet on Charles. That way I usually win," her cousin said soothingly. "His departure is not really unexpected. He has been restless for days."

The younger woman nodded. She gazed into her cup as though she could read her fortune in the tea leaves there. "I simply wish he had told us good-bye before he left. And waited until morning. There was no need for him to dash off to London so late in the day."

The maid who had been sent for more hot water set the pot down with a clatter, causing both women to stare at her. The girl, her face red, begged their pardon and bolted from the room. "I think you should talk to Jeffries, Elizabeth. The servants need some additional training," Louisa suggested.

As soon as she was out of the room, the maid looked carefully down the hallway and burst into a run, her cheeks a bright red with excitement. When the girl reached the kitchen, she saw her closest friend and motioned her closer. "Master Beckworth just left to go to London. And he was in a taking. Now who has been making up stories?" she asked smugly.

"Probably just going home. He lives there, you know," her friend said scornfully. "He stayed longer than usual this time. I thought it was about time he left." She tossed her head and returned to the table where the lamps she had been polishing waited.

Her friend sauntered over to her. "You simply do not want to admit you can be wrong," she said. Her voice carried a gloating note. "Just wait and see what happens. Then everyone will know who to believe." She looked around at the other servants, hard at work and determined to avoid her. "You'll see."

By the end of the week even Elizabeth knew something was wrong. Miller had managed to shield her from most of the gossip, but finally even the older servants realized they could not protect her forever. Reaching a decision, they took Mrs. Beckworth's dresser into their confidence. That lady, as protective of her mistress as Miller was of Elizabeth, knew exactly what must be done. "Give me a few days," she promised.

Later that afternoon when Elizabeth walked into the small salon where Louisa sat working on a piece of needlework that had been started during Elizabeth's first Season, she did not realize how nervous her cousin was. "Jeffries said you wished to see me. Have you received a letter from Charles?"

"No. And I am rather provoked by the dear boy. He truly should have more consideration of others." Louisa laid her needlework on the table beside her and regarded her finger, now covered in drops of blood, with amazement.

"Louisa, give it up," Elizabeth said, laughing. Every time her cousin tried to sew, the cloth became so bloodstained no one would ever choose to use the item. "Or let me finish it."

"Never. But you are sweet to offer, dear one." She wrapped a clean handkerchief about her finger, frowning all the while. Louisa stabbed her needle into the cloth and hit her finger again. "Botheration." Throwing the needlework onto the table beside her, she moved the handkerchief farther down her finger.

"You usually do not work on this unless you have been upset," Elizabeth said suspiciously. "Have you had a letter from Mama lately?"

"Not since the last one she sent asking us to Brighton. Are you certain you do not wish to go?" Louisa asked hopefully, her soft blue eyes wistful. Elizabeth shook her head. Sighing thoughtfully, Louisa unwrapped her finger and inspected it carefully before laying the handkerchief, now stained beyond saving, beside her.

As scatterbrained as Louisa sometimes seemed, she was quick at picking up hints, and there had been too many things happening lately to make her comfortable. Servants gossiping in the halls would drop into an utter silence when she walked by. And except for a few loyal ones, their attitude toward Elizabeth had changed.

As Elizabeth chatted about the latest news, Louisa took a deep breath. When Louisa had checked to make certain no servant was lingering around the door, she turned. All thought of careful words forgotten, she blurted out, "Elizabeth, did you spend the night with one of your brother's friends?"

Elizabeth seemed to freeze for a moment. Her face flushed red and then white. Grace forgotten, she plopped down, forgetting to straighten her skirt. She opened her mouth, but no words emerged. Louisa simply stared at her. Elizabeth tried again. "What did you ask?" Even to herself, her voice sounded peculiar, almost rusty.

"Did you allow one of your brother's friends to spend the night in your room?" This time the question was flat with each word measured out carefully. Louisa sat down in a chair facing her cousin.

Her hand at her throat, Elizabeth stared in horror. "What do you mean?" she asked finally. Her low voice still sounded as though she had not used it lately. With effort she kept the blush from rising in her cheeks.

"Just what I said. According to the servants, the reason Charles left so suddenly was that he heard the rumors that have been circulating about you. Of course, I know they are not true, but they are damaging." Louisa pulled her long lavender muslin sleeve farther over her hand and regarded it closely, too embarrassed to look at Elizabeth while she made the accusation.

When she did look, Elizabeth's face was crimson. Her breath came in gasps. Her cousin, startled, put a hand over her eyes, devastated by the implications of what she saw. "You didn't?" she cried, her face dismayed.

"You don't understand." Elizabeth took a deep breath, trying to control her panic. "I didn't even know he was there until I woke up."

"What are you saying?" By now Louisa's face was a pasty white and her hands were shaking.

"I did spend the night with a man. At least I think I did. But not in the way you mean," she said hurriedly.

Her cousin took a few deep breaths, trying to calm herself. When she felt she had control of her voice, Louisa said harshly, "Tell me everything."

Once again Elizabeth blushed, sending a wave of red from her rounded neckline to her hairline. "I really do not know very much."

"How can you say that? You were in bed with a man. You must have some recollection of how the situation came about!"

"But that is just the point. I don't." Elizabeth reached up to dash tears of anger from her eyes. "When I woke up, he was there." She sank back onto the settee and covered her face with her hands.

"And just who is the 'he' we are discussing?" Louisa rose, her back stiff and her voice stern. Though her stomach was rolling with panic and disappointment, no one would have guessed it from her calm exterior.

"Lord Dunstan." The name was said so quietly that Louisa had to strain to hear it.

"How could you?" her cousin asked almost under her breath. Then she said more forcefully, "And the cad left that very day. I suppose he decided that you could handle any problems that rose. You aren't . . ?"

"No. Nothing happened, Louisa. At least I do not think it did. I woke up and discovered him in my bed. He hid while the maid made up the fire, and then I helped him leave. No one saw him; I am certain of that. I checked the hallway very carefully, so did he." Elizabeth's voice cracked with emotion. She looked at her cousin with tears in her eyes.

"You apparently did not check closely enough." Louisa sank into a chair again. For a few moments silence filled the room as the cousins regarded each other. Then Louisa asked, her voice filled with reproach, "Why didn't you tell me as soon as this happened? I would have helped you. We could have . . ."

"You do not understand, Louisa. I thought no one would need to know. As far as I was concerned, the fewer people who knew about this, the less chance there would be for a scandal. And you know how I feel about scandal." Elizabeth clasped her hands together so tightly that her knuckles were white. "How did you find out?" she asked, her voice trembling slightly.

"The servants." Louisa's voice was thoughtful. "I have no doubt that Charles heard the same story. That would explain his sudden disappearance."

"Charles? What do you mean?" Elizabeth's face was as white as sheets bleached by the summer sun.

"My dresser said that Porter asked Jeffries about the gossip before he left. How could you be so foolish?" Louisa closed her eyes, trying to put the events in order in her mind.

"I did nothing. He was not there when I went to bed. He was there in the morning, but I know no one saw him leave. I got him out as soon as I could. The only people up were the servants, and he was in his room before the footman arrived to start his fires." Elizabeth had gone from distressed to panicked.

"And how would you know that?" Louisa's usually sleepy blue eyes were sharp.

"He told me when he asked me to . . ." Elizabeth broke off hastily. She got up and began to walk aimlessly around the room, aware of a need to escape from those clear blue eyes.

"Asked you to what?" her cousin asked, her voice as calm as she could make it.

Needing to defend her actions, Elizabeth turned to face Louisa. "To marry him." She watched in dismay as a look of relief passed over her cousin's face. "But I said no."

"You did what?" This time Louisa's question was almost a shriek.

"I told him no."

"Then you better write and tell him that you have changed your mind." Louisa rose and stood before her cousin, the difference in height bothering her not at all. She shook her finger at Elizabeth. "Have you no sense? Do you wish to be cast out of society forever? Of course you will accept him. Write him immediately."

"I won't. He does not want a wife, and I do not want a husband. I did nothing wrong. Why do I have to pay the price?" Determined, Elizabeth ignored the memory of the warm feeling that crept over her each time she received a letter from Dunstan. "The gossip will go away. All I have to do is stay here and face it. Remember that is what you told me before."

"Not this time." Louisa crossed to stand beside the window, looking out into the bright sunshine. "This time the gossip began with the servants. Their memories are long. And how long before the rest of the county finds out?" She turned to look at the girl she regarded as her daughter. "You yourself said only a few weeks ago that this was a merciless area. What do you think will happen when your neighbors hear the gossip?" she asked in a quiet voice. "And they will hear."

Elizabeth's face paled. Then she straightened

her spine. "They know me too well to believe such rumors," she said firmly, hoping that she was right.

"But these aren't just rumors, are they?" Elizabeth sank into a chair, her head lowered. Louisa crossed to stand behind her, her hands longing to smooth Elizabeth's tousled curls, to smooth the hurts away. "Besides you know that certain members of this county's society enjoy nothing more than destroying a reputation. At least write Lord Dunstan and tell him that your secret has been discovered," Louisa suggested. If Dunstan had felt a need to make an offer before their secret was known, surely he would offer again. And this time she would make certain Elizabeth would agree.

"No."

"Elizabeth, that is not fair to the man. If someone mentions the gossip in his presence, you do not want him to be surprised. At least give him that courtesy." Louisa thought for a moment and then added, "He is a man with scandal in his past. I am certain he will want to avoid one in the present."

For a moment Louisa was afraid Elizabeth would refuse again. then the younger lady sighed. Louisa smiled slightly as Elizabeth rose and walked toward the desk. "My dear, it is the only way," she said quietly as she watched Elizabeth pull the paper from the drawer. "We will wait for his answer. Then we will write Lady Ramsburg so that she can make the arrangements for the wedding."

Elizabeth looked up with a frown, holding the freshly sharpened quill in her hands. "I will not write Lord Dunstan. It is only too evident that my first impressions of him that morning were the correct ones."

"What do you mean?"

"It is obvious to me that he made certain that the knowledge would be made public."

"How do you know that?"

"Who else knew? Only he and I were there."

"Didn't you say the servants were up?" By now Louisa was wringing her hands. She had been so certain this morning that a few simple words would explain the whole confusing problem.

"I told you no one saw him leave."

"Someone must have." Louisa stopped for a moment. "Or they could have seen him arrive," she said thoughtfully. "What time did he enter your bedchamber?"

Elizabeth cleared her throat. She tried to say something, but all she could get out was a croak. Then she tried again. This time Louisa heard her whisper. "I do not know."

"I suppose with that handsome scoundrel in my bedroom, I would forget to look at the clock, too," Louisa said, her tone more humorous than she would have dreamed she could make it.

"No. No!" Elizabeth's voice was so agitated that Louisa, who had been wandering about the room thoughtfully, turned to look at her in amazement. Elizabeth stood up and moved to her cousin's side. She grabbed one of Louisa's hands and held on tight as though afraid she would be lost without it. "I simply do not know. All I know is that he was there when I woke the next morning." Her low, husky voice pleaded with Louisa to believe her.

"He was in bed with you when you wakened?" Louisa asked quietly. "And you do not remember when he arrived?" Elizabeth nodded. "What was he wearing?"

Elizabeth's face flamed. Louisa looked at her and tapped her foot impatiently. "I do not think he was wearing anything," Elizabeth said hurriedly.

Louisa gasped. Her face flamed and then took on sterner lines. "Elizabeth, you will write that letter to Lord Dunstan immediately."

"I will not. I do not plan to be married by a fortune hunter." Elizabeth stiffened her back and crossed to the window where Louisa had been standing only a short time before. But she did not see the gardens or the sunshine. Once again she could see Dunstan on the floor, the pillow in his lap.

"Well, at least she did not tell me she never plans to marry," Louisa muttered to herself. She looked at her cousin carefully and then smiled. "Elizabeth, dear," she began this time, her voice concerned and loving, "we must find some solution to this problem. Perhaps we could quiet the gossip that is bound to happen in the county if you only announced your engagement."

"And have him leave me like Jack did? Is that what you want?" Elizabeth turned back to the room, her face set in stern lines. "I have been rejected once. It is not an experience I wish to go through again. And what would happen if he insisted that our marriage go through as planned? No, Louisa, I will not write to the man." She crossed to the desk and picked up the pen, meaning to break it. She stared at it for a moment and then sat down, pulling the paper before her once more.

"Elizabeth, I do not like that look on your face. to whom are you writing?" Good as Elizabeth had been as a child, almost too good, Louisa knew that look only too well. "Elizabeth, answer me!"

"To Mama. You wanted to visit her. I am writing to accept her invitation." Louisa's mouth dropped open, but she shut it quickly. "You wanted to visit Brighton this summer. Can we be ready to leave in two days? I will tell Mama we will be there within the week.

Louisa watched as Elizabeth sanded the note, crossed to the bellpull, and then gave it to Jeffries.

"Send this off immediately," she said firmly. Then she turned to where her cousin stood, stunned, uncertain of the wisdom of Elizabeth's decision. "Are you coming with me, Cousin?" Elizabeth asked, her voice carefully neutral.

"Elizabeth, this will not stop the gossip," Louisa finally said. "The servants? Do you mean to leave all the servants here?" Elizabeth simply shook her head and left the room. "But, Elizabeth, you cannot simply run away," Louisa protested as she hurried after her.

13

Two days later, as they watched the luggage coach lumber away, Louisa was still protesting. "My dear, at least let me write Lord Dunstan. As soon as we reach Brighton, the news of what has happened will be one of the on-dits of the *ton*."

Elizabeth ignored her until they too were underway. Then she turned to her, her hazel eyes clear and untroubled. "Jeffries and I had a long talk after you told me what the servants were saying. He and I chose the servants to go with us very carefully. Except for Miller and your dresser they will all return to the manor as soon as they have delivered us to Lord Ramsburg's summer home."

"Even overnight may be too long. What if they talk?"

"Jeffries has assured me that everyone knows the seriousness of the situation. I think we will have to trust his judgment." Elizabeth sat back and closed her eyes, surprised at her own reactions. The last two days had proved to her that her stepmother's and cousin's predictions were right. She could do whatever needed to be done. She sighed. If only she could get that dratted man out of her mind. But his smile and blue eyes were as clear as though he sat on the seat in front of her. Finally, by concentrating all her efforts on the task, she managed to relax and drifted off to sleep.

By the time they reached Brighton, both ladies ached from the ride. The damp evening mist hid the house and shops from their view as the coachman drove them down Steine, as eager as his passengers to see the prince's fancy dwelling. In the mist even the pointed domes of the royal stables were hidden from view. As the carriage pulled into Marine Parade, Louisa sat back and dropped the window curtain. "Oh, how lovely to be near the sea again," she said, clasping her hands in her lap.

"You talk as though we lived miles inland instead of an hour's drive from the coast," Elizabeth said, faintly disappointed by the quiet that surrounded her. "And if this"—she waved her hand at the scene outside her window—"is the exciting life that Brighton promises us, then I truly will be happy here."

"Remember, my dear, it is early yet. When everyone arrives . . ."

"There will be no room for any of us to enjoy anything," Elizabeth said dully, wondering not for the first time how she had convinced herself that coming to Brighton was the right move. Then the carriage stopped. As soon as the coachman dropped the knocker, the door to the town house opened, and servants rushed out to assist them from the carriage. Elizabeth took one look at the tall man directing the servants and turned back to Louisa, "What is the butler's name?" she asked, panicked as she always was when she could not remember the name of a person she should have known.

"Smythe." Louisa's tones were as soothing as the lady could make them, considering how tired she was. "He was at the estate at Christmas," she said, reminding herself that Elizabeth could not help her bad memory for names. The poor dear had tried hard enough.

"Well, I do not know why they had to pension off Old Thompson," Elizabeth mumbled. "I knew his name." She allowed herself to be handed out of the carriage and rushed into the house.

"Louisa, how good to see you once again," said Lady Ramsburg, a petite blonde whom most people thought in her thirties rather than past forty. Long ago she and her late husband's connection had decided that a surface formality made their lives run more smoothly. "Elizabeth, darling, how wonderful to see you again. I had quite given up hope to have you with me this summer." This time her face was a study of delight. "How surprised I was to get your message. And pleased, very pleased. Now I am certain that you will want to rest for a while. Then I have promised to share you with one or two other hostesses. Company in Brighton is still rather thin, but as soon as the last ball of the Season is held in London, you can be sure that this will become one of the liveliest cities in the country." Leading them up the stairs, she linked her arm with Elizabeth's. "You must tell me everything you have been doing, my dear." She took a step up and looked back at the two ladies, evaluating their clothes carefully. "Not terrible, but not the latest in fashion either. Tomorrow we will call on my modiste, a clever woman who has discovered that Brighton in the summer is more worthwhile than London," she told them.

Louisa followed along behind, smiling indulgently and making the right replies. As soon as she had been shown into her room, she sank into a chair. She pulled the pins from her hat and waited.

Before long a quiet scratching sounded on the door. A moment later Lady Ramsburg slipped in and closed the door quietly behind her. "Tell me how you managed to get her here, Louisa!" she demanded, her face still flushed with happiness.

"This was none of my doing, my lady." Lady Ramsburg's face went blank for a moment, and then she frowned. Louisa said quietly, "There is a problem."

"Tell me." Elizabeth's stepmother sank to the chaise and leaned back, one hand thrown dramatically across her forehead. By the time Louisa had finished, she was sitting up straight, her artistic pose forgotten. "Damn and blast! Men! Why do they always have to create problems. If Elizabeth had only accepted him when he first offered." She looked at her confidante, anger in every line of her body. "I suppose there is no choice. Write him tomorrow, Louisa. He will not appreciate being made the butt of *ton* gossip any more than we will." She got up, straightened her pale blue gauze robe carefully, and then asked, "What do you think happened that evening?"

The question was one that Louisa had given much thought to. But as before, she had no facts on which to base her decision. "Nothing. I am certain it was nothing."

"Nothing or not, he will marry her. How could she be so foolish as to turn him down, the heir to an earldom too?"

"Have you ever known Elizabeth to do anything sensible if it involved a man?" Louisa asked, her voice dry.

"No. I tried to persuade her that Jack was a bad choice, but she was determined to have him. And look what that brought her. This time she will be governed by us." Lady Ramsburg crossed to the door and stood there a moment, a determined look on her face.

Louisa, who had seen that same look not long before on Charles's face, was wary. "We have never been successful in the past. What makes you believe we will do better this time?" she asked, glad to have someone to share her worries.

"She is older this time. And she did choose to come here. That must mean something," the smaller woman said with a smile. "Rest now, Louisa. I will send a maid with a tray for your supper. And do not worry. Everything is in my hands."

A few doors down the hall, Elizabeth was telling herself much the same thing. "I can do this. I am not afraid." But every time she thought of facing society again she felt ill. Quickly she undressed, slipping a wrapper of her favorite turquoise on and allowing her stepmother's dresser to brush her curls into some semblance of order. Finally she sat on the chaise and accepted a cup of tea, hot and creamy just as she liked it.

Her quiet reverie came to an end just minutes after it began. Her stepmother, armed with information from Louisa, was at hand. "How wonderful that you finally accepted my invitation. If only Charles were here to complete this little party," Lady Ramsburg said wistfully. "Do you know where he is now? I have written him in London, but I have received no reply."

Elizabeth kept her face from turning red by force of will alone. She said calmly, "The last word I had from him was that he was returning to the capital. I am certain that he will write to you very soon. You know how he forgets important things like letters."

"Well, I suppose you are right. But how vexatious he is. Did he tell you, Elizabeth, that he has

absolutely refused to consider any of my suggestions for a wife? And most of them were absolutely perfect for him. Perhaps you could persuade
him to marry." Lady Ramsburg perched on the
edge of one of the rose pink satin chairs she had
added to the room recently. She looked at Elizabeth expectantly.

Her stepdaughter, no longer as calm as she had
been only moments before, now sat on the edge of
the chaise. "If you are hoping that I will persuade
Charles to marry simply so that the estate can
have an heir, Mama, you had better be ready for
disappointment," Elizabeth said firmly.

Lady Ramsburg allowed herself to wilt a little,
sinking deeper into her chair. Her chin wobbled
gracefully. Elizabeth watched, fascinated. "Of
course, I should have known," the older woman
said in a voice that held a disturbing tremble.
"You and Charles have made a pact. I am never to
be a grandmother!" She threw her head back
against the chair and paused for a moment, her
hand over her brow.

Elizabeth stood up, clapping. "Bravo, Mama,
bravo!"

The older woman flushed angrily and stood up
so that she could stomp her tiny foot. "How
unfeeling!"

"And how long have you been practicing that?"
Elizabeth asked with a cheeky grin. "More important, what did poor George have to give you so
that you would cease your posturing with him?
You are very good, you know."

Breaking into laughter, her stepmother stepped
closer to her and pulled her to the chaise. "You
unfeeling girl. Never have I needed to use such
wiles on my husband. He loves me. And I have
reason to doubt my children do."

"What a corker! And I suppose we beat you, too?"

"Sit down, you miserable creature, and tell me more about what you are doing here. Your letter was far from revealing."

"But I imagine Cousin Louisa has given you as much information as she knows," Elizabeth said dryly. She had known that her stepmother would refuse to be put off. But she had hoped to have at least one night of rest before she had to face her. "Besides, I am certain that you are expected somewhere this evening. I would never forgive myself for disappointing your hostess."

"George has gone ahead. He will send the carriage back for me presently. And my hostess knows that I was expecting you. Now, tell me everything." She sat back, leaning on the back of the chaise.

Elizabeth glanced at her once and then looked away. From first glance, Lady Ramsburg looked as dainty and fragile as a Sevres vase. But her closest friends and her family knew that steel was hidden under her skin. She could dance the night away or argue politics with the sharpest minds in the nation. And the next day she would appear as fresh and vibrant as the evening before. During her Seasons, Elizabeth, who discovered that she had to have a nap each afternoon if she were planning to stay awake until dawn, had envied the lady her stamina. That stamina made her a fearsome opponent. Giving in gracefully, Elizabeth spilled out the story. "You can see that I had to refuse him, Mama. He is nothing more than a fortune hunter." The tone begged her stepmother to agree with her.

For a few minutes Lady Ramsburg was quiet. Elizabeth, accustomed to the lady's methods of thinking everything out clearly, waited impatiently for a reply. She got up and began walking around the room. Lady Ramsburg simply used her absence as an opportunity to swing her legs from the floor and onto the chaise. After minutes that seemed as drawn out as a year of mourning, the younger lady could wait no longer. "Have you decided to disown me, then?" she asked, half fearful of the reply.

Lady Ramsburg ignored the remark and sat there silently for a few minutes more. When Elizabeth was certain that if her stepmother took one minute more to answer, she would scream, the lady asked quietly, "What did you say the gentleman's name is?"

"Lord Dunstan." The words flew into the silence.

"Hmmm."

"What is that supposed to mean?"

The older woman looked up impatiently, obviously still deep in thought. "What did you say?"

"Mama, speak to me. Tell me what you are thinking." For miles Elizabeth had been preparing herself for the peal that Lady Ramsburg would ring over her, and all the lady did was sit there. It was more than her already stretched nerves could bear. "Why did you say 'hmmm'?"

"Because I was wondering about something." Lady Ramsburg looked at her stepdaughter fondly.

"What?"

"For one thing, why do you think Lord Dunstan a fortune hunter?" she asked quietly. She smiled at the girl who was as dear as any natural daughter could be, encouraging her.

"What else could I think? Oh, I had my doubts. Mama, he has written such kind letters. But why else would he offer for me?"

"My dear, have you looked in your mirror lately?" her stepmother asked dryly.

"But I am on the shelf."

"Not all gentlemen are impressed by girls in their salad days. Remember what a stir I caused when I came out of mourning." She preened herself slightly, her sparkling blue eyes so like her son's.

"You are beautiful as well as healthy and well-born, Mama. Of course you were sought after. And you know how to talk to people. All I have is money and a miserable habit of forgetting people's names."

"I thought you were much better at Christmas, darling. Does the problem still trouble you?"

"Not as much as it used to. Our county is very stable. And I manage to learn people's names eventually" Elizabeth turned around to hide a yawn. "I wish I had your talent; you seem to have no trouble remembering anyone's name."

"I have a system. I listen for names carefully. Remember what I told you before your first Season. Repeat the rules with me," Lady Ramsburg said in a firm, not to be denied, voice.

"Listen to the name. Look at the face. Find some characteristic to remember," she said firmly.

"But it does not work for me," Elizabeth said in despair. "If you or Cousin Louisa weren't with me, I could never remember a name. I even called John, Lord Ravenwood, Henry one night. Amelia was so embarrassed." Elizabeth sat down, her face gloomy once again. "Now I have to face the same problem. People will not be as kind to a lady my age as they were to a young girl."

"Let me think about it for a while," Lady Ramsburg said, already turning a plan over in her mind. "And you should reconsider Lord Dunstan's offer."

"What?"

"He would make you an excellent husband, Elizabeth," her stepmother said calmly. "And you need not worry about his being a fortune hunter. Several mothers in our set whose daughters must marry a fortune have set traps for him; he has eluded them all. You know the kind of ladies I mean. If he were a fortune hunter, they would have known."

"Perhaps he is simply able to fool them," Elizabeth suggested. Her stepmother's left brow raised slightly. Elizabeth gritted her teeth in annoyance and wished she had been able to master that trick. "But I do not want to marry anyone," she said stormily.

"Then you should have been more careful. In our class, a lady marries before she allows a gentleman into her bed. But no decision must be made tonight, Elizabeth," Lady Ramsburg said firmly. The maid entered with a supper tray, and the older lady stood up. "Have supper and then have a soothing sleep. Tomorrow will be soon enough to write your letter." She smiled brightly, reminding Elizabeth of a benevolent angel, the one who always makes certain little girls do exactly what they are supposed to do. "Tomorrow will be brighter," she promised as she kissed Elizabeth on the cheek.

To Elizabeth's surprise, the promise held true. Although both Lady Ramsburg and her cousin were far from pleased with her decision not to write Lord Dunstan, from the first moment that their carriage pulled into North Street, with its shops with goods from London, Elizabeth's life seemed brighter. Perhaps it was the admiring words of the modiste, who sighed enviously over Elizabeth's shape while promising gowns within the week. The light misty green of the silk Elizabeth had chosen for a new evening gown made her eyes look greener and more mysterious. Even Cousin Louisa had mentioned it. And if the color had made her wonder what a certain lord would think of her in it, Elizabeth did not say a word.

That evening on the Steine all of the ladies were greeted warmly. With the prince still in London and most of the noble families following his example, the officers of the Tenth Light Dragoons quickly made their way to Elizabeth's side. One, a tall redhead, actually went down on one knee in front of Lady Ramsburg and begged her to introduce them.

"Get up, you wretched boy. Even if I do introduce you, you will not be fit to walk with," Lady Ramsburg laughed. At her words the young captain was on his feet and looked at her expectantly. "Oh, I suppose I must introduce you if I plan to visit peacefully with anyone this evening," she said reproachfully, her blue eyes filled with mischief. "Mrs. Louisa Beckworth, Miss Elizabeth Beckworth, this is Captain, Lord Anthony Hathaway. Lord Hathaway, this is my stepdaughter and our cousin."

Smoothly the gentleman took their hands, kissing each in turn. Although his kiss upon her hand was everything that was proper, Elizabeth knew that the look in his eye as he gazed at her in her favorite blue dress was anything but. She pulled away as quickly as possible and stepped back a pace or two. "What did you say your name was?" she asked quietly, trying to put her stepmother's advice to good use.

"Anthony," he said quickly. Then he noticed two pairs of blue eyes staring at him, their disapproval plain. "Captain, Lord Hathaway, Miss Beckworth. And where are you walking this fine evening?"

"Up the Steine to the Marine Pavilion. George

will meet us there with the carriage," Lady Ramsburg explained.

"May I escort you? There are too many people on the prowl this evening for it to be safe for such lovelies as you." He scowled at two other officers who had spotted him and were heading toward the little group. "Shall we go?"

Unfortunately for him, his ploy was unsuccessful. Before the evening was over, the little group was surrounded by a coterie of young officers, each one determined to whisper compliments into Elizabeth's ears.

As she laughed with one after another, she whispered their names to herself. Tomorrow she would surprise her family by remembering every one.

Unfortunately her intentions were better than her memory. The next afternoon the butler announced a group of officers at one time: "Captain, Lord Hathaway, Major Devereaux, and Lieutenant Blakely."

As they entered and thrust bouquets of flowers into her hands, Elizabeth found herself surrounded by strange men, their uniforms left behind for the afternoon. Stumbling and stammering, she thanked each one, carefully avoiding calling their names. Finally, Lady Ramsburg and Louisa came to her rescue. "Elizabeth was frightened as a child by a strange man," her stepmother said, laughing. "As a result, she cannot remember gentlemen's names. Let me reintroduce you. Perhaps today we will begin by height."

"No, height will not work," Louisa said in a mock serious tone. "What if they appear one by one?"

"Perhaps if she knew each of us as individuals," the major suggested. "The rest of you can go home. I will stay here." The others roared, vowing to stay until their memories were indelibly imprinted on Miss Beckworth's brain.

"If anyone should stay, it should be I," Lord Hathaway declared. "I met her first."

"The best reason for you to leave. You have known her longer," the other two protested.

"Tell him to go away, Miss Beckworth," the lieutenant begged.

Stunned by their reactions to the misfortune that had plagued her since a child, Elizabeth giggled. The other ladies exchanged a satisfied glance and carefully added their balance to the situation. "I will never remember anyone's name if the person leaves," Elizabeth said with a laugh in her voice. "The only way I can learn a name is to see the person often."

"An invitation," Lord Hathaway said in delight.

"No! No! I simply meant that . . ."

"We know what you meant, Miss Beckworth," the major said hastily, his eyes on her chaperons, both of whom were frowning. "We promise to visit you often. And you must promise to allow us to be your escorts up the Steine."

"Yes, do promise," the lieutenant said earnestly, already certain that he was falling in love with her.

"I will even promise to be a gentleman," Lord Hathaway said in his usual mocking tones.

Lady Ramsburg looked at the clock, and the gentlemen stood up hastily. "We will see you this evening," she promised.

14

Charles, changing horses frequently, reached London in record time, but it was still too late for the confrontation he was planning. Tired, he turned his winded horse over to a groom, stumbled up the stairs into his rooms, and fell into bed, not even taking the time to remove his boots.

When Porter arrived in the middle of the next morning, Charles was still asleep. His valet's eyebrows rose, but he worked quietly to set the room to rights, preferring to have his master asleep than in the temper of the day before. He had just finished the unpacking when Charles turned over. The younger man stretched as if trying to remove the wrinkles from his clothes. Then he reached down to rub his feet and discovered his boots.

"Porter! Help me get out of these," he called. Porter was beside the bed immediately. Charles jumped. "Do you have to walk so quietly?" he asked with a frown.

The valet simply stood there and looked at him. Realizing the futility of trying to outstare a servant who had known him before he was breeched, Charles stuck out one leg. After a few minutes of struggle on both their parts, his boots were once more on the floor. "We shall have to have new sheets, Master Charles," Porter said reproachfully, looking at the long tears in the ones on the bed.

"If you must sleep in your boots, please, sir, at least remove your spurs."

Charles glared at him for a minute. Then he lay back and enjoyed wiggling his toes for a few minutes. He stripped off his shirt and his riding breeches and stretched again. Turning over to enjoy the freedom he had missed the night before, Charles faced the clock. He sat straight up in bed. "Is that the right time," he asked, his voice stern.

"Yes, Master Charles. I set it as soon as I arrived." Porter raised his brows as if to question him further. But Charles was already out of bed, heading for the dressing room.

"Find me something for an afternoon visit, Porter. Nothing too tight. I want to be able to move my arms." His valet stared after him and then walked slowly to the clothespress in the corner, his face solemn. "And find my dueling pistols."

With those words a frown appeared on Porter's face. "I believe I left them in the country," he said quietly as he held fresh undergarments out to his master.

"Then you will go out and purchase more this afternoon," Charles said firmly, his voice more like his father's than Porter had ever heard before. "And don't look at me with that frown on your face. You heard the rumors. What am I supposed to do? Ignore them?"

"Perhaps a talk with the man. Rumors are often untrue. Do you remember how your mother heard that you had offered for Miss Balingcourt last summer? She came back to London ready to plan the engagement party only to discover that someone was only making mischief."

"A wedding is far different from what Lord Dunstan did." Charles threw his shirt over his head, hiding a chest that many bits of muslin loved to stroke. "It is not the same," he said through the linen. He yanked the sleeves into place and stuck his head through the placket.

"Let me button your sleeves, Master Charles," Porter said with a sigh.

"How many times do I have to tell you to call me Mr. Beckworth?" Charles asked, his voice angry. "I am a grown man. I deserve my rightful title."

Porter simply looked at him for a moment, much as he used to look at the naughty boy waiting for his father. "And men are willing to talk their problems out and to discover the truth behind the rumors," his valet reminded him. He held the rich chocolate brown coat for Charles to slide his arms into, handed him his hat, and stood back, noting not for the first time what a pleasant picture his master made. At least he usually did with his smiles and laughs. This morning his frowns marred his appearance.

"I do not know when I will return," Charles said sternly. He took a deep breath and headed for the door.

But in spite of his determination, he was not successful. Dunstan was nowhere to be found. For the next few days Charles's troubles had nothing to do with a duel. Avoiding society matrons with marriageable daughters became almost an art. Seeking more congenial company, he finally repaired to White's. Finally, one evening as he sat around a table playing cards with several gentlemen, one of the older men said, "Haven't seen that grandson of Darington's lately. Must say the young are more casual about collecting debts than our generation ever was. Had a bet with him for a pony. He won. But I can't find him to pay him."

"He is out of town. A trip to see his grandfather." The tall man in a corbeau coat with a blue-striped waistcoat spoke, his face bland.

"More likely on an errand," another said quietly.

"Errand? What errand?" the older gentleman asked. "By God, he is not in trade, is he?"

"Trade? Only if he trades in secrets, sir."

The man in corbeau looked at that speaker, his eyes fierce and unsmiling. "Are you certain?" he asked. His voice and his eyes were like hail in the summertime, harsh and startling.

The younger gentleman looked at him for a moment. What he saw made him say quickly, "No. Just a joke." The others laughed. But the older gentleman and the man in corbeau exchanged a glance of understanding. Charles, too caught up in his own worries, missed the exchange.

As soon as the group dispersed, Charles found a way to take a place beside the younger man. "I heard you mention Lord Dunstan. Is it true he is away from London?"

After a quick look around to be certain no one was looking, the younger man whispered, "Yes. And no man visits his grandfather as often as Dunstan does." He winked at Charles. "Play a few hands?"

Unable to think of a good excuse quickly, Charles sat down. He watched as the young man dealt the cards. After inspecting his, he asked, "What did you mean about Dunstan and his grandfather?"

Once again the young man took a quick, furtive look around the room. "Never know who is watching," he said as he settled back in his chair. He looked at his hand once more and played. Then he leaned forward, his face filled with the news he was anxious to impart. "Dunstan's often out of town. Something to do with the government," he said in a soft, confidential tone.

"You mean he's a spy?"

"Shhh!" Once again his partner looked around the room before he turned back to look at Charles.

Charles, confused, leaned forward. "Well, is he?"

"Maybe." He took another quick look around the room, this time spotting the tall gentleman dressed in corbeau. "He has been out of town several times recently. Why only a month or so ago, he was gone for almost a fortnight."

Charles leaned back, a smile on his lips. "And you think that is suspicious?" he asked.

"Certainly. Don't you?"

Looking at his hand, Charles chose his new card. "Not at all. Lord Dunstan was visiting me," he said calmly. His spirits rose as he watched the other man's face fall. "Does your tale have more foundation than that?"

Reluctantly the other man admitted that it did not. As they finished the hand, Charles took a childish satisfaction in being able to best him. As he had forced the other man to back down, so would he force Dunstan to do the right thing by his sister.

The next morning Charles left his lodgings as he had every morning since he had arrived back in London. Heading toward the Clarendon House, he nodded to acquaintances, stopped in to see the design of a new tie pin, ordered some cigars to replace those he had blown a cloud with in the country, and placed his order for a dozen new shirts. Finally arriving at Dunstan's home, he banged the knocker.

"Come in, sir," the butler suggested. "I mentioned your visits to Lord Dunstan as soon as he arrived. He asked me to show you to the library whenever you called."

Ready to hear the butler announce once again

that Lord Dunstan was not at home, Charles stood there for a moment, confusion in his face. Then his resolve stiffened. He squared his shoulders proudly, handed his hat and cane to a waiting footman, and followed the butler down the hallway.

"Mr. Beckworth, my lord," the butler announced. Dunstan, who had been opening the stack of mail that had accumulated during his absence, sprang to his feet. He smiled and advanced across the room, holding out his hand. "Charles, when did you arrive in town? And how is your sister?"

The last word was too much. Charles, his face as dark as a thundercloud, leveled him with a right to the jaw. He stood over Dunstan with a feeling of satisfaction. He rubbed his right hand with his left, his knuckles stinging.

After his first impulse to get up and pummel Charles to the floor, Dunstan just lay there, his eyes wide and his hand on his jaw. He started to get up. Charles stepped closer and drew back his arm again. Dunstan sank back. "Why did you do that?" he asked, his voice less distinct than before.

"As if you did not know, you blackguard!"

Dunstan sat up warily, keeping a careful eye on his opponent. "What are you talking about?"

"My sister. I suppose you thought you could keep me from finding out. Come on. Get up. Let me show you what I think of the idea!" Charles stepped closer, his face still filled with anger.

"She told you?" Dunstan slid against the heavy desk. Keeping the edge in his hand, he worked his way behind the desk to the chair and stood up carefully. Still slightly unsteady from the blow, he leaned against the desk. "And you disapprove?"

"Disapprove? What did you expect me to do?"

"I expected you to at least give me a chance to explain." His jaw already beginning to turn the color of his eyes, Dunstan gave up his position by the desk and headed toward Charles. Once again Charles milled him to the floor.

"I will have my second call on yours, Lord Dunstan," Charles said firmly, dusting his hands lightly as he walked toward the door.

"Charles, you stop where you are!" Dunstan stood up once again.

The younger man turned, his face impassive. "Are you refusing to meet me, sir?" he asked.

"Of course I am . . ."

"Then you leave me no recourse but to destroy your reputation as you destroyed my sister's." Never had Charles been firmer, more steadfast in his resolve.

"What are you talking about?" Dunstan rushed toward the younger man and swung him about. "How can my proposal do that?"

Charles, certain by now that Dunstan would not oppose him, swung his fist once again. This time it was he who was on the floor, his hand to his jaw. He glared up at his one-time friend and started to rise. "No. Stay there!" Dunstan commanded, his blue eyes flashing as he pushed Charles back down. "Now tell me what you are talking about!"

"As if you didn't know," Charles said, sneering. He cautiously sat up, his eyes on Dunstan. The older man stood there, his face puzzled. This time he only watched Charles rise from the floor.

Turning his back on Charles, Dunstan sat down in a large blue leather chair. The younger man simply stared at him for a moment. Then he took the chair opposite. "Now tell me what you are talking about." This time Dunstan's words were individual bullets instead of a barrage of words. "And do not try to tell me I know. I don't!"

His whole plan to force Dunstan to marry his

sister disappearing like London fog in a good south wind, Charles cleared his throat. Dunstan walked over to a table near the door and poured glasses of wine for both of them. He handed one to Charles and waited. The younger man downed his in one gulp. Then he leaned back, confused. "I came to see you to gain satisfaction," he mumbled.

"By satisfaction I suppose you mean to challenge me to a duel. Is that what you meant by having our seconds call on one another?" Charles nodded, his frown still evident. Dunstan downed his own wine and crossed to the decanter, filling his glass again. The younger man looked longingly at the wine but refused to ask. "How my grandfather will love this!" Dunstan said, his voice biting.

"What does your grandfather have to do with my sister?" Charles asked, the blow to the jaw and the wine combining to confuse him.

Dunstan just looked at him. Then the older man began again. "You came to see me about your sister. Is that right?" Charles started to speak, but Dunstan stopped him. "Just nod." He nodded. "Is it because I asked her to marry me?"

Charles stopped in the midst of standing up, surprised. "Marry you?" he croaked, his voice breaking as it had not for years. He stood up and crossed to the table with the wine. He poured himself a glass and drank it quickly. Then he turned to the older man. "Did you say you asked Elizabeth to marry you?"

"Yes."

"Before or after you woke up in her bed?"

Dunstan flushed, took a deep breath, and said as calmly as he could, "After. But I had . . ."

"I suppose you felt it was the right thing to do," Charles said bitterly. "Better to have a wife than a scandal."

"Yes." Dunstan poured himself a glass of wine and took a sip.

"Well, you should have acted more quickly."

"What do you mean? I asked her before I left her room."

Charles stood up, squaring his shoulders. "You have never explained why you were there. And do not tell me Elizabeth invited you. I know my sister too well for that."

"Didn't she tell you? Isn't that why you are here?"

"No. I am here because you have ruined my sister's reputation, and you are going to pay for that," Charles said, his anger apparent.

"Ruined," Dunstan repeated. "You know everything, I suppose. I told her someone would find out. She should have married me right away. I told her that." His face was somber. He ran a hand over his eyes. "I tried to convince her that her way was folly."

"That's right. Blame my sister for the spread of the gossip. You, on the other hand, did everything right." Charles glared at the older man, wishing he had his pistols. "I suppose you are proud to admit that you spent the night with my sister?" Dunstan shook his head. "How could you? Dunstan, you are my friend. At least I thought you were," Charles said bitterly. He had hoped in his heart that the rumors were false, that Porter was right.

"I didn't mean to . . ."

"That's even worse. You seduced my sister on a whim?"

"No, I didn't seduce her. At least I don't think I did." Dunstan began to pace. Trying to get the facts straight in his own mind, he walked quickly around the room. Charles, by this time thoroughly dispirited, watched him. Then Dunstan turned to face him. "You remember that day. By the time the ladies arrived home, we had been gambling for hours."

"And you were winning as usual," Charles said, his tone less bitter than before.

"Your cousin came down for supper, but Elizabeth stayed in her room." Dunstan looked at Charles to see if he were following the story. Charles nodded. "After supper we started playing cards again. I remember that part of the evening clearly."

"Are you trying to tell me that you seduced my sister and you do not even remember doing it?"

"Yes."

Charles laughed bitterly. "I have heard of weak stories before, but yours is the weakest. And I suppose that because you cannot remember you have no obligation to her."

"No. I told you that I offered to marry her. I asked her the very next morning, right after the maid left."

"So that's how the story got out. The maid found you in bed."

"No!" Dunstan got himself under control with an effort. "We were not in bed. I was under the bed."

"Naturally. And I suppose you had been under there all night long." Charles let all his scorn drip into his voice.

"Of course not. The first thing I remember about that morning was being kicked out of bed." Charles stood up, his fist drawn back threateningly. "Sit down. It isn't as bad as it seems."

"You are not the one with a sister whose reputation is in shreds," Charles said, his face dark with anger once more.

"No, but I am the one who wants to marry her,

Charles. I don't know how I woke up in her bed. Don't look at me like that, Charles. Do you remember how you got to bed that evening? You had had more to drink than I." Charles shook his head. "Neither do I." Dunstan sighed. "She will not listen to reason. But I can't get her out of my mind. And every time I ask, she says no." He straightened his shoulders and faced Charles. "Whatever happened was not planned, I promise you that."

"That should make me feel less like killing you?"

"No. I understand. If I had a sister, I would try to protect her like you are protecting Elizabeth. Damn, Charles, I am sorry this happened."

"Because you will have to marry Elizabeth now?"

"No. I want to marry her. I merely wish I had met her again earlier and had a chance to court her properly." Dunstan slumped forward, his face in his hands.

Almost against his will Charles moved toward him. Then as if embarrassed, he moved back to the opposite chair and took a seat. "You asked her to marry you that morning?" Dunstan nodded. "And she said no." By thinking aloud, he hoped to find a solution.

"Of course, she did. Would we be sitting here now in this dilemma if she had said yes?" Dunstan ran his hands through his thick brown hair. Then he rubbed his jaw. He sank back in his seat and closed his eyes briefly. "When did the rumors start? Right away?" He sat up suddenly. "Elizabeth did not mention them the last time I saw her? Did she know?"

"The last time you saw her? Have you been back to the manor?"

"I stopped by the manor several weeks ago and asked her again, but she wouldn't listen. But I keep trying."

"You saw Elizabeth after you left the house party?"

"Yes."

"And you are still willing to marry her?"

"Willing? Charles, I would make her my wife today if she would accept me." By now Dunstan was standing, his face bright with anticipation. "Do you think there's a chance?"

The younger man smiled, his eyes dancing. "Will you return to the country with me?" he asked, already planning his entrance.

"To the manor?"

"To Elizabeth." The heavy burden of responsibility lifted, Charles beamed. "And if she won't have you this time, we will take your offer to a higher authority—my mother."

15

"In Brighton? What is Elizabeth doing in Brighton?" Charles demanded as he stood in the entry hall of the manor. Dunstan and he had arrived only minutes before, determined to make Elizabeth agree to the wedding.

"I believe Mrs. Beckworth and Miss Beckworth are visiting your mother, sir," Jeffries explained, his manner hiding his interest in their unexpected arrival. Not for a moment did he allow his glance to stray from his master to the other gentleman.

"But Elizabeth sees my mother only at Christmas. What could have caused her to go?" Charles turned to Dunstan as if the older man could give him the answers. "My sister has been refusing to go to Brighton for weeks now. Cousin Louisa was determined to get her there, but I was certain that Elizabeth would never give in."

"I trust you did not put a wager on it," Dunstan said dryly, noting all the servants loitering about the hallway. He raised one eyebrow and started to comment but thought better of it.

"Did the ladies expect you, Mr. Beckworth?" Jeffries asked, his face carefully blank.

"No. But I knew they would be here. Elizabeth refuses to go anywhere." Charles was frowning in concentration, trying to make sense of his sister's behavior. "When did they leave?"

"Two days after you left for London. Miss Beckworth decided quite suddenly."

Dunstan and Charles exchanged worried glances. "Heard the rumors, did she?" Charles asked, his face as impassive as the butler's. Dunstan waited, his hands shoved in his pockets, fingering the special license he had had the forethought to get before he left London. While Charles had slept in the coach that afternoon, he had been reliving every moment with Elizabeth, dreaming about the first night of their marriage. He closed his eyes for a moment, wishing he could recapture his dreams. Charles's question, however, brought him back to reality with a thud much like the one he had experienced only weeks before.

Jeffries simply looked at his master. Charles finally said quietly, "Prepare rooms for both of us for tonight. And send in a bottle of wine and some glasses to the library. Dunstan, we need to talk about the change in plans and find some means of getting her to agree." The two gentlemen walked down the hallway, leaving a stunned group of servants behind. For once Jeffries was pleased at the ability of the staff to pass along gossip. The news of the marriage would be around the estate by nightfall.

In the library Charles took the tray from the footman and put it on the table, pouring both himself and Dunstan a glass of claret. Handing him a glass, he asked, "How would you like to visit my mother?"

"Your mother? I have not met her in years. What will she think of me, of us, when I appear to stay with her?" Dunstan asked, putting the fragile glass down so hard he almost cracked the stem.

"No, not stay with her. With Louisa and Elizabeth there the house will be full. When Mama and Lord Ramsburg began going to Brighton, Mama insisted that they purchase a small house. She said she did not intend to house every cousin with a marriageable daughter who wanted to pursue husband hunting at little expense. Wouldn't be going there if it weren't so. For the last year she has filled her house with young ladies anxious to be my wife."

Dunstan gave a bark of laughter, his memory of the lady was of a petite blonde who looked angelic. "To whom did she say this?"

"To us. Told us we were welcome. She had rooms for all of us but not to plan to bring guests. More comfortable at an inn anyway. No matchmaking mamas around." Charles laughed ruefully. "Well, will you go with me?"

"We will stay at an inn?"

"Or we could take lodgings." Charles said. Dunstan nodded, his face somber. "I will need to discuss a few things with Carstairs, my agent." He laughed ruefully."And I had better have a talk with my grooms before I have a revolt on my hands." His eyes glittered dangerously as he remembered the conversation that had sent him to London. "And at least two will be leaving if they were not smart enough to have left while I was gone."

The trip to Brighton was disturbing for Dunstan. He knew he would be seeing Elizabeth again soon, but what would she say?

As Dunstan and Charles left their inn in Brighton a few mornings later, the question of Elizabeth was on both their minds. They were silent in the coach. Then Dunstan asked, "Should we have sent a message to your mother that we had arrived? What if they are not at home?"

"They will be. Mama is at home from eleven to one today. There may be a few callers, but they will not stay long. It will be easier, too, because

Elizabeth cannot refuse to see you." Charles smiled mischievously. "And Mama will ask us to luncheon."

When they entered Lady Ramsburg's drawing room a few minutes later, both of them were surprised at the crowded room. At one end of the room was a settee where Elizabeth and Louisa sat, surrounded by a bevy of men in uniform. At the other end Lady Ramsburg visited with friends. Waving off the butler, who would have announced them, Charles walked toward his mother, bent and kissed her cheek. "Charles, dear one, when did you arrive?" she asked, her face lighting as it usually did when she saw her son.

"Last evening. Mama, may I present Robert Clarendon, the Viscount Dunstan. He came to Brighton with me." Dunstan bowed.

For a moment Lady Ramsburg's face seemed almost a mask, her eyes widened until they were almost too large for her face. She inspected him carefully, wondering if his presence meant the beginning of more problems. Then she nodded pleasantly, deciding to reserve judgment until later. She glanced at Charles, her look thoughtful. "I am surprised to see you again, Lord Dunstan," she said quietly, continuing her inspection. He maintained his poise with effort, realizing that Elizabeth must have told her everything. He fully expected to be asked to leave, but what she saw reassured her. She smiled, one of those breathtaking smiles that had made her so popular both in her Season and as a widow. Dunstan stood talking to her quietly for a few minutes, his eyes wandering from her face to the group across the room only occasionally. Noting the direction of his gaze, Lady Ramsburg finally said, "Would you like to renew your acquaintance with my daughter, Lord Dunstan?"

This time it was his face that changed. He smiled, his dark blue eyes sparkling. "Yes," he said quietly.

"Charles, take this young man across to your sister. Then you come back so that I can talk to you," Lady Ramsburg said. Charles understood exactly what she meant and nodded, hoping that she would agree with his plan.

When they crossed the room, Elizabeth was still unaware of their presence, but Louisa had noticed. She did not tell her cousin what she saw, preferring to wait and observe Elizabeth's reactions. Elizabeth was laughing at the antics of the officers. To her surprise, she felt comfortable around them, not even worrying when she occasionally forgot a name. The officers seemed to take the situation lightly, laughing with her, rather than showing any annoyance. Had she realized the amount of money that was won or lost when she remembered or forgot a name, Elizabeth would have been horrified. Lord Hathaway had instigated the bet. Noting the arrival of two more people, he signaled the others unobtrusively. Quickly and quietly the wagers were made by pre-arranged signals.

The officers stood back, allowing the gentlemen to approach Elizabeth one by one. "Charles," she said delighted, "does Mama know you have arrived?" He bent and kissed her cheek and then Louisa's.

"She welcomed me with open arms," he assured his sister. The officers who had bet against Elizabeth's recognition of him shrugged. Then Charles stepped aside. "I brought a friend with me, Elizabeth."

Lord Dunstan walked up to her from where he had been standing behind two officers. "Miss Beckworth," he said, his eyes fixed on her face. He kissed her hand, his lips lingering for a moment.

From the first moment she saw him, Elizabeth felt her heart race. She blushed slightly, but her eyes never left his. When his lips touched her hand, a fire began racing through her. "Lord Dunstan," she said, her voice even lower, more husky than usual. Almost as if he were drawing it from her, she smiled, her face and eyes reflecting her delight at seeing him again. Their fingers lingered in each other's a moment more.

Louisa, determined that Dunstan should have another chance, rose. "Charles, I am certain your mother has hundreds of questions to ask you. And rather than answering them twice, you can tell us both at the same time. Why don't you, Lord Dunstan, take my place? I am certain my niece wishes to talk with you." She walked away, leaving confusion behind her.

Quickly Dunstan took his place beside Elizabeth. The clock chimed the hour. Startled, everyone looked up. Realizing that their visit had extended beyond the polite limits, the officers made their farewells. "I must protest, Miss Beckworth," Lord Hathaway said as he made his farewell.

"Why?" she asked, her eyes twinkling as she waited for his answer. The tall redhead, though careful to make certain she knew he was not in love with her, enjoyed knowing that he had her attention.

"You are not proceeding in a fair manner." Elizabeth raised her eyebrows but did not answer. "You did not forget Lord Dunstan's name." The other officers, their faces solemn though their eyes were laughing, nodded.

"But I have known Miss Beckworth for several years," Dunstan said, not certain he liked all the attention they were giving the lady he planned to marry.

"Then I suppose you must be forgiven, Miss Beckworth," the captain said, his face breaking into smiles. The others agreed. Then they made their bows to the ladies. "Until this evening," they promised.

"Until tonight," Lady Ramsburg said, noting the disgruntled look on Dunstan's face. As soon as the officers had gone, she turned to the other two gentlemen. "We will have to tell you farewell, gentlemen," she said kindly. "We are expected for luncheon elsewhere." This time even Charles looked disturbed. She patted his hand consolingly. "You may escort us along the Steine this evening and stay for supper afterward."

Before Dunstan and Charles could do more than utter a few words of farewell, they were outside, their hats in their hands. They looked at each other and then laughed ruefully. They walked slowly down the street. "Should have told the carriage to wait," Dunstan said, searching the street for a hackney. Reaching the corner, they stopped for a moment, their eyes on the passengers alighting just down the street.

"Can I interest you in a bird and a bottle, your lordship?" Charles asked as he held open the door of the hackney. Dunstan laughingly agreed. For the rest of the afternoon they walked about Brighton, inspecting lodgings for their stay. One night at the inn had convinced them they needed something more permanent. Finally they discovered comfortable rooms with adequate stabling for both the carriage and their horses. Paying their shot at the inn, they were installed there without delay, leaving Graves and Porter to arrange for a cook and someone to clean.

While her brother and Dunstan were finding a place to stay, Elizabeth attended the luncheon with her cousin and stepmother. Although she tried to keep her mind on the conversations at the table, she kept feeling Dunstan's lips on her hand, seeing his thick brown hair and blue eyes, so deep and mysterious. More than once she had to apologize for her inattention. Both Louisa and Lady Ramsburg noticed. As drawn as she felt to him, she still was not certain she was ready to trust her future to any man.

Arriving home, the ladies retired to their rooms to rest until teatime. Elizabeth, her mind in a whirl, lay down. The soft crisp sheets beneath her reminded her of a morning several weeks earlier. Too disturbed and confused to sleep, she lay there for a time, remembering every word Dunstan had said to her that morning as well as the morning weeks later. His eyes had followed hers, making her heart race as it was racing now. Her breath came faster when she remembered the feel of his lips on her hand. What would it be like to feel those lips on hers?

Elizabeth slid from the bed, too restless to stay there any longer. Why did he make her feel this way? She remembered his letters, the way he had told her what he had been doing, his proposals. Even when she had been engaged to Jack, her feelings had not been so strong. The thought of Jack brought her pacing back and forth to a halt. Her fiancé had told her he loved her, yet he had betrayed her. Would Dunstan behave differently? The question made her sink to the chaise, her face in her hands.

Finally she sat up again, her back straight. Her decision never to marry had been correct, she told herself, ignoring the fever in her blood whenever she thought of Dunstan. She would enjoy her stay in Brighton, enjoy the company of the gentlemen who seemed to find her amusing, and worry about going home to the manor later. Firmly she put away any thought that the scandal would be discovered in Brighton, refusing even to consider the possibility. Putting Dunstan out of her mind was impossible.

When Miller arrived a short time later, the gown she had been pressing thrown over her arm, she discovered her mistress seated in front of her mirror, pulling on her curls. "Why did I ever let Amelia persuade me to cut my hair? Miller, is there anything you can do to make it longer?" The latest *la belle assemblie* lay open in front of her. She stared at herself in the mirror and then turned to read about the latest, longer hair styles. "He must have thought I looked a quiz," Elizabeth said in despair.

Miller carefully laid the dress out where it would not become wrinkled and crossed to her mistress. "You always look lovely, Miss Beckworth," she assured Elizabeth. Then she walked around her, her eyes narrowed thoughtfully. "Which style did you prefer?"

"Oh, I do not know. They all look as though the hair must be much longer." Elizabeth pulled out one curl and let it bounce back.

"We could try this one," Miller told her, pointing to a style that allowed curls around the face, but pulled the rest of the hair high on the top of the head. She put her curling stick near the fire to heat.

"Hmmm. It is different." Elizabeth looked back in the mirror. She pulled her hair up and looked at each side. "Yes, let us try that.'

By the time her hair was arranged to her satisfaction, it was time to dress for their promenade. Miller pulled the petticoat over Elizabeth's curls, careful not to disarrange any. She looped the bows, tying them into knots. Then, glancing at the deeply cut neckline of the dress, she selected a different

chemise, one that had a tie around the top to hold
it in place as well as the ties to separate and lift
her mistress's breasts. That garment in place, she
lifted the thin golden muslin undergarment over
Elizabeth's head. A few moments later the white
muslin gown with sprigs of gold and green followed. Tying the last bow, Miller stood back to get
a view of her mistress. Her curls, except for the
few at her neckline and around her face, were
caught up with golden ribbons, leaving her long,
slender neck bare and elegant.

Elizabeth too looked at herself in the mirror.
She eyed the long expanse of neck and shoulders
with hesitation. "Get me a cashmere shawl," she
said, not certain she liked the look she saw. Miller
handed her the one that echoed the colors of her
dress, draping it artistically about her. This time
when Elizabeth looked in the mirror, she smiled.
"Thank you, Miller," she said quietly. The maid
flushed and smiled.

Like Elizabeth, Lady Ramsburg and Louisa had
not rested much that afternoon. After they had
rested for a time with carefully prepared masques
of strawberries and cucumber on their faces, they
met in Lady Ramsburg's room for a talk. "Is he
here to offer for Elizabeth again?" Lady Ramsburg
asked, her blue eyes faintly shadowed with worry.

"He certainly is not here because of Charles,"
Louisa said, patting her skin with her hand to be
certain that it was as smooth as she wanted. "And
I would think that Charles too gives every sign
that you may be correct. If he is a true gentleman,
I expect that he will do the right thing."

"He certainly forgot he was a gentleman when
he entered her bedroom."

"Perhaps he had had too much to drink," Louisa said soothingly. "You know what gentlemen

are like then. And he has tried to do the right thing. He has offered what reparation he can."

"Will she have him?"

Louisa looked at her cousin for a moment, her face registering her surprise. "Does she have any choice?"

"Ordinarily I would have said no, but Elizabeth has never been one to make the decisions expected. All we can do is to be certain that Lord Dunstan has his chance. If he is wise, he will convince her to marry him before he asks her the question." Lady Ramsburg lay back on her chaise, her face somber.

"What if the scandal begins here?"

"It will if we give it enough time. With company thin right now, we can give the gentleman a chance. She may accept him tonight, and our problems will be solved."

Louisa looked at her cousin, disbelief written on every line of her face. The room was quiet for a few moments. Then Lady Ramsburg said, "He is a handsome rogue, isn't he?"

Elizabeth would have agreed. No matter what her mind told her, her heart was telling her to be gracious to Dunstan, to smile at him and to encourage him. At first that evening she listened to her heart.

When the ladies entered the drawing room that evening, the two gentlemen were waiting. Charles, dressed in a corbeau-colored, double-breasted tailcoat with a deep *M*-shaped collar over a gold and white striped waistcoat and sage green breeches, hurried to his mother's side and gave her a kiss. Dunstan stood to one side, his eyes on Elizabeth. Dressed in a dark blue coat and buff breeches, he wore a lighter blue waistcoat embroidered in fine silk.

Elizabeth could hardly keep her eyes off him.

The blue he wore almost matched his eyes, making them brighter than ever. Even when she was not looking at him, she could feel him staring at her. Unlike the times before when she had been the center of attention, his gaze did not make her feel uncomfortable.

Their plans already made, Lady Ramsburg called her party to order. "Charles, you will escort Louisa and me. Dunstan, will you escort Elizabeth?"

He nodded, his face breaking into a smile. "My pleasure, Miss Beckworth," he said quietly, his eyes reinforcing his words. She lay her hand on his arm, wondering at the warmth that seemed to spread through her body.

Their journey by coach to the Steine was pleasant, each member of the party adding some conversation. The walk in the cool evening air, in spite of the damp, was pleasant. Strolling along, they talked. At first Dunstan and Elizabeth had walked along in a silence which neither enjoyed. Finally Dunstan asked, "Have you been enjoying your visit to Brighton?"

Elizabeth smiled and answered, explaining the entertainments that had already been given. The silence broken, they continued their conversation until suddenly they were joined by two officers. "Major, Captain," they said, Dunstan less than gracious.

"We have been looking for you, Miss Beckworth. Usually you are much earlier," the captain said, looking at Dunstan with a frown.

"Mama is convinced that too much salt air in the evening is making her look hagged," Elizabeth said. The officers laughed loudly, taking in the petite figure that seemed to radiate health and happiness. "Therefore our walks will be limited ones."

They groaned and began protesting. Almost without his being aware of what had happened, Dunstan found himself standing alone, the two officers now on either side of Elizabeth. Disgruntled, he walked over to where Charles and the other ladies were standing, visiting with friends. Introducing him, Lady Ramsburg brought Dunstan into their conversation. Although he laughed and talked, his eyes followed Elizabeth when he thought he was unobserved.

"What do you think of the prince's summer home, Lord Dunstan?" asked Louisa, nodding at the Marine Pavilion behind him. He turned and looked at it, his eyes assessing the rounded dome and peculiar towers that rose behind it.

"That, my lord, is the royal stables," Charles told him with a laugh. Lord Ramsburg walked up about that time, having arrived with the carriage. "I wish I could see the inside. The horses are said to live in the greatest luxury."

"And what did that cost us?" Dunstan asked, his face disapproving. "I suppose we did pay for it? And I thought the prince was known for his taste in art."

"Do not let the people of this town hear you disparage the prince or his construction, Lord Dunstan," Lady Ramsburg laughed. "To them he is a saint."

"With the money he has brought into their town, who could blame them for thinking that," Louisa added, her face solemn.

"Not only Brighton merchants have had their pockets lined," Lord Ramsburg explained. "Look at all the shops that are filled with London merchants here to take advantage of all of our custom."

Charles laughed, his eyes bright. "I really do not mind what the people of Brighton think of the prince. What I want to know is whether you can get us inside, George?" he asked his stepfather.

Just then a crack of laughter from the group surrounding Elizabeth startled everyone. Dunstan looked at the little group only a few feet away, anger in his eyes. Elizabeth was laughing, her face filled with happiness. The shawl had slipped from her shoulders. The redheaded captain, his head bent to hear what she was saying, could not keep his eyes from the creamy expanse that had been revealed. But Elizabeth was oblivious to that; her eyes danced with merriment. Dunstan took a step or two back to the group. Then Lady Ramsburg, reading the fury in his face, called, "Elizabeth, my dear."

Her stepdaughter was at her side immediately. "The twilight is beginning to fade and my skirts are becoming quite damp. I believe it is time to leave," Lady Ramsburg said clearly. The officers groaned and protested, but she would not change her mind. "Nine o'clock is late enough to be out for a walk," she said firmly as though she had not been one of the last to leave the Steine on many evenings.

"Do not forget that you have promised to ride with me tomorrow afternoon, Miss Beckworth," the major said, a smile in his voice. Dunstan glared at him.

The trip back to the Ramsburgs' summerhouse was a quiet one. Dunstan stared at Elizabeth, Charles, George and the other two ladies had little to say, and Elizabeth, having noticed Dunstan's stares, was growing angry. Fortunately, supper was waiting when they arrived.

"Charles has mentioned that you work for the government, Lord Dunstan. Are you interested in politics?" Lord Ramsburg asked, his face revealing his interest in the matter. After the conversation he and his wife had had earlier that evening, he was determined to evaluate the young man for himself.

"I am more interested in helping England win this war, my lord," Dunstan said, his usually pleasant face very stern. "My grandfather did not want me to serve in the army; therefore, I must do my part in other ways."

"Just like Mama. She stands in my way also," Charles said bitterly. "If I had my way, I would be traveling with Wellington now. You do think the Duke of York made the right choice for a commander, don't you, George?"

"A good choice. Not always popular with the leaders in the Houses, but a good soldier," his stepfather agreed.

"I am tired of hearing about the army," his mother complained. Even Elizabeth had to admit that she had begun to have her doubts about the wisdom of Charles's serving abroad. "If you do not have an heir, you must not endanger your life," Lady Ramsburg added, beginning another of her campaigns.

"If you start your matchmaking again, Mama, I will leave," Charles said, the light of battle in his eyes. Prudently, Lady Ramsburg was silent. Dunstan looked from one to another, his face serene. His mind was still seething. How dare Elizabeth allow another man to look at her the way the captain had been?

When the ladies left the men to their port, retiring to the drawing room for tea, Dunstan turned to Charles. "She will never have me. Did you see how she ignored me most of the evening?"

"You just arrived. Give my sister time. I thought you wanted to court her. You cannot do that if you are glaring at her constantly," Charles said, his face serious.

"Take it slowly," Lord Ramsburg said, noting the somberness of their expressions. "Ladies must be given time to make up their minds." He smiled reassuringly.

"Is that what you did with Mama, George?" Charles asked, his face breaking into a wide smile. He remembered that Season well.

His stepfather laughed. "I took one look at her and decided that I must have her. Getting her to agree took time. Shall we join the ladies?' he asked.

The ladies had been discussing the gentlemen. "Do you think Lord Dunstan is handsome, Elizabeth?" Lady Ramsburg asked, her eyes fixed carefully on her task of pouring the tea.

Her stepdaughter blushed. "I suppose some people would think him handsome," she said. Her heart kept telling her that she was one of those people, but she ignored it. But she could not ignore the memory of him on the floor beside her bed, his blue eyes reflecting his surprise. She gazed dreamily into space, totally ignoring questions addressed to her.

When the gentlemen entered and Dunstan glared at her again, that dreaminess disappeared. As they played a few hands of cards later, she pointedly ignored him, taking Charles as a partner and leaving Dunstan to partner her cousin. Lord and Lady Ramsburg looked on indulgently as the brother and sister began to quarrel. Finally Louisa threw down her hand. "Enough," she said firmly. "Gentlemen, good night. Elizabeth, go to your room." The two involved in the argument looked up, their faces surprised. Then they broke into laughter.

"Were we retreating into childhood again, Louisa?" Charles asked when he could breathe again.

"You sounded as you did then. So stern," Elizabeth added, her hazel eyes twinkling. Dunstan, his sense of humor tickled, watched as she leaned over and kissed her cousin, wishing that it had been he whom she had kissed. His eyes darkened again when the shawl slipped once more.

"Good night, children," Louisa said firmly, making her own departure. Her leaving was a signal that the evening was over. Quietly Charles and Dunstan made their good-byes.

Dunstan stopped in front of Elizabeth. "Will you be receiving guests tomorrow morning, Miss Beckworth?" he asked, his eyes never leaving hers. She nodded, afraid of what he would say. "Then I will see you then," he promised.

Unable to sleep that night, Dunstan left their rooms and walked along the seashore, his coat turned up to keep out the damp. As he walked, he thought of Elizabeth. Every time he thought he had a chance with her, something happened. Once again he fingered the license in his pocket. Once again he thought of how the officers that evening had bent to hear what she had to say. By the next morning his lack of sleep and his anger had combined to put him in a dangerous mood.

"Put it off. Send a message that you are indisposed," Charles urged when he saw the determined look on Dunstan's face. "Wait until you are more in control."

"Have you changed your mind about wanting me as a brother-in-law?" Dunstan asked, his face cold. The dark brown jacket he wore made his face look stern.

"Of course I have not. But, Dunstan, you are not at your best. Wait to approach Elizabeth when you are." Charles poured him a cup of tea, hoping to get him to drink it. Dunstan refused.

When he arrived at the Ramsburg home that morning, his temper was on edge. Once again he was shown into a morning room. Once again Elizabeth waited for him alone.

He made his bow more carelessly than before.

Elizabeth tried to deny that her heart had begun
to race when he walked into the room, but she
could not. Dunstan, his face serious, enjoyed the
picture she made in an apricot muslin tied with
darker ribbons of that color. Her curls fell art-
lessly about her face. This morning her neckline
was high.

For a few moments they simply stared at each
other, letting themselves look their fill. Then Dunstan walked to where she sat and took the seat
opposite. "Miss Beckworth, Elizabeth," he said.

At the same moment she said, "Lord Dunstan."
They both stopped. For a short time there was total
silence as each waited for the other to begin again.

Finally he spoke. "Elizabeth, Charles has told
me about the rumors. Why didn't you write to
me? We both knew something like this might
happen."

"And what do you propose to do about it now
that you know?" she asked, her face as blank as
she could make it.

"Why, make you my wife, of course," he said.
She could tell that he was surprised that she had
had to ask. She took a deep breath, causing the
bodice of her dress to rise and fall dramatically. "I
have a special license. We can be married today,"
he said, keeping his eyes fixed on her.

"Marry me. Just like that." Elizabeth's dreams of
a marriage with a husband who loved her just for
herself faded. "Why?"

The question caught Dunstan unaware. He
thought for a moment trying to find some reason
that would appeal to her. Finally he simply said,
"We have to marry."

"Have to marry?" Elizabeth stood up and crossed
to the window, pulling back the curtains to gaze
with sightless eyes on the lovely garden below. She

turned to face him. "Lord Dunstan, the words 'have to' are anathema to me. I have reached an age when I can please myself."

"And it does not please you to marry me? That is what you are saying?" he asked angrily. He rose and walked to her side, his anger evident in every movement of his body.

Realizing that he had missed the point she was trying to make, Elizabeth began again. "Lord Dunstan, please try to understand. If we are forced to marry simply because society dictates, will our marriage be successful?"

"Others have been," he said biting off every syllable.

"Have you looked around you, Lord Dunstan? How many of your friends are happily married? I can count mine on one hand, and that includes one couple I know very well. If we marry simply because we are expected to marry to eliminate the scandal, what hope do we have to fare any better?" She waited for a moment, hoping that he would answer her, would convince her that he was not simply following the dictates of society.

When he did reply, her hope was shattered. "I suppose you are unwilling to give up the admiration of those fawning officers who were with you last evening. Did you deliberately let your shawl fall so that the captain would enjoy the view more?" He glared at her.

Elizabeth took a deep breath and straightened her spine. "Are you objecting to the dress I wore last evening, Lord Dunstan?" she asked in a voice so low and quiet that Charles, had he been present, would have warned him to take heed. "I do not remember your objections when you greeted me last evening." Her eyes were shot with green fire.

"You were not making a display of yourself in

public then," he said sternly. He walked away from her and then turned abruptly. "I suppose you also make it a practice to lure gentlemen into your bedroom so that you can have the pleasure of turning them down when they do the right thing?"

The red flags in her cheeks were only one indication of her anger. "Lord Dunstan, I suggest you leave," she said firmly, tapping her foot and reminding herself that a lady did not strike a gentleman. "I regret that my answer is a disappointment to you." She held back her tears with an effort, her face strangely calm.

Dunstan, who would have given his all to call back the hasty words that had spilled out, stood there for a moment. His blue eyes were wide. He started to cross to the door and then came back, his face set in somber lines. He put his hands on her shoulders, keeping her there when she tried to pull away. "You must listen to me," he said, the despair in his voice evident. "I did not mean to offend you. I want you for my wife. And I will do anything I need to to assure that you will accept me." At first Elizabeth held her breath, thinking he would declare his feelings. "Both you and I know that what happened that night was not planned, but because of that night, our life is planned. I cannot let you go." His hands tightened as she tried to pull back. "But I will not repeat my offer until you are ready," he said. Then he pulled her to him and kissed her, his lips as warm and as sweet as he could make them. "Think about me," he said quietly. Then he left the room.

16

During the next few days, Elizabeth Beckworth thought about Lord Dunstan more than she would have imagined was possible. As angry as she had been with him, she could not forget his lips on hers, his hands holding her firmly but tenderly in place. And he was everywhere. As Charles's friend, he was in the drawing room in the morning, with them for their walks along the Steine, and in demand at the parties that began to occur more frequently, being attentive to her as well as the other ladies with whom he danced, talked, and laughed.

Even that first afternoon when she had still been so angry with him, he had disarmed her. Entering the house as she and the major were leaving for their ride, he had bowed, his eyes friendly instead of condemning her as they had that morning. He had handed the bouquets he was carrying to the butler and smiled at her, telling them to enjoy their ride. She had looked back puzzled, not at all certain that she needed his approval yet rather unhappy because he had given it.

Had she been able to see him a few minutes later, she would not have been so confused. He had entered the drawing room with a sad look on his face. "Who died, Dunstan?" Charles asked, laughing.

His friend just looked at him with reproach. Charles, who had already had to listen to the story of Elizabeth's refusal more times than he wanted that morning, apologized. "I told you I would speak to her for you," he said, his face serious. "Tell Mama and Cousin Louisa the whole and see what they say." He had tried to persuade Dunstan to approach them earlier that day, but he had refused.

When the last of the afternoon guests had left and they were alone drinking tea, Dunstan finally gave him the nod. "Mama," Charles began hesitantly. Then as if making a decision, he hurried on. "Dunstan wishes to ask your advice."

His mother looked from him to the older man. Louisa, her face carefully calm though her eyes were sparkling, looked up from the plate of tea cakes she was inspecting. She and Lady Ramsburg exchanged looks. "Yes?" Lady Ramsburg said, patting the place beside her on the settee. Dunstan sat beside her, the despair showing on his face.

"I have made such a muddle of this," he said quietly. This time the looks that Louisa and she exchanged were worried ones. "When Elizabeth agreed to see me this morning, I was certain that she meant to say yes."

"But she did not?" Louisa asked, setting her teacup on the table beside her and leaning forward slightly.

"No. She told me that she did not believe in marrying only because that is what society expects. She said most marriages made for those reasons were unhappy ones. And she chose not to marry under those conditions and under those odds." He closed his eyes, dreading the next part but knowing that if they were to give him any advice, they had to know. "I was angry. I said things I knew were not true." Lady Ramsburg raised her eyebrows, waiting for him to explain. He blushed. "I accused her of dressing improperly, of flirting." He could not and would not tell them anything more. He fell silent.

For a moment the room was in silence. Then Lady Ramsburg asked, "Had you discussed the situation with her earlier?" He shook his head. "You walked with her last evening, said a few words to her earlier yesterday, and then asked her to marry you this morning?"

Dunstan nodded. "I told her that Charles had told me about the rumors." The two ladies closed their eyes in despair. "I told her that she should have accepted my first offer."

"Lord Dunstan, no wonder she did not accept you," Louisa said, her hands clasped in front of her as though she were trying to keep from throwing something at him.

"What do you mean?" Both gentlemen wore puzzled looks.

Patiently Lady Ramsburg explained. "Elizabeth knows what society expects in a situation like this one. She does not have to be reminded. She wanted to be reassured, to know that you offered for her, not just for the woman you had wronged." Louisa nodded. "I wish you had approached me first," she said, sighing.

"Is there anything he can do to make her change her mind, Mama?" Charles asked. He had already decided on his own course.

"Be patient, be pleasant, and be attentive," Lady Ramsburg said firmly. "No more accusations or talking about what society expects. Let her see you as a man who wants her to be his wife because he cares for her. You do care for her?" Three pair of blue eyes stared at Dunstan. Red crept into his face. He nodded. All three of the watchers sighed. "We will need to make certain that you receive the right invitations. Come, Louisa, we need to write a few notes."

Dunstan and Charles stood there for a moment. Then Dunstan put his hand over his face as if trying to wipe away bad memories. Charles slapped him on the back, "I told you Mama would help," he said, his face smiling.

"Yes," Dunstan said quietly. "Now, if your sister will respond. I am tired. Make my excuses for me, Charles. I will see the ladies tomorrow." He walked out of the room, his usually straight shoulders sagging just a little.

Charles, left to his own amusement, stayed at his mother's. He would talk to his sister that very afternoon. When Elizabeth returned, she found him in the drawing room waiting for her. One look at his face was enough to rouse her anger. "How could you do it, Little Bit?" he had asked, his face registering his disapproval.

"Do what?" She took off her top hat and put it on the table and then ran her fingers through her tousled curls.

"Refuse Dunstan." Charles stood there looking down at her. "What will happen now if these rumors spread to Brighton?"

"They will not," she said firmly as if she could stop them just by wishing. "Jeffries assured me that he would put a stop to them."

"Your butler must be truly remarkable, Elizabeth. To stop rumors after they have already spread. Be realistic. Accept Dunstan."

"Little brother, my life is my own. I will decide when and if I will marry. And it will not be because society says I must." She glared at him, wishing that she were younger so that she could throw something at him as she often had when she was a girl. "Now, I am going upstairs to dress for the evening. I would suggest that you return home to do the same."

"Little Bit, please . . ." he began.

"Charles, stop. We will never agree on this," she said sadly, wishing that just one member of her family understood how she felt. "Little brother, I understand that you want to protect me, but this time you cannot. I refuse the protection you provide. I must face this in my own way." She looked at him, just a hint of tears in her eyes.

"Will it distress you if Dunstan remains in Brighton?" he asked, not certain what he would do if she said yes.

The thought of Brighton without Lord Dunstan was somehow more than she could bear. "No," she said quietly. Before he could ask the other questions she saw in his eyes, Elizabeth left.

The next few days were curious ones; she had seen Dunstan every day. But he was the perfect gentleman. Never by word or deed did he remind her of the secret they shared. Sometimes it was almost disconcerting, she told herself. Her memories were vivid even if his were not.

Dunstan's memories were as vivid as her own. However, following Lady Ramsburg's suggestions, he was allowing Elizabeth time to get to know him, to understand how he felt. The task was not an easy one. Following the pattern he had established that first evening, Dunstan took long walks along the beach at night, his eyes on the waves, but his mind on Elizabeth.

As if his presence were not enough, his bouquets arrived regularly, although not just for Elizabeth. Lady Ramsburg and Louisa received their share and it was often his flowers they carried as they went out in the evenings.

More and more people had left London, joining the early comers at the seashore. As more people arrived, entertainments grew more frequent. Soon their evenings included early balls, a card party or two, and some musical evenings. Elizabeth found these evenings more agreeable than the ones she spent at home, except when she had to watch Dunstan dancing with younger ladies. When there were no guests other than Dunstan present, Lady Ramsburg insisted that they practice their card playing, claiming she was sadly out of practice. More and more, Dunstan and Elizabeth were partners. As they sat across the table from each other, he would look at her, his blue eyes never leaving her face. He would ask her questions about her childhood, often encouraging her cousin or stepmother to tell him details she found too embarrassing to relate. Charles, who often chose to play chess with his stepfather, would lean over her shoulder to add his version, often more colorful than anyone else's. At times Elizabeth felt Dunstan knew more about her than she did herself.

Dunstan, not as open about his early years, told them about school and about his grandfather. "He has always reminded me of a hawk," he said once, his eyes unfocused and staring off into the distance. "He knows everything that is going on. No one can keep a secret from him." Elizabeth gave him a sharp look, fearing to ask just what he meant. "If I took a gun out without permission, he would be waiting for me when I returned," Dunstan laughed, rubbing his hip in remembrance. "It is because of a friend of his, Lord Seward, that I am involved in the war effort at all."

"But you said he would not let you buy a commission," Charles reminded him, his face scornful.

"No, but he found me something else to do. Not just make-work but a real job, something that is essential to the effort."

"How is it that you are able to spend so much time here, then?" Elizabeth asked, not certain if she wanted to hear the answer.

"My job can be done almost anywhere. They send the packets to me, and I return them," Dunstan explained.

"You should see the post he receives," Charles said, laughing. He held up his hands to reveal the size of the stack. "And most of it is from matchmaking mamas like mine eager for his company."

"Charles!" his mother said indignantly. Elizabeth frowned at him; the idea of Dunstan's receiving invitations from mothers of marriageable daughters disturbed her. She tried to put it out of her mind but was unsuccessful.

"Do not 'Charles' me, Mama. Did you believe I would not notice the bevy of young ladies and their mothers who now arrive for morning calls and stay to luncheon?" He raised his eyebrows quizzically.

"How could I ignore my friends when they arrived in Brighton?" she asked, her blue eyes dancing. She smiled at Louisa and at Elizabeth as if asking them to agree with her. "And if their daughters happen to be with them . . . ?" Her voice trailed off artistically.

"If you do not want to see my back, Mama, have done," Charles said; for once his face was serious. Lady Ramsburg just laughed, but she took the message to heart. She did not intend to lose the company of her son again. "What I would give to have my closest relative my grandfather!" Charles said theatrically, bending down to give his mother a kiss to soften the blow. "You are lucky, Dunstan."

"I do not find your mother much different from my grandfather," Dunstan said with a smile. "He matchmakes as often."

"I told you that I was not unique, my son," his mother said, putting on her hurt look. She dabbed her eyes with a tiny scrap of lace and then ruined the effect by looking under her lashes to see if they were appreciating her performance. All those at the table at the time burst into laughter.

After that evening, Elizabeth lost her reserve with Dunstan. She laughed with him as she did her officer friends, accepted him as a partner for dances, and walked with him in the garden. Not by word or deed did he reveal his continued interest in her.

Uncertain about his attitude toward her, her interest increased. When he did not escort them to their evening entertainment, Elizabeth unconsciously searched for him, restless and unable to truly enjoy herself. When he walked in, she would smile at her partner and relax.

To her surprise, Elizabeth discovered that her popularity did not wane when the other ladies arrived from town. In fact, her coterie grew. From the first moment that she arrived, her hand was claimed for every dance. In spite of the heady popularity she enjoyed, Elizabeth was prudent. No one received more than his share of dances. But she always found room to include Dunstan's name on her program.

"Go away, Lord Dunstan," Lord Hathaway said one evening. "Miss Beckworth says she has no more dances free. If you disappear, then I will have yours."

Elizabeth giggled, sending waves of pleasure

through Dunstan. "I am desolated to have to refuse you, my lord. But I want those dances myself," Dunstan said. He took her program and looked through it carefully. "But the major has two also. Shall we award you one of his?"

"And have me on duty forever? No, sir, I will bear this cruelty, sweet temptress." He bowed low over Elizabeth's hand, clasping it for a moment longer than he should have. He turned to Dunstan. "You, sir, are an unfeeling brute." His posturings finished, Lord Hathaway asked, "Do you join me tomorrow for luncheon, Lord Dunstan?"

"With pleasure, sir." Having recognized that most of the officers in Elizabeth's entourage were only interested in light flirtations, Dunstan had been able to greet them as friends, escaping to their quarters when he had grown despondent. Elizabeth, feeling rather left out, tapped her foot, reminding him of the dance. He smiled and presented his arm. "Shall we dance?" he asked, his smile telling her how much he admired her. She was dressed in sea green that evening, the color of her dress reflected in her eyes. The dress had a split skirt, revealing the elaborate lacework on her undergarment, and the lacework was repeated at the neckline of the low bodice. As he led her onto the floor, Dunstan could not tear his eyes from hers, following her even when the pattern separated them. When her next partner claimed her, Elizabeth could still feel Dunstan's eyes on her, following her through the dance.

He returned to her side later that evening for the supper dance. As soon as the music had ended, he led her to the edge of the dance floor, watching her as she fanned herself with the ivory fan she carried. The evening was unusually warm. And because someone had started the rumor that the Prince of Wales had arrived in Brighton that evening and might honor the ball with his presence, the doors and windows to the room were carefully closed because everyone knew his fear of the night air. Elizabeth glanced longingly at the doors onto the terrace. Dunstan, realizing her thoughts, glanced back at the other guests waiting to enter the supper room.

"Your mother has promised to keep us a place at her table," Dunstan said softly. "Shall we walk on the terrace until the first crush is finished?"

Elizabeth looked at the crowd of people waiting to enter the next room and back at the doors longingly. "Someone will see us," she whispered.

"Not if we slip through these doors." He opened the terrace door just a crack, letting a hint of breeze touch her. "I am certain there are others outside as well. And we will not be gone long."

Elizabeth glanced around the room, but everyone else was laughing and chattering, waiting to enter the supper room. Once more a faint breeze ruffled her skirt. She slipped through the door, and Dunstan followed. He slipped her hand through his arm and put his own over it protectively. As it usually did, the slightest touch of his hand made her heart beat faster. They walked to the end of the terrace in silence, enjoying the cloudless night with its myriad stars. The breeze, slightly stronger now, molded her dress about her, reminding Dunstan of the glimpse of her he had had when he awoke that morning months earlier.

When she turned and would have begun to walk back to the doors, he stopped, his hands still over hers. She stopped, too, turning back to him in surprise. "Dunstan?" His lips found hers and his arms pulled her tightly against him. Two kisses. That was all. Then he released her and slipped her hand back through his arm as though nothing had happened. He walked her back to the supper room and filled a plate for her. The happy smile in his eyes was the only sign Dunstan gave of what had happened.

Elizabeth spent the supper hour picking at her food, her eyes rarely leaving his face. Her heart beat faster as she watched him watch her. "I do not know what Lord Dunstan is doing," Louisa Beckworth told Lady Ramsburg later, "but Elizabeth is enthralled."

"But will her enchantment lead to marriage?" Lady Ramsburg wanted to know. They glanced at Dunstan, now standing talking to Lord Hathaway and Charles, and then at Elizabeth, dancing with the major. When they looked back at Dunstan, his eyes were fixed on Elizabeth. Louisa Beckworth and Lady Ramsburg exchanged glances and sighed happily.

Before long, everyone in Brighton was wondering the same thing. The gentlemen placed their bets, noting that Lord Dunstan never had to worry about a place on Miss Beckworth's card. As invitations were sent, each hostess realized that if she wanted one of them to be present, the entire party must be included or no one would come. For the first time in her life totally oblivious to the interest of the *ton*, Elizabeth enjoyed herself. Unlike her Seasons when her stepmother and father had expected her to select a husband, she lived for the moment, taking each compliment in stride, discounting the praises of her admirers. They as well as she knew that she was not interested in anything but a light flirtation. Therefore, she was safe, or as safe as any bachelor could imagine. Only with Dunstan was she different.

One reason for the difference was Dunstan himself. After that evening on the terrace, Elizabeth had expected him to change, but he had not. The next morning he was punctual as he called to take her riding. "Good morning, Elizabeth," he said quietly. Although she was never certain when she had granted him the right, he had begun to call her by her first name. But she did not correct him.

"Good morning, Lord Dunstan." Her eyelashes fluttered down over her eyes, this morning a clear green because of the jade green riding habit she wore. She settled her black beaver top hat more firmly on her curls and smiled up at him. He tossed her into the saddle and checked her stirrup. Satisfied that she was secure, he mounted his own horse. Cantering until they reached the long stretch of beach, neither said much. As soon as they reached the open sand, Elizabeth leaned forward, patting her horse's neck. "A gallop, my lord?" she asked, her eyes sparkling.

"A gallop. And the winner may choose the prize," he said, his eyes on her mouth. She smiled, bending low on her horse's neck. They raced neck and neck until slowly Dunstan's large stallion began to outpace Elizabeth's mare. Recognizing defeat, Elizabeth pulled up, walking her horse slowly to allow her to cool down.

Soon Dunstan was beside her. "What prize will you claim, my lord?" she asked, just a hint of wonder and fear in her voice.

Before he could answer her, a loud hello echoed down the beach. "Mama said you had gone out for a ride, Elizabeth," her brother said with a smile. "I was certain you would not mind if we rode with you." He gestured to the three officers who had accompanied him.

Elizabeth and Dunstan exchanged one glance,

and then he said in a voice that did not reveal his disappointment, "We are happy to have you join us, gentlemen." Aware of a discontent she could not name, Elizabeth added her welcome to his. Together the party rode back up the beach to Brighton.

Later that evening as they enjoyed a quiet evening at home, Elizabeth and Dunstan watched as Lord and Lady Ramsburg played cards against Charles and Louisa. Then Dunstan asked, "Would you like to walk about the garden?"

Elizabeth glanced outside to the lingering twilight and nodded. For a few minutes they walked along the paths between the flowering plants, simply enjoying the night air. "I enjoyed our gallop today," Dunstan said as though he had just thought of it.

'When I am in town, I miss my rides. I wonder why the *ton* frowns on ladies galloping?" Elizabeth stopped to pull a wilting rose from its stem, scattering the petals of the pink rose along the path.

"Not all ladies are as accomplished riders as you," Dunstan said quietly. He too stopped and watched her inspect the roses carefully as though she were looking for something of importance. The late twilight was just fading, and the moon had not yet come up. The air was heavy with the sweet smell of flowers. The lengthening shadows hid her face and made alluring hollows on her neck.

She looked up, her eyes laughing. "Accomplished? As I remember, sir, you are the accomplished rider. You won."

"So I did." Dunstan allowed just a hint of surprise to echo through his voice. Then his voice grew deeper. "I do not think I collected my prize."

She looked up in surprise. He took a step closer,

his blue eyes laughing down at her. He paused for a moment as if giving her a chance to run away. She stood her ground. He took a step closer. Soon he was close enough to put his arms around her. Once again he waited for her to protest. When she did not, he pulled her close to him, letting her hear the racing of his heart. She pulled back slightly and tilted her head back so that she could see him. The temptation was more than he could bear. Slowly he lowered his head, his lips slightly parted. Then he kissed her, softly at first and then deeply, his tongue caressing her lips, urging them to open for him. His arms held her tightly against him; the thin layers of material between them did little to dull the fever in their blood. He pulled away, noting with satisfaction the way her body followed his as if protesting his departure.

Finally they stood alone once again. As he had before, he tucked her hand back into his arm and walked back into the house. If the others noticed the slightly dazed look on her face or the crumpled cravat he wore, they did not mention it.

Each time Dunstan took her into the garden or walked with her along a terrace, kissed her and then let her go, Elizabeth yearned for more of his kisses. Her dreams were vignettes of that morning so many days ago. But this time she did not kick him out of bed. She would awake, her body aching for the caresses that she had dreamed of. She would dress for the evening, longing for the moment when he would take her arm and lead her from the room to the darkness outside.

Dunstan too lived for those moments, ached for her in a way he had never felt before. Often he walked alone for hours trying to free himself of her spell. Then he recognized what he had to do. When the agony of letting her go grew too strong,

Dunstan stopped kissing her, walking with her in the garden late in the evening. More and more he turned his attention to the other ladies. Ashamed of herself and yet angry, Elizabeth began to feel uneasy, restless.

"Are you angry with me?" she finally asked one evening while they were dancing.

"No." He looked down at her, wishing he understood what she was thinking. He longed to run his fingers through the curls clustering about her face.

"Oh." The silence between them grew. As the music finished, she let him walk her back to where her cousin was seated. Louisa, her face flushed with anger, wielded her fan in short, jerky strokes. Catching sight of her cousin's face, Elizabeth hurried to her side, "What is wrong?" she said anxiously.

Louisa glanced around as if expecting other than the pair of them to be close at hand. "My dear, the most horrible thing has happened," she said in accents of doom.

"Is Mama ill? Is Charles hurt?" Elizabeth sat down beside her, patting her hand. "Do tell me."

Louisa glanced up to see Charles approaching, his face as dark as a thundercloud. "You tell her," she demanded, dabbing at her face with her scrap of lace handkerchief.

"Tell me what?" Elizabeth asked so forcefully that a lady nearby looked up startled. Elizabeth blushed, but she asked again, "Tell me what?"

"Edgerton has returned," Charles said, his mouth a straight line. "He asked our hostess to point you out in case you had changed."

"Who?" Elizabeth asked, more to give herself time than because she had not heard the first time. Dunstan's face now wore a frown that was darker than Charles's.

"Your former fiancé. Apparently someone wrote him that you were pining away for love of him. He has decided to offer for you once again," Charles said, his voice flat with anger. Elizabeth could only stare at her brother, her eyes wide.

"Here he comes," Dunstan said. His voice like his face was cold and hard. He straightened up, looking about the room for Lady Ramsburg. He did not find the lady, but he did catch the eye of Lord Hathaway, who cut his conversation short and walked across the room, moving more rapidly than he appeared to be.

"Elizabeth, my dear. How lovely you look," Lord Edgerton said, picking up her hand and kissing the palm. Elizabeth resisted the impulse to wipe it off. She said nothing. "Still having trouble with names, Elizabeth?" he asked, smiling down at her. He made his bow to Louisa, who ignored him. "I was certain you would remember mine. We shared so much together."

Charles could bear no more. "Edgerton," he said coolly. "What a surprise to see you in England once more. How did you manage it? Your family buy the other man's family off?"

The barb was so close to the truth that Edgerton flushed. He swung around quickly, half expecting to see the young boy that Charles had been when he left. At the sight of those hard, cold eyes and those shoulders, he straightened up, his eyes flashing angrily. He glared at both Charles and Dunstan and then turned back to Elizabeth.

With Edgerton's attention focused on Dunstan, he had not seen Lord Hathaway arrive. He swung back only to watch Elizabeth walk to the center of the ballroom on the captain's arm. "Who is he?"

he asked, his eyes angry. He watched as Elizabeth laughed at something the tall redhead had said. His mouth narrowed to a fine line.

Louisa smiled. "Just one of Elizabeth's suitors," she explained. "Isn't it wonderful that she is finally recovering from the shock of your father's death, dear boy?" she asked Charles. He nodded, his eyes still fixed on Edgerton's face. "And we owe it all to Lord Dunstan." She smiled up at Dunstan and patted his arm affectionately.

"Dunstan. I knew a Lord Dunstan seven years ago. What happened to him?" Edgerton asked, a bite to his voice. The years of hard living showed in every line of his face.

"He is dead," Dunstan said bluntly. He and Charles exchanged glances. Together they searched the floor for Elizabeth's next partner, determined that Edgerton would have no chance with her that night.

"You do not much resemble him," Edgerton said spitefully.

"Thank you, my lord."

"I did not mean it for a compliment." Edgerton strolled off, his eyes on his former fiancée.

"What are we going to do?" Dunstan asked Louisa, his face still wearing a frown. His eyes followed Edgerton around the floor.

"Nothing," she said, watching her cousin circle the floor. "Elizabeth must take care of the situation herself."

The dance finished, the captain led Elizabeth from the floor. Edgerton was waiting. "Shall we dance, Elizabeth?" he asked, holding out his arms. "Remember how well we danced together?"

"This dance is already promised, my lord. Perhaps you should ask someone of a lower class. I am certain she would not refuse you," Elizabeth said proudly as she took her escort's arm. "I only dance with gentlemen." She smiled up at the major, and they walked toward the dance floor.

Edgerton flushed. His eyes flashed. "She will pay for that," he muttered to himself, not willing to give up the thought of her very large dowry.

"Did you say something, my lord?" Lord Hathaway asked, his arms folded across his chest. He looked at the other man, noting the slight paunch and fleshy jowls.

"No." Edgerton looked around the floor, hoping no one else had seen his humiliation. They were the center of all eyes. Chalking up yet another grievance against Elizabeth, he made his way to the card room, where he had promised to meet a friend.

"Did Miss Beckworth greet you with open arms?" his friend asked.

"No, but she will," Edgerton said, his teeth clenched in anger. Time after time during the next few days, he approached Elizabeth. Time after time she turned him away. Charles especially stayed close to her side, ready to protect her if she should need it.

But he was not present when Edgerton faced her once again. "As cold as ever," Edgerton taunted finally. "I wonder if your friends will believe your actions or my words when I begin to tell my tales."

"What do you mean?" Elizabeth asked, her blood running cold with fear. The white gown she wore was no whiter than her face.

"How sad it is to me to find such a passionate young girl repressed into such a sour old maid. When I remember how sweetly you responded to me, how sad I am that you ignore me now, how will you be received then?" he asked, expecting her to collapse in fear.

"Shall we see, my lord?" Elizabeth smiled at him, a cold, hard smile of a lady who was not willing to be coerced. She glanced over to the chair where her stepmother sat, her eyes on Elizabeth though she carried on a conversation with someone else and then to where her brother stood, gathering strength from each of them.

He drew back in anger. "Watch how your escorts disappear," he said menacingly. "You are mine. You will always be mine!" Elizabeth watched as he walked across the room to where Lord Hathaway and the major stood. She took a deep breath and waited for the repercussions.

17

With effort Elizabeth presented a calm appearance to the world. Her callers and bouquets arrived every morning as they had been. She went riding or walked along the Steine. Even the presence of Lord Edgerton, who did everything he could to attract her attention, did not seem to ruffle her composure.

To her family's delight, her behavior became the standard by which proper ladies were judged. Several young ladies whose behavior had been less than perfect last Season had to listen to their mamas extolling Elizabeth's aged virtues. The addition of Edgerton to the ranks of her admirers angered her and caused a few of the older ladies who had hoped to ensure comfortable marriages for their daughters to watch her with narrowed eyes. The presence of the officers they could ignore. Most of them were without private incomes and would expect their wives to follow the drum. But to watch while three of the most eligible men in Brighton made Elizabeth, a lady long on the shelf, the center of their attention was too much. If she had had the decency to encourage her brother to notice other ladies, they could have forgiven her. Edgerton, after all, was not what they would have chosen for their daughters. But she did not. Within a small circle, discontent grew. But even they agreed that Elizabeth's treatment of Edgerton had been completely correct.

Elizabeth did not realize the problems that were fomenting around her. Avoiding Lord Edgerton, enjoying a harmless flirtation with the officers, and watching Dunstan whenever she thought she was unobserved took all of her time. As more and more people arrived, her social schedule increased.

One afternoon at tea, however, Lord Ramsburg appeared, his face beaming. "It has come," he announced.

"What?" Lady Ramsburg asked, her face glowing with happiness as it usually did when he appeared. She reached up to smooth back the gray hair at his temples.

"The invitation to view the royal stables. But we must go before the prince arrives next week. The prince's factotum suggests that we may wish to have a picnic on the grounds." He sat back and took a cup of tea.

"A picnic? Nonsense, my dear. Far too common. Now, a breakfast. Yes. Louisa, a moment of your time," Lady Ramsburg said, the look on her face causing some concern to her children.

"The stables?" Elizabeth asked. "But Amelia and John are arriving in a day or two," she began. Then she looked at her brother's face. He was smiling broadly. "Oh, well, perhaps they could join us. Is there a limit to the size of the party, George?" she asked.

"None at all. And with the weather so pleasant now, the grounds will be lovely."

"And what a wonderful opportunity to return the hospitality of some of our friends," Lady Ramsburg said. Although they had held dinner parties since their arrival, their house did not possess a ballroom, a definite lack as far as the lady was concerned.

"Nothing too large, my dear. We would not want to frighten the horses," her husband said with a laugh.

When the morning for the expedition arrived, the weather was clear, the sky was a beautiful blue, and in spite of their casual attitudes, most people were excited about the expedition. While they toured the great domed structure with its stalls, still only partially filled, the servants were outside on the grounds preparing the meal.

"Take out the stalls and this would be a wonderful ballroom," Elizabeth said as she craned her neck to look up at the dome.

"Never. Only think of having to decorate it," her friend Amelia said as she reached out a hand to stop her eldest son from dashing into a stall. "It is interesting, though. So different."

"Come. We have seen the place. Let us leave it to the men," Elizabeth said, laughing. Her stepmother and cousin had already finished their cursory inspection and had returned outside. "This young man needs fresh air and running room. Don't you, John?" She picked him up and laughed as he tried to squirm free.

Outside, the blankets had been spread. "They will be inside for hours still," Amelia said as she sank to the waiting blanket. "Let John go to Nurse, and you and I can have a quiet talk. Your letters have been less informative than usual lately."

Elizabeth took her place beside her friend and was silent for a moment, watching Louisa and Lady Ramsburg stroll across the carefully groomed lawn. Then she sighed. "I wrote you about Jack." She paused for a moment.

"You don't feel anything for him, do you?" Amelia asked, horror in her voice.

"No, of course not. But everything has changed since he arrived. At first Brighton was simply wonderful," she said, tossing her hands over her head and lying back, laughing. "I never had this much fun during our Season."

"You are not supposed to, my sweet. You are supposed to be seriously looking for a husband," Amelia reminded her. "That is difficult, as I'm sure you remember."

Elizabeth sat up suddenly. "Amelia, that is what is wrong with our way of life." Her face was serious.

"What do you mean?"

"As girls we are plunged into society before we know who we are. Or at least most of us are. You knew exactly what you wanted the moment you saw John. But I wasn't ready."

"That is a very broad statement, Elizabeth. For years the social system has proceeded along very definite lines. If there were errors, don't you believe they would have been found?"

"But there are. Look at how many young girls make disastrous marriages. How many of your friends are as happily married as you and John?"

This time Amelia lay back, her eyes closed. Elizabeth waited. Her friend opened her eyes, glanced to see where the nurse and her son were, and said quietly, "A few. Not many. But would the marriages be better if the girls had waited until they were older? Most older ladies never find husbands."

"But if everyone waited?"

"What would we do in the meantime? Living with my mother made me unhappy at times. If I had had to stay home longer with nothing to do?"

"In the country most of us have occupations.

Didn't your mother insist that you oversee the washing or jam making?"

"Elizabeth, even the dirtiest households will not keep a young girl busy constantly. And jam making is a seasonable occupation. Besides, my friend, all of these occupations are merely ways of preparing young ladies to be the mistress of their own households."

Her friend opened her mouth to continue the argument. Then she too lay back down on the blanket. "If Miller were to see me now," she said, a laugh in her voice.

"My maid would be in hysterics. She spent hours choosing the right dress for the occasion. You would have thought I was meeting the king instead of viewing the prince's horses."

"I know what you mean. Miller produced this dress as the only suitable choice. I feel totally out of place."

Amelia sat up again. "You look lovely. And if you are out of place, so are the rest of us." She settled her dress about her, the lovely soft blue reflecting the blue of the sky. "What modiste made your dress?"

The next few minutes were spent discussing clothes, the gown Elizabeth was wearing in particular. "And where did she find the material?" Amelia picked up a fold to run the sheer cream-colored muslin, so fine it felt like silk, through her hands.

"She did not say. I suppose it was smuggled. But I feel certain my spencer is made of the finest English wool," Elizabeth said, laughing, not in the least dismayed.

"And good French embroidery by the look of these tiny stitches. Convent bred at least." Amelia was inspecting the design sewn onto Elizabeth's sleeve. "She is just the one I want to make me a special dress."

"For the prince's ball?"

"No, for something much more private," her friend said with a wicked laugh. Her light blue eyes sparkled with mischief.

"Amelia, what are you plotting now?"

"Never, my dear. You are too innocent to hear," Amelia said, her eyes sparkling even more as she watched her husband look around for her. "John, we are over here," she called.

Elizabeth stood up hastily, letting her skirts cover the silk stockings that matched her gown. Her cheeks, already pink from the sun, glowed with color. Dunstan, who had followed Lord Ravenwood, smiled as he saw her. He walked quickly to where she stood.

He had just taken her hand in his when Louisa Beckworth appeared. "The servants have everything ready. Come, fill your plates," she said, smiling at them.

"May I be your escort, Elizabeth?" Dunstan asked as he watched her friends lead the way.

"With pleasure, Lord Dunstan." "Robert," she whispered in her mind, but she was too shy to say it aloud. He filled her plate for her with fruit, a slice of ham, and fresh tiny peas with mint. Seeing her comfortably seated, he returned with his own, filled almost to overflowing.

"Are you hungry, my lord?" she asked, curious that he could eat so much without gaining an ounce.

"Starved." His deep blue eyes gazed into hers, making it clear he was not talking about food, willing her to answer him. She blushed and turned her attention to her plate once more. "Long walks along the beach at night give me an appetite."

"Do you go alone? Isn't it dangerous?"

"No. I have yet to see anyone. But I admit I stay close to the town."

"Why have you taken up walking, my lord?"

"Because I cannot sleep." He let his long eyelashes drift over his eyes for a moment, took a bite, and chewed for a while. Then he said quietly, "A beautiful lady haunts me." He smiled.

Quickly her eyes returned to her almost empty plate. She did not remember eating anything. "Is there only one? I have watched you dance with several," she said huskily. Then embarrassed by her behavior, she lowered her eyes. Later she glanced up shyly, using her eyelashes to hide behind. "Are you angry with her?" she finally asked, her voice trembling slightly. She waited in anticipation as he finished his food. He took their plates and handed them to a servant. Then he sat down beside her again. Across the lawn, several similar scenes were taking place. Gentlemen and ladies sat together, laughing and talking. Amelia whispered something to John, and he kissed her cheek.

Elizabeth longed to smooth the slight wrinkle from the dark blue sleeve in front of her. But she hesitated. The silence grew. Then Dunstan cleared his throat. "I am not angry with the lady," he said finally. "But I am impatient." She looked up at him in wonder. "Soon I will have to return to my usual life even if she has not given me an answer." He paused for a moment, hoping that she would say something. When she did not, he continued. "My grandfather and my superior both demand to see me."

"When do you leave?" she asked, a little of her joy in the day dimmed.

"Not today or even tomorrow. I hope to persuade my lady to accept my suit before I go." It was the closest he had come to asking her to marry him in weeks.

Elizabeth sat there, her eyes staring into his dark blue ones. She opened her mouth. "Elizabeth, Mama said to tell you it is time to leave," Charles said as he walked up, totally oblivious to the scene he had just interrupted.

Dunstan stood up reluctantly and offered Elizabeth his hand. He pulled her up, letting her rest against him for a moment before releasing her. "Will you think about it, please?" he whispered in her ear, letting his lips touch it caressingly. She shivered slightly and nodded. Beside the carriages where they waited, the two older women smiled. Amelia, glancing around to make certain they had all of her son's toys, let her eyes linger on the pair speculatively for a moment.

At the ball that evening Dunstan dreamed. He had made his plans. He had the supper dance. After completing the dances that his good manners required, he stood quietly, his eyes following Elizabeth. As he waited impatiently for his first dance with her, he reviewed his decision. He was certain she had been ready to give him the answer he wanted that morning.

Midway through the evening Elizabeth had chosen to sit out a dance, wilting into a chair while her escort fetched her a glass of punch. Her hostess, like the prince, feared the night air; therefore the ballroom was overheated. Elizabeth watched Dunstan move through the graceful dance, his figure elegant and supple. Totally absorbed, she did not at once glance up when someone sat beside her.

"Miss Beckworth," a man said. He watched her start.

"Mr. Hartley. When did you arrive?" She looked

about the room for her brother, but he was dancing. Elizabeth straightened her shoulders, wondering why a man whom she had asked to leave
her home should be paying attention to her. He
made her nervous.

"Earlier today. Do me the honor of the next
dance, Miss Beckworth." Hartley's request was more
a command.

"My next dance is taken, sir."

He let a small frown crease his brow. "Then the
next," Hartley demanded.

"My card is full, sir. Perhaps the next time."
Elizabeth smiled, but it obviously was a dismissal.

"Full and sitting out a dance," he muttered as
he left her. He walked across to the punch bowl
and turned to face her again, displeasure in every
line of his face. His eyes widened as he watched a
young officer hand her a cup and take a seat next
to her. They widened even more when they saw
who her next partner was. "Lord Dunstan."

The lady standing near him turned and smiled
at him. "Such a handsome man. And so in love,"
she said as if in reply. "We look anxiously for an
announcement every day. They make a lovely couple. Don't you agree?" Hartley nodded, his eyes
searching the room. Finally he found the person
he was seeking and made his escape.

"Charles. We have been missing you in London," he said as he pounded his friend on the
back.

"Hartley. I wondered when you would arrive."

"We were taking bets on whether you had convinced your mother to buy you your colors and
had gone to the Peninsula without a word to anyone," Hartley said, watching to see the younger
man's reaction. Charles stiffened. "London has
been devilishly dull without your wit."

As usual when he began thinking about the army, Charles's face darkened. "She still will not hear of it. The Tenth is here in Brighton, though. Some of Elizabeth's coterie have taken me under their wings, shown me around." Charles looked around the floor, finding his sister in Dunstan's arms. "As soon as she accepts him, I will be on my way," he promised.

"Accepts him? What do you mean?" Hartley asked, his face carefully composed. He had known that Elizabeth was in Brighton, supposedly untouched by scandal. But he had not expected to find Dunstan there. Or so accepted by the family.

"He offered months ago. But she refuses to give him his answer. He has my mother's and my blessing already. All he needs is hers." Charles smiled broadly. "Even Edgerton has given up all hope."

"Edgerton?"

"Her former fiancé. Returned to England this spring and expected Elizabeth to be willing to marry him again," Charles said. His voice was filled with indignation.

"And where is this fiancé now?" Hartley asked, his voice cool and calm, although his heart was beating as if he had run a race.

"Former fiancé. He is still here, and everyone is talking about him. His top loft is empty if he thinks Elizabeth will have him. Just making a spectacle of himself and embarrassing her."

"I must congratulate you on your expert maneuvers, Charles," Hartley said as warmly as he could. "I never believed you would succeed." Without me, he added to himself.

"Will you be in Brighton long, Sebastian?" Charles asked, his eyes searching the floor for the lady who had promised him a dance.

"As long as it is amusing," Hartley said, a wicked smile playing about his lips.

As the music stopped, Charles gave him their direction and then hurried away. Hartley stayed where he was for a moment, watching as Dunstan escorted Elizabeth to another man, a tall redhead. He turned to go into the card room, but out of the corner of his eye he noticed someone else staring at her, anger in her eyes. Casually, as though he were searching for someone, he walked across the room to her side. Taking the seat next to her, he once again searched the floor, finding Elizabeth dancing. He sighed heavily.

"Is there something wrong, sir?" the older lady asked, eager to be the first with the latest gossip.

"I had hoped to dance with Miss Beckworth."

"The lady's card is filled long before the dance begins," the lady said scornfully. "And at her age too. I do not understand what Lord Dunstan and the others see in her. There are far more lovely and younger ladies about."

"She is popular?" Hartley's voice revealed his feigned astonishment.

"Her card is always full," his informant said bitterly.

"I am surprised. And after such a terrible scandal too. I had not expected to see her in company."

"Everyone knows Lord Edgerton was to blame. Any man who would fight a duel over an opera dancer and then run away with her is beyond the pale, no matter how many years have passed."

"Edgerton, just so. I do not suppose . . ." He sighed again.

Interested, she turned toward him, her face alive. "It was Edgerton you were referring to, wasn't it?"

"No." Once more Hartley sighed. He looked around the room until he found Dunstan standing at the edge of the dance floor, his eyes on Elizabeth. Just for a moment he let his hatred of the man show on his face. Then he pushed it firmly away.

"Lord Dunstan?" she asked, her eyes growing wide. Hartley sighed again but did not deny it. "And Miss Beckworth?" He nodded. "What kind of scandal?" she asked in delight.

Jumping quickly to his feet, Hartley said quietly, "Nothing. Nothing at all." And he walked quickly to the card room, determined to seek out Elizabeth's former fiancé. Finding him, Hartley drew him over to a secluded table. A few minutes later Edgerton jumped up, his face malicious in his enjoyment of the news Hartley had just given him. "I will do my part," he promised. Hartley watched for a moment as Edgerton walked back to the ballroom; then he found an interesting game to join.

Had he seen the ripples of his action spread around the ballroom that evening, Hartley would have laughed. By the end of the evening both Elizabeth's and Dunstan's names were on everyone's lips. Even before the supper dance, Elizabeth noticed the stares. When the second of her partners, a young man who had just recently joined the *ton*, made his excuses and asked to be released, she found Louisa. "I want to leave early tonight. Will you come with me?" she asked, not certain why she felt the need to retreat.

"What is wrong?" her cousin asked on the way home. But Elizabeth could not explain.

At the ball, Dunstan, disappointed once more, drifted over to the chairs where the chaperons sat and few of the less fortunate girls. Asking one of the young ladies to dance, he was surprised when she refused. When the second also declined, he grew thoughtful. Making his excuses, he walked back to his lodgings.

Lord and Lady Ramsburg and Charles stayed until the band stopped playing, but not because they were enjoying themselves. They had heard the rumors very early. In fact, several disgruntled mothers had taken care to drop a few words where they could hear. Their faces calm, they had made the rounds, noting the silence when it fell, tracing the rumor to one of its carriers.

The lady, her face flushed with anger, said belligerently, "I suppose Miss Beckworth was ill, since she had to leave the ball early. Her early departure had nothing to do with guilt."

"Nothing," Lady Ramsburg said, hoping that it was true. "Our barrister will be in touch with you," she said menacingly.

"For what?"

"To charge you with slander. We will see how you enjoy being held up to ridicule."

"No, you cannot. My daughter would be ruined."

"You are spreading rumors that could ruin my daughter's life."

"Not me. A gentleman told me."

"A gentleman? Which one?" Lord Ramsburg said, his voice sharp and forceful.

"I did not see him clearly," the lady admitted.

"But you saw my daughter and Lord Dunstan across the room?" Lady Ramsburg asked, her voice cold.

"I was not wearing my glasses," the lady admitted. She pulled them from her reticule and put them on. "If things are distant from me, I can see perfectly. But I can't see people clearly when they are too close. And he was sitting beside me."

"Give it up, my dear. I believe her," Lord Ramsburg said, putting an arm around his wife's waist. She let her head rest on his waistcoat for a moment.

Then she turned to the other lady and said, her eyes as stormy as her voice, "You, my lady, should be careful of repeating what you hear. You have done more harm than you could ever dream of." She turned around. "Take me home, George."

Charles had traced the rumors to another source —Edgerton. Accompanied by Lord Hathaway, Eliabeth's brother tracked his man to the terrace, where Edgerton was blowing a cloud. His face dark with anger, Charles stalked up to the older man, his gloves in his hand. Striking Edgerton across the face, he demanded, "Name your seconds!"

"What?" Edgerton tried to bluster his way out of the situation. Having been through a duel before, he had no desire for another. Besides, Beckworth was known as an excellent shot and a good swordsman.

"Name your seconds. Lord Hathaway will act for me."

"Must be in his cups," Edgerton told Lord Hathaway as the older man moved closer to the stairs leading into the garden. "You know I cannot accept his challenge."

"Too cowardly, are you? Or was that a provision in your return to England?" Charles moved forward, his fist drawn back to strike.

"Apologize, Edgerton, or take a stand like a gentleman," Hathaway said. "Admit you are lying."

Edgerton looked around the terrace as if hoping to find someone to rescue him. No one appeared. Remembering his years of exile, he stammered a few words and then took a few deep breaths to clear his wine-soaked head. Charles took a step closer. Edgerton stumbled backward and fell down the low steps, landing on his back. The other two men stood above him menacingly.

"Will you meet me?" Charles asked, disgust in his voice.

"Why are you blaming me? I was simply repeating what I had been told," Edgerton said, remembering the threats Hartley had made. Charles was large, but Hartley was more frightening.

"Who told you?"

"Some lady." Edgerton slithered along the ground, putting distance between him and Charles. "I'll tell everyone that she lied. All I wanted was Elizabeth. I thought she would have to accept my offer if everyone started talking. I'll tell them I lied."

Charles and Hathaway looked at the man groveling before them. Their faces hardened. "Do that!" Charles said. They turned on their heels and left, not wanting to be tainted by Edgerton's cowardly behavior a moment longer.

By morning Edgerton had left Brighton. Rumors flew widely, the most popular being that he had been called to the bedside of a dying relative in Scotland.

In spite of Edgerton's promise that the lady would retract their words, the damage was done. Both Elizabeth and Dunstan found their acquaintances deserting them. Invitations and callers began to disappear as everyone waited to see what would happen. When Dunstan heard about Edgerton, he sought out Charles angrily, demanding an explanation why the man had been allowed to escape unscathed. Charles simply ignored him. When he tried to see Elizabeth, she refused.

Her original determination to face the scandal forgotten, she locked herself in her room, refusing to face anyone except Miller. After the first wild despair was over, she sat up, determined.

Then she began to pack. "We are going home, Miller," she said firmly when her maid answered her bell. "Tell the footmen to bring down the trunks."

"They are serving the family supper now. Will the morning do?" her maid asked. Her face did not reveal her disturbance.

"No. As soon as the table is cleared and they have had their own meal, tell them to bring them down. We can begin to pack tonight."

"Shall I tell Mrs. Beckworth your plans?"

"No. I will." Elizabeth took a turn or two around the room. Then she asked, "Who is present for dinner tonight?"

"Lord and Lady Ramsburg and Mrs. Beckworth. And the two young men."

"My brother and Lord Dunstan?" Elizabeth asked, willing the answer to be different than she knew it would be.

"Yes, Miss Beckworth." The maid waited patiently, watching her mistress wear a path in the rug.

"As soon as they are finished, ask my cousin to come up to me." She paused and smiled at her maid. "Thank you for being so patient with me the last few days."

"It was nothing." The maid blushed and quickly made her escape.

The message she delivered to the family was not one they wanted to hear. "Tell her to come down immediately!" Charles demanded.

"Nonsense. Thank you, Miller. You may go," Lady Ramsburg said soothingly.

"I will not let her run away again. Doesn't she know that she is running right back into the same situation?" Dunstan asked. His face was drawn with worry.

"If she retreats to the manor this time, she may never leave again," Louisa said somberly. They all looked at her, worry evident on all their faces. "Last time she was willing to talk to Amelia. You remember what happened yesterday?" They nodded. "If she will not see her best friend or any of us, what will happen when she returns home? You remember what she was like before. Not you, Dunstan, but the rest of us. She crept back into her shell, and it took years before she had the courage to crawl back out again. I am not even certain how she managed this time. If it happens again . . ."

"I won't let it happen. Doesn't she realize that this time the rumors affect me as well as her? She has to listen to me. I received two letters today: one from my superior and one from my grandfather. My superior suggested that I take a leave of absence until this unpleasantness is forgotten. He will be in Brighton soon and will discuss the situation with me. My grandfather demands my presence at home. And if I go home without Elizabeth, he will have me married to Cecile before I can say no!"

"Calm down. Everyone stay calm." Lord Ramsburg stood up, his pleasant face serious. "We will simply have to get her to talk to us." Everyone nodded. Remembering the last few days and the countless pleas, they wondered how they would ever convince her. "She expects you to go up shortly, Louisa. Can you persuade her to listen to you?"

"Louisa? George, Elizabeth can twist Louisa around her finger without even trying," Charles said, giving his words less of a sting by giving his cousin a hug and a kiss. "Louisa is simply too sweet."

"My dear?" Lord Ramsburg looked at his wife.

Before she could answer, Dunstan stood up, his pale face determined. "Let me."

"In her bedroom. Never!" Louisa said firmly. "We would never keep it from the servants. Then think what a scandal there would be."

Dunstan exchanged glances with Lord and Lady Ramsburg. "It may be the only way," he explained. "We have to do something soon. Lord Edgerton arrived in town this morning. According to the officers of the Tenth, he is delighted by the situation. And some of his remarks go well beyond anything that has been said before." The others, except Charles, who had already heard what was being said and had had to be forcibly restrained, gasped. "Before long, the only course open may be a duel. And none of us want that." The others nodded.

"But it seems so underhanded," Charles complained. "Once she has been alone with you this evening, she can't refuse you."

"She has before. If I can persuade her, is there a clergyman nearby who will perform the service? I still have that license we bought in London, Charles." After a quick consultation Lady Ramsburg nodded. "What are our plans if she refuses again?"

"I have a plantation in the West Indies. We could send her there. I will send someone to Bristol to ask about ships." Lord Ramsburg turned back to Louisa, regret in his eyes. "I know that this is not what you like, but will you go with her if it comes to this?"

"Of course," she said sturdily, trying to hide her despair. "If Elizabeth needs me, I will accompany her to the North Pole if necessary."

"I am afraid the climate is not quite that cool in the West Indies," Lord Ramsburg said gently. "Thank you."

"I can try to persuade her," Charles said, still uncertain of their plan.

"Like you did me?" Dunstan asked, rubbing his jaw. Now that there was something he could do, his spirits were rebounding.

"No. But she might listen to me." No matter how hard he tried to persuade them, everyone else agreed with Dunstan.

"Good luck, dear boy," Louisa said as he stood up. Lady Ramsburg clasped Dunstan's hand for a moment while Lord Ramsburg pounded him on the back. Unspoken between the four oldest people in the room was the knowledge that Dunstan was to use any means he could to persuade Elizabeth. Dunstan took a deep breath, straightened his shoulders, and faced the door. Before his resolve was gone or his nerve disappeared, he walked quickly up the stairs.

18

When Miller opened the door a short time later, her eyes widened. Dunstan held the door open wider and motioned her to leave. For a moment he thought she might refuse. With a quick look over her shoulder, the maid started through the door. Her eyes seemed to promise retribution if he harmed her mistress.

"Louisa, would you mind if we left for the manor tomorrow?" Elizabeth asked, her back to the door as she sorted letters and invitations at her desk. "Louisa?" She put down the bunch she had in her hand and turned. "Dunstan!" She took a step or two backward and pulled her wrapper closer around her. Feeling the desk behind her, she turned her back, trembling slightly.

He crossed the room slowly, feeling like an intruder. One trunk, its lid open, blocked his passage. Quickly he moved it out of his way, watching as Elizabeth reacted to the sound. Still she kept her back to him. When at last he was behind her, he stood only inches away, letting her feel his presence. Nowhere did he touch her. "Elizabeth, you cannot run from this forever. We must talk."

"Talk? I let you talk me into seeing you again, and look at what happened." She started to turn around, but felt him behind her. She huddled closer to the desk.

"Let us not lie to each other, Elizabeth," he said as calmly as he could. "The reason we are in this situation now is that someone saw me leaving your room that morning."

"As you told me they would. What did you do, pay them to watch?" This time even his presence did not keep her near him. She pulled away, crossing to stand beside the chaise. She closed her eyes and sank down. "Dunstan, I did not mean that." She sighed and wiped a tear from her eye.

"I know, my dearest."

"Your dearest? Most likely only your latest." In the days she had been in her room, Elizabeth had had much time to think and to let her imagination run rampant.

"Elizabeth!" Dunstan reached out and picked her up. "I expected more of you than that." As he emphasized his words, he gave her a little shake. "You know that is a lie."

For a moment she glared at him, daring him to release her. When he did, she sank back to the chaise, her head in her hands. "I know. Damn and blast! Dunstan, why is this happening to us? What have we done?"

Wanting to take her in his arms, Dunstan resisted the urge, fearing it might be too soon. He sat beside her on the chaise and picked up her hand, lacing his fingers with hers as he had often done in the garden. Letting the silence flow around them, he sat quietly, only his hand and his body beside her reminding her of his presence.

When she was as calm as she could be, Elizabeth turned her head to stare at him. Her fingers tightened on his. "Why do things like this have to happen?" she asked plaintively. Again only the silence answered her. His fingers answered hers. "Does Mama know you are here?" she asked curiously, for the first time realizing how strange the situation was.

"Yes." He resisted the urge to kiss her lips as they made an *O*. "She is worried about you. We all are."

"Everyone but the *ton*, I imagine. Once again I am the center of their conversation." Pulling her hand free, she crossed to the window to look out into the darkness where she knew the garden lay.

"But this time you are not alone." Dunstan followed her, once again standing only inches away from her. "Society has decided that we are both to blame." He laughed ruefully.

"But they will accept you. You are a man. Such things are accepted from men." He watched as her shoulders slumped.

"No. You are wrong there. Today I received a letter from my superior." He felt her start. "Yes, even in London they are talking about us. I have been informed that I am now on a leave of absence and only to return when the situation has been resolved and society has forgotten. By spring, he hopes."

She turned around and put her hands on his shoulders, her face sad. "I am sorry," she whispered as she saw the pain in his eyes. He leaned forward until their foreheads touched, taking comfort from her nearness. For a few minutes they stayed that way. Then she pulled away again, pausing by the trunk to run her hand over its curved, brass-bound lid. "They will forget," she said in as calm a voice as she could manage.

"Not completely. Now I am known as a rake. Me a rake. Blast it, Elizabeth. I lived a comfortable, well-ordered life until you appeared in it. If you had only come home a day later." He ran his hand through his hair.

"So now I am the one who caused the problem?" Elizabeth's eyes flashed with fury. "May I remind you that I was in my own bed, sir!" She stamped her foot, much like her stepmother was fond of doing. "Why do men always blame women?" she asked, throwing her hands up into the air.

"I am not blaming you, you termagant. I simply said that you have complicated my life." Dunstan tried unsuccessfully to get closer to her, but she pulled away and stormed across the room. "But I like complications," he added soothingly.

"Then you should enjoy this," Elizabeth said, tossing her head and sending all her curls bobbing. The wrapper, only loosely tied around her, was creeping open, giving Dunstan teasing glimpses of her breasts and legs.

"Elizabeth, stop trying to twist my words."

"That is another thing. Who gave you permission to call me Elizabeth? No wonder people are talking when you are so familiar."

"Familiar. My dear, have you forgotten what we have shared. I could be much more familiar if I wanted. I wonder if the officers you flirted with so assiduously would enjoy knowing what you look like in the morning. Your breasts rosy and peeking through the thin lawn of your nightrobe. Your waist so small above your rounded hips. Your scent, the smoothness of your skin."

"Be quiet. Be quiet," she shouted, angry that he should destroy such a beautiful memory. "You are no gentleman."

"Oh, but I am, my dear."

"What do you mean by that?" she asked suspiciously, tears of anger still pooling in her eyes.

"If I were not a gentleman, I would have dragged you to a clergyman the morning I awakened in your bed. Then this would never have happened.

Instead I listened to you." He reached out with a long arm and dragged her over to him. "Come here." When she was close enough, he pulled her into his arms and sank down on the chaise. "Now be quiet." He ensured her compliance by kissing her, softly at first. Then his tongue began to tease her lips, urging them to open.

Her eyes fluttered shut. She sighed, giving him just the opening he had been hoping for. His kiss deepened as it had that evening in the garden. His tongue tangled with hers, sending flashes of fire along her spine. Startled, she tried to pull away. One hand on his chest slid inside the shirt placket to the warm skin beneath. "Robert," she whispered, pulling him closer, her arm around his neck.

He pushed her back into the chaise, letting his body hold her in place. While his tongue invaded her lips, one hand sought and found her breasts. Gently he ran his thumb over a nipple, feeling it harden in his hand. Elizabeth twisted restlessly beneath him. "Ah, sweet," he breathed as he kissed her again. This time it was her tongue caressing his lips. "Yes, love, yes." He reached up to push her wrapper from her shoulders, to free her so that he could enjoy her more completely.

By this time, Elizabeth was no longer thinking, only feeling. His lips, his hands ignited flames within her, flames she ached to have put out. She twisted restlessly beneath him. Her hands found his waist and pulled his shirt free, wanting to be closer to him. Dunstan pushed one knee between her legs, letting her feel his weight. He reached up to take his shirt off, but it caught. He sat up, impatient to be free. He stood up and almost fell into the open trunk where he had pushed it to the foot of the chaise. The incident had a sobering effect.

Pushing his shirt back into his breeches, Dunstan breathed deeply for a few minutes, keeping his eyes carefully off the chaise. Finally when he had himself once more under control, he sat back down. Elizabeth reached for him once more, but he moved out of reach. She opened her eyes. "Dunstan?" The question was more than his name. He simply looked at her, noting the flush on her breasts, the delightful tumble of her clothing.

Elizabeth sat up slowly, her faced flushed with embarrassment, pulling her wrapper about her tightly. As soon as she was covered once more, Dunstan sat at the foot of the chaise. "Dunstan?"

"I truly prefer Robert, love." He smiled at her, but kept his distance.

"Robert," she said hesitantly. Then as if determined not to let this opportunity pass her, she asked. "Why?"

"Why what?"

"Don't play games with me, Robert. Why did you pull away? We were so close."

"Closer than you realized, love." He reached out to smooth a curl from her face. She grabbed his hand, kissing his palm. He let his finger trail down her jawline, following the curve of her cheek. "You are so lovely," he told her, his eyes gazing deeply into hers.

"Then why did you pull away?" Elizabeth tried to pull him closer, but he refused to move.

"It was the hardest thing I ever had to do," he said quietly, his eyes shadowed. "But I could not go on."

Her face paled. She dropped her eyes, fighting tears. "I see," she whispered, determined that he would not see her cry.

"No, love. You do not."

"Don't keep calling me that!"

"What?"

"Love. How can you call me that when you said you could not go on. I suppose I really am a fallen woman now," she said angrily. She swung her legs over the edge of the chaise, ready to make dash for the comparative safety of the dressing room.

"Shaken, my dear, not fallen. That is why I stopped. Why I couldn't go on," he explained. "If I had taken you then, I would never have been able to let you go."

"Let me go where?"

"To the West Indies or the manor."

"Robert, you are not making sense. Shall we begin at the beginning?" Elizabeth suggested, her pulse rate finally slowed to normal. "Sit down beside me," she said, her voice coaxing. He shook his head. "Then bring that chair over here."

When he was safely in his own chair, Dunstan took a deep breath. Before he lost control again, he plunged in. "We have some decisions to make tonight," he said clearly. "Or at least you do. I know what I want to do already." He glanced at her to be certain she understood him. She nodded, causing her curls to bob again and her wrapper to slip a little. He turned away quickly.

"And what is that?" she asked, her voice low and husky. She picked up a scarf from the top of the trunk and began to fold it into smaller and smaller squares.

"Let me explain your choices, and then we will talk about mine." Elizabeth looked up at that, her eyes noting the strain and pallor in his face.

"Go on."

"You know our situation." She nodded solemnly. "Unless we take action immediately, we will be ostracized by society. It does not matter that the rumors are not specific or that they were probably made up by a jealous woman who thought you had too many beaux. The harm has been done."

"Do you mean to tell me that all this grief did not have any basis to it? That I have stayed in my room because someone was jealous of my beaux?" Elizabeth stood up, her eyes flashing. "Who did it? Does she realize what she has done? Tell me her name. I will visit her and let her discover first-hand the effects of gossip."

"It would do no good. Besides, the lady has already left. And you and I know there is a good reason for our reactions. We know what we did."

"You do? All I remember is waking up with you in my bed."

"A bump on my head and elsewhere"—he rubbed his hip,—"were my first memories of that occurrence. You had longer to react than I did."

"What did you expect me to do? Allow the maid to see you in my bed? With the curtains open, she was certain to see you."

"Agreed. But the problem remains that we and probably someone else know that we were in bed together that morning. Charles said the rumors at the manor began when the coachman and groom returned from London."

"And the rumors here did not begin until the last ball of the Season was over in London," Elizabeth said thoughtfully. "If Jack had not come down earlier, I would know for certain it had been he." Elizabeth crossed to the chaise again. She ran her hand over the silk fabric covering it, remembering the warmth of Robert's skin beneath her hand.

"I think we can absolve Edgerton of the deed, but he has certainly added his share to the problem," Dunstan said, frowning.

"What do you mean? What has he been doing?"

"What he has been saying is more the question. The major and Lord Hathaway, have agreed to talk with him privately and discourage any future remarks."

"Did you warn them he was dangerous?"

"They know. They also said to tell you that they do not believe the gossip. But their colonel has prohibited them from visiting you. He is not as generous as they." Elizabeth smiled. "I have already begged their pardon for my ridiculous behavior," he added.

"After I overcame my anger, I decided that you were sweet to be jealous," Elizabeth said, giving him a long glance from under her eyelashes.

"Sweet? That is not what you said," he reminded her. "I wish you had told me sooner."

"You were much too sure of yourself as it was. The ruthless way you dragged me off to the garden." Once more Elizabeth fluttered her eyelashes at him.

"And you always let me. Had you protested after the first time, I would have stopped," he told her seriously. "Elizabeth, I lived for these few moments alone." He smiled at her and she smiled back. Then their hands reached out to each other, and they were on the chaise again in each other's arms. A few kisses were all that Dunstan allowed them. Then he sat up again and pulled her up beside him. "Enough of that."

Elizabeth allowed him to put her off again. "But who in London hates us enough to want to harm us?"

"The person may not hate us. He may simply be a gossip who cannot keep from repeating what he has seen or heard."

"You think it is a man?"

"I don't know. All I do know is that twice rumors have begun about us. And I do not plan for there to be a third time. I hate being the center of everyone's attention."

"You too?" Elizabeth asked, turning to look at him in wonder. "All my life I have tried to stay out of the public eye. Unfortunately, I have not always succeeded."

"I was succeeding nicely until you came into my life," he reminded her. "For eighteen months I had been blessedly scandal-free."

"My fault again. You did choose to crawl into that bed," she said firmly. Then she asked, "Why eighteen months?"

Then the whole story poured out: his father, his brother, his grandfather. "He has decided that it is time for me to marry," Dunstan explained for what he hoped would be the last time. "He has even picked out my bride."

"Your bride?" Elizabeth's eyes flashed at him.

"She is his choice, not mine," he reminded her. His smile warmed her like a fire on a cold day. "But if we do not solve this problem satisfactorily, I may not be able to resist him much longer," he explained. "Or if I do, I will need to leave England."

"Leave England? Why?" she demanded, her heart racing in fear.

"I have decided that if he turns me off as he threatens to do, I will join our forces on the Peninsula," he said quietly, his mouth in a firm line. "But that is still only a possibility. Let us get back to our problem. How can we stop the gossip and prevent it from recurring?"

"Your superior has truly put you on a leave of absence?" He nodded. "And your grandfather is using the situation to force you to marry a girl you do not want?" He nodded again, pleased to see her mind more on him than herself. "Perhaps we should run away together," she said only half in jest.

"I have a better idea." He reached out and took her hand, holding it between both of his own. "Marry me."

"Robert, you know how I feel. Marriages that are forced rarely work out happily." She sighed deeply, but she did not pull her hand away.

"Remember the day at the royal stables?"

"How could I forget? The ball that evening is burned into my brain," Elizabeth said bitterly.

"Forget about the ball. Concentrate on the breakfast we shared." His thumb stroked the top of her hand lightly. "What would you have said that morning if I had asked you to marry me?" he asked quietly, his eyes never leaving hers. Her eyes fell before the ardor in his. "What would you have said?" he asked again. "Picture yourself there with me beside you. What would you have said?"

"Yes." The word was so soft that Dunstan had to strain to hear. He reached out and gathered her into his arms, covering her face with kisses. Resolutely she pushed him away. "But things have changed. Robert, do not feel you must offer for me. I would rather live in obscurity than have you beside me and unhappy."

"Haven't you been listening to me, Elizabeth? I want you for my wife. I was attracted to you as early as your first Season, but with my prospects your father would have laughed at me. As soon as I saw you again, I realized that you were even more lovely than you were as a young girl and that I wanted you to be mine. Now, call your maid and change your clothes. As soon as the clergyman arrives, we will be married."

"Tonight?"

"I am not letting you change your mind," he said firmly.

"What about your grandfather? Shouldn't he be here? Will he forgive us if we exclude him this way?"

"I refuse to wait another night to make you mine. Besides, we can always tell him we were ready to start practicing to make his first great grandchild." She blushed and hid her face against him. Dunstan took a deep breath and stood up. He crossed to the bellpull and gave it a tug. "I will see you downstairs before long," he said quietly.

Elizabeth was never certain how she had managed to get ready that evening. Miller laid out her newest ball gown, an oyster white embroidered with pearls and lace around the bodice and hem. Handing her mistress her silk petticoat, Miller pulled it into place, tying it only with a bow instead of the usual knotted bow. The dress was so low that only the most delicate chemise could be worn beneath it. Miller tied it into place, once again with only a bow. Taking her curling stick, she pulled each curl into place. Finally Miller dropped the dress carefully over Elizabeth's head.

Lady Ramsburg and Louisa entered during the last delicate operation. They watched misty-eyed as the maid smoothed the last wrinkle. Then they handed Elizabeth the gifts they had brought. Lady Ramsburg had brought a hair ornament made of pearls and lace to match her dress. "I had hoped you might wear this at your engagement ball," she explained. She watched in satisfaction as Miller added it to her stepdaughter's curls.

"And I brought you these," Mrs. Beckworth explained. "My own dear husband gave them to me the morning of our wedding. We met secretly in the garden, and he put them around my neck himself," she said as she clasped a string of pearls around Elizabeth's neck. "Be as happy as we were, my darling."

"Your father would have been so pleased to welcome a fine young man like Dunstan into the family. He never cared for Jack. Did he ever tell you that?" Elizabeth nodded. "This is truly the best way, my darling," Lady Ramsburg said quietly. "Now, if Charles and the groom have returned, the wedding will take place."

"Returned? Where did they go?"

"To their lodgings to change clothes. With you in your finery, the gentlemen could not remain in afternoon dress. Oh, Louisa, isn't she lovely?" Smiling happily, the two older ladies brushed tears from their eyes. Hearing a knock, they opened the door.

"Is the bride ready? Her groom is impatient," Lord Ramsburg announced. He smiled at Elizabeth as he put her trembling hand on his arm. "If you two ladies will go down first," he suggested. He watched his wife kiss her stepdaughter's cheek and brush away a tear. Then Louisa did the same. Before the tears truly began to flow, they hurried away.

Elizabeth took a deep breath. She closed her eyes briefly. Then she opened them and smiled brilliantly. "Do not be startled, my dear, when you see our guests. Your stepmother suggested, and I agreed, that this wedding be as normal as possible. We invited some of our closest friends, Lord and Lady Ravenwood, a few of the young officers you like so much, and Dunstan's superior. He was waiting to talk to your young man when he went home to dress." Lord Ramsburg kept up his commentary as they walked down the stairs, describing in detail how the chef had risen to the occasion and how the gardener had willingly provided flowers for the ceremony. "Give them to her now, Miller," he suggested. The maid dropped the train of Elizabeth's gown and hurried to do his bidding. "Now, a big smile and we are ready." She looked at him and smiled sweetly.

The ceremony itself was a blur. A tall man in priestly attire stood in front of a bank of flowers and asked her questions. She responded. Dunstan responded. All she could remember was Dunstan's hand on hers giving her comfort, strength. The service concluded, they turned to accept their guests' best wishes.

Elizabeth remembered one guest asking the significance of the hour. "Such a strange time for a wedding."

"To honor a memory," Dunstan explained, his eyes never leaving hers. The lady had sighed, delighted to be included in such a romantic adventure.

Although the wedding had been arranged hastily, the wedding supper was a masterpiece, the chef declaring that his honor demanded great sacrifices. For Elizabeth, even though she ate almost nothing, the time flashed by. For Dunstan the toasts seemed endless. Finally the last course was served, the last toast drunk, and they could leave.

As Elizabeth talked with Amelia, Lord Seward drew Dunstan into a quiet corner. "A wise choice. Your lady is very lovely," he said diplomatically. Dunstan, his eyes on his new bride, simply nodded and smiled. "Will you be returning to London immediately?" Seward asked, his face carefully bland.

Dunstan, familiar with his tactics, recognized that hint in the older man's voice, looked at him sharply. "I plan to take my bride to meet my grandfather. We will stay at Clarendon until it is time for the Season so that they can get to know each other. Do you need me in London?"

Before he could explain fully, Seward noticed Lord Ramsburg approaching. He said quickly, "No. The country is the right place for now. Expect a letter from me soon." He paused, his face stern. "Remember that what you do for me must be kept a secret—even from your wife." Dunstan watched Seward walk toward the group where Elizabeth stood surrounded. His eyes were troubled. Then Lord Ramsburg hurried up.

"I have arranged for you to borrow a house from a friend of mine. He will be in London for some time," he said smiling broadly. "The coachman is waiting and has his instructions. But do not run." He refused Dunstan's thanks and watched carefully as the newlyweds said their good-byes.

His earlier worries forgotten, Dunstan crossed to Elizabeth's side, taking her hand in his. "Well, brother, are you willing to give her into my hands?" he asked Charles, half in jest, half seriously.

"Be good to her, Dunstan," Charles said seriously. He bent down and hugged his sister as he had done many times before. Then he held out his hand to Dunstan. Having said their other good-byes earlier, the couple quickly left the party.

"Where are we going?" Elizabeth asked once they were under way.

Her new husband laughed ruefully. "All I know is that Lord Ramsburg borrowed someone's house for us. I didn't think to ask where it was."

Elizabeth let her head rest on his shoulder for a moment. Then to her delight, she was draped across his lap, his lips on hers as though he were starving for her sweetness. She wrapped her arms tightly around his neck and opened her lips slightly.

The carriage came to a halt before either of them were ready. "We are here, your lordship," the coachman said loudly. He knocked on the carriage door once more. As a hand from the inside pushed it open, he stood back. The gentleman exited first, throwing the coachman a coin that glittered gold in the lamplight. Turning back to the coach, Dunstan lifted down his wife, swinging her over the cobblestones to the entranceway beyond. Laughing, they entered their temporary home.

A few minutes later, the door to their rooms closed safely behind them and his lady's maid dismissed, they were alone again, the months of dreams and longing adding to the emotion both felt burning within. The firelight cast warm shadows around the room, removing the hint of dampness that was always present along the seashore. Elizabeth stepped back, not certain what was supposed to happen next. Dunstan let her retreat slightly and then followed her, wrapping his arms around her. "Mine," he whispered in her ear, letting his lips and tongue explore its curves.

"What?" she asked, her voice trembling with emotion.

"You are mine," he said again, the emotion in his voice making the sentence louder than he had intended. He pulled her back against him, holding her tight, kissing her neck and ear until she melted against him. Then he let her turn in his arms. They looked at each other for a moment before they kissed. As it had happened earlier that evening, their kisses quickly grew more passionate, tongue and lip blending, caressing.

This time Dunstan felt no restraint. His hands wandered over Elizabeth, seeking to discover her hidden mysteries. She too was without fear, without hesitation. Her hands pulled his cravat loose so that she could reach his chest, could run her fingers through the pelt matted there. At first, hands and lips were enough. But passion quickly flared out of control.

With effort Dunstan pulled back. Elizabeth tried to keep him close. "We have too many clothes on, love," he whispered in her ear. "Turn around." Without embarrassment, like a child being undressed by her nurse, she stood quietly as he unhooked her, slipped her gown from her shoulders, and helped her step out of it. The cool evening air hitting her skin sent shivers through her, breaking the spell for the moment. She stepped back, silhouetted against the firelight. For Dunstan it was his dream brought to life.

He reached up and with one hand ripped open his shirt. He discarded his jacket and pulled the shirt over his head. With only his breeches and his stockings still on, he walked slowly forward as if giving her the chance to pull away, to refuse him. He held out his arms, and she came willingly, brushing her fingers over his tender nipples, laughing in delight as they hardened when she touched them. Then she leaned forward, resting heavily on Dunstan. Her arms stole around his neck, bringing his lips down so that she could kiss him. For a moment Dunstan was startled. Then he laughed and swung her up into his arms.

Crossing to the bed, he placed her carefully in the middle, sitting beside her on the edge. Letting his kisses follow his gaze, he kissed her breasts, half hidden in the flimsy material of her chemise. But Elizabeth wanted more. Once again her arms pulled his head down to hers, her lips burning with an ache that only his could relieve. His hands slipped lightly over her breasts, teasing them until her nipples jutted proudly against the soft fabric. "How does this come loose?" he asked, wanting to feel her breasts heavy in his hands. Within seconds the offending garment was gone, leaving her clad only in her silk petticoat.

"You have more clothes on than I do now," she whispered. Then she sighed in delight as his lips found her breasts. Her hands stroked his back, delighting in the feel of muscles rippling under his skin. She ran her hand lightly down his spine, causing him to shiver. He bit her breast lightly. "Robert!" she cried.

Rolling to his back, Dunstan breathed heavily for a while. Then he turned onto his elbow and reached for the bow on her petticoat. Feeling sinful for enjoying his gaze so much, Elizabeth lay there peacefully, waiting for his hands and lips to return. When they did, it was far different from anything she had felt before. Using kisses so light they felt as though a butterfly's wing had brushed her skin. Dunstan gave his homage to her body, stopping only when she pulled away in embarrassment.

Then she pushed him back on the bed. "Let me kiss you," she said quietly, sending shivers of delight through him. Her lips wandered as his had done, stopping only when she found clothing. "You have too many clothes on," she said once more.

Hesitantly, not certain how she would react, Dunstan slid off the bed. He stripped the rest of his garments away and stood there for a moment, letting her grow accustomed to him. Her eyes widened. She held out her arms, smiling at him. Then he slipped back into bed, pulling her to him, letting her feel his passion. His shy bride met every caress openly, letting him enjoy her as she enjoyed him. As they drifted into sleep sometime later, Elizabeth giggled.

"What is it?" he asked, pleased with the happy sound.

"If I had known that marriage was so enjoyable, I would have accepted your first offer," she whispered, letting her hand twine itself in the hair on his chest.

He pulled her closer so that she rested partly on him. "Shameless hussy," he said as he kissed her again.

19

"Elizabeth, we must leave now," her husband of less than a week reminded her. He watched indulgently as she kissed her family good-bye. "Remember you are welcome at Clarendon whenever you wish to come," he told them all

Louisa Beckworth smiled up at him. Since Elizabeth had returned home from her brief wedding journey radiant, her cousin had been happy. But when she discovered what Dunstan and Charles had done, she was delirious. Realizing that Louisa needed a home of her own, Charles and Dunstan had reached an agreement. As soon as their lawyers had finished the arrangements, the manor was hers. And if she wished a snug little house in Bath, the rents would provide it. She cried when she had first heard it and tried to convince them it wasn't necessary. "But it is, darling Cousin," Charles had said quietly. "After trailing after us for years, you need some place of your very own." Elizabeth smiled proudly, pleased that her husband was so thoughtful and that her brother had matured so much over the summer.

Had she realized his motivation, she might not have been so proud. After deeding half of the property to Louisa himself, he had agreed to sell the other half to Dunstan for a comfortable sum, large enough to buy his colors if he could manage it without his mother discovering his actions until they were final. Charles watched Dunstan hand Elizabeth into the carriage, waved them on their way, and returned to his lodgings. He and Porter were on their way to London before nightfall.

In Dunstan's carriage there was a comfortable silence for a time. Elizabeth wiped her tears away finally and took her bonnet off. Dunstan drew her down to his shoulder, his hand soothing her much as he would have done a baby. Listening to the steady beat of his heart, Elizabeth drifted off to sleep. In a few minutes Dunstan followed.

When they awoke sometime later, they were still in each other's arms. Dunstan woke first and watched fascinated as Elizabeth breathed steadily, her breasts rising and falling. His arms tightened. She stirred. "Are we there yet, Robert?" she asked sleepily, unwilling to move.

"No. You know I told you that the journey would take longer than a day," he said, his hand tracing the shell-like surface of her ear. "Are you one of those travelers who needs reminding?"

"Stop that," she said, turning her head away. Her protests were less than forceful. She pulled his hand down and clasped it, measuring her fingers against his, marveling as she always did at the contrast between them, his so large and hers so small.

"But I enjoy it," he said so close to her ear that she could feel his breath.

"We can't. Robert, you know what happens when you do that," she whispered, her eyes on the flap in front of her. "They can hear everything."

"We will be quiet. Come let me show you," he said softly, turning her in his arms.

When they stopped for luncheon, Dunstan told his coachman, "Arrange for a chamber so Lady

Dunstan can refresh herself. We will have a luncheon served there. And you two do not need to hurry." Elizabeth blushed, thankful for the dimness of the coach. On the box the servants exchanged knowing looks.

On the journey the servants grew accustomed to long stops. Only in the early morning hours did they make good time. As they neared the end of their journey, Elizabeth grew quieter. Finally she asked, "Does your grandfather know about our marriage?"

"Yes. I wrote him." Dunstan fell silent. She had been with him as he was writing. He waited for her to continue.

"Is he going to be very angry?"

"With you? No, my dear, he will take one look at you and welcome you. With me it may be different. During the last few months I have not been his idea of a dutiful grandson." Dunstan laughed ruefully.

"But I do not want him to be angry with you. What happened was as much my fault as yours. More mine, really. Had I listened to you at the beginning . . ."

Dunstan pulled her into his arms. He gave her a shake. "If you keep trying to take all the blame, I will be angry. If I had been more persuasive. . . ." He bent and kissed her, a long, passionate kiss that caused Elizabeth to flame once again for him.

Elizabeth finally pulled away, breathing unsteadily. She sank into her corner of the carriage and took hold of the strap. He reached for her again, but she held him off, her face serious. "Did you tell him about my problem with names."

"No, love. We will let him find that out for himself." This time he would not be held off. He picked her up and put her on his lap. "Robert," she complained, "I will be all rumpled when I meet your grandfather." Her protests were weakened by the way her arms crept around his neck. Sometime later, she whispered, "I wish you had told him."

"Hmmm?" He had found the ties of her bodice and was working to undo the knots.

"What will he do when I call him or his friends by the wrong names or fail to recognize them at all?"

"Elizabeth, we will explain as soon as we see him. If your problem was accepted in Brighton, how can he be upset? Now, I would like some cooperation, if you please," he demanded in a mock serious tone. Putting her uneasiness aside, Elizabeth gave him her full attention.

Their luncheon stop having been even longer than usual because Elizabeth had insisted that Miller find her something fresh to wear before the luggage coach left, it was late afternoon when they arrived at Clarendon Hall. Elizabeth, excited and afraid, held on to Dunstan's hand as they rolled up the long road to his home. "The gardens were planned by Capability Brown," he explained. "My grandfather is proud of them. Those and his apple orchards are his greatest interests. The Hall is not large, but it is comfortable. It is built of stone from the Cotswolds."

As they rounded a curve, the trees that had been blocking her view disappeared, and there in a lawn of rolling green broken only by formal garden and well-groomed bushes was the Hall, its mellow Cotswold stone glistening in the sunlight. The panes of glass from its many large windows caught the rays of the sun and sparkled. "Dormer windows. One of my friends had them in her schoolroom. I was so jealous because she could sit there and look out while all I had was a regular window," Elizabeth said, looking up at the roof. "What are those rooms?"

"You will need to ask the housekeeper about that. I spent most of my time away at school or out on the land." As the carriage pulled to a stop, she clutched him frantically. "You will be fine," he assured her lightly. "Smile."

When she stood before the earl a few minutes later, Elizabeth tried to keep that smile intact. But it was an effort. The earl kept them standing in front of him for several minutes, his eyelids closed as though he were sleeping. Then he tilted his head backward, and Elizabeth saw her husband's eyes in another man's face, slightly faded, it was true, but still recognizable. The earl continued to look at them, taking in each detail of their appearance. Elizabeth was glad she had taken the time to change at luncheon. Her jade green traveling dress made her eyes appear a deep green, and her bonnet she knew framed her face well.

"So this is my new granddaughter," the earl finally said, rising and walking toward them. Elizabeth stared at him for a moment as she realized that the only way he could see clearly was keeping his head at that angle. The earl's face was as devoid of emotion as his voice. "Your name is Elizabeth?" he asked.

"Yes, my lord." Once again Elizabeth sank into a curtsy.

"None of that, girl. None of that. Let me see you." She stood still as he walked around her, inspecting her as he would a horse. She looked at Dunstan, a fine white line beside her mouth, but he avoided her glance. His circuit completed, the earl waved them into waiting chairs and took his own again. "My friends inform me that the two of you were involved in some kind of scandal." Elizabeth blushed, certain he knew exactly what everyone had been saying.

"Grandfather, I wrote you about it. Told you how I felt. Both Lord and Lady Ramsburg believe we will hear no more about it," Dunstan said firmly.

"Lord Ramsburg. Works for the government, I believe." Elizabeth nodded, not willing to trust her voice.

"Good reputation. Hard worker. Plays deep, I hear." The earl's tone clearly revealed that he expected no answer. He looked from Dunstan to Elizabeth again, noting their clasped hands partly hidden by Elizabeth's skirts. He stood up. "Must admit, not the one I had wanted for my boy, Elizabeth. Too old. Should have married long ago."

Elizabeth flushed angrily and started to speak. Dunstan squeezed her hand to keep her silent. "I met her during her first Season, Grandfather. But you know what the situation was then. Her father would have shown me the door."

"Hmmm. Good man, your father. Respected him. Too bad about his early death."

Elizabeth settled back in her chair. She nodded, tears glistening in her eyes.

The old man crossed to the bellpull. "Well, suppose we have to make the best of it. Invited some friends to meet you. Only a dinner party. With a bachelor household have no call for balls. Have to change that, I guess."

"You invited some friends tonight, Grandfather?" Dunstan stood up, angry.

"No, for tomorrow." He turned to the butler, who appeared in the doorway. "Have my grandson and his bride shown to their suite. We keep country hours here, Elizabeth, but I had the meal set back when you arrived later than expected.

Say in half an hour." She nodded. "At what time tomorrow do you wish to interview the housekeeper? Be good to have someone to deal with her. Usually see her at eight."

"Eight will be fine, my lord," Elizabeth said as calmly as possible.

"But what am I to call him? And why didn't you explain about my appalling ability with names? Dunstan, I will never remember all of the servants." Before he had shown them to their rooms, the butler had introduced the servants, omitting only the chef and his helpers, who were busy at that time.

"You managed in Brighton. I am certain you will manage as well here," her husband said soothingly.

"But there I had help."

"I will be with you," Dunstan promised.

But the following morning he left for the orchards before she could remind him of the appointment with the housekeeper. When the woman entered the room, Elizabeth tried desperately to remember her name. Fortunately, her housekeeper, as if sensing her problem, said, "I am Mrs. Finch, my lady. The earl said you will be giving me orders about the household."

"Mrs. Finch, before I give any kind of order, I need to know more about the Hall, your routine, the things the earl likes or does not like. From what I have seen so far, I admire your efficiency."

"Thank you, my lady." The older woman beamed with pride, savoring the words to share them with the other servants. "I try. Where would you like to begin?"

"Where would we be least disruptive of your morning routine?" The question earned her another mark of approval.

"Since everyone has been served, I believe the kitchens. I suggested that the chef prepare something light for luncheon. His plans for the dinner party are quite elaborate. Would you care to inspect the menus?"

"I am certain, Mrs. Finch, that they are satisfactory. But perhaps we can discuss them with the chef." Elizabeth said the housekeeper's name to herself again as she followed her down the stairs. By the time they had completed their tour of the Hall, Elizabeth knew the housekeeper's name, but she had no idea of anyone else's but the chef's. Like her stepmother's chef, he was called Jacques. Mrs. Finch had told her after their interview with him had concluded, "I am certain his name was originally Jack, but with all the rage for French chefs today, what is a poor Englishman to do? That war with Napoleon has disturbed people's minds."

Elizabeth had nodded solemnly, holding back a laugh. She was not laughing as she picked at the meal on her luncheon tray. The gentlemen had decided to inspect one of the farther farms, choosing to stop for lunch at the local inn. As soon as her mistress had finished, Miller took the tray away. She watched Elizabeth rub her neck for a moment and then stood behind her, her hands massaging the tight muscles of her mistress's neck. "Rest for a while. The maid assigned to our room said that the dinner party was being planned for forty. You will need to be fresh."

"Yes." Elizabeth sighed. "Forty new names," she moaned.

"Rest. And when you are ready to get up, I will have a bath waiting for you."

Elizabeth nodded. She climbed up into her bed, sinking into the cool white sheets redolent with lavender. "Miller, are they treating you well?" she asked drowsily.

"Very well."

Elizabeth drifted off into a sound sleep, waking hours later. She stretched and rolled on her side, taking in the preparations Miller had made. A large copper tub rested on the hearth. Heaps of towels stood nearby. "A bath," Elizabeth said smiling. She stretched lazily and was trying to decide if it was time to rise when Miller walked in, a gold silk gown on her arm. Quickly placing the freshly pressed dress where it would be safe, Miller rang for the hot water.

Before long, Elizabeth was ensconced in a tub filled with water exactly the right temperature and scented with her favorite sandalwood and roses. She lay back and let the tensions ease away from her. She was lying there, her eyes closed when Dunstan entered from his rooms. Waving Miller away, he picked up the sponge she had been using and ran it lightly down Elizabeth's shoulders. "You have already washed my back, Miller. I will do the rest myself," she said quietly, her eyes still closed.

"Does that mean you won't let me help?" her husband asked, running the sponge over her breasts.

"Dunstan, when did you return?" As though she were accustomed to receiving men as she bathed, Elizabeth smiled. She reached out and caressed his cheek.

"Not soon enough. To think that I missed any of this sight," he said as he bent and kissed her.

"You are going to get wet," she said breathlessly when he raised his head.

"A problem with an easy solution." His boots and jacket already off, Dunstan stripped his shirt off in one easy motion. His buckskins quickly followed. "Have you any other objections, my lady?" he asked as he stood beside the tub.

"Not one," Elizabeth said, holding up her arms. In a moment he was holding her wet body close to his, his mouth plundering hers.

That interlude was all that kept Elizabeth going that evening. As she had known it would be, the evening was an ordeal. She smiled and greeted people, the whole neighborhood it seemed, realizing that the next time she met them she would not be able to call them by name. Only one new person remained vividly in her mind, angelic, blonde, laughing, Cecile Westin.

"Cecile!" her husband had said, delighted. "When did they start letting you come to adult parties?"

"When I convinced them that I needed to be presented next Season. Thanks to your marriage, Robert, I will be going to London."

"My marriage?" Just then the next person arrived. Cecile Westin moved on, her large blue eyes twinkling mischievously.

"I thought you did not like her," Elizabeth whispered to Dunstan as she waited for the next person to reach her.

"Nonsense. I just did not want her for a wife. Can you imagine what kind of marriage we would have had? I would have had to dandle her on my knee. But she is a sweet thing. The Westins are our closest neighbors. You will enjoy getting to know Cecile."

Elizabeth smiled, gritting her teeth. Her imagination was only too vivid. And while Dunstan might think of Cecile as too young for marriage, Cecile did not. Elizabeth had seen those looks in other girls' eyes before.

Finally the evening was over. As the guests departed, promising invitations to a variety of events,

Elizabeth and Dunstan smiled and accepted their best wishes, promising their attendance. Right before they went up to bed, the earl said, "Went well. Think you impressed them, Elizabeth."

"They may not be so impressed next time," she mumbled under her breath.

"What do you mean?" The words meant only for herself had caught the earl's attention.

"Elizabeth has trouble remembering people's names, Grandfather. She is worried that she will embarrass you," Dunstan said, smiling down at his wife.

"Should think it might. Have to put my mind to the problem. Is it only the gentry, Elizabeth, or everyone?"

"Everyone," she said with a sigh. "I called Lady Jersey Lady Arundson once. It was at a luncheon. My mama, Lady Ramsburg, almost fainted. Fortunately, Lady Jersey laughed. My secret was no problem in Brighton. People thought it amusing."

"Hmmm. Then mustn't be a secret here. Will spread the word. Wouldn't want anyone embarrassed." Thoughtfully, the earl walked up the stairs.

For a few days no one mentioned anything about her failure at remembering people's names. In fact, Elizabeth thought the earl had forgotten. Then one morning she walked into the breakfast room. The footman bowed. She nodded. Sinking into her chair, she waited until he brought her her tea. Then she noticed. There on the pocket of his jacket a name was embroidered. "Harris?" she asked. "Is that your name?"

"Yes, my lady." He poured her tea and stepped back. "Is there anything else?"

"No. Yes. Where did you get that?" She pointed to the new jacket he wore proudly.

"The earl had new jackets made for us, my lady.

All of us have one. We are to keep them, too, even after you have learned our names," he said proudly.

"Thank you, Harris," she said, dismissing him. For the rest of the morning she walked through the Hall, stopping servants and reading the names they wore on jackets or aprons. Only the chef and his assistants had something different.

"The earl, my lady, presented us with these instead," the chef explained, settling his toque blanche more firmly on his head. Then Elizabeth noticed that each hat had a name neatly stitched on it. "He ordered a full dozen each for us," the chef added.

"You are as thoughtful as your grandson, my lord," Elizabeth said to the earl when they met before luncheon. She reached up and kissed him on the cheek.

"Humph! Anyone would have done it," he said gruffly, but Elizabeth noted his cheeks redden and knew he was pleased. "Never thought about the problem before. Have you had it from childhood?" He held out his arm to her and led her into luncheon.

Summer gave way to autumn. The first round of dinner parties over, entertainment stopped for a time as the harvest began. Elizabeth found she was happier than she had ever been in her life. Few things marred her life, and one was Cecile Westin. The young seventeen-year-old rode about the countryside freely. And often when Dunstan returned from the fields, he would have her on his arm, laughing up at him. "Look what I have found, Elizabeth. Cecile was riding over to see you when she saw me instead. Is there enough for another person?" he would ask, knowing the chef was always prepared.

The earl smiled indulgently. Elizabeth too smiled and gritted her teeth. Those afternoons when Cecile appeared for luncheon, she stayed usually until right before teatime. "Tell me about London, Elizabeth," she would say pleadingly. "Grandmama has not taken part in the Season in so long, I am afraid I will do something wrong. Tell me about the patronesses and which modiste to use." Reluctantly Elizabeth would comply. After a time, however, she had to admit that she agreed because she hoped that Cecile would be a success. If she were, then surely she would not spend so much time with Dunstan. She also admitted to herself that the girl was charming.

In spite of the time he spent on the land with his grandfather or Cecile, Dunstan also found time to be with Elizabeth. One day the two of them explored the house, making notes for improvements they wanted to make. When they entered a large, open room filled with a large rocker, a small table and chairs, and a box of forgotten playthings, they looked at each other and smiled. They wandered through the suite, running hands over the hobby horse that waited there. When they reached the low bed draped in holland covers, they paused and pulled them off, looking at the polished wood and crisp sheets beneath.

Their eyes met. Dunstan closed the door and turned the key. They were in each other's arms, pulling at clothing frantically. They sank down to the low bed, not willing to let the other go for even a moment. As they lay there quietly sometime later, their clothes in disarray, Dunstan whispered, "Someday our children will sleep here." He ran his hand through her curls. "I hope they look like you."

"Never. They must have your eyes and your

smile." She ran her finger around his lips. "And your memory," she added quickly.

"Hmmm. Children. How many would you like?" he asked as he leaned up on his elbow so that he could look down at her.

"Do you have a choice? I thought they just came," she said. "Some women at the manor had them as often as once a year."

"And grew old before their time. No, my dear, when that time comes, I will make certain our children are not so close together," he said solemnly.

Elizabeth lay there listening to his heartbeat, her eyes dreamy. "Our children," she said with a sigh. "I wish," she began. Then she sat up, her face excited. "Robert, wouldn't it be wonderful if we had a baby of our very own? Do you think . . ."

He pulled her down and kissed her, his eyes lit with passion once more. "I think if we want a baby, we should work at it more diligently," he said with a smile as he kissed her neck.

"What kind of practice?" she asked innocently. When he told her, she blushed. Then she reached up to pull him closer.

The crops that year were rich. Barns groaned under the weight of the grain. Apples too were plentiful. As the workers poured onto the land to finish the picking, Elizabeth worked to provide their meals, mostly served outside. Then it was time for the harvest festival.

When the last sheaf was cut and the corn dolly made, the workers followed the last cart into the barn, their tired faces pleased. Then showered with water, they went to the feast that had been prepared. Served at long tables outside, the workers ate the traditional supper of boiled beef and carrots, bread baked in the shape of an ear of wheat, rabbit pie. Dunstan had spent his days with his gun, roaming the fields where the harvest had been going on. As the rabbits ran from the reapers, he had killed them. His grandfather and the other landlords in the area did the same. By the time the day for the harvest supper arrived, every large household in the area had enough for the baking. Washed down by apple cider from their own presses and then by plum pudding, the meal was followed by dances and merriment.

As soon as the meal began and Elizabeth had made certain that there was enough for everyone, Dunstan sent her away. "I have to stay. There are usually fights," he explained. "Tempers have built up during the long hours of work." Already Elizabeth had seen them flare. She watched for a few minutes as the people downed cider, encouraging one another to have more. She nodded and let Dunstan lead her into the house.

"Are they making you leave, too?" Cecile asked when she joined them. Her usually sunny face wore a frown. "They never let me stay," she complained. "And I like cider and plum pudding."

"Come with me. I saved some just for our supper. Why don't you join me?" She exchanged a look with Dunstan, noting once again the fond look he cast at Cecile.

"May I? Dunstan, will you tell my grandfather where I am?" she asked, her face all smiles again. He nodded and watched them walk away.

"Is being married pleasant?" Cecile asked, her face serious.

Elizabeth gulped. "Yes," she said unsteadily. "Why do you ask? Are you planning to marry?"

"No. Not right away. I want a Season or two first. I would have married Dunstan if Grandfather had insisted. But fortunately he married you. You don't mind that our grandfathers tried to make him marry me, do you?" She stopped and looked at Elizabeth. "I think I would make a very bad wife."

"Why?" This time Elizabeth let just a hint of smile cross her lips.

"Because I hate to stay at home, to work inside. I would far rather be outside on horseback." Cecile paused, a worried look on her face. "Do you think that will hurt my chances of having a successful Season?"

"I am certain it will not. Remember to insist that your grandparents take your mare. Although most of your time will be spent going to parties, riding in the park is popular. Oh, you will not be able to enjoy the gallops you have here, but a ride is a good way to visit with friends."

"Just what I had told them. Will you explain it to my grandmother? She will not listen to me. I am so glad you came, Elizabeth," Cecile said, giving her a hug. I did not have to marry Dunstan, and I am going to London!"

For the most part, Elizabeth too was glad she had come. When Dunstan was beside her, holding her close, she never had any doubts. The gentry had taken her problem to heart, and although they did not laugh about it as much as the people in Brighton had, they were kind, so kind that Elizabeth relaxed in their presence and discovered that their names came easily.

After the first few weeks of marriage, both Elizabeth and Dunstan established a routine. They would work separately in the morning and ride about the countryside, visit neighbors, or spend time with each other only in the afternoons.

But even that changed. One morning Elizabeth ran down the stairs to join her husband at breakfast. She was the only one there. "Lord Dunstan left a message for you, my lady. He said he will return in a day or so," said the butler, his tone condescending. Of all the servants he alone still disapproved of her.

"Where did he go?"

"I cannot say. Do you wish breakfast, my lady?"

For Elizabeth the day had lost its brightness. She went about her duties as methodically as usual, but when she was finished, she was lost. Picking up one of the latest novels from the Minerva Press, she tried to while away her extra time with some suspense, but the book failed to hold her attention. She picked at her food and snapped at her maid so that by the time Dunstan arrived at home, not only she but everyone was pleased to see him.

"Where did you go?" she asked brightly as she watched him wash the dust away.

"On business." Dunstan rotated his neck, trying to loosen the stiffness he felt from hours in the saddle. "It is wonderful to be home."

"I was so surprised to find that you had left. We had seen each other less than an hour before, and you did not mention anything about having to make a trip." Elizabeth's tone was petulant.

"I did not know," Dunstan sighed, wishing she would give up questioning him, even indirectly.

"When you go on your next journey, I would like to go with you," she suggested.

"That will not be possible." Dunstan watched Elizabeth's mouth change into a straight line.

"How often will you be gone?" She got up and ran a hand over his bare back, sending shivers of delight down his spine.

"I do not know. Elizabeth, can we change the subject? I am tired. All I want right now is a hot meal and a bath. I've been on horseback for days." He closed his eyes and rotated his neck again.

Elizabeth flounced across the room, out of charity with her husband of less than four months.

As his absences grew more frequent and his explanations more brief, Elizabeth began to have doubts. Their marriage seemed to be falling into a pattern she had seen all too often. Her husband was still passionate, but it was passion at his convenience.

Most days, however, Elizabeth enjoyed her life. She accepted the fact that Dunstan cared about his family's financial future. She watched for him when he was away and hurried downstairs to welcome him home, to arrange the hot meal and the bath she knew revived him.

One afternoon she saw him ride up after an absence of almost a week. She ran downstairs, but he was not in the hallway. She noticed his hat and whip on the table beside the partially open door of the study and hurried toward the door. She had her hand on the latch, ready to push the door open, when she heard the earl ask, "And where have you been, Robert? You may fool your wife with stories about being gone on business, but I know better. What are you involved in this time?" The conversation, had Elizabeth known it, was really a battle of wits between the earl and his grandson. The older man enjoyed trying to discover what errand Seward had Dunstan running and where he went. But she only heard the words.

Elizabeth took several steps back, away from the door, her heart pounding. All those weeks she had thought she knew her husband, and she had been mistaken. Turning, she raced up the stairs, determined to hide her stricken face from the servants, determined too to avoid her husband until she had her emotions more under control. She choked back a sob.

A short time later Dunstan appeared in their rooms, a peculiar look on his face. "You were not downstairs to greet me. Are you ill?"

"Dunstan, you are home," she said as warmly as she could force herself to be. "I was involved in this novel and did not realize you had arrived. I am fine." Her smile, though forced, reassured him.

"Hmmm. It is so wonderful to be home." He embraced her, pulling her tight against him. It was all she could do to keep from going rigid in his arms. That night as she lay beside her sleeping husband, a man too tired to do more than kiss her good night and put an arm around her, she worried.

20

While Dunstan and Elizabeth enjoyed their seclusion in the country, Charles had returned to town. As he waited for the lawyers to work out the last details of the contract for the manor, he renewed his round of activities with his friends.

"The wanderer returns. Ho, Charles!" one of his friends called as he walked into his club.

"Who is in town?" Charles asked, taking the seat that was offered at the table.

"Bit thin of company yet. Everyone's gone to Brighton," his friend Jonathan added. "Where you been, Charles?"

"Brighton. I have been dancing attendance on my mother and sister."

"Your mama still trying to marry you off, Charles?" Jonathan asked. He poured himself another glass of wine and tried to sit up straighter.

"Yes." Charles downed his glass and refilled it. "This summer she concentrated on my sister and was too busy to have time for me."

"Elizabeth? Would never think Lady Ramsburg could pull that off. Must be at least thirty."

"Not thirty. But Mama managed. The wedding was last week. Announcement will be in the papers soon."

"Who'd she marry? I heard Lord Edgerton had returned."

"Don't mention that man to me." Charles shook his fist as if in anger. "She married Dunstan."

"Dunstan. The one at the house party?"

"The same. Are there enough people around for dinner and cards this evening?" Charles asked, trying to count heads around the room.

"Bound to be. Where?"

"My place. About eight." Charles ambled off in search of a few more friends to make up his party.

Card parties, cockfights, bets over being able to walk backward the longest—all these filled Charles's days and nights. Soon he was coming home later and later. And the lines that had disappeared from his face began to reappear. Some evenings he spent at the theaters whose companies had chosen not to tour the provinces, companies of whose actresses played before small audiences. To Charles, the small crowd at the theater was not a deterrent. It simply meant that there were fewer men in the green room to share the girls among.

Before he had been in town long enough to be bored, Charles turned around one evening to see Hartley walking up. "Sebastian, I thought you were still in Brighton."

"Not even the prince stays there in September. We missed you, Charles. And truly I was disappointed not to receive an invitation to the wedding. How are your sister and her husband?" Hartley asked with a smile. His tone was everything it should be—pleasant, interested.

"They are at Clarendon Hall. She said something about staying there until the holidays. I have a snug party planned in my rooms tonight. Care to join us?"

Hartley smiled and bided his time, his hand running reassuringly over the signed note in his pocket. He attended the party and managed without much effort to include himself in whatever Charles was doing. He was there by his side the evening that the Covent Garden theater burned down. "Which of these pigeons shall we take home to our nests?" Hartley asked as he watched the dancers huddle across the street from the flame-engulfed building. "Do you think they will be more welcoming tonight than the last time we tried?" He raised his eyebrow in a question.

Charles laughed. "We looked a sight. Where did you find those wigs and clothes, Sebastian?"

"Anything can be had with money, Charles. Haven't you discovered that yet?" The phrase was Hartley's motto, something he never allowed himself to forget.

"Those girls certainly were not ready to go with us for our looks," Charles reminded him. "And they were not worth the price they were asking, either. Remember how angry they were when we took off the wigs? Is either of them over there?"

"No. We had better make our choice soon before the merchandise is picked over," Hartley said, making his way toward the little group.

"You go ahead, Sebastian. I see someone I want to speak with over here."

Laughing, Hartley had bid him a good night and left. Charles glanced back at the burning theater and walked down the street, his eyes thoughtful.

Late the next morning his face was wreathed with smiles. "It has finally come," he said as Hartley walked through the door.

"What? Have you finally bought your commission?"

"No. But it will only be a few days now," Charles said as he signed a document and sanded it.

"Did your mother finally agree to purchase them for you?"

"No. This is the final deed I must sign on the manor. I will be on my way to the Peninsula soon."

Hartley took a seat, his face deliberately unconcerned. "You sold the manor?"

"Only half. I deeded the other half to my cousin, Louisa." Hartley closed his eyes briefly and then opened them again. "Dunstan and I decided she needed a place of her own. He wanted to buy the whole thing to give her, but I refused. Said I would match his gift. After all, she is a relative of mine."

"How thoughtful." By this time Hartley had himself well under control. ."And you plan to use the money from the sale to buy your commission. Does your mother know?"

"No. And I do not want her to know. As soon as the Little Season begins, they will be back in town. If she found out, she would get her friends to refuse my money."

"Perhaps you could use an agent," Hartley suggested, his face as thoughtful as his voice.

"What do you mean?"

"If someone else approached the right person and your name did not come into it until the very end, she could do nothing to stop you." He looked up and smiled. "I know just the one."

"Capital. Sebastian, you have the best ideas. As soon as the funds become available, I will let you know. How can I ever repay you?"

"You could pay off your debts, Charles." This time there was a bit of a sting in Hartley's voice.

"What are you talking about?"

"Surely you haven't forgotten this note you signed, giving me one quarter of your sale price for the manor." He took out a piece of silk and unwrapped it, revealing the agreement. "Do you remember it?"

Charles nodded. He closed his eyes for a moment, wondering how he would explain the loss of so much money to his trustees. Then he smiled brightly, remembering that the money for the manor was his without restrictions. He would need to watch his expenditures, though. He did not plan to use capital for all his purchases. "As soon as the funds clear, you will have your share. What were we playing that night? I usually don't play that deep."

"An intriguing game but boring. I have already forgotten it. How are we going to amuse ourselves today?"

Charles was as good as his word. No sooner than the funds had been deposited, he posted Hartley a check. He also reminded him of the commission and told him to get busy. He wanted to be a captain in the Horse Guards.

Within a few days Hartley had the news Charles had been waiting to hear. "Your commission is assured. As soon as the funds are delivered, your orders will be sent. Charles, they told me that you should form your stable carefully. They recommend sturdy mounts that will last. Shall we go to Tattersall's for a look."

"You go ahead? I may take a run into the country for a few days. I know just the horses I want. I will give you a note for the bank so that you will have funds when you need them. What was the amount?"

Hartley named a figure, adding a percentage for himself. Even though the money from the manor had been considerable, it would not last long. "You will not be able to assume the commission until after the New Year, something about paperwork."

"Yes, my stepfather always says the army moves

more slowly than a snail." Charles laughed. "I suppose that is one of the things I will need to get used to. Should I have my uniforms made yet?"

"I would wait until you have talked to your colonel. He will be able to recommend a tailor."

"You're right, Sebastian. You have probably saved me from some terrible solecism."

"How long do you plan to be gone?" Hartley asked. For a few minutes longer the two men talked; then Hartley told Charles good-bye and headed toward the bank.

Charles made his preparations quickly. Then he and his valet made their way out of London, stopping first at Lord Ramsburg's estate.

"What is this sudden interest in acquiring a stable, Charles?" his stepfather asked suspiciously.

"I thought it was time for me to take more interest in my estates. And since your horses are strong, I thought that adding one or two to my stables would improve my stock." He looked at the two stallions he had chosen, one a black with no spot of white anywhere and the other a bay.

Not thoroughly convinced, Lord Ramsburg looked over the horses, strong animals capable of running for hours. "If it is hunters you want, I have some that are better jumpers."

"No, these are exactly what I want. Your head groom mentioned that you are planning to put them on the block."

"Yes. Neither is up to my weight for long stretches. I have gotten some good colts from them, though. Since I am in London so much lately, I have been neglecting my stables. It is a shame to do that to good horses." Lord Ramsburg let the black nuzzle his hand. "They are yours if you want them, Charles."

Delighted though she was by his visit, his mother

was angry with him, too. Putting his new horses through their paces, he ignored the young ladies she invited to luncheon and dinner. "Give it up, my dear," Lord Ramsburg urged one evening as he sat in a chair and watched her maid add the last touches to her ensemble. "Right now Charles is horse mad. And horses and young ladies usually do not mix."

"He is so frustrating. Can't he understand that I am doing this for his own good?"

"Are you, my dear?" He stood up and offered her his hand. "I rather thought it was for your own."

Finally Charles made his escape, sending his horses to his own estate. "I am going to visit Elizabeth and Dunstan, Mama. Do you wish to accompany me?"

"And miss the Little Season? I will see them here for Christmas. I wrote to invite the earl also. And Louisa. Give them my love, dear one." She patted his cheek, rather glad for once to see him on his way. "Now, who will be presenting young ladies this Season?" she asked as she watched him ride away.

Had she chosen to accompany him, Lady Ramsburg would have received her heart's desire. On his first day at Clarendon, his eyes widened when Cecile Westin walked in on Dunstan's arm. "Elizabeth, present me at once," he said, poking her in the side. His voice trembled slightly.

She raised her eyebrows at his serious tone. She looked at the other side of the room, where her husband and Cecile talked with the earl. Dunstan had returned only the day before from one of his business trips. "Dunstan, bring our guest over here," she said, her voice sharper than she had intended it. "Cecile, this is my younger brother, Charles

Beckworth. Charles, this is Cecile Westin." She stepped back, amused but cynical.

Charles took the young girl's hand as though he were handling the rarest Venetian glass. "Miss Westin," he said softly as though he were afraid a noise might cause her to disappear.

"Mr. Beckworth." They stared into each other's eyes for a moment, only breaking the gaze when they realized that the room had fallen silent around them. "Do you plan to stay long, Mr. Beckworth?" Cecile asked, trying to make her voice sound unconcerned.

"Until it is time to leave for the holidays. We will be going to my mother's and stepfather's. You, Dunstan, and the earl will be accompanying me, won't you, Elizabeth?" He took his eyes off the angelic vision before him to look at his sister. "You have not changed your mind?"

She looked over at Dunstan, her glance cool, and assured him they had not. Then she watched as Charles led Cecile to a chair and carefully seated her. "Do something, Dunstan," she whispered as she watched her brother take a seat nearby the vision.

"What? Charles will have to handle this himself," he said, laughing.

"But what will Mama say?"

"If you can arrange this match, she will probably give you her blessing," he reminded her.

"But he can't moon at her like that. We do not want another scandal." She glared at her husband, upset but not wanting anyone to notice her agitation.

"Plan some outings. Go to Wells shopping for Christmas trinkets. Let them help you plan the party for the tenants. Since we will be going to your mother's, we will need to have it before we leave. You will think of something."

And you will find some excuse to leave again, she thought.

But Elizabeth rallied. Enlisting the aid of her housekeeper, Cecile's grandmother, and the mothers of several of the other young ladies in the area, she took them shopping in Wells.

The caravan left early one morning. Elizabeth drove in her carriage with her brother and the Westins. Three other carriages followed with a mixed party in each. After a day of inspecting the shops and a luncheon in the private parlor of an inn, they came back by moonlight to Clarendon Hall for a late supper. From the notes of thanks she received from the young ladies and gentlemen involved as well as their mothers, she was an inspired hostess.

"And all I did was walk around with Mrs. Westin, two steps behind Charles and Cecile. I did order most of what we need for the party. It will be delivered next week," Elizabeth told Dunstan. She was sitting on the chaise, rubbing one foot.

"If you wear yourself to a nubbin, I will be upset. You need to spend more time with me," he complained.

"You are the one who is always gone. I should be the one complaining. You told me to arrange this expedition; I would never have thought of it," she reminded him. "Then you leave on business." Her voice was edged with bitterness. "What are you doing when you are gone? And what kind of business is it?" she demanded. The sharpness of her voice was in contrast with the smile on her face. Dunstan had her foot in his hand and was scrubbing it soothingly. At least it began that way. The he kissed her instep, sending shivers up her leg. "Dunstan," she protested, not willing to release her anger.

"Hmmm?" His kisses continued up her leg.

"It is almost time to go down for dinner. Dunstan," she breathed huskily, pulling her foot away. "Besides, you have not answered my question. "What kind of business are you spending your time—our time—on?"

He got up and turned the key in the lock of the door. "Do we have to discuss it now? I have something else in mind," he said as he pulled her close to him and refused to let her go.

The Christmas season that year was the most exciting time the country had seen in many years. Each hostess tried to top the previous one. The Westins, reviving an old family custom, invited everyone, old and young alike, to make plum puddings. They had warned everyone in their little group to wear old clothes or at least ones that could be washed. Invading the kitchens, everyone in the group took a turn stirring their own puddings. Laughing, each family added their special trinkets as well as fruit. Dunstan held up the small golden ring before he threw it into the bowl. "Whoever finds this in the pudding will not be unmarried this time next year," he said loudly. Cecile blushed and bent her head over her own bowl. Charles rushed to offer his help. Even Elizabeth managed a laugh.

Through skating parties and informal dances, Elizabeth and Dunstan watched as Charles devoted himself to Cecile. His attentions finally grew so pointed that Elizabeth sent for him. "What are your intentions, Charles?"

"What do you mean?"

"What game are you playing with Cecile, Charles? I warn you that if you hurt her, her grandfather will see you in Newgate if he can."

"Hurt her? I plan to marry her, Little Bit." Charles sat down on those words, startled himself.

"Then you already have her grandfather's permission to address her?" his sister asked when she regained her breath.

"No." He stood up and took a turn around the room. "I will. But Cecile is afraid that if I ask his permission now, he will not take her to London for the Season."

"You have already spoken to Cecile?"

"Not really. We were talking after that redheaded girl and her fiancé announced their engagement. That is when Cecile told me."

"Does she know you plan to make her an offer?" Elizabeth asked directly.

"Yes. I am certain Mama will love her as much as I do."

"And what about her grandfather? Charles, she is only seventeen."

"Oh, I don't intend that we should marry immediately. We both agree we are too young for that. Cecile wants a Season or two, and I still want my commission." He sat down and smiled at her as if expecting that she would agree with everything he said.

Elizabeth bit her tongue to keep the angry words from spilling out. That night when she and Dunstan were alone, she was not as reticent. "They plan to go on enjoying life day by day, never worrying about tomorrow. Robert, he sat there and told me they have an arrangement. But they do not plan to marry for a year or two. A year or two. It will never work."

"Elizabeth, Mr. Westin may well refuse the offer. He has told me many times that the reasons he chose me for his granddaughter were my land and my title."

"How humbling for you." She glared at him. "But Charles has land and money in his own right."

"All of it miles from here. Her grandparents are not willing to let her go that far. You are worrying for nothing." He pulled her into his arms. "We will be leaving for Christmas with your stepmother very soon. If the attraction between them lasts until the Season, then we will worry." He took the brush from her hand and laid it on her table. "Aren't you wearing too many clothes?"

Although Elizabeth did not refuse him, there was something missing that night. As they lay on their sides, their backs carefully turned to each other, both wondered what was going wrong. Determined to hide their uneasiness from others, they put on their smiles the next morning. Only the very observant could tell those smiles rarely reached their eyes.

At the Christmas festivities at the Ramsburg estate, Charles was once again the despair of his mother. "Should I tell her, Robert?" Elizabeth asked as she put the emerald pendant that had been his gift to her about her neck, thinking not for the first time that he must care for her because he had chosen his gift so carefully. "She is trying so hard."

"And enjoying playing matchmaker so much. I heard her tell my grandfather that she was certain that I was the perfect husband for you the first time she met me." He laughed. "The look she had in her eyes that first day in Brighton told me differently. Had there been any other honorable solution to our situation, she would have refused my suit and had me thrown out."

"Mama?"

"Your stepmother is made of stern stuff, my dear. Cousin Louisa, however, saw nothing but the romance."

"Perhaps I should drop a hint or two," Elizabeth suggested. "Something to prepare the way." He bent to kiss her, but she pulled away slightly so that his kiss landed in her hair.

"You know your stepmother better than I. Do what you wish, my dear," he said as he stepped back, frowning. During the last few weeks she had pulled away from him more than once. Hiding his anger and doubt, he took her arm and led her to the group assembled below.

When they entered the room, Louisa sighed. "Is there something wrong, Mrs. Beckworth?" the earl asked solicitously. Since his arrival he had gravitated toward her whenever he could. And Louisa with her kind heart found him quite distinguished no matter how her cousin objected.

"But you can never tell what he is thinking," Lady Ramsburg had protested. "He seems so secretive."

"That is one problem he cannot help. Think how restricting his problem must be. And so uncomfortable to hold his head at that angle all day. Maybe that is why he is occasionally out of sorts."

"George is trying to persuade him to take his seat in the House of Lords. He says the earl has the best mind for grasping facts that he has ever seen."

With these memories fresh, Louisa smiled sweetly at the earl. "I am so pleased that Elizabeth and Dunstan are so happy together."

"How can you tell?" he asked. Elizabeth always seemed to be so stiff around him, her face blank.

"When he enters the room, have you seen him look around until he finds her? And she does the same. They are in love."

"Love. Ha."

"You do not believe in love?" Louisa asked, a hint of disbelief in her voice.

"Not much good comes of it," he told her firmly. "Most marriages made for the sake of love that I have known have been disasters. Give me something more substantial any day. Property, advancement—those are good reasons for marriage."

"I disagree. My husband and I married because we loved each other. And our marriage was a happy one."

"If he had lived, I believe you would have grown apart," the earl said, not at all happy to have his ideas questioned.

"And what is your basis for thinking that?" she asked. "Have you made a study of marriage?"

"Only those around me. Most of them are less than felicitous." The earl frowned as he watched Elizabeth walk onto the floor with someone other than her husband. The look in Dunstan's eyes revealed his annoyance. When a gentleman of her acquaintance asked Louisa to dance, the earl scowled. Then she stood by the door, his head tilted back, his eyes on the grandson and his wife.

"At least Dunstan and Elizabeth are not making themselves the center of all eyes," Charles said, noticing that the couple was at opposite ends of the room. "I would never wear my heart on my sleeve like they were doing for a time." The earl coughed to cover his laughter. Even he had been aware of Charles's infatuation.

"I presume you are referring to your sister and my grandson?" the earl asked.

"You have seen them. Staring into each other's eyes as though they were alone. Just yesterday I surprised them in the library. Startled, that's what I was, to see them kissing that way. They are married." Charles's voice was filled with disgust.

"And married people are not allowed to kiss?"

"Not in public. And look at them now." The

earl looked back to the dance floor. The music had ended, and Elizabeth had returned to Dunstan's side. "Gazing into each other's eyes like young puppies. Someone will have to speak to them before they go to town."

The earl took another look at his grandson and his wife. The sight did not reassure him. Glaring would have been a better word than gazing. "Whom do you suggest for the job?" The question brought Charles's commentary to an end. "Perhaps you can convince them."

"Not me. They will never listen to me. Mama or you, that's the best. They will listen to you."

"I believe I will pass the opportunity on to your mother. Have you been to the card room tonight?"

The rest of the evening the earl spent in the card room, only emerging when it was time for supper to be served. Once again his eyes followed Elizabeth and Dunstan, noting that even though his grandson filled her plate, there was a coolness between them. But Elizabeth's eyes seemed to follow Dunstan everywhere. Even when he was speaking to someone else, she knew where he was, what he was saying. The earl sighed, his eyes hooded once more.

21

The trip back to Clarendon had been a reminder of Elizabeth and Dunstan's first journey. The earl, who enjoyed his privacy, had chosen to take his own coach, and the servants had traveled with the luggage. Once again the couple had dallied along the way, arriving hours after the earl. They dashed into the Hall, flushed and laughing. They handed their cloaks, hat, and bonnet to a waiting footman, being careful not to look at each other. Dunstan, freed of his apparel faster than his wife, waited impatiently. As soon as she was free, he grabbed her hand and started pulling her toward the stairs.

They had only taken two steps upward when the butler appeared. "Lord Dunstan, this message arrived for you a short time ago. The man who delivered it said it was urgent." As though he were handling a dangerous snake, the butler held out the letter. It reeked of roses.

Dunstan stared at it, his eyes narrowed dangerously. Elizabeth took one look, glared at her husband, pulled her hand free, and ran up the stairs. "Elizabeth," Dunstan called, but she ignored him. He heard the door slam, but by then he had read the message. "Send word to the stable to saddle our fastest horse." He grabbed his hat and cloak and looked up the stairs longingly. "And tell the chef to pack me something I can eat while I ride. Tell my wife and my grandfather I should be home within the week." He drew his cloak around him and pulled his hat over his ears.

"Roses," Elizabeth fumed. "Cheap scent and a cheaper woman, no doubt. And to think I had forgiven him." And she probably would again. But their first enjoyment of each other was lost. "My husband is not even my own. I have to share him as I shared Charles's mother." Her sense of abuse grew by the day. By the time Dunstan returned, Elizabeth's anger had grown to epic proportions.

He arrived four days after he had left. He needed to be shaved. His clothes looked and smelled like he had slept in them as he had. After four days of a mistress who found fault with everyone, his servants took one look at Dunstan and decided to make certain they were far away when he and Elizabeth met.

Perhaps recognizing the problems he might be facing, Dunstan chose to have his bath in his dressing room. Then clean, shaved, and fed, he sought out his wife. He had seen her face when the butler put that letter in his hand and had spent the last four days trying to decide what to tell her. Fortunately, the decision had been taken out of his hands. He had been recognized and almost taken. Only the quick work of another agent had saved him. After Seward had heard his report, had blasted him for his carelessness, he had also given Dunstan permission to explain things to his family.

Taking a deep breath, Dunstan entered their bedroom. He had heard Elizabeth's voice a moment ago. When he walked in, she was in front of the fire, her brown curls wrapped in a towel. "So the prodigal returns—again," she said bitterly. "How soon will you leave this time?"

"Elizabeth? Love?"

"Interesting that you should call me that. It must make it easier to convince the woman you are with that you are talking to her."

Dunstan walked in front of her, his blue eyes flashing. "I have never been unfaithful to you, Elizabeth."

"And I imagine you will tell me that you have never had a mistress either. A friend you went to school with has a passion for roses."

"That is not what I said. Besides, any mistress I had was before I met you."

"Before my first Season, then?"

"No, before I met you again last spring," Dunstan said between clenched teeth. He kept reminding himself that she had a right to be angry, but that did not make him feel any better.

"Interesting how your story changes." She twisted around so that her back was toward him.

He walked over to her, grabbed her shoulders, and turned her to face him. "You are going to listen to me now. And you can believe what I say. If you don't believe me, I have witnesses."

"They must have seen some interesting sights," she said in her most biting tones.

"What they saw was my capture by a French spy. If the other men working for Seward had not been there, I would be dead." Her face blanched. "I could not tell you before because Seward would not let me. We have been trying to catch this agent for months. She worked out of Bristol and did great harm to British shipping."

"She?"

"The agent's name is Angelique Martine. She worked the brothels in Bristol, choosing her prey carefully. Somehow she learned my name and sent me a message offering to sell information about Napoleon's plans for the invasion."

Elizabeth pulled free, not at all certain whether to believe his story but hoping it was true. "I suppose she got away.'

"No. She will be brought to trial in a very short time. And, woman or no, she will hang." Dunstan stepped back, watching his wife's face.

"Did your grandfather know?" she asked, wondering what she would do if he said yes. A faint glint of anger simmered in her.

"No. Oh, he made a game of guessing, but I did not tell him anything." Dunstan took her hand. "If I had told anyone, don't you know that I would have told you?"

Elizabeth looked at him, noting the way he looked into her eyes, apparently unafraid of what she would see there. She sighed, remembering how Edgerton had betrayed her trust. Could she trust her husband's story? She closed her eyes. "Will this happen again?"

For the first time Dunstan felt hope. "I cannot promise that it will not. At the present time it seems an impossibility. Too many people know who I am. A spy or spy catcher is only useful if he or she is anonymous." He watched her carefully.

She took a turn around the room, picking up small objects here and there and moving them to another spot. Then she stopped. "I thought I was losing you or would be forced to share. And one thing I refuse to accept is sharing my husband." Her voice was very quiet and calm, almost too calm. Its normal huskiness had an edge. Her face revealed little of what she was feeling, what she was hoping.

Dunstan looked at her set face and realized the importance of that statement. In a tone as serious as hers, he replied. "I will never leave you. If my country needs my services, I will go," he said, his voice ringing with honesty. "But what I can promise is that as long as there is life in my body, I will come back to you."

Elizabeth said nothing, letting the silence grow. Then she sighed. "You were working for Lord Seward?" she asked as if for confirmation. He nodded, refusing to add his pleas to the facts he had presented. He watched as she walked aimlessly around the room, her face thoughtful. Finally she stopped and faced him, her decision made and her resolve firm. "Where were we before you left?" she asked. He smiled broadly and reached out to pull her into his embrace.

After the turmoil of the first few days of January, the next week or so was calm. Elizabeth reviewed her plans for refurbishing the Hall, and Dunstan helped the men check on the stock. They would be leaving for London before very long; Cecile had insisted that they both swear blood oaths that they would be close at hand to support her. Mrs. Westin had added her mite to their decision. "I so dread going out in company again. What if Cecile becomes infatuated with a fortune hunter? Her grandfather would never forgive me."

Nor would Charles, Elizabeth said to herself. Aloud she merely said, "You will be a wonderful chaperon. Cecile loves you so much that she will follow your lead in matters of society. And my family will be there to help you."

"So kind of you. I cannot tell you how much I have been worrying about . . ." The conversations became so common that Elizabeth knew almost to the word what Cecile's grandmother would say and would have to bite her lip to keep from answering the next question.

Outwardly Elizabeth's and Dunstan's lives settled into peaceful patterns as January continued. On the surface everything appeared to be perfect.

His duties relatively light in the winter cold, Dunstan spent much of his time watching his wife make decisions—the color of curtains, the design for the china, the color of paint for the trim in the smallest guest bedroom. The only room that did not receive her attention was the nursery. Each month she waited anxiously. Each month they were disappointed.

One afternoon after a game of chess with his grandfather, Dunstan tried to find Elizabeth, tracking her from the storerooms in the basement to the library and finally to the morning room. Surrounded by long lists of improvements, Elizabeth sat at the desk she had rescued from the attic, frowning at a piece of paper. "So this is your bolt hole today," Dunstan said with a laugh.

"Hmmm." She looked up and gave him a rather absent smile. Then she reread the letter one more time.

" 'Hmmm' is all you have to say to your husband who has been absent from your side since breakfast?" he asked. He had not received his customary smile. To his dismay Dunstan was beginning to discover that Elizabeth's smile or absence of it could change his appreciation of the day.

"Robert, did Charles mention anything about the army to you at Christmas?" Elizabeth asked. Her eyes were gray with worry.

"All he talked about was Cecile or his new horses. What has he done now?"

"According to one of Mama's gossipy friends, he has bought a commission in the Horse Guards. Mama is beside herself with worry. Since my cousin was killed, Charles going off to fight is one of her worst fears. She did not give him the money, that is for certain. And his money is doled out monthly." She put up a hand to rub the back of her neck.

Robert moved behind her, moving her hand so that his could massage her tension away. "You said yourself that he needed something to do. Maybe the army will be good for him. I tried hard enough to get Grandfather to agree when I was younger. I saw myself leading men into battle, rescuing people on the battlefield. I am certain he is the same. The reality never made an impression on me. When he meets soldiers who have been in battle, he may change his mind." He kissed the base of her neck, but she did not respond to the caress.

"He met my friends in Brighton. Their stories did nothing to discourage him."

"Elizabeth, he is a man. He has the right to make decisions about his own life."

She turned around and glared at him. "But what if he is hurt?"

"You did encourage him, Elizabeth. Now it is too late to tell him that you have changed your mind." He stepped back and pulled her to her feet facing him. "I wonder if he told Cecile what his plans were?"

"Mama did say it was a rumor. Maybe it isn't true." She put her head on his shoulder and her arms around his neck. "Robert, I have just discovered the most lowering thing about myself," she said quietly.

"What?" He bent and kissed the cheek that he could reach, the kiss so soft that she would not have known about it had she not been looking.

"I am a coward." He pulled back to look at her. "Oh, I do not mean about meeting strangers. I knew that."

"Then what do you mean?"

"With people I care about. I want to know where they are and what they are doing and that they are safe."

"But even knowing where people are does not mean they are out of harm's way. Elizabeth, we have no guarantees," he said, quietly increasing his hold on her.

Her grip about his neck tightened convulsively. He simply held her for a moment, wondering at her, surprised by the fear that seemed so close to the surface. Then she stepped back. "You will think me a rattlepate, going on that way," she said with a laugh that covered the emotions still too near the surface. "Were you looking for me?"

"Yes, I received a letter from Seward today."

"Robert! Is he sending you into danger again? He promised." She drew away from him, wondering where he would go this time, what danger he would be in. Perhaps it would have been easier with only the worries about other women.

Dunstan smiled slightly, pleased that she was not ready to see him out of her life for even a short time. "I never said he had promised anything, Elizabeth. He rarely does."

"Then what did he want?"

"Seward suggested that we return to London."

"Immediately?"

"No, only as though we were leaving early for the Season. He is not certain, but he feels something important is about to happen. He suggests we begin to make our preparations."

"This early? There will be no one in town."

"Lord Ramsburg said he and your stepmother would be returning almost as soon as all their guests left. It will give you a chance to visit with her."

"And listen to her complain about Charles." She made a face. Then she said thoughtfully, "She will worry less if I am there. Oh, I do hope the news about Charles proves false."

"If it is not, she will need your support even more. Will leaving early cause you too many problems?"

"Not if I start planning immediately." She crossed to the bellpull. "Send Mrs. Finch to me as soon as possible," she told the footman who answered. "We will need to make some decisions about what we need to take with us. And finish our measurements for all the windows and doors here. With the figures I will be able to visit the fabric warehouses in London and make my selections." She crossed to the desk and made a brief note.

"I can tell that my presence is redundant." He walked over to her and kissed her cheek. "Send someone to call me when you are ready for tea."

"Hmmm." Elizabeth closed her eyes for a moment when he was gone, wondering how she had been able to refuse him that morning so many months ago. If she lost him now, it would destroy her.

When Cecile Westin walked in on the earl's arm a short time later, Elizabeth winced as she noticed the bright rosy cheeks, clear complexion, and sparkling blue eyes of her husband's friend. "Cecile wanted to ask you some questions about the Season, Elizabeth. So I invited her to tea," the earl said as he seated the young girl. "Shall I have someone bring it now?"

"May we talk first?" Cecile asked, flashing her dimples. "I have more serious matters on my mind."

The earl smiled indulgently. "Then I will leave you ladies for a time."

No sooner was he out of the room than Cecile flew out of her chair. "Elizabeth, you simply must do something."

"About what?" After the news of the day, the very last thing Elizabeth wished to deal with was another crisis of Cecile's.

"My clothes." She broke off as Elizabeth began to giggle. "You would not be laughing if my grandmother dressed you, Lady Dunstan." Cecile said indignantly, forgetting that the blue velvet walking dress trimmed in fur that she had been in *ault* over just a week earlier had been her grandmother's choice. "She wants to have Mrs. Thompson in the village make most of my clothes. That way we will not have to go to town so early."

"Mrs. Thompson's clothes are always in the height of fashion. I daresay there are establishments in London that would rejoice to have her work for them."

"But what if someone asks for the name of my modiste? What shall I say? Mrs. Thompson in the village sews for me? How humiliating!"

Elizabeth kept her face serious with an effort. "Perhaps you could pretend you did not hear?" she suggested.

"A proper hoyden I would look then. Some of Grandmama's friends do not accept less than an answer. I can see them sitting around me, each one trying to get me to divulge the name. And the worst of it is that Grandmama will tell them."

"I see. Perhaps you can say she is very exclusive, has decided to live retired, and now has agreed to work only for you."

Cecile ran over to her and embraced her heartily. "You truly are the best person, Elizabeth. At first when Charles said so, I could not see it, but you are. My own personal modiste. Perhaps I will start my own fashion. Now all I have to do is convince Grandmama."

"Convince her of what?" Elizabeth asked warily.

Just then the door opened. Dunstan walked in. Cecile rushed to his side and threw her arms around his neck. Elizabeth closed her eyes for a moment, the sight too painful to accept. She had taken his word that his absences related to his job, but what if he had been lying? What if there was another woman? Elizabeth knew Cecile was not the one, but there could be someone else. "Dunstan, Elizabeth has had the most wonderful idea. I am going to take my own modiste to London with me." His arm around Cecile, holding her at his side, Dunstan looked quizzically at his wife. "Isn't she clever? I will have the most original clothes this Season."

"But, Cecile, I only suggested you say you had your own modiste."

"I can hardly wait to tell my grandmother," the young girl said with a rush.

"Tell her what, minx?" the earl asked as he walked into the room. "Should I warn her?"

Quickly Cecile explained the idea, taking his arm. "Do you think she will agree?"

"What I know is that tea will be served almost immediately. I told my butler to see to it directly." The earl smiled and sat beside Elizabeth on the settee. "You ladies have had enough time to talk. We gentlemen demand equal time."

"Elizabeth, do you know what Charles's favorite color is?" Cecile asked.

"Anything that Cecile wears," Dunstan said in Elizabeth's ear. "Or should we give her more ammunition against him?"

Despite what Charles had said, Elizabeth had her doubts about her brother's success in that quarter. How could someone prefer Charles to Dunstan? She glanced at her husband, noting the way his riding breeches hugged his body. Since he was married, perhaps Cecile was willing to accept Charles after all. Elizabeth admitted that the two young people had been immediately drawn to each other.

Late that afternoon, Elizabeth was once more immersed in lists. After her meeting with Mrs. Finch, she had decided to take some of the supplies that were so plentiful in the country with her to town. The extra household meant that more animals would need to be slaughtered. She was frowning at the list in front of her when the earl came in. He took a seat and watched as she went on with her planning, oblivious to his presence. When at last she finished and rose to go, she stopped, startled.

"I did not mean to frighten you, my dear," the earl said softly as he took in the picture she made in her jade green kerseymere dress trimmed in white velvet.

"It is I who should apologize. Did you want me, my lord?"

He crossed to her side and took her hand, wanting to reassure her, to tell her of his support, to make her more secure. He had watched the circles under her eyes grow larger. And even though they had begun to disappear in the last few days, he had finally decided to have a talk with both of them. Elizabeth, unsure of herself, dropped her eyes. "Yes. We need to have a talk, my dear. Sit down beside me here." Hesitantly, wondering what had caused him to seek her out, Elizabeth sat down on the settee. "Elizabeth, I owe you an apology." She looked up in surprise. "No, do not try to deny it. I have been less than welcoming to you, my dear." She blushed but said nothing. "Yes, well, old men are sometimes reluctant to admit that their ideas are not the best ones."

"What do you mean, my lord?" she asked, her voice very soft.

"I mean that Cecile is a brainless flirt who would have driven Robert mad in a year. You, however, are just what he needs." She blushed and then turned pale, not certain she agreed with him. "When he brought you home as his bride, he was happier than I had ever see him. And you are the reason. No, do not deny it. My dear, welcome to the family."

He held out his hand to her. She took it and held it within hers for a few moments, her heart racing with happiness at his words and yet aching with sadness too because she knew that first happiness had been lost. Emotion filled her throat, keeping her from speaking. "Now, do you suppose that you could call me Grandfather as Robert does?" He held out his arms, and she flew into them, her tears running down her cheeks faster than she could brush them away.

That evening as she told Dunstan what had happened, she cried again. "What is wrong?" he asked, taking her in his arms and patting her tenderly.

She simply shook her head and cried harder. Dunstan continued to hold her until her tears ceased. Handing her a handkerchief, he watched as she dried her cheeks and blew her nose. "Tell me why you are crying," he said, using a dry edge of the handkerchief to wipe her tears away. She held him tighter, buried her face in his shoulder, and refused to speak. He simply held her.

In the next few days Dunstan rejoiced as Elizabeth turned to him more naturally, their problems less apparent. As she relaxed, she could laugh at Cecile, flirt with her husband. Then Charles's letter arrived. The rumors were true. He had written to both his mother and his sister. His commission had been approved, and he was to take his place with his regiment.

As much as the news worried Elizabeth, when Cecile found out, she was a virago. "He knew that he had bought this commission when he was here before Christmas?" she asked, her face much redder than usual. At Elizabeth's nod, she went pale. She closed her eyes for a moment. "How does one become an *imcomparable*?" she asked when she opened them.

"Cecile, are you all right? Do you wish smelling salts?" Elizabeth asked, her hand on the younger girl's shoulder. Cecile shook her head. She sat down, smoothing the soft pale blue velvet riding habit she was wearing as though she were petting a cat. "Is this a surprise to you?"

"When we discussed the future, Charles mentioned buying a commission. But the boys around here do that all the time. I thought he was merely trying to impress me. How can he court me if he is in the Horse Guards? He will be sent to fight Boney and I will never see him again." Her voice was tragic in its intensity. "When will he be posted to the Peninsula?"

"Not before the start of the Season," Dunstan said in a soothing voice. "Any dances you have promised to him he will be there to claim."

"If I choose to give them to him. I shall have to make my plans more carefully now," Cecile said, the light of battle in her eyes.

"Do not do anything rash," Elizabeth cautioned. "Do you wish to send Charles any word when I write him?"

"No." Then she paused, her mouth set in a straight line. "Yes. Mention that I was surprised. Also tell him that I have decided to find someone who will be closer at hand to promise my dances to."

Elizabeth added other remarks to Cecile's and sent the letter to Charles, wishing that he were not so far away. "You would have boxed his ears had you been in the same house, Elizabeth," Dunstan reminded her. "And do not tell me again how young he is. Let your mother worry about him. You worry about me." She smiled and nodded her head, but his words triggered new anxiety. What had he done? Why should she worry about him?

Her mother too was in tears. But Lady Ramsburg in tears was a formidable individual. Recognizing the futility of persuading Charles to sell out, she took another route. Back in London, she began giving dinner parties, including as her guests a diversity that had not been seen before, adding the military to her select guest lists.

"Robert, listen to this," Elizabeth said in an excited voice late one winter afternoon. " 'And he listened and agreed. Charles, as the heir to two titles, not one, had no business on the battlefield, not without heirs. He promised to make certain that Charles was assigned to London.' " She smiled at Dunstan. "Isn't it wonderful?"

"I am not certain Charles will think so. Does she plan to tell him? Your brother may be very angry with her meddling," Dunstan said as he pulled Elizabeth onto his lap. "Did she send any other news?" Elizabeth shook her head, deliberately omitting her stepmother's constant references to her desire for a grandchild. To Elizabeth's regret that dream was no closer to coming true. He pulled her head down for a kiss, banishing all thought of either her mother or Charles. Their kisses deepened.

Then the door to the library flew open. Cecile burst in. She came to a complete halt, her eyes wide. Elizabeth, her face as red as the ruby she was wearing, tried to get up, but Dunstan would not let her.

"Did you knock?" he asked Cecile, his voice cold and angry. She shook her head. "Then, perhaps you should leave."

Meekly the young girl turned. Then she swung around again. "How delightfully comfortable that looks. Will I be able to try it?"

"Not until you find your own husband," Elizabeth said as coolly as she possibly could, smothering the giggles she felt would overcome her in a moment.

"Good-bye, Cecile," Dunstan said pointedly. "Come again when you have learned some manners." Slightly abashed, she left the room. Almost before the door had closed behind her, Dunstan had his lips against Elizabeth's, but she could not help giggling. "Did you see her face?"

"Who would care? We are in the privacy of our own home, and she was the one who showed poor manners."

"You do not understand country society if you believe that," Elizabeth said as she wrapped her arms about his neck again. Before the first kiss ended, a knock sounded on the door. "Come," Elizabeth called from her safe position on the settee. She smoothed her wrinkled skirts as best she could. Dunstan snorted and turned his back in disgust.

"Good, you are still here," Cecile said as she walked into the room. Dunstan threw up his hands and left the room muttering under his breath.

Elizabeth controlled herself with effort. "What do you need, Cecile?" she asked, trying to muffle her laughter.

"Did you tell Charles what I said? Have you heard from him?"

"No."

"Why hasn't he written?" the young girl asked indignantly.

"I really do not know. Was there anything else you wished to ask?" Elizabeth stood up to escort her unwelcome guest to her waiting horse. Then, catching sight of the curiosity on the girl's face, she realized her mistake and said, "No, Cecile. Ask your grandmother." She walked her to the side door, where her groom waited. As soon as Cecile was mounted, Elizabeth turned back into the house, returning hastily to call. "Charles will be posted to London. We can discuss the news on your next visit." The girl looked unhappy, but Elizabeth merely waved her on her way.

Quickly Elizabeth made her way to her suite, stopping only once to give her maid orders. She opened the door and hurried in. As she had suspected, Dunstan was there. "I thought you would never get here," he complained as he took her in his arms, letting her feel how badly he wanted her. "Will anyone else disturb us?"

"No." She let herself relax against him, her arms clasped around his waist.

"Has Cecile gone?" he asked with a wary look on his face. His hands were busy with the hooks on the back of her dress.

"Yes." She pulled his shirt free of his pantaloons and ran her hands up his sides. The hooks undone, he slid the dress from her shoulders. "Ummm," she murmured quietly as his lips explored her breasts. Together they walked toward the bed, each intent on the other.

As they lay beside each other sometime later, Dunstan whispered, "I love being with you." Elizabeth felt a pang. For a moment she had thought he was telling her he loved her.

She bit her lip and then smiled. "I love being with you too," she whispered back. Dunstan hugged her close, wondering why her words brought him so little happiness.

January became February. Charles, though not pleased at being posted to London, had written Elizabeth. She was to tell Cecile that his dances were his. Any attempt to alter the plan would be met with the fiercest resistance. And he would see her in London soon. The first letter was followed closely by a second and then a third.

Other letters arrived from town with the news of the latest royal scandal, this time involving the Duke of York and his former mistress, Mary Ann Clarke. "Damn woman. No sense," the earl complained. "Sat in a carriage with his enemies and told about arranging promotions for those who were willing to give her a commission. Suppose she thought talking would get her an allowance. Stupid, both of them. Did she hope to win him back by betraying him to his enemies? May be a brilliant leader, but the Duke of York deserves whatever they do to him. Criminal fool for getting involved with Mary Ann Clarke in the first place. And those damned love letters. Sound like a lovesick fool. He should have had more sense. As bad as his brother!"

"What will happen? Do you think the duke knew what was happening?" Elizabeth asked, her hazel eyes gigantic with surprise.

"That is what Colonel Wardle has proposed to find out," the earl explained. "The Opposition plans to get as much out of this dirty linen as they can." He stood up, the London newspaper in his hand. "Can't understand how the Commons got hold of this. Someone looking to make a name, I suppose. Should have been handled in the Lords.

Then we would see if it were spread over the blasted papers."

"Can you be ready earlier than we planned?" Dunstan asked Elizabeth. His face was worried. "I would like to be closer at hand during this." She looked from one serious face to another and nodded. Then she hurried from the room to find Mrs. Finch and give her the news. Before the next day was over, the first coach of supplies and linens made its way toward London.

Later Elizabeth sat in her morning room going over the last few details with Mrs. Finch. "And you will send a messenger with capons and trout at least once a week. When the peas are ready, send them in quickly. And the strawberries," she added, covering her yawn with her hand. "Pardon me," she said and then yawned again. Because she was determined that all the plans for redecorating be complete before she left for London, Elizabeth had been rising earlier each morning, ignoring Dunstan's protests as she stole from his arms. Mrs. Finch looked at her with concern, noting the dark circles under her mistress's eyes.

"You have worn yourself out, my lady. Perhaps you should rest now. We can finish this tomorrow," the housekeeper suggested. Elizabeth agreed and made her way to her bedroom.

She was asleep when Dunstan found her. Startled, he just stood there for a moment and watched her sleep. Her reddish brown curls that he loved to run his fingers through made a splash of color against the crisp white sheets. Dressed in a soft white wrapper, her face and hair were the only spots of color in the white bed. He looked at the dark circles evident even under her lashes, acknowledging that he had helped to put them there. He looked at the letter in his hand and then at her. "Elizabeth," he said quietly. She stirred but did not awaken. "Elizabeth." This time his voice was louder. She opened her eyes slowly, confusion evident in her eyes. "Wake up, Elizabeth," he said as forcefully as he could.

Finally she was awake. Noting the somberness of his face and the letter in his hand, she asked quietly, "What is wrong?"

"We need to leave for London as soon as possible." He held out his hand to help her up.

"Why? Does Lord Seward need you?"

"No, it is Charles." She lost the little color her face had had. Her hand went to her throat, and she tried to speak but could not. "He is somehow involved in the scandal surrounding the Duke of York."

"Charles?" Elizabeth took a deep breath and sank to a chair, too weak to stand.

"Your stepmother has written asking that we come immediately."

22

In the hours after Lady Ramsburg's letter arrived, everyone worked frantically, trying to compress several days' tasks into one. By evening they were exhausted. As they met shortly before supper, one thought was uppermost in all their minds. "How did Charles become involved? He does not run in the duke's circles. Why is this happening?" Elizabeth asked. Accustomed as she was to her younger brother's reckless behavior, she could find no logical explanation for the situation.

Both of the gentlemen tried to soothe her. "Damn scandal mongers. Trying to drag everyone down to their level. Just like the Commons. Probably a mistake," the earl said, patting her on the shoulder.

She exchanged a glance with Dunstan, her face shadowed. "Mama does not make mistakes like that. Nor does she look for problems where none exist. If she asked us to return to London, the situation is serious." She looked at Dunstan for confirmation of her facts.

"A most unflappable lady, Grandfather. Look at the way she handled the problem of Charles's commission," he said, his face very thoughtful. "If she says there is a problem, we should believe her." He frowned. "That commission . . ." He and his grandfather exchanged a somber glance.

"Think it is that serious, do you?" the earl asked,

his eyes on his grandson's face. Dunstan nodded. "Suppose I must come to London as well. Pleasant young man, that Charles. Might be I have a few friends who would help."

"Oh, Grandfather, would you really come?" Elizabeth asked as she hugged him.

Never one to show much emotion, he stepped back and nodded. "Won't slow you up, though. Get things in order with my agent, the planting and all that. Then I will follow in a few days." Dunstan clapped his grandfather on the shoulder, happy to have his support. He had been trying unsuccessfully for years to get the earl to visit London for longer than a week or two at a time. "May even take my seat in the Lords while I am there. Lord Ramsburg said he could use my help. Opposition rather strong. The Prince of Wales has no more sense than his brother."

When Elizabeth and Dunstan left the next morning, most of the household turned out to say goodbye. Mrs. Finch, her hands filled with her reminders, nodded as Elizabeth gave her last minute instructions. "I will join you as soon as I can," the earl promised. "Tell the young rapscallion to keep his chin up." He shook Dunstan's hand and then smiled at Elizabeth.

She kissed his cheek and started to climb into the carriage. Then she hurried back. "Grandfather, see Cecile before you leave. Tell her what has happened. I meant to write, but did not have the time. If she and Charles have already made plans, she may want to change them."

"I will," he said quietly. "But didn't Cecile say that she never wished to see Charles again?"

"That was before Lady Ramsburg kept him from going to the Peninsula," Dunstan added dryly. "Charles said they had an understanding."

"Hmmm. I wonder if her grandparents know about this," the earl said. He helped Elizabeth into the carriage, clasped Dunstan's hand once more, and watched them drive away. When he turned to enter the Hall, his face was grim.

In the traveling coach, the atmosphere was equally somber. Both Dunstan and Elizabeth found the long hours breeding grounds for fears. What would happen to Charles? For Elizabeth too, there was the constant worry about Dunstan's work for the government. Would being in London mean she would see him less. They sat next to each other, only their hands touching, lost in their own thoughts for a long time. Then Elizabeth sighed. "What is it?" Dunstan asked, pulling her closer.

Her heart raced as it always did when she was close to him. Then she smiled at him and shook her head. "Nothing." She put her head on his shoulder and closed her eyes. Exhausted from her activities of the last few days and the worry that had kept her sleepless the night before, she drifted off to sleep. Dunstan put his arms around to hold her in place as the coach bumped over another stone. Then, his head resting on her hair, he too drifted off to sleep.

Unlike the previous journey when they had laughed and loved their way to the Hall, this one was rapid. Pausing only for a quick meal and a change of horses now and then, they traveled late into the night. As a result, by the time the sun had set the next evening, they were in London. Dunstan handed Elizabeth out of the carriage. He stretched, enjoying the release from the jolting of the coach. As they walked into the house, he asked, "Do you wish to see Lady Ramsburg tonight?"

Elizabeth shook her head. "It would take too long to find her. By the time we changed and dined, she would have gone out for the evening." She stopped, her face horrified. "You do not think she would avoid the *ton*, do you?"

"No. You read her letter. She was worried but not in despair. But with London so thin of company still, it should not be hard to discover her. Is that what you want?"

"We can see her in the morning." She took off her bonnet, handing it to a waiting footman.

"I suppose I could go to my club and try to find out what is known there," he suggested almost against his will. All he really wanted was a bath and a good supper.

"Not tonight," Elizabeth pleaded. It was all the encouragement Dunstan needed. He nodded. "Have our servants arrived?" she asked the butler, who was waiting for orders.

"About an hour ago, my lady," he said rather haughtily, his composure slightly ruffled over the many new additions she had thought necessary to the staff. Elizabeth, for once, did not worry about him. She would learn his name eventually, she supposed, too tired really to care about anything at that moment.

"Tell Graves and Miller that we wish baths as soon as possible. And send our suppers to our rooms on trays." She stopped for a moment and looked at Dunstan. "What is his name?" she whispered in her husband's ear.

"Brown," he whispered back, amused.

"That will be all, Brown," she said. "I will interview the servants later." As they walked slowly up the stairs, she asked, "Do you have a housekeeper?" She brushed her finger along the banister and then looked at her glove, annoyed to find a spot of dust.

"Worry about the house tomorrow. After you have visited your stepmother, you can take everything in hand," he suggested.

Their baths finished, supper eaten, they lay in bed later that evening. Although tired, neither was sleepy. "What are you thinking, Elizabeth?" Dunstan asked. He was propped up on his elbow, inspecting her. She wore a very puzzled look.

"How different everything seems." She looked up at him. "Last year I would have been terrified at having to remember so many new names, so afraid to have anyone discover my weakness. Now?" She shrugged her shoulders.

"You were certainly bold enough this evening," he teased. "Whispering in my ear in public!"

"The man already distrusts me because I have disrupted his routine. What would you have me do, insult him by not remembering his name?" she asked defensively. She pulled away from him to lie closer to the edge of the bed.

"Never." He pulled her back to the middle and lowered his head until his lips were only a breath away from hers. "You are to do anything you want," he said and kissed her. He put his arms around her and rolled over on his back, never taking his lips from hers.

"Do you expect me to sleep comfortably on this hard mattress?" she asked, laughing a little and punching him. She pulled back so that she could look at him more closely.

"No. Sleep was not what I had in mind," he said, a light she recognized in his eyes. "Shall I demonstrate?"

Waking in his arms the next morning, Elizabeth

smiled lazily, noting the way his lashes swept over his cheeks. A maid scurried in adding more coal to the embers on the hearth. The crisp, cold air of the morning made her appreciate Dunstan's warmth. She closed her eyes again.

In her stepmother's drawing room later that morning, Elizabeth drew on the strength she had found in her own home. Louisa and Charles were there when they arrived. Louisa was worried, but her greetings were warm. Charles, his face older and more careworn than Elizabeth had ever seen, was subdued. He sat quietly, deliberately silent as the others told them what they knew.

"Charles received a letter," Lady Ramsburg said, her voice more harsh than usual.

Louisa rushed to explain. "Obviously from a blackguard. Such handwriting, small and crabbed, and on dingy paper as well."

"George told us the man had probably tried to disguise his normal hand," her stepmother said, her anger very close to the surface. "I wanted to go to the Runners, but Charles would not agree." All four of them looked at Charles.

He flushed angrily. "What did you want me to do? The least hint of any problem with my commission, and I'll be called to testify in front of the Commons," he said bitterly, silently wondering why this was happening to him.

"And it has not been just one letter either, has it, Charles?" Louisa asked. He shook his head. "The writer demands money, pounds and pounds. Five thousand at first."

"He went up to ten when Charles ignored the first letter," his mother added. "This time he included names and dates."

"What have you done so far?" Dunstan asked, his face thoughtful.

"I went to my colonel," Charles said, his voice as lifeless as his face. "He told me to pay up. He did not want his regiment besmirched anymore than it already was. I tried to explain my situation, that my funds were tied up, but he only told me to find a way, go to the moneylenders if necessary." He ran his hand through his hair, the first sign that he was the Charles Elizabeth had known. Even his clothing, a dull brown coat with buff pantaloons and a green waistcoat, reflected his despair. Elizabeth took his hand and squeezed it. His fingers were cold, but he returned her grasp, holding as though she were a lifeline. "Then I came to Mama."

Dunstan turned to his mother-in-law. "What has happened since then?" he asked, his face carefully neutral.

"We paid the money," Lady Ramsburg explained, ignoring their disapproving gasps. "I was not going to allow Charles to be miserable."

"Then what is the problem?" Elizabeth asked, her eyes puzzled.

"Obviously ten thousand was not enough," Dunstan told her, looking to his mother-in-law for confirmation. She nodded, her face strangely unanimated.

"This time he wanted twenty thousand," Charles said, no emotion in his voice. "He means to bleed me dry."

"He does seem to be rather greedy," Dunstan said.

Louisa, already familiar with the story, continued. "After that we suggested the Runners again."

"I had George inquire, but then we received a letter telling us the price had gone up again and that we were to stay away from the Runners," Lady Ramsburg added.

"Now we are trying to discover who knew where Lord Ramsburg was going and why he was there?" Louisa said. She picked up the needlework she had in her lap and jabbed the needle into the cloth and into her finger.

"That is something we have been trying to discover, but without much success," Lady Ramsburg said quietly. "George has made inquiries, but we must be discreet."

"As usual I have made hash of things," Charles said, his face grim.

"How can you say that?"

"Did you know that Mrs. Clarke was involved when you bought your commission?" Elizabeth asked indignantly.

"Charles, this is not your fault. I do wonder, though, who dislikes you so much," Louisa said, her face as pink as the gown she wore.

"Dislikes me? You think it is someone I know."

"It must be," Louisa said calmly. The others looked at her, new respect in their eyes.

"Of course. Someone who knew what you were planning," his mother said thoughtfully.

"Charles, who knew that you planned to buy the commission?" Dunstan asked.

"My friends."

"All of them?" Dunstan asked, his face carefully blank. Charles nodded. "Then here is what I propose to do," his brother-in-law said. "Write the blackmailer. Tell him that you have no ready cash."

"He will expect me to go to the moneylenders," Charles said, his face revealing his uncertainty. His voice, however, was no longer flat.

"But we will have more time before he carries out his threat. Is that what you wanted, Robert?" Elizabeth stood up and crossed to her brother.

She stood behind him, her hands resting lightly on his shoulders. She looked over at her husband, encouragement in every line of her face. Their eyes met and held.

"That is exactly what I want. It will give us more time to talk to people. All of us must behave as though nothing were wrong." He looked at the ladies in the room; each one nodded in agreement. "Charles?" he asked.

"I am not certain I can carry this off, Dunstan." The ladies glared at him. "I mean I am not good at playacting."

"There will be no playacting about this. You do not have to worry. We will take care of the situation." Charles looked around the room, aware once more of the love he felt for his family. He glanced at each face, aware of the determination he saw in them. Then his normal optimistic attitude began slowly to come to the surface. By the time luncheon was over, he was laughing as usual.

Putting her redecoration plans aside for the moment, Elizabeth threw her support behind her stepmother and cousin. "We need some way to get everyone together," Lady Ramsburg said. "Some reason that no one will question. I wish that you were making your bow to society this year."

"At my age? And after the scandal in Brighton? Mama, that would occasion much discussion. It is too bad that Cecile is no relation of ours. She is the granddaughter of the earl's closest friend. But she will not be in town for a week or so yet."

Louisa had been sitting quietly, their words echoing through her brain. Her face brightened. "But Elizabeth can be presented—as a bride. With all the gossip about the Duke of York and that Clarke woman, last summer's scandals will be long forgotten."

"How could I have overlooked that?" Lady Ramsburg smiled brilliantly. "Louisa, you are so clever. My ball to present the newlyweds will be the start of the Season. We shall invite everyone, even the most remote connections. How could I have missed such an opportunity?"

"You would have thought of it yourself, I am certain. We must get Elizabeth on the list as soon as possible. Will you be her sponsor?"

"Does this mean I have to wear court dress again and all those feathers?" Elizabeth asked. During her first Season she had been presented to the queen and had been frozen with fear the entire time, certain her headpiece would fall off at any moment.

"Yes," Lady Ramsburg said absently. "Give me yours and Dunstan's list as soon as possible. We will dine with the closest of the family beforehand with the ball to follow. Louisa, do you think Gunter's is still the place to go for . . ." Elizabeth stared after her two relatives as they walked away, leaving her alone in the drawing room. Then she laughed softly and followed them.

While Elizabeth was trailing after her stepmother and cousin, Dunstan had returned to his office while Charles spent his days at the Horse Guards. Deciding that having more than their own resources at hand would be wise, Dunstan sought out his superior. "Good to have you back, my boy. You will be happy to know that the pretty little spy you caught in Bristol is no more." Lord Seward leaned back in his chair. "I have something else I want to give you to work on now that you have returned." Dunstan shifted uneasily in his chair. Lord Seward looked at him, his gray eyes stern. "Out with it."

Quickly the viscount explained. "As you can see, my lord, I could not deny him my help," he finished quietly.

Seward sat there for a moment, his fingers tapping each other lightly. "I hope that when this incident is over there will be no more. You do what you must, but make certain that your connection with this office is not widely known."

"Shall I stay away until this is over, my lord?" Dunstan asked stiffly.

"No. I need you. You can read the reports and write summaries. And tell me what the *ton* is talking about." Dunstan winced. "Not the scandals, about the war. Now get to work."

During the days Dunstan wrote his reports; in the evenings he escorted Elizabeth to the dinners and card parties that marked the beginning of people's return for the Season. Elizabeth too spent her days involved in business. From visiting fabric warehouses to find the materials to refurbish the hall, to ordering a new wardrobe for the Season, to running errands for her stepmother, she was busy from morning to night. Although she once would have dreaded them, even the evenings with their entertainments did little to stir her fears. Having Dunstan and the earl close at hand had helped. And Dunstan, as if he could read her mind and her fears, found reasons to be constantly at her side.

The earl had arrived in town a week after their own arrival. Bearing messages from both Cecile and the Westins, he had been a welcome sight, especially to Charles. As soon as his duties at the Horse Guards were completed, Charles spent the rest of his days at Clarendon House, prompting Dunstan to ask when he planned to move in. "I prefer to keep my own lodgings," Charles had said calmly. "Wouldn't want to impose." His eyes twinkled merrily.

As soon as the earl had arrived, Dunstan and Elizabeth had poured out the whole story. He had just listened, his face impassive, his eyes hidden as they usually were when his head was held at a normal angle. After they had finished, he sat for a few minutes and then asked, "Have you made any progress in discovering this person's identity?" He tilted his head to one side to look at them. They shook their heads.

"We are waiting for an answer to the letter Charles sent."

"Have you checked the place to which the money was sent?"

"Charles and George, Lord Ramsburg, did that at the very beginning. The man there simply sends them on," Elizabeth explained.

"Did you get the new address?" The earl's mind was sorting through possibilities.

"No. It is never the same twice. The letter comes. Then we suspect the man gives some sort of signal. Haven't been able to detect it yet. Then someone, different each time, appears to take it away," Dunstan said quietly.

"Interesting," the earl said thoughtfully. "Is this in London?"

"Near where Covent Garden theater used to be."

The earl raised his head at that, realizing the tenements that surrounded the place. "Strange. Did you try bribery?"

"Yes," his grandson said. "But the man is too afraid to talk. There's something there that we do not know about."

"I shall talk to Charles. The boy must know something that he has not told us," the earl said, his voice serious.

In the times when he was not busy with his seat in the House of Lords and Charles was not on duty, the earl made Charles relate the details of his life from the first moment he arrived back in town from Brighton. Certain that there was something both he and Charles were missing, he made copious notes each time and then compared them to the ones he had made earlier.

"This Jonathan, is he one of your closer friends?" the earl asked one afternoon after they had spent hours going over the story again.

"No. Oh, we run in the same circles. We play cards together, box the Watch. He looks me up whenever I am at my club," Charles explained again. Although at first he had protested when the earl demanded that he tell the story over and over again, Charles had early learned that refusing the earl was useless and was not a way to maintain a peaceful environment.

"Who is your closest friend? Everyone you have mentioned seems only an acquaintance."

"He is with the army on the Peninsula," Charles explained. "After that I suppose I spend more time with Elizabeth and Dunstan and you. Or Sebastian," he added as an afterthought.

"Sebastian?"

"Sebastian Hartley. I met him when I came to town for the first time." Charles shifted, uncomfortable in the high collar of his uniform. He wished that he had taken the time to go by his lodgings and change into something more comfortable. But he had been released late, and he knew the earl was waiting. Charles did not plan to repeat the last time he had not been prompt. The old man had torn a strip from him as though he were his own grandson. In fact, Charles was beginning to believe he was. His grandfathers having died rather young, he had never known anyone like the earl before and was rather fascinated by him.

"Hartley. Believe you have mentioned that name before. Stop squirming, young man." Charles sat still while the earl sorted through the papers. "Yes, here it is. Let me see." He read for a moment and then tilted his head back. Charles had his finger inside his collar, trying to loosen it. "Knew that collar was too tight the first time I saw it. But you had to learn yourself. Next time have the tailor build in some extra room. What good is a uniform if you cannot move in it? Go on now. Change. Give me a chance to review this," he ordered as briskly as any general Charles had met. "But do not dawdle."

When he returned sometime later, Dunstan and Elizabeth had arrived. Elizabeth was saying, "Everything is ready. The acceptances have been pouring in. Louisa was right. No one seems to care about last summer. Even Mama was wrong. She thought so early in the Season the party would be sadly thin of company. Now she declares it will be a sad crush." The men laughed. "When you are standing in the receiving line tomorrow evening, you will not be laughing," she said with a grimace. Just then she saw Charles. Her face brightened. "I had a visitor today, Charles."

"Yes?" His face showed his disinterest.

"She was most disappointed not to see you."

"One of Mama's friends ready to tweak my cheek and tell me what a handsome young man I am," he said cynically.

"She does think you are handsome. Don't you think so?" she asked the other two. They nodded solemnly. "But I think Cecile is rather young to be one of Mama's bosom bows."

"Cecile? Do you have her direction? Would it be proper for me to call? Is she coming to the party?" Charles's words fell out of his mouth as though shot from a cannon.

"Too bad you did not stay in uniform, Charles," the earl said, a twinkle in his eye. "I understand some girls are impressed by them."

"Not Cecile. Elizabeth, where are they staying? Are they receiving visitors?"

"Yes. And here is their direction. I knew you would want to dart off immediately when you heard." His sister handed him the card and sat down, not at all surprised when he rushed from the room.

Settling back to pour the tea, Elizabeth handed the cups around and had the footman serve the sandwiches and cakes. "Have you discovered anything new, Grandfather?" she asked when the servants had left.

"I am not certain. Charles goes about meeting people every day. And from what I can see, no one dislikes him. Very pleasant to have around. Few close friends. Does keep mentioning Hartley."

"Hartley!" Dunstan and Elizabeth said at almost the same moment. They exchanged a look. Dunstan signaled Elizabeth to go ahead.

"The man is a bounder," Elizabeth said, disgust in her voice. "He likes Charles because my brother sometimes is very foolish and drinks and plays deeply. He has led Charles into some dangerous business. Mama and I were very disturbed."

"Is that all?" the earl asked, his face thoughtful.

He had dipped his pen in a nearby inkwell and was making notes.

Dunstan opened his mouth, but Elizabeth continued. "The man ravished one of my maids last spring. And caused a dustup between Charles and me. Then when I asked him to leave the manor, he was offended. He seemed to think I had no authority. He tried to persuade Charles to change my mind. But Charles sorted him out somehow. He left later that same day in one of the coaches."

"You did not tell me any of this," Dunstan said, his face as dark as a thundercloud.

"It happened before we married," she said quietly, not certain she liked the jealousy that was rampant in her husband.

"Yes, but . . ." Dunstan looked at his wife, took a deep breath and held his tongue.

"Do you know something else about the man, Robert?" the earl asked, dipping his pen into the ink again.

"He is as bad a man as you and your mother feared, Elizabeth. Comes from an old family, not much money and what he has, he gambles away." Dunstan and his grandfather exchanged glances, remembering only too well what happened in that situation. "Supplements his income by associating with the young men, those just in town for a bit of town bronze. Takes them under his wing and introduces them to dangerous living."

"Any evidence of blackmail, my boy?"

"Not as far as I can tell." Not pleased to have to admit his actions, Dunstan went on. "When I got back to town after the house party at the manor last spring, I knew something was wrong. I had someone in our department do some checking for me. I didn't like what I saw." His eyes were on

Elizabeth's face, checking for the disgust he was certain he would see there.

Her eyes remained clear. In fact, she smiled the slow, temperature raising smile she reserved only for him. He let the breath he had been holding out slowly. "He gets the young men in deep waters. And there is always a profit in it somewhere for him."

The earl turned to Elizabeth. "Has he been invited to the party?"

"Mama protested, but Charles insisted. Then Louisa convinced her by reminding her of the purpose of the party. He was one of the first acceptances. But why Charles? They are friends."

"Hartley has no friends," Dunstan reminded her. "He cannot afford them."

23

While the earl made copious notes about Hartley, Charles made his way to Grosvenor Square, where the Westins had rented a house for the Season. Handing his card to the butler, he waited to see if he would be admitted. Then he saw the flowers on the table in the entryway and cursed softly. He would order some to be delivered every day, he promised himself. If she would only agree to see him.

From the moment the butler announced Charles's name, no one was in doubt whether or not he would be received. "He has come. I knew he would." Her earlier anger with Charles for buying a commission forgotten, Cecile got up to look in the mirror above the mantel. "Is my dress all right? Is it too wrinkled? Does it make me look too young?" Cecile still had not forgiven her grandmother and Mrs. Thompson for not agreeing to her plan. Instead of the dashing gowns she had pictured herself in, they had chosen ones that revealed her youth.

Mrs. Westin looked at her granddaughter, pride in every line of her face. "You look fine, my dear," she said, nodding her head once again as she noted how well the simple white muslin with the golden brown spencer and bows became Cecile. Although she was not about to allow Cecile to be thought fast, she had decided to allow her to try some original color combinations. "Show Mr. Beckworth in," she said quietly when Cecile was once more in her seat. "Remember, my dear, that country manners are not appropriate for London. Mr. Beckworth is being kind enough to call. That does not mean that he will show the same partiality that he showed you in the country."

Cecile's blue eyes grew big, flashing with anger and a little dismay. To her relief Charles, though dressed in more formal clothing than he had worn in the country, was much the same. He bowed politely, taking her grandmother's hand and kissing it. Cecile privately admitted that had he done the same to hers, she might have swooned. Then he made his bow to her.

Taking a chair opposite to Cecile's, he smiled. Her heart raced. Charles, too, was having difficulty controlling his emotions. From the moment he had seen her, looking so much the young lady with her hair pulled high on her head and then tumbling into curls, his heart had been beating erratically. "I am pleased that you arrived in time for Mama's party tomorrow. Have your dances all been promised?" he asked as soon as he could.

"We only arrived last evening," Mrs. Westin explained. "I am certain Cecile has a few dances left." In truth, Mrs. Westin was not at all pleased that her granddaughter would be attending a ball before her own presentation. Had it not been for her husband's insistence that to miss the ball would be an insult to their neighbors, she would have refused the invitation. Mrs. Westin's dreams were filled with the horror of sitting with the chaperons and seeing her granddaughter ignored.

"May I have the first and the supper dance

too?" Charles asked, knowing the limits he was allowed.

"Will you not have obligations to your family?" Mrs. Westin asked, filled with pride to think Cecile would open the ball with such a handsome young man. If his friends followed suit, Cecile's success would be assured. Having had only one child, Cecile's father, it was her first turn to play chaperon, and she was nervous.

Now that Charles had confirmed his dances Cecile saw no reason to worry. Self-assured, she assumed London would be as enjoyable as the country had been. "Please, Grandmama, say I may," she begged prettily. Her eyes never left Charles's face. The smile she wore was only for him.

"I assure you that I will not neglect my duties," he promised, wondering how soon it would be proper to speak to Cecile's grandfather. Then the thought of what was still unresolved returned. His smile slipped slightly.

With both young people longing to have a few minutes alone, to return to the carefree days of before Christmas, they made polite conversation. Finally it was time for Charles to make his good-byes. He opened his mouth and to his surprise asked, "Did you bring your horse to town, Miss Westin?"

"Yes, Lady Dunstan urged my grandparents that it would be just the thing."

"May Miss Westin ride with me tomorrow about eleven?" he asked the older lady. "It is not a very fashionable time, but I think she would enjoy seeing the sights without the crush that happens later."

Mrs. Westin looked at her granddaughter sitting on the edge of her chair and then back to Charles. "I understand that riding in the park with a groom behind is considered very ladylike today. Yes, Cecile, you may go."

"Thank you." Charles stood up. "Until eleven tomorrow, then."

"Until tomorrow."

The door had hardly closed behind him when Cecile was on her feet, running to the window. "Do not be peeking out of that window," her grandmother said sternly, remembering her own youth. "It is very unladylike."

"Isn't he wonderful, Grandmama? I wonder if he will be wearing his uniform?"

The next day Charles was prompt. Wearing his uniform, he stood proudly. Cecile took his arm and then allowed him to throw her into the saddle. "Has your mare a skittish disposition, Miss Westin," he asked as they rode away.

"Never before." Cecile, looking radiant in a rose-brown riding habit, bent over and patted her horse's neck. Her blonde hair was pulled back under her brown velvet top hat to hang in curls down her back. She looked up and smiled. Charles felt warm in spite of the cold of the day.

When they reached the park, they cantered along, leaving the groom to follow. Although Cecile was interested in seeing everything from the cow being milked on the Park green to the beggars, her first interest was in Charles. "Quickly, tell me everything," she said, casting an eye over her shoulder to see where her groom was. Fortunately, he was more interested in the ladies who were selling their wares nearby than he was in watching his mistress.

Charles, in as few words as possible, gave her the basic story. "As you must realize, Cecile, I will not be able to approach your grandfather until the situation has been solved," he concluded.

She looked at him ready to dispute his remark, but something in his face held her quiet. Acting much more responsibly than Elizabeth or Dunstan would have believed possible, she said in a soft voice that the groom could not hear, "Do what you must, Charles. I will be here."

Only the knowledge that they were in public kept Charles from wrapping her in his arms and kissing her on the spot. He flushed and nodded. Then he took her home.

Instead of a pleasant afternoon on horseback, Elizabeth was at Ramsburg House, supervising the placement of the giant urns of greenery that her stepmother had chosen to decorate the ballroom. The last one in place, she had walked into the morning room, ready to tell the ladies farewell for a few hours. The crisis she found there made her change her mind. "Chicken patties, Louisa. They have sent chicken patties," Lady Ramsburg was saying as she wrung her hands. "We shall be the *on-dit* of the town. I will never use this caterer again. How could he have confused my order with that of the Lord Mayor?"

"He has sent someone to the Lord Mayor. His chef is probably as distraught as yours," Louisa said soothingly. "The chef and I have checked everything else. It is just as you ordered it." And very delicious, she added to herself. She and the chef had decided that someone must sample each item.

"Chicken patties instead of lobster! What would people think of us?"

"Probably that you were setting a new style, lobster being what everyone else serves," Elizabeth said, knowing just how to appeal to Lady Ramsburg's vanity.

"True. Darlings, what would I do without both of you," her stepmother said, her composure restored. "Now, go home, Elizabeth. I will expect you at six. And you, Louisa, may retire to your room if you wish. I will cope," she said theatrically. Louisa and Elizabeth exchanged a smile and made their departures.

For Elizabeth, who had grown accustomed to very little time to herself, the afternoon stretched endlessly. The earl was visiting a friend, and Dunstan was somewhere in the government offices. After letting Miller wash her hair, Elizabeth drifted around her room, too restless to settle for long. The last few weeks had been so hectic that she and Dunstan had done nothing but dash from one engagement to another.

She threw herself on the chaise. When they had arrived in London, their suite had not contained one. To her surprise Dunstan had visited a furniture warehouse the next day and had one delivered. But she had been the only one to use it. She sighed, wishing that her husband were with her. Even if he did not love her, his arms were warm and his lips sent fire through her veins. She sighed again.

"Why the sigh, love?" Dunstan asked, crossing from the door into his dressing room.

"Robert! I was wishing you were here," she said opening her arms to him. He sat down beside her, taking her in his arms.

"I have missed this," he admitted a few minutes later.

"You have been neglecting me shamefully," she said with an artistic pout.

"What time do we have to be at your stepmother's this evening?" he asked, taking a look at the clock that chimed five on the mantel. When she told him, he too sighed and released her. "I suppose Miller is on her way now?" he asked. She nodded. "I wish that the evening were over, and we could stay right here."

"No more than I. All those names." She sighed again. The scratch at the door brought their few moments together to an end. As Elizabeth dressed, she wondered if they would ever be completely alone. They were always surrounded by others. Miller held out garments of silk so fine that Elizabeth believed she could read a book through them. They felt cool against her warm skin. When she looked in the mirror, she gasped. The petticoat was concealed but did not hide her legs. Miller tied the last tie into place. Then she slipped the gown for the evening over Elizabeth's head. The undergarment was as fine as the petticoat, made of the softest silk that clung to Elizabeth's curves lovingly. Had she worn it alone as the modiste had told her she could, Elizabeth knew that she would have felt as though she were in public unclothed. And Dunstan would have forced her to return to her room and change her gown, she admitted as she took a long look at herself in the mirror.

The tunic followed. Also of silk but this time shot with gold so that when she moved, it caught the light, it was heavier. Banded about the neck, the high waistline, and the hem with a heavier gold design, it hung in graceful folds. Ribbons made of gold caught up her curls. Elizabeth had looked through her jewels earlier, hoping to find something that would finish the ensemble, but both she and Miller had agreed that nothing looked right. Finally she had chosen her diamond ear drops and a diamond clasp for her hair.

Before Miller could hand these to her, Dunstan walked in, handsome as always in his favorite dark blue with a white waistcoat and knee breeches, sapphires sparkling from his cravat and his hand. He carried two boxes with him. Elizabeth stood up to welcome him. "Do you always find blue to match your eyes?" she teased.

"Always," he answered. He held out his hand to her, telling her to turn around. "Beautiful," he said a moment later, his eyes telling her more. "These are for you." He exchanged a knowing look with Miller, the maid having told him what her mistress planned to wear.

Elizabeth sat down quickly. She opened the first box, a long, thin one. Inside was an ivory fan mounted on gold sticks. "Dunstan," she breathed as she slipped it over her wrist and opened it once or twice, looking at him coquettishly over its edge.

"Go on," he urged.

The second package was bigger. Elizabeth looked at him and then opened the box, her eyes growing wider. "Will they do?" he asked anxiously.

"Yes, oh yes!" She pulled the topaz and diamond ear drops from the box and fastened them into her ears. Miller took the matching brooch and clipped it into place on the ribbons in her hair. After pulling her gloves on, Elizabeth put on the matching topaz and diamond bracelets, turning her wrists to catch the sparkle. "You spoil me, my dear," she whispered as she stood up to put her arms around his neck, marveling at how wonderful one man could feel.

Fashionably late, the earl, Elizabeth and Dunstan strolled into the drawing room only minutes before the guests arrived. For the next few hours they chatted with their friends, not really noticing the excellent dinner that was put before them. When the ladies left, reminding the gentlemen not to linger too long over their port, Dunstan moved closer to his grandfather. Under the cover of the general conversation he asked, "Are you certain you will be able to force him into action if he is the one?"

"No. But at least we will have given it a shot." Lord Ramsburg glanced over at the earl. The older man nodded. "Drink up. It is time to rejoin the ladies."

Until the guests had been received, neither Dunstan nor his grandfather were able to put their plan into motion. They smiled and clasped the hands of those people arriving, accepting their wishes for happiness. Occasionally Dunstan would look at Elizabeth and smile. Laughing with a friend from Brighton, assuring him that his name, of course, was not forgotten, Elizabeth made a charming picture, all flashes of white and gold. Only her hair and eyes gave a contrast.

Just a short time before Lady Ramsburg gave the signal for the band to begin playing, Hartley walked in. He was all graciousness to his host and hostess. The mask rather slipped when he reached Elizabeth. Surveying her in her gold, topaz, and diamonds, he smiled harshly and hurried past, merely nodding his head before going on to the earl. Dunstan was so angry that he took a step after him, but Elizabeth pulled him back, her hand resting on his arm for a few minutes until he calmed. Then it was time for the opening dance. Leading Elizabeth to the center of the floor where their set was forming, Dunstan walked proudly. "Joining them there were Lord and Lady Ramsburg, the Earl of Clarendon and Mrs. Louisa Beckworth, and Charles Beckworth and Miss Cecile Westin, a young lady just come to town," wrote one of the gossips to a neighbor who had been unable to attend. "My dear, they glittered." And they had. With every eye on them they danced the first measures. Then everyone joined them in the dance.

The sight was not a pleasing one for Hartley. Charles had been surprisingly cool of late, perhaps because of the beauty who was on his arm in the dance. He looked besotted, thought Hartley. The thought made him brighten for a moment. Then Elizabeth turned, her face animated as she looked up at Dunstan. She laughed at something he whispered. Hartley's face grew hard as he thought how the two of them had managed to cheat him out of half of his share of the manor. The money had lasted such a short time.

Before the evening was over, the earl had his answer. Trusting his luck, Hartley walked about the ballroom sowing seeds of discontent. Matchmaking mothers were usually his target. And in them he found ready soil. Disgruntled already because of the loss of the viscount, they gazed with anger upon the wealthy Mr. Beckworth, known for dancing only once with any young lady, as he danced again with Miss Westin.

The next afternoon Dunstan, Charles, Elizabeth, and the earl met, Charles's presence being the hardest to command. He had promised to ride with Cecile that afternoon. Only the earl's command had worked. Charles grudgingly appeared.

Quietly the earl explained what he had learned. His friends had volunteered to help and had been stationed about the ballroom, changing places occasionally so that they would not be noticed. Hartley had been busy spreading discontent, his friends had reported. "But Hartley is my friend," Charles protested. Only when he was told that Hartley had made disparaging remarks about Cecile did his protests stop. "Why did he do that? Cecile has just arrived in town. His remarks could ruin her."

"No. I spoke to Mr. Westin and Lord Ramsburg. Both are talking steps to assure it does not. You are determined to marry Cecile, aren't you, Charles?" the earl asked. "That is what you told me earlier." Charles nodded. "When the announcement of your engagement appears in the paper soon, that talk will soon die down. The matchmaking mamas know when to stop talking, you see. No one enjoys the town laughing when the man you were hanging out for is engaged to another. Speak to Mr. Westin and Cecile tomorrow, Charles."

"But why would Hartley do such a thing? I thought we were friends. He helped to arrange my commission so that Mama would not find out until it was too late."

"You never told us that," Dunstan said angrily. He looked at his grandfather for his agreement.

"How?" the earl asked.

"What do you mean?" Charles asked, his face puzzled.

"How did the transaction work?"

Quickly Charles explained. He had told Hartley what regiment he wanted and given him the money. The commission had followed.

"How did you give him the money?"

"A draft on my bank. The funds for the manor had just been turned over to me. I was plump in the pocket." Charles sat down, his face angry.

"Did Hartley know that, too?" Dunstan asked, knowing Hartley's reputation.

"Yes. I had to pay off a bet to him. He had to wait for the money until the manor was sold."

"It must have been a considerable sum," Elizabeth said, her face disapproving.

"It was. Do you really believe it was he?"

"Yes. It had to be someone who knew you well, someone who knows the *ton*," the earl said. "Have you been unaware that Hartley resents anyone who has money?"

"Not really. He was certainly angry enough with Dunstan for winning so often at the house party. Said some foul things about your luck. But never thought he resented me," Charles said slowly. Dunstan and Elizabeth exchanged glances. "But why would he try to blackmail me?"

"What better way to get more money from you? You have not received another letter from him, have you?" the earl asked.

"No. At least I do not think so. I left to go on duty before the post arrived today. Porter always goes by Ramsburg House sometimes before noon and picks it up. He had not returned when I left after changing."

"Does Hartley know the way your trust works?" Elizabeth asked, crossing to look at him. With the three of them opposite him, Charles felt as though he were on trial.

'Yes. I used to complain about it all the time. And he knows that I have spent all my ready blunt on a stable of horses, which I do not need simply to parade in the Park or ride through the streets." Charles glowered at all of them.

"Poor little brother. Shall I tell Cecile you are still longing for excitement on the Peninsula?" Elizabeth asked as though he were still in dresses.

"Ask away. Mama will never let me go, and Cecile knows it. Maybe by my serving here in England, it will release someone else to fight," he said calmly, raising both Dunstan's and the earl's opinion of him considerably.

"Well done, brother," Dunstan said, clapping him on the back. Charles flushed. "You have more bottom than I gave you credit for."

"Thought I would sell out, did you? I thought about it. Then I decided that was no way for a Beckworth to act. Besides, if Hartley sees that my name is brought into this scandal, I will be asked to resign," Charles said, ruthlessly honest for once.

"Can this inquiry by the full House continue much longer?" Dunstan asked his grandfather.

"In the Commons one never knows. Handled badly. That is what I told your stepfather the other day. Should have been handled in a committee. This dirty linen should have been kept in the basket. The woman is an obvious liar," the earl said forcefully. "We must work quickly. Send Hartley another letter at the old address telling him you have discovered his identity. Ask him to meet you." He looked from his grandson to Charles. "You set the place. Not too seamy but far enough away from society so that neither of you will be recognized. Tell him you will reveal his perfidy if he persists."

The next two days were nerve-racking ones for the four involved. As more people returned to town for the Season, their social obligations increased. Dunstan, hoping for some time alone with his wife, arranged to work at home in order to be on hand if he were needed. But Elizabeth's days were filled with visits and luncheons, which, once accepted, could not be canceled. The afternoon she did arrive home early, she found Charles already there, waiting for the earl's return. "It was Hartley, then?" she asked as she walked into the room where Charles sat with a letter in his hand.

The turquoise dress she wore was one of Dunstan's favorites. Its neckline was modest, and Elizabeth's hair always seemed brighter when she wore it.

"He does not admit it. But then I did not mention his name in mine either. We are meeting later today. I had to cancel another drive with Cecile," Charles said despondently.

"Then she will be even happier to see you tonight. Where are you going?" Elizabeth asked. When Charles mentioned a musical evening for which they had sent regrets, Elizabeth said, "You must find time to bring her here. We have hardly seen her since she came to town."

"Her grandmother keeps her very busy. Always taking her someplace new. I will bring her soon." Charles looked at the clock again.

"What time are you meeting him?" Dunstan asked.

"At five. Do you think the earl will be back by then? What should I say?"

"Not anything foolish. Hartley probably believes that you are bluffing. He may not expect to see you at all. Are you armed?"

"Armed? Robert, what are you saying?" Elizabeth demanded. "If there is going to be trouble, he should not go."

"He must, my dear, if he plans to free himself from this fear of scandal." Dunstan's hand on her shoulder reminded Elizabeth of the decision they had made last summer. They looked into each other's eyes, searching for something that was hidden.

The clock struck the half hour. Charles stood up slowly. "I do not want to be late," he said slowly as if he had to force the words from his mouth. "My groom should be outside now waiting."

"When you get there, Charles, turn your team over to the ostler and take the groom into the public room with you. Will Hartley recognize him?" Dunstan asked, his face suddenly serious.

"Be careful, little brother," Elizabeth said with a catch in her throat. She threw her arms around Charles's neck and hugged him close.

"I will, Little Bit," her brother said in her ear. He shook hands with Dunstan and walked out the door.

Elizabeth burst into tears and threw herself in her husband's arms. "Don't cry, my dear. Charles will be just fine," he said quietly as he held her close.

24

When Charles returned two hours later, his face was as gray as a winter sky. Even without words all three people looking at him knew that the meeting had not gone as planned.

"Are you hurt?" Elizabeth cried, running to meet him. She was dressed for a ball in a new silk gown in a rich color much like the reddish color of the urns from Greece that were being exhibited in London.

"No." He turned to the earl. "My lord, it would be best if I talked to my sister and brother-in-law alone for a time. I am sorry, but some of what Hartley said concerns them. They may tell you later if they wish, but I cannot."

The older man nodded, accepted his cloak and hat from the butler, and turned. "Shall I make your regrets to our hostess?" he asked. Dunstan looked at Elizabeth and then nodded.

"Come. Let us go to the library. Bring some wine," Dunstan said. Nothing was said until the servant was gone and the door closed firmly behind him. Charles made certain, opening the door to check for listening servants and then shutting it again.

"He was surprised," he began bluntly, crossing to stare into the fireplace, where the embers burned hot. "You were correct in that." He whirled around to face them. "And he hates us, you especially, Elizabeth. You and Mama tried to persuade me to stop seeing him. And you cost him money." Charles closed his eyes and walked to one of the large leather chairs. He sat down as though he could not bear to stand any longer and put his face in his hands. "He took great pleasure in telling how he planned to ruin all of us. When he is called before the House of Commons to testify, he will tell them I bribed him to buy his commission. He has a copy of my draft and a copy of my commission with the price at the top. Then he plans to tell how I plotted with him to ruin my sister in order to gain the money to buy the commission. Cecile's grandfather will force her to cry off now." Because he was tired and upset and his head was in his hands, his words were muffled. But Dunstan had heard enough.

"Tell me what he meant when he said you plotted to ruin your sister?" Dunstan said as he grabbed his brother-in-law and pulled him to his feet. Not even the sight of Charles's eyes with the light gone out of them could still his anger. Elizabeth, her hand pressed to her mouth, stood still, her eyes wide with horror.

"I told him I did not know what he was talking about. Then he reminded me of the note I had signed." Charles stood there waiting for Dunstan to hit him, too despondent to put up resistance.

"What note?"

"The one promising him one fourth of the profits if you married and I sold the manor."

"Charles, you didn't?" He glanced up once, but the look on his sister's face was too much to bear. He looked at the floor again.

"I thought it was a bet. I paid him off." Charles stumbled back to his chair, his hand over his face.

Dunstan, his face disapproving, brought him a glass of brandy. Charles grasped it tightly, his fingers white against the bowl. He downed it in one gulp. The room was silent as they waited for him to continue, certain he had not finished his story.

When he had himself under control again, Charles raised his head. His sister was still standing where she had been, staring at him. Dunstan was seated nearby. "He said I agreed to the scheme. I do not know. I was too angry with you, Elizabeth, and too far gone in drink to know what I was saying or doing. At least I hope I was," he added truthfully. Elizabeth's eyes grew wider as though she knew what was coming next. "My job was to apologize and get you to drink a glass of drugged wine, Elizabeth. Listen to me! I betrayed my own sister, caused her ruin." He took a deep breath and closed his eyes. Then he said quickly. "He used the others too. They plied you with brandy, Dunstan, and kept you gambling until everything was ready."

Dunstan got up slowly and crossed to his wife. He put his arm around her as if to shield her. His face was angry but controlled. "Hartley enjoyed telling me this," Charles said with a bitter laugh. "He enjoyed what he did. And I called the man a friend. A friend? He is a devil. He enjoys making people suffer. I could see it in his eyes tonight. Why couldn't I see it before? How many lives has he wrecked?"

"Too many. Far too many," Dunstan said quietly. "Finish your story.

"It will never be finished. Not when he can do this again. And he will. It is how he lives, how he enjoys life."

"Charles, we will worry about what to do with

Hartley later," Elizabeth said, her voice a throaty quaver. "Tell us what happened." Her lips were a white line as she bit them to keep them from trembling.

"According to him, I took the wine to your room, and he followed me, to be certain of its location, I suppose. After I left and went to bed, he helped you upstairs, Dunstan. According to him, you were on the go but had not passed out. He took you to Elizabeth's door, began to loosen your clothes. You opened the door and walked in, telling him that you had learned to undress yourself when you were a child. Shut the door behind you. Made him angry, you did. He went to bed and waited until the next morning. Nothing happened. He decided that you had not been as drunk as he had believed. That when you realized you were not in your own room, you left. He thought one of the servants helped you to bed." Charles crossed to the brandy decanter and poured himself another glass.

Elizabeth collapsed on Dunstan's chest, breathing hard. His arms tightened convulsively about her. No matter how the marriage had happened, she was his, and he did not plan to let her go. Nor would he let her feel regret or shame. He kissed her curls softly.

"That is not all. When you asked him to leave, Elizabeth, he decided that whether or not anything had happened, he would make people believe it had. He decided to ruin you. When the carriage broke on the way to London, they stopped at the White Hart and found Susan working there. With some inducement, he did not tell me what, he persuaded her to tell the coachman and the groom that she knew you had had a man in your room. She was not lying. Dunstan, Hartley had seen you walk in. Of course, Elizabeth was totally unaware of it. You know the rest."

"Was he the one who spread the story in Brighton?" his sister asked, her eyes on her husband's face trying to decide his reactions.

"Yes. And he planned to do the same thing to me. But the earl stopped him. Now no one can stop him. Told me it would take fifty thousand pounds. Fifty thousand! And then he would want more later." Charles sat there and stared into the glass of brandy, wishing that he could escape his problems as easily as the brandy disappeared.

For Elizabeth the shock was beginning to wear off and anger had set in. She pulled away from Dunstan and walked over to her brother. She took the glass from his hand forcibly. "You have had enough of this. Haven't you learned your lesson yet? How do you expect to protect Cecile?" She set the glass down so hard it rocked. She walked up and down the room in front of him, letting all her emotions free. "I was in your care, and what did you do? You sold me for a commission. Charles, I am ashamed to be your sister. And Cecile will be ashamed to be your wife. If I were she, I would definitely want to cry off. Look at you, sitting there, drowning your griefs. What good will it do? What good will it do?" By her last words she was crying and hitting out at Charles, who simply sat there, taking his punishment as he thought he deserved.

Dunstan grabbed her, pulling her into his arms. "Stay here," he told Charles as he took his wife from the room, carrying her into the small salon across the hall. "Stop this, Elizabeth," he demanded, giving her a shake.

"Did you hear him? My own brother was party to putting a man in my room. How many people have known? Were they all laughing at us?"

"Didn't you hear what he said?" He gave her another shake, more forceful this time. "Hartley thought I escaped his plan."

"But I did not. I was asleep and yet I was ruined. Of course, I could not remember that evening. My own brother drugged me." She burst into tears again. Dunstan tried to draw her into his arms, but she pulled away. "The whole story will be spread out in the House of Commons. We shall be written up in the papers just like the duke and his mistress. Our families will be ruined." She hit her husband as she had hit her brother.

Finally Dunstan had had enough. Capturing her hands, he gathered her close, stopping her words with his lips, allowing her only moments to breathe between kisses. Gradually her tears ceased, and she lay against him quietly, listening to the beat of his heart, fast and hard. When he thought she was calm enough to listen, he said, his words ringing clear and true. "You are my wife, mine. Do you understand?" She nodded, her hand creeping between the buttons on his waistcoat and shirt to rest on his chest. "No matter why we married, we are married. I will never let you go. And no one will hurt you." His voice was cold and determined. "I will take care of Hartley." He stepped back, letting her go. Then he rushed into the hall, calling for his coat. Seeing his evening cloak lying on the table, he picked it up and threw it around him, his face set in angry lines. He rushed out of the house.

"Dunstan, Dunstan!" Elizabeth cried. When he did not return, she darted into the library. Charles looked at her warily, not certain what to expect from his sister even though only hours before he thought he knew her better than anyone else. He looked around for Dunstan, not really wanting to deal with Elizabeth on his own. "Charles, you must do something immediately. Dunstan just left the house in a rage. Go after him. He may kill Hartley and be sent into exile. Charles, I like England, and I want my husband alive. Go after him."

Before she had finished her speech, Charles was out the door, not certain where he was going. "Did you see a man come out of this house in the last few minutes?" he asked a linkboy standing near the steps. The boy nodded. "Where did he go?"

"Caught a hackney, my lord. Told him to go to St. James."

"Find me another quickly and there's another of these for you," Charles said, tossing the boy half a crown. The lad's eyes opened wide. "St. James, his club? Or Hartley's lodgings?"

"Be back in half a minute, guv. Stay right there." The boy was as good as his word, Charles was on his way within minutes, and the linkboy had enough to feed his family for several days.

When Charles finally found Dunstan outside the building in which Hartley had taken rooms, he was wrapped in his cloak, the black blending into the shadows. Had Charles not been looking for him, he would have missed him. Sinking into the shadows himself, though not as effectively as Dunstan, he said, "Elizabeth was worried about you." Dunstan laughed. "She said to tell you she preferred to stay with you in England. And she has no desire to be a widow."

"A widow? Have you any idea what she was talking about?"

"I believe that she had some idea that you were rushing out to challenge Hartley to a duel."

"An interesting thought, but so unprofitable. In a duel he might win."

"I thought you would be ready to call me out."

Charles leaned his head against the building wearily. "To think that is what I almost did to you."

"You simply provided the opportunity. But if you are so loose tongued every time you are in your cups, it is lucky you are not in Spain. No matter now, although Elizabeth may not forgive you so easy. No, it is Hartley I plan to have. How, I am not certain." He looked up and down the street, but the only people in sight were two gentlemen walking unsteadily up the stairs to a house down the block. He drew his cloak about him more closely, cold in the damp night air. "Is there an inn nearby?"

"Bound to be. If not, the club is close at hand."

"Not the club. If Hartley walked in and I saw him, Elizabeth's fears might be realized. No, we need a quiet place where we can talk this out." They walked down the street together, for all the world like friends out for an evening of riotous living.

Finding an inn that looked clean, they requested a private parlor and called for a bird and a bottle. "Though I suspect it is the former we need more than the latter," Charles added. He had taken Elizabeth's remarks seriously and had to admit their truth.

"Don't turn Methodist on me, yet, Charles," Dunstan laughed. "The bottle is simply to wash down the bird, which may be tough." To their surprise, the meal was a fine one, and the claret as smooth as any Dunstan had in his cellars. "Make a note of the name of this place, Charles. When we need to escape our wives, we will have a snug hideaway."

"First I must have a wife. Westin will never let me marry Cecile if this gets out," Charles said, letting his depression sink over him again.

"Nothing will come out," Dunstan said firmly.

"For Elizabeth's sake as well as our own, we must find a way to stop him."

"Oh, he has offered to take the full blame himself. Didn't I tell you?"

"No. What price did you say he wanted?"

"Fifty thousand," Charles told him.

Dunstan whistled, his face thoughtful. "He definitely plans to beggar us," he said. "And, more than certain, that is only the first payment. That type is never satisfied."

"I can attest to that," Charles said dryly. "I wish I had investigated before I paid him anything."

"No regrets, Charles. Keep your mind in the proper sequence. Let us plan our revenge."

"How?"

"I am not certain. Give me some time."

"We don't have any. He could be called to testify any day now. And if he is . . ." Charles stared at his brother-in-law wishing that he were able to react as coolly. Dunstan's calm face hid a mind that was at work.

"We will tell Grandfather and Lord Ramsburg part of the story. No need for them to know how Elizabeth and I decided to marry."

"No," Charles said forcefully.

"Don't worry. They will forgive you. You may feel the bite of Grandfather's tongue for a while, and that is not pleasant, I can assure you, but eventually you will be back in his good graces, especially if we can defeat Hartley."

"But I do not understand why they must know anything more than they do."

"We need their help. They may be members in the House of Lords, but they both know people in the Commons. They may be able to find out when Hartley is scheduled to testify."

"So we know how much time we have." Charles's face lit up with understanding.

"Exactly." Dunstan leaned back and smiled wickedly. "Let us find Elizabeth and tell her what we have planned."

"You tell her. I think I will avoid her until she forgets what I have done."

"That long? You will send us an invitation when you and Cecile marry?" Dunstan teased him, ready to relax now that he knew that there was some sort of plan.

"Cecile and I . . . Cecile. I was to escort her and her grandmother to some cursed musicale tonight. She will never forgive me." Charles pushed back his chair with such force that it fell over. He hurried to the door, leaving Dunstan to settle their account, and broke into a run, heading for his own lodgings not far away.

"Remember to change first," Dunstan called as he followed him into the street. Then he checked the street for a hackney.

Elizabeth was still in the library when he returned. The earl was with her, had been with her some time. To Dunstan's dismay, she had told him the whole story. His grandfather was sitting in one of the large leather chairs, his head propped up on the back. Since the chair faced the doorway, as Dunstan was certain his grandfather had planned, those blue eyes so like his own were the first things he saw as he walked in the door. Disconcerted for a time because of the angry look his grandfather wore, Dunstan hovered in the doorway until Elizabeth rushed to his side. "I told Grandfather everything," she explained. Dunstan looked over her head at his grandfather. "Did you find Hartley?" she asked anxiously.

"No, dear one. You can stop packing. There will be no duel."

"In my day that would have been unthinkable,"

his grandfather said is a voice that was neither angry nor upset.

"In your day, Boney did not have Europe in a stranglehold, Grandfather. And I have no desire to see the New World. Besides, duels are so public." He glanced at Elizabeth when he said it, remembering belatedly her own experience with duels.

"Do you have something else in mind?" the earl asked. This time his voice held a note of curiosity.

"What do you and Charles mean to do?" Elizabeth asked, her brows drawn into a frown. "Why isn't he with you?"

"He was promised to Cecile and her grandmother." Dunstan seated his wife on the settee and went to stand behind her. "We will see him tomorrow." Then he turned his attention to his grandfather. "Our plans are still tentative. But you can help us if you will, Grandfather. Can you get a schedule of witnesses for the inquiry in the House of Commons?"

"How far in advance would you want it?"

"Two days or three?"

"I will try for a week. At the rate those Commoners are going, they will not be finished until Easter. They keep calling that Clarke woman back, listening to those stupid love letters the duke wrote her. How could a grown man be so besotted, so foolish? And the way they lap up what she says. Anyone can tell she is lying. Anything else, my boy?"

"Do not mention this to Seward. With my history, he will bid me adieu in a moment."

"Think you do yourself a disservice there. He told me this week what a godsend you were." The earl stood up slowly, showing the strain of the evening and his age.

"But you have taken your seat in the House of Lords, Grandfather. What else could he say to one who votes on bills he wants passed?"

The earl was silent for a moment, just looking at him. Then he nodded his head. "I will ask about the schedule in the morning," the earl promised as he walked out of the room.

"You have been remarkably silent for the last few minutes, Elizabeth," Dunstan said, crossing to sit on the arm of a chair opposite her. "Did you wear yourself out talking to my grandfather?"

"Are you very angry with me?" she asked, her eyes on his hands. "I thought he had a right to know. And I was the one who would be ruined if the story got out." She looked up at him under her lashes.

"It was your story. You told it," he said quietly.

"But you wish I had not."

"I did not say that." He stood up and took a turn around the room before coming back and facing her. "Elizabeth, what I would have liked is for you to discuss it with me first. If you wanted him to know, we could have told him together."

"But he does not blame you. He understands that what you did was not deliberate."

"He is not the question. We are." He took his seat beside her on the settee and picked up her hand. "If we are to make a success of our marriage," he began. She looked at him, startled. "That is what you want, isn't it?" She nodded. "Then we must work together." Dunstan kissed the hand he held, and a shiver ran up her spine.

"I am sorry I did not wait for you," she said softly. "But I was so upset—mostly with Charles. The story just came flowing out."

"You have every reason to be disturbed. If the situation was not as bad for him as for us, I would have leveled him myself."

"Somehow Charles always manages to survive unscathed," she told him, remembering their childhood.

"I want all of us to emerge from this unscathed," her husband said firmly. He glanced at the clock as it struck the hour, surprised that it was only ten. Then he looked down at his wife. He stood up and offered her his hand. "Could I interest you in an early bedtime, my dear?"

Miller, dismissed summarily, closed the door behind her, smiling. Inside the husband and wife looked at each other, their faces serious. "Can you forgive me, Elizabeth?" Dunstan asked.

"For what?"

"Letting myself be hoodwinked like that, like the veriest baby. I should have realized what he was doing. I never liked the man."

"Neither did I. We have excellent tastes in enemies, my lord."

"And in spouses." He pulled her to him. Realizing that the dress had no ties, he quickly found the hooks down the back and had her dress off in moments. He gasped as he saw her standing there in her petticoat and chemise, the firelight casting interesting shadows through the silk. "I like this," he ran his hand over the front of her chemise, stopping to touch the nipples he could see so clearly through the fine fabric.

"Why do men wear such complicated clothing?" she moaned as she struggled to unbutton his waistcoat and shirt. Her task was made harder by the fact that he was kissing her breasts. "Robert." His name was merely a sigh on her lips, but he looked up. It was enough. She pulled away from him and stripped his coat and waistcoat away. Then she ran toward the bed, threw off the rest of her garments and climbed in. He was quick to follow.

Their lovemaking that evening was fevered, frantic, as if their fears were driving them. "Mine," Robert said over and over again. When she would pull away for a moment, he would follow as though he were afraid to lose her. And for the first time, even without the words, she felt secure. Though they did not get much sleep that night, the next morning they awakened renewed.

That renewal helped them both in the coming days. Hartley somehow made it a point to be where they were, how they never discovered. Keeping their faces carefully blank, they passed him, ignoring him as though he were not there. Issuing the cut direct helped Elizabeth control her anger.

Charles was not as lucky. Dancing attendance to Cecile, he was on stage constantly, wincing the first time he saw the man every evening. Hartley, as though recognizing his reaction, began to vary his time of arrival. Though he customarily arrived at the last moment, he began arriving much earlier. After the first jolt Charles was able to control his emotions. After dancing the first dance with Cecile, he would dance the duty dances the hostess required. After that he would repair to the card room for a hand or two, never more. Then he would return to the ballroom for another dance with his love and remain until the supper dance when he was her partner again.

One evening while Charles was in the card room, Hartley saw his chance. He approached the lovely Miss Westin, whose engagement had lessened the number of admirers who surrounded her. He smiled at the young man who stood beside her, waiting for the music to begin. "My lord," Hartley said mockingly, his tone and his facial expression reminding the young man of the vowels that Hartley held. "Will you release Miss Westin so that

I may dance with her?" he asked, his tone daring the young man to refuse. Cecile, confused, looked from one to the other. Elizabeth, her chaperon for the evening, had hurried away to fix a torn hem as soon as Cecile's partner had arrived. When Elizabeth returned a few minutes later, she looked around the dance floor for the younger lady and then stared horrified. Rushing into the card room, she found her husband and Charles engaged in a quiet hand. "Come see what that man is doing now!" Elizabeth said, her voice snapping like her eyes.

"What are you talking about?" Charles asked. "I do not see why you had to drag me out here. Wasn't your husband . . ." He stopped, his eyes on the couple. As he watched, his face grew grim.

"Have you told her anything about him?" Dunstan asked, his voice more quiet than even he had expected.

"No. Oh, I told her that he was a bad 'un, but that is all."

"And that probably made her more curious," Elizabeth said bitterly. "How did he get his name on her card? This was not his dance."

"But I did not. You are her chaperon. Where were you?" Charles demanded. "What will her grandfather say?"

"More important, what will you say? I know the chit." Dunstan said, "and she is remarkably hot at hand. If you tell her not to do something, you can be certain that is exactly what she will do."

"Perhaps I should have a talk with her," Elizabeth suggested. "Leave her to me."

But when she tried to explain how evil Sebastian was the next morning, Cecile was merely intrigued. "What kind of trouble?" she asked, her eyes on Elizabeth's face.

"I would rather not say," she began. The stubborn look on Cecile's face, however, was enough to convince Elizabeth that that tactic would not work. "He tried to ruin me!" she blurted.

"Did he attempt to ravish you?" Cecile asked, her voice properly horrified.

"No. He tried to force a strange man into my bedroom to do that. He did take advantage of one of my maids." Elizabeth's voice revealed her disgust with both Cecile and Sebastian Hartley.

"Are you certain? Grandmama says many maids use their wiles to capture the gentlemen's attentions." Cecile looked at Elizabeth, noting the way the older lady's eyes narrowed. "He is a wonderful dancer, and he behaved like a perfect gentleman with me last evening." Cecile sighed, pleased with her logic.

Making a note to congratulate Dunstan on his accurate reading of the lady's character, Elizabeth made one last attempt to convince her of the impropriety of being seen with Hartley any further. "Cecile, did Charles tell you that Hartley has threatened to blacken his name in all of society so that no family would accept him as a suitor for one of their daughters?"

"No, he did not. Besides, Charles is engaged to me. He does not want anyone else."

"But your grandfather might withdraw his consent if the scandal becomes known," Elizabeth told her quietly.

Cecile, her face flushed with anger, was indignant that anyone would alter her plan for her life. "And how does Mr. Hartley intend that this should happen?"

"He claims Charles is involved in the scandal surrounding the Duke of York."

"But he is an old man." Then Cecile stopped,

her eyes flashing. "Does that mean Charles was involved with that woman, that Clarke person?"

"Not that we know of. Hartley is the link, though. When he is called as a witness in the inquiry concerning the Duke of York, Hartley intends to reveal Charles's involvement. Think what your grandfather will say then."

Cecile's small, angelic face was cold. Her voice echoed that chill when she asked, "What can we do to prevent this from happening?"

"Dunstan is at work on a plan. We simply need to avoid the man and tell our friends to avoid him. Do not mention why, of course. Simply hint them away."

"As you tried to do me?" Cecile asked, recognizing her folly.

"Yes. Will you help?" Elizabeth asked, her face serious.

Cecile thought for a few seconds. "Yes. Now that I have found Charles, I intend to keep him. No one or nothing will get in my way."

Her commitment made, Cecile found ways of implementing it. Elizabeth never asked how, but soon Hartley found himself not as welcome. Invitations began to be mislaid, especially in those households where young ladies were. At the balls where he could be found, Hartley found it difficult to find partners except among the matrons and wallflowers. One or two of the latter dared their mothers' frowns and refused as well. Accustomed to making others uncomfortable, Hartley began to feel pressure of his own.

25

Within the week Hartley became aware that something was wrong. Once accepted in almost any circle, he now found himself relegated to the status of those annoying individuals to whom one owes some type of obligation. For Hartley the position was not a desirable one. Self-assured though he was, he began to feel uncomfortable, to feel that people were watching his actions more carefully than he wanted them observed.

For the third morning his mail contained no invitations, only letters from his creditors dunning him. His valet took one look at his master's face and found a pressing errand that needed to be run. Hartley threw the letters on the floor. He paced the room, his boots marking the covers of the bills. His face was angry.

He walked quickly from one side of the room to another, never noticing that as he brushed against the table he was knocking his carefully amassed curios to the floor and later grinding them under his heels. His frown grew darker and darker as he considered how he might retrieve himself from the disasters he saw looming in front of him.

Finally he stopped. A smile that, had anyone been present with him then would have frightened even the bravest man, crossed his face. He walked to the desk, ruthlessness in every line in his body.

Although Dunstan, Elizabeth, and Charles had been aware of Hartley's failing fortunes, not one of them believed that he would simply give up his plans. So they waited. The earl made the wait easier when he acquired a list detailing the witnesses to be called during the next five days. Hartley's name was nowhere to be seen.

Dunstan, with Charles as his companion, began a round of the less reputable hellholes in London. After playing a few hands and seeming to drink deeply, they would mention Hartley's name, wondering why he was so slow in retrieving his vowels. Pretending to be on the go, they put their hands over their mouths and looked around the room as if to confirm that no one had heard them mention Hartley's name. Only at one establishment did their routine change. As they walked in, a tall man appeared beside them.

"You were told never to return, my lord," the man said, looking down at the pair, his eyes hard.

"I do not plan to play," Dunstan explained. Charles simply stood there, surprised at the size of the man. "Is there somewhere we could talk?" The afternoon still early, the man agreed, his face impassive.

"What do you want with me?" he asked.

"How would you like an opportunity to earn a sizable amount of money?" Dunstan asked, his face as blank as that of the man in front of him.

"Doing what? I do not plan to hang from a gibbet for you, my lord." Sitting, the man did not seem so tall.

Quickly Dunstan explained, slowly but carefully building the ideas into a workable whole. "Would you mind leaving England?" he asked. Charles, who had heard the plan before, had used the time to inspect the man from head to toe.

"You would be well paid," Charles said finally.

"So his lordship explained." The man stood up, leaving Charles and Dunstan, still seated, feeling like children. "Return tomorrow. I will have my answer by then."

"Where did you find him, Dunstan?" Charles asked as he watched the man walk toward the door and bend to go through it. "What a fighter he would be!"

"And how much better for our purposes." Dunstan looked around the room, noting the way eyes were on them at all times. "Come. Let us find more comfortable surroundings."

Hartley might be staying home more than he liked, but neither the earl nor his family had that choice. Determined that no one would guess that anything was wrong, they danced their way through balls, listened to various musical performances, and even attended a lecture or two. "Too bad Napoleon got to Egypt first," the earl said after hearing one intrepid traveler describe the ruins he had seen in Egypt. "Might be an interesting place to visit. Always thought camels fascinating creatures."

"If they are as wicked as that man said, I hope I never see one," Elizabeth said firmly. She lifted her dress a little and gave it a shake. The talk about insects of the desert had made her feel uncomfortable.

"Why did you choose such a dry lecture?" Charles asked the earl. The older man gave a bark of laughter.

"Never thought you had it in you, Charles," the earl said as he clapped Charles on the shoulder. "Dry lecture. Good pun." Charles simply stared at him in confusion. Dunstan and Elizabeth exchanged a glance and broke into laughter, too.

They were not laughing the next afternoon when Charles appeared, a letter in his hand. "He asks for a meeting at the same tavern. This time he told me to bring you," Charles said, his face somber.

"Everything is ready," Dunstan reminded him. "When does he wish to meet with us?" They fell silent when the butler entered the room, asking for Lady Dunstan. She listened to him for a moment and then hurried from the room.

As soon as she and the butler were gone, Charles took a deep breath. He answered as though there had been no interruption. "This evening. He suggests that we may wish to bring some blunt. The amount, though smaller than before, is considerable."

"I will do my part," Dunstan promised. "Do you need me to frank you, too?"

"No. Mama and I talked recently. We decided that I should have some at hand. In fact, she has been most generous of late. Her only suggestion was that I use George's safe. Had to agree my lodgings were not safe enough for the amount she suggested." Charles looked around the room to make certain no one was within hearing. "What do we do now?" he asked as Elizabeth walked back in the room, Cecile close at her heels.

"About what?" the young lady asked, her face showing not a trace of strain. Enjoying her Season and hailed as one of the beauties, Cecile had taken the problem with Hartley rather philosophically, preferring to let the *ton* eliminate him.

The strain was beginning to show on Elizabeth. Her brows were drawn together in a frown. "What have you two been plotting?" she asked, her eyes trailing from Dunstan to her brother. She knew they had not told her everything.

Not wanting to alarm Cecile, neither Dunstan

nor Charles would answer. Their faces as placid as they could make them, they laughed, declaring themselves innocent.

Cecile too had noticed something. "Is it Hartley? What has that man done now?" she asked. She tapped her foot, waiting for an answer. Elizabeth looked at her, thankful her brother was too besotted to take offense at his fiancée's attitude. With both of them so anxious to have their own ways, she had visions of the quarrels they would have when they married. She shivered slightly, glad to be safe from those arguments. She looked at Dunstan once more. His face, though, carefully noncommittal, was peaceful.

Fortunately Charles knew exactly the approach to take with Cecile. "Your plan is working, my dear," he said. Ignoring the other two, he put his arm around her and squeezed her waist. As usual, she grew pink and giggled. "Hartley is growing nervous. I imagine he is feeling the displeasure of the *ton* more every day." He bent down and kissed her cheek, marveling at her smooth skin and shell-like ears.

"Charles, her grandmother has entrusted Cecile to my care. Do not try to abuse her trust," Elizabeth said, her voice stern. Dunstan looked at her and laughed. She closed her eyes, realizing that she had sounded just like Louisa. Weakly she began to laugh, too.

Both Charles and Cecile stared at them, their eyes wide. "We are engaged," Charles said, his feelings of propriety bruised.

"Even Grandmama allows a kiss on the cheek," Cecile said pompously. She looked at Charles, remembering other kisses not so innocent. "You said you would be busy this afternoon, Charles. Have your plans changed?" she asked. He nodded. "Will you see me home?"

"Yes. I need to speak to your grandfather too. Is he at home this afternoon?" Charles asked.

"He is always at home. Grandmama is quite in despair with him." Cecile walked over to where Elizabeth sat, the smallest expression of regret on her face. "Will it be possible to visit the new modiste you found tomorrow, Elizabeth?" she asked, more anxious to be with Charles than to shop.

Her hostess nodded. Cecile made her farewells quickly. Charles looked at Dunstan. "Is there anything I should do before we leave?" he asked.

"No, I have everything in hand. Meet me here at ..." Realizing that Charles had never given him the time of the meeting, Dunstan paused.

"Half past six," Charles said. "That will be time enough."

"Does this mean that you will leave me alone again this evening?" Cecile asked. "Really, Charles, this is too bad of you. I had a new dress to show you, and I am supposed to sing."

"You two had best be on your way," his brother-in-law urged. He walked them toward the door, intent on escaping before he had to explain to his wife.

"Come for luncheon tomorrow, Cecile," Elizabeth said. "We will visit the modiste afterward. You gentlemen may join us if you like," she added quickly. "Either at luncheon or shopping."

"Or for both," Cecile said, smiling up at Charles.

Having shopped with Cecile before, Charles said, "I think I may be on duty tomorrow afternoon." He tugged at her arm. "If you wish my escort for long, we will need to leave now." Their good-byes finished, the two walked from the room.

"I also must be leaving," Dunstan said before Elizabeth could begin the questioning he knew was coming. "If you need me, send someone to the office. And tell my grandfather that I would like to see him before Charles and I leave this evening," he said as he paused in the doorway. Blowing her a kiss, he was gone.

Though she had grown better about dealing with her fears, that afternoon Elizabeth could not rid herself of the thought of Hartley. Like some pale toad usually hidden from view, he signaled danger, not for herself this time but for Dunstan. She was certain of it. She had read the note Charles had left behind, had dropped carelessly when he had put his arm around Cecile. She had picked it up, at first simply so the servants would not find it. She had not meant to read it. But she had.

She had stared in horror at the words. Veiled only faintly was the threat. If they did not come, if they did not bring the money he demanded, Hartley would reveal their secrets to the world. He took great pride in reminding Charles of that fact, relating in more graphic detail exactly what the consequences would be if he did. She closed her eyes.

She was still sitting in the chair with her eyes closed when the earl walked in. He looked at Elizabeth, noting the gray tone to her usually clear skin. "What has happened? Is it Dunstan?" She held out the letter wordlessly. He too read the letter. "Is Dunstan here now?"

"No. He went out. He said that he needed to talk to you before he and Charles left for this, this rendevous tonight. They plan to leave at half past six. Try to talk them out of going," she begged.

"Have you lost sight of everything, my dear. This is exactly what they have been preparing for. Have faith in them," the earl said firmly.

"It is Hartley I do not trust. That man is evil."

At six o'clock that evening she was repeating the

same thing to Dunstan. He merely shook his head and wrapped a new cravat around his neck. Five already lay on the floor beside him. Graves stood beside him, another six across his arm. He carefully lowered his chin and looked in the mirror. "I think that will do it, Graves," he said. When the valet had left the room, Dunstan walked over to where Elizabeth sat curled up on the chaise, her eyes dark with fear. "My dear, there is no other way. We must meet the man." He glanced at the ormolu clock on the mantel, ready to be on his way. "He is nervous. Nervous men make mistakes."

"Nervous men also strike out." She sat up then and tried to present a calm appearance. But one single tear trickled down her face.

Dunstan saw it and sat down beside her, pulling her into his arms. "Do not cry, love. I promise you I will take care of myself."

"Be certain you do, my lord." She tried to laugh lightly, but it sounded more like a cry. "Oh, Robert, I could not bear to lose you too," she said as she wrapped her arms around his neck.

His arms closed around her, holding her pressed to him. For a moment the only sounds were of their hearts beating and their breathing. Dunstan kissed her lightly and put her farther back on the chaise. His tone light, he said, "Lady wife, have faith in me. I do not plan to leave the lady I love alone in this world." He smiled and stood up and was gone before she could utter a word.

"He loves me," she whispered and lay back, her hands clasped to her heart.

Lost in her dreams, Elizabeth floated through her evening meal with the earl. At first his frequent glances at his watch did not bother her. But as the hour grew later and neither Dunstan nor Charles had returned, her face grew more somber.

When midnight had come and gone, the earl stood up. "Go to bed, Elizabeth," he suggested.

"But what if . . . ?" She paused and closed her eyes, not willing to speak her fears aloud for fear of their coming true.

"I will leave someone on duty throughout the night. If any word comes, he will call us."

At first she still refused to go upstairs, but then she agreed, realizing that if her fears were to come true, she would need to be strong not only for herself but also for her mama, Louisa, and Cecile. She went up to bed, donning the sheer nightrobe she had had Miller lay out. She listened to the hours tick away on the clock, wishing she could push them along faster. Finally about dawn, she drifted off to sleep, only to awaken a short time later with horrible dreams. She rose, deciding to read, but the novel she had enjoyed a few days earlier seemed hopelessly stale. She put it to one side and stared off in the distance, her eyes unfocused and dull.

When Elizabeth drifted into the breakfast room later that morning, the earl noted the circles under her eyes. He too had slept uneasily. Quietly he had the footman bring fresh tea and watched as she drank her first cup.

They were sitting there quietly when they heard the knocker at the door. Both stiffened only to slump a few minutes later when Lord and Lady Ramsburg, followed by Louisa Beckworth, hurried into the room. "What happened? We waited up, but Charles never returned. What time did they arrive?"

"They did not come home last night," the earl said quietly, his eyes on Elizabeth. Her face was almost as white as the dress she wore.

"Have you eaten?" Elizabeth asked. When they

told her they had not, she slipped from the room to order fresh food. She returned a few minutes later, her eyes slightly red. Noting her stepdaughter's shiver, Lady Ramsburg told a footman, "Send Miller to me."

The maid appeared minutes later, her face disturbed. When she saw the assembled group, she paused. "Yes, my lady?"

"Fetch your mistress a pelisse or a shawl. I know when she ordered that dress, she must have bought a spencer to accompany it."

She had, but Elizabeth had taken one look at the bright jade-green spencer and had refused to put it on, declaring that the color was offensively bright. Now it was easier to agree.

Their breakfast over, the ladies retired to the morning room. The gentlemen entered the library. Both groups were silent, preferring to keep their thoughts to themselves. An hour passed. Then two. Suddenly there was a commotion in the hall. Both groups rushed out, their faces anxious. When the saw Cecile and her grandparents, their faces fell.

"What is wrong?' Mr. Westin demanded, taking in the situation faster than either of the others.

"Dunstan and Charles did not return last evening. Did Charles send you a message, Cecile?" Lady Ramsburg asked.

"No. What do you mean did not come home? What were they doing? Why do you all look so serious?" the girl asked, her face anxious. She took a step forward without lifting her skirts and tripped on the hem of the blue-figured muslin she wore. "Tell me," she begged.

Elizabeth looked at the earl, her eyes begging him to explain. Quickly and quietly he did. He pulled the sleeves of his corbeau-colored coat over his hands and laced them together. The Westins

looked at each other and then at their grand-
daughter. Her eyes were wide and filled with tears.
"Nothing has happened to Charles, I know it. If
something had happened, I would have felt it.
Convince them I am telling the truth, Grandmama.
Tell them," she said, her voice shaky.

Her grandmother put her arm about her, leading her into the drawing room nearby. When they
returned a few minutes later, Cecile was dry-eyed.
The clock chimed again. Realizing that her guests
had no intention of leaving until they had heard
some news, Elizabeth met with the housekeeper,
giving orders that a simple luncheon be prepared.
"Soup, of course. And whatever else is available.
Tell the chef to make it simple and to remember
that I trust his judgment implicitly."

They were sitting at their meal sometime later,
the ladies pushing the food around on their plates,
and the men eating little more. This time no one
heard anything except the rattle of dishes and
quiet conversation until the door to the dining
room flew open.

"Just as you suspected, Charles. They are all
here," said Dunstan, striding in as though he had
no troubles in the world.

"Where have you been?"

"What happened?"

"Why did you not send us word?"

"Is it over?" The questions flew so quickly that
neither of the gentlemen could answer them. Elizabeth said nothing, her eyes fixed on Dunstan's
face. His eyes never left hers.

"Give a hungry man a chance," Charles said in
protest. "We only stopped to change horses. And
Dunstan's men have refined that action to an art,"
he said. "Food. Give us some food." He sat down
by Cecile and watched in delight as she filled his

plate. Dunstan walked to Elizabeth's side as if drawn.

"Take my seat, dear boy," Louisa said quietly, giving a footman a signal to bring another chair. Then she quickly set some chicken and fruit before him. Dunstan took Elizabeth's hand and held it tightly, not even letting go to eat.

When the men had eaten their fill, everyone retired to the drawing room. "Do not keep us in suspense much longer," the earl said sternly. "It is obvious that you were successful. Tell us about it."

Charles began, rising to his feet. "Hartley was so certain that he had us in a trap. He was not even worried because there were two of us. He should have been." Charles chuckled wickedly. "Reminding us that the time was growing shorter and that sooner or later he would be called as a witness, Hartley once more presented his demands." Lord Ramsburg coughed, but when Charles looked at him, he waved him on.

"Since we were so reluctant to give him money, he suggested that we allow him to 'win' it from us. Why he thought one idea would be more palatable than another, I have no idea. We allowed him to think we had no other choice." Charles laughed bitterly and then leaned over to give Cecile a kiss on her cheek.

"Charles, continue with the story!" his mother said. Her face was stern. The others nodded. Elizabeth tightened her fingers around her husband's. He looked at her and smiled.

"We agreed to play and retired to a private parlor after first calling for brandy. Dunstan, this was your plan. Do you wish to tell this part?"

"You are doing a fine job. Continue."

"Dunstan had bribed the innkeeper and imported his own man to serve us. Not one of the servants but a rough-looking man. He kept our glasses filled. But Dunstan and I were drinking well-watered brandy. Hartley was not. At the beginning, as Dunstan had planned, we lost to him, handing over thousands of pounds. He was so confident that he admitted he had shaved the cards. That is when he made his mistake."

Dunstan cut in at that point. "He began to boast about his ability to ruin a reputation. He was so certain that we were not going to do anything that would harm ourselves or those we love. He even laughed at our helplessness."

"He was laughing so hard he did not even notice when the servant substituted a bottle of brandy that was drugged," Charles added. "He drank it without suspecting anything."

"Drugged?"

"Why?"

"Is that legal?"

"How would that help?" Elizabeth asked the last question.

"We were prepared to be rough with him. But we decided to use the sleeping draught before we tried anything else. He slept all the way to Portsmouth." Dunstan smiled, a wicked twinkle in his dark blue eyes. "And it seemed such poetic justice."

"I do not understand any of this," Cecile complained.

"Portsmouth. Ships sail from there to faraway lands," Lady Ramsburg explained kindly.

"Oh. What happened next?" Cecile looked from Charles to Dunstan, her brown eyes wide.

"A ship to China was waiting. Grandfather agreed to invest in the trading venture so that the ship would be standing by if we needed it," Dunstan said as he smiled at the older man.

"You sent him to China?" Elizabeth asked, breaking into a full smile for the first time in a long time.

"Yes, we did. You should have heard me talking to the captain when he was in London," Dunstan said laughing. "I was the heartbroken nephew, mourning my uncle's lapses into insanity. According to my story, his doctor had recommended a total change of scenery, somewhere out of the ordinary. His father, a crony of the Prince of Wales, had naturally thought of China, the source of so many treasures."

"And the man believed you?" Lord Ramsburg asked.

"With the generous percentage of the cargo we allowed him, he had no reason to question my motives. It was obvious that we would spare no expense to insure Hartley's well-being. We even sent along his nurse."

"Nurse?"

"What do you mean?"

"You sent a woman to China with Hartley?"

"No, a man. And what a man. You should have seen him. He is so tall that he has to bend to enter normal doorways. He will be rather uncomfortable on board ship," Charles said, his eyes alight.

"Like the captain, he will be well rewarded," Dunstan reminded Charles. "This morning we put them aboard ship. We warned the captain that my Uncle Hartley had rational moments, that he was sane at times, but that he suffered from delusions of persecution."

"You sent the man off like that? What will he say when he awakens?" Louisa asked, her face worried.

"If he is sensible, he will take the letter his nurse has for him and use the money enclosed to start a new life. The ship will make port at one of the trading compounds. The captain has orders to leave Hartley there. The captain will spread the word to the other ships. Without a great many inducements most captains avoid madmen."

"Then he is gone forever," Elizabeth asked, her face thoughtful, "or at least for a very long time?" Dunstan looked at his wife and nodded. Then he looked at Charles. On the road back to town that morning, both men had decided not to tell the others about the nurse's other function. Realizing the great wealth to be made, the man had agreed for a price to stay in China with Hartley, to keep an eye on him. He had guaranteed that the man would never return to England. Neither Dunstan nor Charles had asked him what he meant; they knew.

The afternoon was far along when all the questions had been answered and all the comments had been made. Both Dunstan and Charles were yawning. Elizabeth and the earl too hid yawns behind their hands. Finally everyone got ready to leave.

"Escort me home, Charles," Cecile asked prettily, her cheeks flushed with pride as she looked at him. He looked to her grandparents for permission. They nodded. He held out his arm.

Lord Ramsburg walked toward the door. Then he stopped. "I almost forgot to tell you," he said, surprise in his voice.

"What?" the earl asked.

"The inquiry is almost over. The last group of witnesses has been called, and Hartley's name is not on the list."

"What?" Charles shouted. "I paid that man five thousand pounds so he would not talk and several hundred more to get rid of him, and he would not have been able to hurt us anyway? That double-crossing excuse for a human being!"

Dunstan, Elizabeth, and the earl exchanged looks, letting Charles rant and rave without comment. Knowing firsthand Sebastian's ability to wreak havoc, they were just as happy to have him thousands of miles away.

"Have done, Charles," the earl finally said sternly. "Cecile needs to go home."

"As do we all," Lady Ramsburg added. She kissed both of her children and left, taking her husband and Louisa with her. A few minutes later the Westins and Charles left also. The three remaining looked at each other for a moment. Then Elizabeth hugged the earl.

"Get some rest," he urged them. "I will see you in the morning. I will tell the servants to bring me a supper tray when and if I ring, if that is all right with you, Elizabeth."

"The idea is an excellent one. I think I shall do the same." She looked at Dunstan, and he agreed. Slowly the three of them moved up the stairway.

When the door to their suite closed behind them, Elizabeth turned to face her husband, her fears and anxiety replaced by excitement. She hid her feelings behind a frown. "Did you or did you not tell me several days ago that the only way our marriage would survive is if we are honest with each other?"

Dunstan nodded, the tiredness he felt in every line of his face. "And then you rush off to meet Hartley, telling me as you leave that you have a plan. A plan I know very little about. Then you do not come home." The memory of her despair during the long hours of the previous night put a sob in her voice. "Dunstan, I can survive almost anything if I know what to expect. You simply dash off, leaving me to my imagination." She brushed tears from her cheeks and waved him away. "Then there was what you said as you left. How dare you leave me like that!"

"You knew most of the plan, Elizabeth. I was afraid you would worry too much if you knew more." He held up his hand to stop her words. "I know I was wrong. I did not trust you enough." She smiled, just the merest curve of her lips. "But what about the other thing?" he asked. "What are you talking about?"

"You told me you loved me and then left me," she shouted, the effects of the last few days telling on her.

"Yes. I have been telling you I loved you for months."

"Never in words." She stamped her foot. "And the day that you do, you leave as soon as you say it." Big tears formed in her eyes, and she brushed them away angrily. "Why didn't you let me say it too?"

Dunstan stopped, afraid to breathe. "Say what?" he asked quietly, hoping the answer was what he wanted to hear.

"I love you. I love you. I love you," she shouted.

He gave a shout of laughter, his exhaustion forgotten. "I love you too." He pulled her close to him, his dark blue eyes holding her prisoner. Then he kissed her, softly at first. Then as though they could truly become one, their kissed deepened. When he pulled away a few moments later to take a breath, Dunstan smiled and asked, "Don't we have on too many clothes?"

When a footman walked by their door a few minutes later, he was startled to hear laughter and soft throaty giggles coming from the room. Then there was silence. Nine months later the nursery at Clarendon held the newest member of the family.

*If you enjoyed this book, take advantage
of this special offer. Subscribe now and . . .*

GET A *FREE*
HISTORICAL ROMANCE
— NO OBLIGATION(a $3.95 value) —

Each month the editors of True Value will select the four best historical romance novels from America's leading publishers. Preview them in your home Free for 10 days. And we'll send you a FREE book as our introductory gift. No obligation. If for any reason you decide not to keep them, just return them and owe nothing. But if you like them you'll pay *just* $3.50 each and save at least $.45 each off the cover price. (Your savings are a minimum of $1.80 a month.) There is no shipping and handling or other hidden charges. There are no minimum number of books to buy and you may cancel at any time.

send in the coupon below